For most of history, most of mankind has either lived under imperial rule; or has wanted to; or has been locked in struggle with empire. It is true today. In this, the supposed age of democracy, both China and the Soviet Union have imperial governments. Both are expanding; between them they encompass more than half the populations of the world. Nor are things so stable at home. Many books, written by liberal and conservative alike, note the drift of the United States toward imperial forms. The President of the United States holds, with his red and gold telephones, control of more power than was ever held by any man throughout history.

Blessing or curse, savior or destroyer: the shadow of empire falls across the Earth even in this enlightened age.

CREATED BY
JERRY POURNELLE

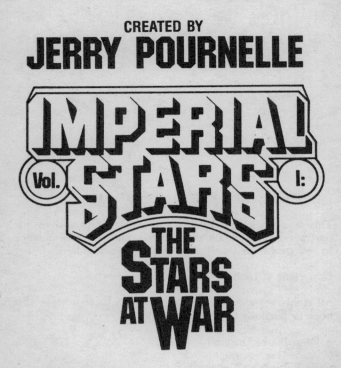

IMPERIAL
Vol. STARS I:
THE
STARS
AT WAR

With John F. Carr

BAEN BOOKS

IMPERIAL STARS: THE STARS AT WAR

Copyright © 1986 by Jerry Pournelle

A Baen Books Original

Baen Publishing Enterprises
260 Fifth Avenue
New York, N.Y. 10001

First printing, December 1986

ISBN: 0-671-65603-1

Cover art by Doug Beekman

Printed in the United States of America

Distributed by
SIMON & SCHUSTER
TRADE PUBLISHING GROUP
1230 Avenue of the Americas
New York, N.Y. 10020

CONTENTS

ACKNOWLEDGMENTS

EMPIRE by J.E. Pournelle was written especially for this work and appears here for the first time. Published by arrangement with the author and the author's agent, Kirby McCauley Ltd. Copyright © 1986 by J.E. Pournelle.

IN CLOUDS OF GLORY was first published in the July 1955 issue of *Astounding Science Fiction* and appears here by special arrangement with the author. Copyright © 1955 by Street & Smith Publications and copyright © 1986 by Algis Budrys.

THE STAR PLUNDERER by Poul Anderson appears here by special arrangement with the author. Copyright © 1954 by Love Romances Publishing Company and copyright © 1986 by Poul Anderson.

TRIBESMAN, BARBARIAN, and CITIZEN by John W. Campbell first appeared in the May 1961 issue of *Analog Science Fiction*. Copyright © 1961 by Street & Smith Publications. THE BARBARIANS WITHIN was first printed in the January 1965 issue of *Analog* under the title "Race Riots." Copyright © 1965 by Condé Nast Publications.

HYMN OF THE BREAKING STRAIN by Rudyard Kipling is in the Public Domain.

THE MIRACLE OF GOVERNMENT by James Burnham was first published in *From Congress and American Traditions*. Copyright © 1957 by James Burnham.

TO A DIFFERENT DRUM by Reginald Bretnor appears here for the first time by arrangement with the author. Copyright © 1986 by Reginald Bretnor.

THE WHIRLIGIG OF TIME by Vernor Vinge first appeared in *Stellar I* edited by Judy-Lynn del Rey in 1974. It appears here by permission of the author. Copyright © 1974 by Random House.

NIGHTMARE WITH ANGELS by Stephen Vincent Benet is in the Public Domain.

Research for certain non-fiction in this work was supported in part by grants from the Vaughn Foundation and the L-5 Society Promoting Space Development, 1060 E. Elm St. Tucson, AZ 85719. Opinions expressed in this work are solely the responsibility of the author.

DEDICATION

For Stefan T. Possony: as good a friend as liberty and civilization have ever had.

INTRODUCTION

EMPIRE
Jerry Pournelle

We live in a modern and enlightened age: surely we are done with empire forever? Stories of future empires are no more than fanciful tales, stories for amusement, the worst form of escapist literature.

Perhaps. And yet—

Do understand. I do not despise "escapist" literature. As C.S. Lewis and J.R.R. Tolkien once observed, it is jailers who are most opposed to escape. Good stories well told are reward enough in themselves. There is "escape" enough in this book.

However, we may also hope to learn something worth knowing. Humanity is a young species. If we are clever, and have a little luck, our line can last for billions more years, and settle the planets of distant stars.

This is no flight of fancy. We could today build ships to take us to the nearest stars. The ships wouldn't be cheap: they'd have to be travelling space colonies, self-contained worlds. They'd need energy sources, meaning we'd have to solve the fusion problem, but that's merely a matter of money and engineering; we don't need any new *science*.

1

The journey would take hundreds of years. The spacefarers who leave Earth would not live to see the new stars close up. For all that, we could do it, and many now reading this could be aboard that first star ship.

We can do that today. What will we do in a hundred years? In a thousand, when we will have spread through the solar system and space colonies are common?

Arthur Clarke said it first: If mankind is to survive, then for all but a very brief part of our history the word "ship" will mean "space ship." We *will* spread through space. We will build a colony on the Moon: if we had a government of courage and imagination we would have that in time to celebrate the 500th anniversary of Columbus's voyages of discovery. As it is, it will take a bit longer; but we will go back to the Moon. We will settle other moons, and asteroids, and the planets; and we will go to the stars. Where mankind goes, government goes.

It is no idle thing, then, to think about what forms of government we will take to the stars. We in this enlightened age think we know; but do we? We are, after all, no smarter than our ancestors. We know more, but that's quite a different thing—and we have forgotten much that we had best relearn before we pay dearly for what they knew and we don't.

Imperial Stars examines the future of government: of wars and rumors of wars; of tumults and revolts; and of peace and rule and law and order among diversities of peoples and cultures and wealth. Through history the characteristic government that includes a multitude of races and peoples and cultures has been empire.

Empires take many forms. The Athenians established an empire and held it through their Golden Age of Pericles: through the age of Athenian democracy. Their suppression of Mitylene, and the siege and destruction of the neutral city of Melos, are among the most cynical and ruthless acts of history; for when the people of Melos pleaded that the gods would favor the cause of justice, and all the world knew that Melos was in the right, the Athenians said:

> *Of the gods we believe, and of men we know that by a necessary law of their nature they rule wherever they can . . . you know as well as we that right, as this world goes, is only in question between equals in power; for the strong do as they will, and the weak suffer what they must.*

It is only in fairy tales that democracies always act from the purest motives, and never have imperial ambitions. Of course the democracy may not survive. The Athenian democracy was snuffed out and her empire dismembered after Sparta's victories; we do not know what would have happened to the democracy if Athens had won. We do know that the Roman Republic gained an empire—and then became one, complete with emperor. Fletcher Pratt begins his justly renowned history of decisive warfare thus: "The Greeks had to go imperial to survive." We like to believe that western civilization has more freedom of choice.

The forms of empire change. The day of empire has not ended.

Empire. The very name holds power, even in this republican land and age. It conjures images of flags and drums, burnished shields and glittering banners; trumpets and courts and ceremonies: of Queen Empress Victoria and her captains and kings; of Claudius the Idiot, who became a god; of Alexander of Macedon, master of the world at thirty-two and dead a year later; of Charlemagne and Roland, Don John of Austria at Lepanto, Canute the Great, Constantine's fiery cross in the sky.

It conjures memories of past glories. Recently I stood at the *limes* at Arnsburg: the outer limits of the Roman Empire at its greatest extent. As I stood in the watchtower and stared out into the German forest I fancied I could hear the distant sound of horns, the measured tramp of the legions, the clatter of hooves of the cavalry patrols. Behind me lay plowed fields and cities; ahead, to this day, is forest and waste. The borders of empire were the boundaries of civilization.

The late Herman Kahn once argued that the natural state of mankind is empire, and the natural size of an empire is the Earth: that empires grow until they encounter something capable of resisting them; and the only institution capable of resisting for generations is another empire. Republics by contrast are short-lived, and either succumb to the pressure of the empire on their borders, or transform themselves into empire in order to remain independent.

There is much essential truth in these observations. For most of history, most of mankind has either lived under imperial rule; or has wanted to; or has been locked in struggle with empire. It is true today. In this, the supposed age of democracy, both China and the Soviet Union have imperial governments. Both are expanding; between them they encompass more than half the populations of the world. Nor are things so stable at home. Many books, written by liberal and conservative alike, note the drift of the United States toward imperial forms. The President of the United States holds, with his red and gold telephones, control of more power than was ever held by any man throughout history.

Blessing or curse, savior or destroyer: the shadow of empire falls across the Earth even in this enlightened age.

But empire may be many things.

"Saith Darius the King of Kings, the Great King: By the favor of Ahuramazda these are the nations I seized beyond the boundaries of Persia; I ruled over them; they bore tribute to me; what was said to them by me, that they did; my laws held them firm. Media, Elam, Parthia, Asia, Bactria, Sogdiona, Chorasmia, Drangiana, Arnchosia, Sattagydia, Gandara, Sind, Armygian Scythians, Scythians with pointed caps, Babylonia, Assyria, Arnbiz, Egypt, Armenia, Cappadocia, Sardis, Ionia, Scythians who are across the sea, Skudia, petasos-wearing Ionians, Libyans, Ethiopians, men of Maka, Carians.

"Saith Darius the King of Kings: Much which was ill

done, that I made good. Provinces were in turmoil, one man smiting another. By the favor of Ahuramazda this I brought about, that the one does not smite the other at all, each one is in his place. My law, of that they feel fear, so that the stronger does not smite nor destroy the weak."

This was no idle boast. Darius the Great King had brought more than a quarter of humanity under his rule. This was Empire, the greatest that had ever existed, and Darius sat supreme at the top of it. His word was law; his messengers carried it everywhere. So he boasts, and so it was.

More important is *what* Darius boasts. Contrast his inscription with one found in Elam by Darius's predecessor:

"I Assur-bani-pal, Great King of All Lands, took the carved furniture from these chambers; I took the horses and mules with gold-adorned bits from the stables. I burned with fire the bronze pinnacles of the temple; I carried off to Assyria the god of Elam with all his riches. I carried off the statues of thirty-two kings, together with the mighty stone bulls that guarded the gates. Thus have I entirely laid waste to this land and slain those who dwelt in it. I have laid their tombs open to the sun and have carried off the bones of those who did not venerate Assur and Ishtar, my lords—leaving the ghosts of these dead forever without repose, without offerings of food and water."

Assur-bani-pal has come to conquer and destroy. Those not of Assyrian lineage may expect no more than slavery and death. Contemporary accounts say that lands the Assyrians passed over suffered "the death of the earth." Assyrian armies left little but waste. Not so the Persians. Darius the Great King has come not to destroy, but to rule; and by his rule shall all benefit, Medes, Persians, Scythians, and Ionians alike. It is the difference between mere conquest and Empire; and long after the King of Kings, Great King, was no more than blowing dust, the memory of his empire remains and flourishes. Cyrus the Great found no mean place in the Bible; and to this day there are those in Iran who wish he or one like him would come again.

The Imperial theme runs long through Western history. We first glimpse it in the Hittites, those strange Indo-European peoples who settled in what is now Turkey. They brought iron weapons into the Bronze Age; they also brought the notion of Empire: the remarkable idea that Hittites and Hurrians and Luwians and Carians might all retain their own gods and customs and kings, yet all serve the same Emperor. They had other odd notions: they believed that kings and emperors were not exempt from right and wrong; that restrained by no man they yet ought to be restrained by law.

We see that notion again with the Achaemenians: Cyrus the Great and his descendents, who forged what we in the West call the Persian Empire. Though their history was written by their enemies, the people of Aryana, Iran, land of the Aryans, come off well in both the Hebrew and Greek accounts. Persian nobles were taught to ride, shoot the bow, and speak the truth. Cruelty was no part of their heritage. Neither was racism: the Persian Empire brought in as citizens Aryan and Semite alike, and if all were subject to the King of Kings, Great King, they were not merely subject alike, but subjects under their own laws and customs.

Alexander of Macedon marched the length and breadth of Persia. He married the Great King's wife and daughters. He defeated the Great King in every battle, until the Great King's own guards slaughtered the man who had once ruled a quarter of the world. Alexander married ten thousand of his Macedonian soldiers to Persian wives. And, of course, in the end the Persian Empire conquered both Alexander and Macedonia. What matter that a Macedonian sat on the Peacock Throne? He was addressed as King of Kings, Great King; scribes and scholars advised him; the Ten Thousand Immortals with golden apples on the hilts of their spears guarded him; and woe to the sturdy Macedonian peasant who dared approach the Emperor as any Macedonian once had the right to approach his King. The King of the Macedonians was but a man. He who sat on the Peacock Throne was King of Kings, Great King. . . .

The Persian throne endured to this generation; and who can say that the ayatollahs will last forever?

And finally we come to the Empire that shaped all our lives: Rome. Rome, whose citizenship was so valuable that Paul of Tarsus had only to say "Civis Romanus sum" to be freed of the jurisdiction of the provincial governor and sent to very Rome for his appeal to be heard. Rome, whose peace lies through our history and legends. Rome, that gave rise to our longings for world government.

We long for world peace and order. We also prize freedom. Yet we know: enduring peace among a diversity of peoples has so far come only from empire. True, the United States has attempted a different experiment: to forge a nation of states. It is also true that the United States has been, and many think can survive only by continuing to be, a melting pot. Empire preserves diversities; democracy erases them. And it has been a long time since we heard serious talk of states rights in this land.

The Roman Empire was born of republican conquests. Conquest and external enemies alike required that the old Roman army of the citizenry in arms be replaced with professional soldiers: a standing army of legions.

The Emperor was born of the Roman Army. When there are no legions there is no need for an Emperor. Yet the very nature of empire breeds the need for soldiers: how else can the empire be held together? And the larger the government, the more likely its need for soldiers: we may write constitutions for a world government, but if we ever achieve one in reality history says that it will be imperial.

History can be wrong. Perhaps we will evolve new

forms of government; or find new ways to make old ones work. It certainly can do no harm to speculate.

Herewith fact and fiction about governments and empires of the future.

Jerry E. Pournelle
Hollywood: Spring, 1986

EDITOR'S INTRODUCTION TO:

IN CLOUDS OF GLORY
Algis Budrys

Algis Budrys was born in Lithuania between the two halves of the civil war we call the World Wars. His father was a high official of the Lithuanian Diplomatic Corps; Algis Budrys grew up in the worlds of diplomacy and intrigue. The Hitler-Stalin Pact gave Lithuania (and two thirds of Poland) to the Soviet Union. The Lithuanian diplomatic corps abroad continued to represent the old Republic in such places as Britain and the United States where the Russian conquest was not recognized; and Budrys grew up as an exile.

To this day the United States has never formally recognized the incorporation of the Baltic Republics into the Soviet Empire; but when we signed the Helsinki Agreement we gave full recognition to the *de facto* borders of Europe and ceased to hold our annual observation of Captive Nations Week. In effect we abandoned a dozen nations to the tender mercies of the Soviet Union in exchange for a paper promise of "human rights" for the subjects of the Soviet Empire. The Russians did not precisely promise not to be beastly;

but they did promise that they would be less beastly than was their prior practice.

To prove their devotion to the Helsinki pact, the Soviets promptly rounded up and jailed the Helsinki Watch Committee, a group of Soviet citizens who announced their intention of monitoring Soviet observation of the accord. They recently traded Anatoly Scharansky, one of the organizers of Helsinki Watch, for a group of legally convicted Soviet spies.

The Helsinki Agreement is said to be a triumph of American diplomacy. Whether or not that is so, it did pretty well end the hopes of exiled Baltic peoples. A few of their representatives in exile continue to operate consulates and embassies, but one hears less about them with every passing year. Their incorporation into the Soviet Empire is well nigh complete.

As the Soviet example shows, empire doesn't always mean drums and flags and an imperial majesty. On the other hand, even when you have all those, you may not have a real empire. The Great Mogul Emperor, descendent of Babur the Tiger, held his throne long after his word ceased to be obeyed outside his own palace; while the British built themselves quite a good empire long before they acknowledged what they had. It was an empire acquired almost by accident through a private company, and regularized only after the Great Sepoy Revolt. Once regularized it endured, of course. It was abandoned only when the Britons tired of rule.

In this classic tale Algis Budrys speaks of a time when mankind has been united, but has yet to find a place among the stars.

IN CLOUDS OF GLORY
Algis Budrys

"We are the men of the Agency—
　We're steadfast, stout-hearted, and brave.
For a buck we will duck
　Through the worst that may come,
And argue the price of a grave.

"Oh, we are the Agency's bravos—
　We peddle the wealth of our skill.
　We will rescue your world or destroy it,
　Depending on who foots the bill."

ANONYMOUS

I

The tidy little orchestra finished the dance set and broke up, leaving behind the quartet nucleus, which began Schubert's "Fourteenth." The party guests dispersed through the room, talking in groups while the servants passed among them with refreshments.

Thaddeus Demaris brooded solemnly in a heavy chair near the fireplace, half-listening to the two well-kept men conversing nearby. One of them was Walker Holtz, the hunter. The other was Captain Romney Oxford, of Her Canadian Majesty's Legation in Detroit.

Walker Holtz fingered the stem of his boutonniere and took a sip of his liqueur. He leaned against the mantelpiece, let his eyes flick negligently over the crowd, and resumed his conversation.

"My dear Captain Oxford, I'll grant you artillery. Artillery and, in certain circumstances, infantry. But not aircraft. The British had the quality and the Americans the quantity."

"I don't see how you can say that," Oxford countered. He took a gulp of his drink and set it down firmly. "What about the Trans-Polar Campaign?"

Holtz raised his eyebrows. "I think it's generally accepted that Vitkovsky was able to commit his reserve fighter wings only because the Alaskan Air Command of the old United States Air Force was snowed in."

Oxford granted the point easily. "Quite so. And then Vitkovsky's transports would have suffered, say sixty percent interceptions over Quebec?"

"You're being generous, Captain," Holtz rejoindered. He inhaled gently over his glass before raising it to his lips. "I would have said fifty."

Oxford brushed the polite quibble aside with a graceful wave of his hand.

In his chair, Demaris smiled bitterly and scornfully. These men with their heads for the facts and figures of ancient military history—how many of them had ever heard a shot fired in anger?

"Well, then," Oxford was saying, scoring his point, "I should like to remind you, Colonel Holtz, that Vitkovsky's plan necessarily allowed for seventy percent interceptions. As it finally transpired, so many surplus troops landed in Illinois that an emergency quartermaster and clerical staff had to be flown in."

Holtz frowned, discomfited.

Demaris stood up impatiently and snatched a liqueur from a passing servant's tray. The heavily flavored cordial bit at his tongue.

And for all the battles won in parlors and drawing rooms, where was Earth's frontier today?

His lip curled. He swung around and stabbed an extended forefinger at the startled Oxford. "I should like to point out," he bit off in the astonished man's face, "that what you have just cited was the USSR's suicidal policy of wasting men, *not* the superiority of its air arm, which was consistently hampered and eventually destroyed by a typical Russian insistence on trying to make a rapier do a bludgeon's work."

Holtz stepped between them, his temples throbbing and his nostrils white. "You are ungentle, sir."

Demaris looked at him coldly, a certain amount of anticipation tightening the curl of his fingers. "And you are a fool and an ass."

The muscles knotted at the corners of Holtz's thin jaw. He drew back his hand to slap. Demaris lifted his cheek a fraction of an inch, his head tilting to present a willing target. The buzz of conversation was dying in the room, smothering under a wave of rapt silence.

Oxford reached out hastily and pushed himself between Holtz and Demaris. "Eh . . . Colonel Holtz . . . I don't believe you've previously met Thaddeus Demaris. The introduction is my pleasure."

The pallid urgency in Oxford's eyes was mimicked by Holtz's sudden slackness of mouth. His arm lowered limply. "Ah? Uh . . . oh, no, Oxford, *my* pleasure, I'm sure—"

Demaris smashed the back of his hand across Holtz's face. The hunter stumbled back, one hand pressed to his nose. Oxford made a noise of protest. Demaris stood motionless, his face set.

Holtz regained his balance. "Really, Mr. Demaris," he mumbled, waving Oxford back, "my sincere apologies—"

Demaris looked at him with something much like disappointment. He spun on his heel and stalked off.

Even the night was dishonest. Laden with perfume, the artificially circulated air stirred a sham breeze across the balconade. A sickle of moon drifted among the gray-silver clouds. Behind him, Demaris could hear the last notes of "Death and the Maiden" fading politely away.

How far in the past was Oxford's and Holtz's war? Three hundred years. And after finishing that war, how far in the future did Man imagine his Empire of Earth lay, stretching out into the stars? One century? Two? With the interstellar drive and the Terrestrial Space Navy to ride it.

And where, now, was Earth's frontier, a full hundred years beyond that well-planned future?

Pluto. That's where it was. Just barely, Pluto.

All right. You could understand that. An empire only goes as far as its enemies will let it. A hundred years ago, the Vilks had drawn the line.

Demaris smashed his flat, horny palm down on the coping of the terrace. The slap of sound startled some of the strolling couples in the formal gardens, but it would have been ungentle for them to stare at him. He knew of their curiosity only by the fact that no face, among all those couples, turned toward him even at random.

His lips twitched back from the points of his teeth.

And with the Vilks fifty years gone in a pyrrhic war with Farla, you could expect the ships of Earth to be going out again. You could expect that.

You could die of the eating hunger in your stomach, expecting it. You could grow old, with strings for muscles and pudding for a brain, expecting it.

You could run up a string of successful, pointless duels. You could go to graceful, inbred gatherings in the elegant, bandbox mansions. You could listen to Schubert quartets and a lot of Delius. But there was damned little Beethoven, and no Stravinsky. There was yearning, and no fulfillment. Nor much of a desire for it. It was considered more gentle to simply yearn.

A servant touched his arm. "Your pardon, Messire—a Mr. Brown is on the vid."

Demaris fought to keep from spinning around violently. "Thank you," he said in a voice that, incredibly, was calm enough. He strolled back into the mansion. Brown! Thank God! He'd been going mad, waiting.

"We spill our all for the Agency—
(Our lives are excitingly gory.)
Pink or blue—any hue—
Save the red of our birth—
At the beck of crisp, green glory."

II

Brown was the code name. Kaempfert was the man. Blocky, with a square face and blunt fingertips, he was one of sixteen men who sat behind their crowded desks in the Agency's sparsely furnished Assignment Room.

"How are you, Bill?" Demaris said, shaking his hand. "How're Leni and the kids?"

"Fine, Thad. Getting healthier every day." He looked down at his stomach and chuckled. "All of us. Sit down. You got here fast. Champing at the bit, Thad?"

Demaris nodded expressively. "I can't take Earth any more." He grimaced distastefully. "Croquet, Mr. Demaris? Liqueur, Messire? Agh! Our society's like a translucent china dish, overlaid with gilt filigree and wrapped in cotton batting. It's beautiful, it's elegant, and safe—but you don't dare use it to eat from."

Kaempfert smiled, his eyes sparkling briefly. Then he flicked a hand toward the files on his desk.

"O.K., then—let's get you out where the red meat is. Briefly, here's the job:

"Farla's as good as gone. She may not know it, yet, but the only thing that's saved her for the time being is Marak's inability to move in without first slapping down Genis—and vice versa.

"So, Marak's asked us for a man who'll keep Genis off balance until Marak can move in on Farla and consolidate. That's you. You'll handle strategy, maybe do some on-the-spot generaling."

Demaris nodded. "Sounds good." He grinned fiercely. "Sounds damn good!"

Kaempfert handed him a file. "Here's most of your poop. You get a full-scale briefing tomorrow at eight. That's Ante Meridiem, son. You're scheduled for Make-up and Indoctrination at eleven."

Demaris whistled softly. "Shooting me out in a hurry, huh?"

Kaempfert nodded, his face grave. "It's faster than I'd like. One day isn't enough to set up an air-tight job. But it's a hurry-up situation. We'll just have to take our chances. If you think somebody's spotted you, you're hereby authorized to take the most logical preventive steps under the circumstances."

Demaris nodded as though in echo to Kaempfert's expression. The necessity was obvious, but nevertheless, the Agency didn't often work that way.

Kaempfert broke the silence. "Well. That's that. Where're you staying tonight, Thad?"

Demaris shrugged. "Hotel of some kind, I guess. I got here straight from the airport. Still got my bags out in the front office."

"Well, how about staying over with us?" Kaempfert stared down at his fingertips.

Demaris laughed. "I guess that's one way of making sure I won't get into a fight before morning. Sure, Bill. Be glad to, and thanks."

Kaempfert looked up at him with the traces of guilt fading out of the corners of his eyes.

Demaris winked at him. "Where'd you get the idea I was the pugnacious type, Bill?"

Kaempfert grunted.

Demaris sprawled his bulk in an easy-chair, his feet thrust out atop a hassock. He felt free and relaxed for the first time in weeks. He'd eaten a quick meal, unconstrained by any necessity for making intricate small-talk. No, he had a lazy evening to look forward to; something he hadn't had since the last time he'd known he was going out in the morning.

He whistled a snatch of "Heroes All" and chuckled softly.

Leni Kaempfert smiled fondly as she shut the nursery door behind her. "Adding a new verse, Thad?"

"Me? I never wrote that thing."

Leni's tongue bulged her cheek. "No?"

"Why, no."

She shrugged agreeably. "O.K. But if Old Man Sullivan ever proves his suspicions, you'll be in deep trouble." She looked at Demaris with mock-solemnity. "The Agency is a serious business enterprise. Let us not go around making snide remarks."

Demaris took a gulp of his drink. "To Hell with Old Man Sullivan!"

"It's his outfit, Thad," Bill Kaempfert reminded him, "We just work there. He runs things the way he wants them."

Demaris reached out spasmodically, as though unconsciously trying to seize hold of his fleeing peace. For an hour, he had forgotten the habitual tensity of his muscles. Now his jaw was hardening again.

"Yeah!" he spat out harshly. "He sits in an office somewhere, where nobody ever sees him, and he runs it. I just go out and bleed dollar bills for him." Demaris coiled his body into a tense crouch on the chair's edge.

"Now, come on," Kaempfert said, "it's not as bad as all that."

Demaris lashed out savagely. "Isn't it? If there were still a TSN—if there were even the faintest chance of working for Earth instead of messing up the stars for Sullivan's profit—would you stick with the Agency? Would you be selling yourself on every streetcorner, no reasonable offer refused?" He could see he was embarrassing the Kaempferts, but what he was saying was true.

Bill Kaempfert grinned uncomfortably. "That's a point, Thad," he admitted. "But you don't knock your bread and butter."

Demaris thumped his empty glass down on the side table. "Would we starve?" he asked. "Would we really wind up begging in the streets? You especially; couldn't you get a job as a personnel manager with any company you wanted?"

Kaempfert shrugged. "Maybe. If I could think up some explanation for not having any references. It's been ten years since I've held a legal job."

"O.K. So you'd have a little trouble. But not that much. Besides, we're off the point."

Kaempfert raised his eyebrows inquiringly. Demaris inhaled raggedly.

"Let's face it, Bill—we're bad enough off now, but we'd cut our throats if we gave it all up and tried to live in this teashop society. We just don't fit. Our personal frontier doesn't stop at Pluto." He grimaced.

"Here we sit. Two prime representatives of a race that used to have guts to spare—that scared the universe half-silly the first time we pushed a rickety tin can to Sirius. And here we sit now—the backwash of the Wave of the Future!"

Kaempfert put up a restraining palm. "Easy, Thad. Most people would figure Pluto was plenty far enough. Most people don't ever even leave Earth. And we may have scared the universe, but we sure didn't impress the Vilks."

Demaris brushed Kaempfert's palm down as effectively as though there'd been a physical contact. "All right. So the barbarians licked us. That was when the TSN was fifteen ships and a handful of cranky torpedoes. Now the Vilks are gone for good. It was an Earthman that licked 'em, too."

Kaempfert nodded. "Old Connie Jones."

"*Exactly!* Connie Jones—an Agency man hired by Farla. So who got the territory an Earthman won? Who moved in where Earthmen should have been the conquerors? It would have been Farla, buying its military brains from an Agency run by Earthmen. It happened to work out that Farla bled itself to death. So who *does* move in? Who takes the territory that's open by default? Does Earth have even that much ambition?

"No, it has to be rabble like the Maraks, or the Geneiids! A pack of jackals. And what does Earth government do about it? Earth government isn't even interested. And what do individual Earthmen do—the ones who still care? Why," Demaris suddenly simpered, "*we* work for Mr. Sullivan's Agency, and *we'd* be only too happy to hire out to one of the jackals, wouldn't we? We're for sale; lock, stock, and barrel, soul, body, and birthright. We do the dirty work for every stinking little race in the galaxy, and meanwhile Earth government sits primly on its solar system and keeps its hoop-skirts dry."

"Thad?"

"Yes, Leni?"

"Thad, what you're angry at is that Bill and I don't protest as much as you do. But we *aren't* arguing. Bill thinks you're right, and so do I. Still, there's no way we can change Earth's present attitude. And we've at least got this substitute.

"And tell me this, Thad—honestly, now, and no heroics—will you quit? Will you ever quit, and settle for a life here on Earth? Going from one duel to the next until nobody dares associate with you and you blow out your own brains for lack of some other man to fight?"

Demaris looked at her helplessly. "No," he admitted.

> *"Though we are men, at the Agency,*
> *We fight in peculiar skins.*
> *Aptly taught, we're not caught—*
> *We've been thoroughly trained,*
> *In the lore of exotical sins."*

III

The Agency building was dingy. Demaris and Kaempfert walked down the grimy hallway and up the splintered stairs to the second floor. They pushed through the chipped glass door labeled "Doncaster Industrial Linens" and were in the Agency's front office.

Demaris still felt the irritating memories of last night's adrenalin. He looked around and shook his head. "There's no place like home sweet home—even if it's a false beard."

Kaempfert shrugged. "Our customers don't know where the cash-and-carry heroes come from. Why should Earth government? Besides, I can just hear what the government would have to say about its nationals fighting alien battles and chancing all sorts of international complications if their origin is discovered."

"Government could use a jolt," Demaris growled.

"Your briefing room's down the hall," Kaempfert said. "You're due there."

Demaris nodded. "Uh-huh." He put out his hand. "Bill—I'm sorry I'm such a pop-off. I didn't really mean to give you a rough time last night. Be seeing you, huh?"

"Sure, Thad. Come home—nothing to forgive."

They shook hands, tapped each other on the biceps, and separated. Demaris walked down the hall, and Kaempfert went through the front office to his desk.

He'd memorized his Marak file. Now he turned it in to the technician at the door of the briefing room, who tagged it with his code name and dropped it into a similarly labeled filing cabinet.

"Strip," the technician said in a bored voice.

Demaris had already begun climbing out of his clothes. He handed the bundle to the technician, who tagged it and put it in a locker. "Stand still, please ... no facial expression, if you please . . . hold it . . . thank you." The front and sideview photographs were clipped to Demaris' check card, and the card was handed to him. "Medical examination over in that corner, please."

Demaris bobbed his head impatiently. The doctor, standing beside his equipment, was thin but not invisible.

He was given a complete physical, with results noted on his card, and returned to the technician, who wordlessly handed him a set of light coveralls, noted their issue on his card, returned the card, and then nodded him over to the desk where his briefing officer had been sitting all this time.

"Mr. Blue?" the briefing officer said as Demaris came over, addressing him by his code name, "My name's Puce." He smiled slightly. "Sit down, please. May I have your card, please? Thank you."

Demaris handed the card over.

"You've studied your file?"

"Memorized it."

"Yes, yes, of course, Mr. Blue. Just a routine question. You know how it is—mass production. We treat everybody the same way—old hand, new comer, special recruit; whatever he may be. It's not as informal as it might be, but—"

"I know."

"Uh. Well. Now, Mr. Blue—if your rank were that of Tjetlyn in the Marakian Interstellar Air Fleet, and I were a Klowdil, which of us would salute first?"

"Neither of us. You'd be my inferior, so I'd pretend to ignore you. If I wanted anything from you, I'd say so. The salute, as such, is unknown on Marak." Demaris gave the answer in a bored voice.

"Yes. Well—as a Tjetlyn, you might be invited to official functions at the homes of Chiefs of State. Would it be proper for you to drink three portions of *drasos?*"

"It would be mandatory—three and as many more as I could hold."

"Good. Very good, Mr. Blue. Now, assuming that you were on leave and fell into the company of a perfectly respectable but not hostile young *pavoja:* What would be your course of action?"

"I'd pretend she was Eileen deFleur—up to the point at which my normal Marakian biological urges would, unfortunately, suffer frustration due to accidental circumstances over which no one could possibly prove I had any control."

Mr. Puce chuckled. "Very good. Now, supposing—"

And so forth, through a veritable nightmare of possible pitfalls which might betray his un-Marakian nature. Demaris threaded his deliberate way through all the vicissitudes Mr. Puce could conjure up for him, and emerged unchallenged—and angry at the redundance of going through this college entrance examination when he knew that Indoctrination would supply him with the unconscious awareness of all these things, driving the knowledge not into his conscious information banks but into his reflexes.

Still and all, he could not deny that the Agency had remained undetected only because of this kind of thoroughness—and that in this case, especially, with no time for the usual three days' checking to be sure, every possible precaution still might leave some chink unguarded.

*   *   *

"All right, Mr. Blue," Puce was saying, "I think that about covers it. Now, if you'll just sketch out a situation map on this board, I think that'll be all—except for Make-up and Indoctrination, of course."

Yes— Except for that mere trifle. Demaris twitched his upper lip as he picked up Puce's stylus and laid out the map.

Farla was a cluster of stars shaped like a badly pitted furnace clinker. Adjoining it on the side away from Earth—which he represented by a contemptuous, zero-shaped speck at the foot of the board—was Marak, with its stars grouped like a rat's head, sniffing at the clinker. To Farla's right, Genis and her stars were a twisted, mold-eaten orange peel. Working quickly, he sketched in the profile view, which included such scattered breadcrumbs as Ruga, Dilpo, and Stain, all inextricably jumbled in by the fact that stars, unfortunately for diagramatics, occupied three dimensions, were anything but stationary, and were governed by countless dozens of little pocket empires that had seized in any and all possible directions once the Vilk yolk was taken off them.

The pure white stars, he thought—the pure white stars live in a garbage heap.

He turned the board around and pushed it toward Puce, who nodded approval. "Yes, that's fine. All right, that does it. Thank you, and good luck, Mr. Blue."

Demaris grunted and stood up, taking his card. Of all the clerks at the Agency, Bill Kaempfert was the only one he could stomach, because Kaempfert was the only one who'd actually done any fighting. He almost turned around to club Puce as the man tried to prove something or the other about himself by loudly—and anything but absently—humming a chorus of "Heroes All."

Then he shrugged and let it go. The fool was proving his adolescence by somehow making the rollicking tune acquire heroic chords.

Demaris walked into Make-up and Indoctrination to the accompaniment of his own misinterpreted music.

*   *   *

Make-up peeled off his skin as neatly as a glove, and put it away for his return. Scalpels clicked against his bones. Weapons sent over a last-resort personal arm that the surgeons buried in his rib cage. Make-up delved into its resources and so disguised the weapon's unavoidable metal that only the most careful comparative fluoroscopy would detect it.

And the Monster chugged on its dolly beside the operating tank, revamping his brain.

When he emerged, at eleven o'clock that night, he spoke English with difficulty. His tongue and vocal cords were not adapted to the language.

The Earthman—the *dakta*—nodded in satisfaction as Demaris sat up groggily.

"Nice control," the *dakta* said to himself, noting the weak but sure movements of Demaris' limbs. Demaris, who had to translate from English to Marakian before he could be sure of the *dakta's* exact meaning, was only a bit slower in reaching the same conclusion. He tested the flexibility of his double-jointed fingers, and worked his double-opposed thumbs for a moment.

"Oh, they'll work fine," the *dakta* assured him. " 'Fdoo seisomysell."

Demaris groped for the meaning of the idomatic phrase, which, like most such, had been tossed off casually. "Par-don," he said. "Would you please speak more slowly?"

"I say—'If I do say so myself.' "

"Oh, yes. Of course. Everything seems to be all right."

"That's quite an accent," the *dakta* apologized, obviously not having caught Demaris' statement.

Demaris strained for clarity. "I say—'Everything seems O.K.' "

"Oh! Oh, yes, sure. We really piled it on—much more thorough than usual. A matter of costuming to lend reality to an actor who might not have learned his part too well."

Demaris shook his head with annoyance at his own incomprehension. He sorted out the *dakta's* syllables in his mind, trying to extract their meaning.

"Would you like me to repeat?" the *dakta* volunteered.

Demaris shook his head in disgust. There was really no point in this clumsy communication. The Monster had superimposed a Marakian personality where an Earthman had been, and there was not much that Earthmen and Marakians had to say to each other.

"Never mind," he said, enunciating as clearly as possible.

> *"We do or die for the Agency—*
>   *As much of the first as we can—*
> *Heroes who, mashed to glue,*
>   *Spent their saved-up back pay,*
> *Are strange to the mem'ry of man."*

IV

The trip out to Marak in the Agency ship took about a week, T.S.T. In that time Demaris recuperated completely, until, by the time the ship ducked down on Marak's nightside, he was at his physical peak. He grinned with delight at the steelhard claws which sprang out from his fingertips at will. He paced his cabin relentlessly, a constant growl of satisfaction rumbling up his throat as he felt his supple tendons coiling and uncoiling in fluid motion.

Yet, the bitterness was still there. Paradoxically, it was sprung from the same source as his satisfaction. If Earthmen could take one of their own kind and turn him into a duplicate of any other bipedal, bilaterally symmetrical being—if they had learned that much, and mastered biology to such a point—why did Earthmen have to wear disguises at all? Why did Earth's fighting men have to fight for every race but their own, and why was Earth itself so helpless?

No, not helpless—spineless.

Some day. Some day, maybe, things would be different.

The growl in Demaris' alien throat became a caged cough of rancor.

* * *

The ship dropped him in a sparse area, flitting down and leaping back to the sky as soon as his contact turned up. Demaris watched it dwindle, and only after it was gone did he notice his contact's hungry eyes following it.

"I haven't been home in a long time," the contact apologized in perfect Marakian. "I've got another three years to go here."

Demaris grunted. "Believe me—six months and you'll be begging to sign up for a new tour."

"I suppose so," the contact agreed. "I don't guess it's changed much?"

"Not the slightest."

The contact expressed himself in listless oaths. "Well," he said with a final profane twitch of his mouth, "let's put the show on the road. I've got a car stashed out in some shrubbery down there."

Demaris fell in behind him. Neither of them spared any particular attention to the thoroughly familiar country-side. They threaded their way through the broken thickets, automatically keeping clear of shrubs that would have left cockleburrs in their glossy fur.

The Marakian Overchief was growing old. His fur was beginning to lose its sheen, and his skin hung loosely around his neck. Nevertheless, his eyes were incisive and his voice was penetrating. He studied Demaris thoroughly for several moments before he said anything beyond a perfunctory greeting. Then he grunted with satisfaction.

"Good. You look as though you can handle things. I don't know where Resvik dug you out, but that's unimportant."

The contact, standing beside Demaris, made a non-committal gesture. "As I've said from the beginning, we're not prepared to go deeply into Koil's past activities. Some of them might be interpreted as having been extra-legal. But he's thoroughly familiar with all the aspects of what's expected of him, and he's got the training required."

The Overchief surveyed Demaris again, and shook

his head in agreement. "He looks it. He ought to, for the price you're asking."

"It's fair," the contact said.

"Oh, yes—I'll grant you that. Well—is there anything else, Resvik?"

"No, sir. I'll get back to my duties. It's been a pleasure, Overchief. Good luck, Koil." He slipped out of the office, closing the door gently behind him.

The Overchief gestured toward a bench, and Demaris sat down, quietly watching the Overchief stalk back and forth behind his desk. The first actual contact with the head of an alien culture was usually the most ticklish part of one of these things. But, again as usual, it seemed to be going smoothly.

"Now—what's your full name?" the Overchief asked.

"Call me Todren Koil," Demaris answered.

The Overchief grinned thinly. "All right, we'll call you that. What we want you to do is harry Genis. Within reason, you can do it your own way. I want their navy kept busy—too busy to deploy against our main push. If you do your job right, they shouldn't even suspect we're moving in on Farla until we're well on our way. I have no expectation that you'll be able to keep their fleet completely tied down after we make our move, but you should be able to hamper them somewhat. That's all we need—an edge. Your job's done the day we put a ship on Farla itself. By then we'll have the old Farlan perimeter well enough defended so that anything they do won't catch us with our fur wet. Clear?"

Demaris gestured affirmatively.

"I don't suppose you're wondering why we hired you?" the Overchief asked. "No. I can see that. Resvik's undoubtedly informed you about the"—he coughed—"high quality of our military leadership. I *don't* expect an affirmative comment from you," he added, not without a strong trace of the bitterness he must have felt. Resorting to mercenaries after his own officer-training system has proved deficient is never pleasant for a military leader. "All right," he said with a savage rumble, "what will you need offhand?"

"Some light, mobile stuff. Not much of it. A squadron of *Pira* Class boats ought to do it. I'll do all my work through your intelligence agency. I'll need liaison and authorization. We may have to supplement their demolitions and infiltration groups—I'll see how their existing forces work out under my methods. I think I can get in a lot of damage before Genis even begins any full scale retaliation. Give me about fifteen days to start the operation rolling. By then, I'll know whether I need to ask for anything else."

"Done." The Overchief touched the switches of his desk communicator. "Send in Tjetlyn Faris," he said.

Demaris felt the tension oozing away from him in direct proportion to his mounting excitement. He could feel himself settling into the old familiar state of pleasant anticipation. It might not be for Earth's sake, but for Mammon's. It might extend the Agency's reputation, instead of Earth's. It might be for cash on delivery—but it was action, nevertheless—action, and, in war, the only peace he could hope to have.

He looked up at Tjetlyn Faris with quicksilver burning through his veins.

Faris was a youngish Marakian of about his own age. He came in the door and stood waiting for the Overchief to speak.

"Sath, this is Tjetlyned Todren Koil," the Overchief said, indicating Demaris. "Todren, Faris Sath. He's your liaison and Second in Command. He'll take you down to our intelligence offices and introduce you to the existing routine. Your authorization will be there ahead of you. From here on, it's your operation to work out between you."

Demaris acknowledged Sath's presence with a shake of his head. The Overchief had made him the Tjetlyn's superior by one grade, but Demaris had no illusions about that. No Agency man ever worked without his employer's setting a watchdog over him.

Deep within the Marakian interior, the Earthman smiled. That didn't always work out the way it was meant to. Old Connie Jones, for instance, working with Farla's paranoid culture, had so maneuvered his personal watchdog assassin that, in the end, the assassin had seen the expediency not only of not killing Jones but of taking the victorious fleet back to Farla and staging a revolution.

Quis custodiet—But that wouldn't work here, nor was it necessary. Marak was not Farla, though the two races were descended from the same ancestor. There was no danger here of an attempt to kill the mercenary once he'd done his work.

Demaris wasn't sure he wouldn't have welcomed that added fillip.

"At your orders, Tjetlyned," Sath said. Demaris shot a look past him at the Overchief and saw that he was pointedly ignoring both of them.

Ugh. He'd been daydreaming at the wrong time. He nodded quickly to Sath, and they slipped out the door together.

> *"Ah, we are the Agency's offspring,*
> *The brood of a sinful old maid.*
> *There isn't one chance that she'd sell*
> *   us out—*
> *Unless things were such that it*
> *   paid."*

(alternate chorus)

V

Three months later, Sath laid a fresh set of reports on Demaris' desk. "Here we are, Koil. Top sheet's the summary." He dropped down on the bench beside the desk and wearily dug a flask out of his belt. "Have some?" he offered, holding up the flask.

Demaris twitched an ear negatively, and took his own brand out of a drawer. "Can't stand that gunk you use." He tilted the flask and touched his tongue to the mild stimulant. Recapping the flask, he yawned broadly. He looked at the report in disgust.

"Same thing?"

Sath nodded. "Yep. In the past fifteen days, our

demolitions teams have immobilized such-and-such a tonnage of Geneiid naval vessels. Our infiltrators have immobilized this-and-that additional tonnage by misrouting supplies, disrupting communications, altering fleet orders, et cetera. We can truthfully report that our organization has been doing an excellent job, and that we are performing far above the expectations set down by Staff."

Demaris grimaced. "And how far behind schedule is the push against Farla?"

Sath coughed. "Well, if you plotted the curve of Staff's failure against our curve of success, they'd be almost superimposed."

Demaris shook his head. "Still the same trouble?"

"Yep. Seems like Genis has just as good an intelligence service as we do. Tit for tat, right down the line."

Demaris clicked his fingertips against the surface of his desk. The situation stank. For every boat that shipped a team of saboteurs into Genis, a Geneiid boat dropped its cargo down on Marak's planets. Like two giants stabbing pins through each other's ganglia, Marak and Genis were immobilizing each other.

War in space—war in terms of planetary englobements, massive landings, and blockades—was impossible. The problem of supply and reinforcement became insurmountable over interstellar distances. As the attacker's supply lines lengthened, the defender's shortened, until eventually the attrition on the attacker became too great. You could only stage a mass attack on a hopelessly weak foe—such as Farla. Otherwise, it was your infiltrators and demolitions men, crippling your enemy at home, who first had to weaken him. And if your sabotage was balanced by equally effective enemy action, then both of you slowly bled away, matching each other corpuscle for corpuscle, neither ever gaining a relative upper hand.

Demaris wondered how long this could keep up. Agency men weren't supermen. Man for man, there was no reason why they should be any better than their opposite numbers. The Agency's selling point was the right man in the right place, at the right time.

Well, so far he was holding his own. But how much longer would the Overchief be satisfied with that?

Demaris grinned to himself, at himself. Face it. What galled him most was his inability to beat his Geneiid adversary. The Agency and its considerations were secondary.

"So, anyway—" Sath was saying, "I just got a call from the Overchief. He wants to see us."

Demaris inhaled slowly.

The Overchief was showing the strain. Farla should have been penetrated and taken by now. Instead, the Marakian fleet lay hamstrung in its berths. That the Geneiids were racked by the same frustration was of little comfort to him.

He waved them to benches with a nervous gesture of his arm. Demaris sat down carefully. For the first time since he'd landed on Marak, he became consciously aware of the weapon buried in his chest. Cautiously, he put a slight bit of pressure on his shoulder muscles, and held his breath. He felt the weapon's barrels slip forward. Then he relaxed. No. If this was a showdown, here, he had no right to fight for his life. The manner of an Overchief's death would be too carefully investigated. If he were caught now, in these circumstances, the weapon's other characteristic was his own only escape. He'd have to detonate its charge.

He realized his mind was making mountains out of molehills, and fought down his apprehension. The Overchief might find fault with Todren Koil, and Todren Koil would react accordingly. But the Overchief had no possible reason to think that Todren Koil had ever been a weak, pink-skinned monster whose only real weapon against the universe was the intricacy of his mind.

The Overchief looked up from his desk. "Glad to see you, Todren, Faris. You're not here for reprimand."

Demaris heard Sath's breathing deepen deside him. His own diaphragm relaxed.

"If it wasn't for you," the Overchief went on, "we'd be in much worse trouble." He got up and began to stalk back and forth. "Genis, as we've found out, just happened to produce a good intelligence man of its own. We didn't expect it—we had no reason to. They're generally no luckier with their officers than we are." He slapped a thigh with an irritated hand. "We've got to remove that officer, or those officers, though the latter possibility gives Geneiid luck altogether too much credit. I want you two to lay out an operation that will accomplish the purpose. I shouldn't even have to say that any resource, short of a fleet action, is yours to call on. All right, I want a summary of your ideas by tomorrow. Faris, I'll speak further to Tjetlyned Todren alone."

Sath inclined his head affirmatively, rose, and slipped out. Demaris looked inquiringly at the Overchief, who was standing with his back to him.

The Overchief turned around. "Todren," he said softly, "this Geneiid intelligence officer—he seems to have popped up out of the ground. We have no dossier on him. Might he be some relative of yours?"

Demaris had been expecting the question for a full minute. He looked steadily at the Overchief. "I have no relatives."

The Overchief stared back, his eyes equally unwavering. Finally, he said: "Well, that is as it may be. I suggest that you devote all possible effort to clearing up the situation."

"Yes, sir."

He slipped out of the Overchief's room and joined Sath. They walked down the hall together.

Just how far, he was wondering, did Old Man Sullivan go in his pursuit of a dollar?

> "We fight for the Agency's money—
>   We draw out our pay with a smile.
> For our gold, we've been told,
>   We should barter ourselves
> In truly professional style."

VI

It did not take a fleet action. Not quite. It took a combined operation of all infiltrators and demolitions teams on Genis itself, and the services of a fast cruiser.

The infiltrators pin-pointed the Geneiid intelligence director and cut him off from communication with possible help. The demolitions men blew their way into his headquarters. A *Pira* boat shuttled him up to the cruiser, and the cruiser, ultimately, delivered him to Demaris. The maneuver completely disrupted the normal schedule of activities against Genis, but Demaris, looking across the room at the captured Geneiid, calculated that it was cheap at the price.

"Well, there he is," Sath commented.

"So he is," Demaris agreed, looking dispassionately at the drugged Geneiid. For the life of him, he could see no trace of Make-up's scalpels on that leathery hide—but then, where were his own scars?

"What now?" Sath asked.

"I'd suggest we put our program back into shape as quickly as possible—and make sure Genis doesn't try to pull on us what we did to them."

"I've already set up defenses against that kind of stunt. You're right—I'll get us straightened out while you handle this beastie." Sath went over to his own desk and got to work. Half the organization had been lost or compromised in the kidnaping. He had to reassemble and reinforce what was left. But it was downhill work, now. Marak had her edge.

Demaris jerked his head at the medical technicians. One of them jammed a hypodermic through the Geneiid's skin and shot in a neutralizer. Demaris stood idly by, whistling between his teeth.

It was a touch-and-go business. He'd tried to put himself in the Geneiid's place, and he'd decided that if he were suddenly kidnaped, he wouldn't use his Agency weapon, until it became completely obvious that there was no other resort.

So far, so good. The Geneiid—he was a Geneiid—was still alive, and he'd been taken with no more trouble than you'd expect. But the man might revive in a panic.

He whistled a bit more loudly.

> *"Oh, we are the Agency's bravos—*
> *We peddle the wealth of one*
> *skill—"*

The Geneiid's eyelids fluttered upward. It seemed to Demaris that the man looked at him with an intensity peculiar for even these circumstances.

> *"Ah, we are the Agency's offspring,*
> *the brood of a sinful old maid—*

The Geneiid sat up and stared malevolently at Demaris. "How did this happen?" he asked in passable Marakian. The technicians giggled, Sath, looking up from his desk, grinned coldly. Demaris smiled without humor.

> *". . . Unless things were such that*
> *paid."*

The Geneiid looked around the office in dawning comprehension that meant one thing to everyone else and something quite differeent to Demaris. "I see—" he said slowly. "What now?"

Demaris reflected that there was the best question he'd heard in a long time. He wondered if the other man thought Demaris was in on a deliberate double-cross. If he did, almost anything might happen. He had no idea how he'd react in similar circumstances.

"I fear, my friend," Demaris said in passable Geneiian, "that the Fates, which might just as easily have conspired against me, have seen fit to trip you up, instead." It wasn't a bad start. From an observer's point of view it was the kind of dialogue you might expect from two opposed professional men in the apparent circumstances.

Well, it was, Lord knew—it was. No matter what your concept of the circumstances might be.

The Geneiid looked at the floor in glum anger. Demaris could understand that. It was only by the grace of making the first move that he himself was not sitting in a Geneiian office somewhere, slowly digesting the fact that he was one of two ends being played against Old Man Sullivan's middle.

"All right," Demaris said. He turned to Sath. "Think there's anything we need to know from him right now?"

Sath shook his head negatively. "Not immediately. I suggest we save him for later. We've got lots of work to do."

Demaris gestured to a couple of armed guards. "Put him away where he'll keep." He looked the Geneiid in the eyes. "I'll be talking to you later."

The man lifted his eyes off the floor, agreeing wordlessly. Rising, he went with his guards.

Demaris plunged into the work of shaping the battered organization for the final, crippling blow. He entertained no thoughts of not completing his job. Mr. Sullivan would not be handed the weapon of a broken contract to wield when Demaris returned to New York and his revenge.

Only gods and television audiences see the pattern of human events. What he did in his office touched on the histories of four races, but, for Demaris, the movement of men and armed forces translated itself into the shifting of reports from IN to HOLD to OUT, and the roar of rockets became the rattle and ping of bookkeeping machines.

For two days, he and Sath reassigned, regrouped, deployed, redeployed, canceled, substituted, implemented, and supplied. Only the games-like transposition of figures from one table of organization to another furnished its own synthetic excitement.

Demaris wondered, in a few brief snatches of stolen relaxation, whether he hated Mr. Sullivan most for double-crossing him or for placing him in a position where the outcome of the battle became a foregone conclusion, now that his personal opponent was prematurely taken. From a strategist, he had descended to a clerk. It was war, but it was not magnificent.

Well, at least it was over at the end of the second day. Between them, he and Sath had shaped Marak's intelligence service into the means for completely hamstringing Genis, now that her own expert was gone.

Certainly, her own expert. As much as Demaris was Marak's own.

He felt his mouth curl sardonically.

Sath dropped the last order into his OUT box, pushed his bench away from his desk, and stretched. Demaris rubbed a hand across his tired eyes.

"It's done," Sath said with relieved finality. "All over."

Demaris growled agreement with his Second's mood. Blinking, he peered around at the office. Half the subordinate staff was asleep on cots pushed into dimmer corners. The other shift half-slumped over its desks. No one had left the office since the Geneiid's capture. Given enough breathing space, Genis might have been able to throw out a desperate taskforce to intercept the Marakian fleet, which had set out for Farla the moment the Geneiian saboteurs lost direction and purpose.

"Call up the Overchief and let him know, will you?" Demaris said to Sath. He felt washed-out. The job was done, and soon he'd be back on Earth.

And this time, after he got through with Mr. Sullivan—provided he could dig him out of this sanctum—there might not even be any more Agency jobs.

Hunting? Police work of some kind? Demaris didn't know. Uselessness was a bitter strain in his throat.

Sath put his phone back on his desk and looked puzzledly at Demaris. "Something's wrong," he said. "I told the Overchief we were set. He just mumbled perfunctory thanks. Then he said it wasn't our fault, but we weren't going into Farla. He wants to see us."

Demaris sucked in his lower lip and scowled. Possibly he was becoming a monomaniac, but he nevertheless wondered what Old Man Sullivan had done now.

* * *

> *"There's something that's cute in the*
> *Agency—*
> *Some sweet little winning appeal.*
> *For its dough it will go*
> *Through your pockets at night,*
> *And what's not glued in it will*
> *steal."*

VII

The Overchief sat behind his desk, half facing the boarded-up window shattered in night-before-last's abortive Geneiid attempt to get their man back.

He moved his hands in an unsettled gesture. "I don't understand how they knew," he repeated, and dropped his hands into his lap.

Demaris, mystified, stared across the room at Resvik, the contact, who had been there when he and Sath came in. Beside him, Sath was also frowning, trying to make sense out of the situation. Resvik was impassive.

The Overchief seemed not to realize that Demaris and Sath had no idea of what he meant. He rambled on.

"Almost exactly to the moment. As soon as we and Genis became preoccupied with each other."

Sath cleared his throat and ventured the question. "Sir—I'm sorry, but I'm afraid I'm a bit fagged out. May I ask you to repeat what's happened?"

The Overchief turned toward Sath. His gaze was weak and unsteady. He squinted across the room. "What? Oh, Sath— Yes. It's Stain. I just got word. Their ships have been in Farla for the past month." He gestured again, his palms slapping down on his thighs. "There is no more Farla."

Demaris felt his facial muscles twitch in an uncontrollable surprise reaction. Then he became expressionless. Beside him, Sath was breathing erratically.

Demaris looked at Resvik with careful deliberation. They were both in immediate, pressing danger. The Overchief's previous line of speculation about him had been very close to truth. But the contact seemed unconcerned.

"They moved in against almost no opposition," the Overchief was continuing. "What they did meet was hopelessly indecisive, unorganized, and lacked any initiative whatsoever. They moved in rapidly, set up bases, and are now completely consolidated. It would take years to undermine them to the point where we could hope to engage them successfully."

Sath had obviously gotten well past his initial shock, and his mind had been working rapidly. "Well, sir, that is a setback, of course. But we have an efficient and well-directed staff, apportioning credit to Tjetlyned Todren, who deserves it. It seems to me that the immediate institution of a vigorous program would—"

The Overchief cut him off with a muddy waving of his hand. "No, no, I appreciate your enthusiasm, Tjetlyn Faris, but this is a defeat . . . a defeat—" he repeated in a barely audible mutter. "We have been bested—"

"But, sir—"

Oddly enough, the Overchief displayed no surprise or anger at Sath's repeated overreachings of privilege. He merely shook his head hopelessly, and Sath must have realized there was no purpose in pressing the point. He shot Demaris a baffled look, but found no help there.

Resvik addressed himself to the Overchief. "Sir, if you'll find the time to conclude that business we spoke of—"

The Overchief started at the sound of his voice. Obviously, he'd completely forgotten the man was there. He stared bewilderedly at Resvik for a moment before he collected himself.

"Yes, yes, of course— Tjetlyn Faris, I'll speak further to Groil Resvik and Tjetlyned Todren."

"Yes, sir." Plainly baffled and shocked at the Overchief's irresolution, Sath slipped out after one more fruitless look at Demaris.

Demaris continued not to speak mainly because he had no idea of what to say. The Overchief had become incomprehensible, and Resvik's position was totally unclear to him. The fact that this was the working of still another scheme of Old Man Sullivan's no longer struck him with much novelty. He wondered, briefly if he would ever discover just exactly where and how far all of the Agency's tentacles extended.

Resvik stood up and came over to him. "Well," he said, "that's that. We're wound up here. I've got the pickup ship coming tonight. You and I and Holtz—"

"*Walker* Holtz?"

"Sure. the Geneiid." The contact grinned cynically. "We can't leave him here for that Faris hot-shot to question, can we? It's a shame he got out of here so fast," he mused.

Demaris rolled his eyes frantically toward the Overchief. Had the contact gone out of his head?

Resvik followed the direction of the glance and sniffed contemptuously. "Him!" He flexed the muscles of his forearm and the nose of a hypodermic pistol slipped out between his fingers. "Four micro-cc's of lobotomol, right into the forebrain. What's he going to pay attention to?"

Demaris stared at the contact. Almost unconsciously, he reached out and eased Resvik's forearm aside until he was out of the line of fire.

VII

Holtz laughed pleasantly as the three of them sat in the pickup ship's lounge. The sound came out of his Geneiian throat with very little of its Terrestrial unbanity.

"I'd say it was quite admirable of Old Man Sullivan," he commented in his barbarous accent. He laughed again. "Picture the complexity—the intricacy of the organization. Mr. Black is planted on the capital planet of an empire—" Holtz's bow toward Resvik, attempted with a Geneiian spinal column, was grotesque. "He is assimilated into the imperial government, probably with the aid of that ingenious instrument in his hand, and thereafter devotes himself to the groundwork of systematically lobotomizing such key figures as display any inordinate talent. When a crisis arrives—as, with Old Man Sullivan's ubiquitous help, it inevitably must—Mr.

Black offers to supply the talent so unfortunately lacking in the native personnel. Then you, Mr. Demaris, and I, perform our duties—and Old Man Sullivan grows richer, and richer, and richer. Fabulous! And what a sublime disregard for human decency!"

Resvik was watching them impassively. Since the three of them had come aboard the ship, five T.S.T. days ago, he had talked only when spoken to. Most of the conversation had been between Holtz, whose attitude was manifest, and Demaris, who had gleaned as much as he could and was now becoming impatient and irritated as Holtz's personality wore thin.

"But can you *picture* it, man!" Holtz demanded. "The intricacy of the enterprise—the beautifully working plan, endlessly repeated with every race that an Earthman can possibly be made to resemble! I need hardly point out that this means practically every race with which terrestrial minds can communicate at all! Beautiful! Beautiful! And if not for your commendable enterprise, Mr. Demaris, neither of us would ever have been in a position to realize it. Why, not even Mr. Black, here, is anything but another cog in this lovely machine—"

Resvik—Mr. Black, if you preferred the other *nom de guerre*—stood over Holtz. "I think that's about enough," he said flatly. He looked from Holtz to Demaris and back again, spreading his contempt between them. "What are you, anyway?" he said at Holtz. "A misfit hunter, trying to find a new kind of quarry to kill. And you"—he turned to Demaris—"a thug, half a cut below an assassin. You stink with neuroses, both of you. You're misfits. There isn't room for you on Earth. Where else would you go, if there was no Agency?"

"Funny," Demaris said, looking up at him evenly. "Here I am, a thug. When I'm not dressed up for one of these things, I look like a killer. I act like one. And the charming Mr. Holtz is the prototype of all gentleman pickers-off of lowlier life. But you, my friend—I'll bet you don't in the least really resemble Machiavelli."

Resvik sat down suddenly, hate brooding out of his eyes at Demaris.

Demaris smiled as well as his Marakian jaws would

let him. "I'd add a nice word about the efficiency of Old Man Sullivan's recruitment teams, if I were you," he said to Holtz.

His hide itched. He scratched fiercely and uselessly at his forearms, then steeled himself by an effort of will and kept his hands motionless. He was having trouble with his vision, too—he'd become accustomed to a slight turn of the head for direct seeing.

"Why do you want to see Old Man Sullivan?" Bill Kaempfert asked.

Demaris set his jaw stubbornly. "I think you've got a pretty fair idea."

Kaempfert began a gesture, exhaled in frustration, and thumped his hands on the edge of his desk. "What am I going to do with you?" he asked, more to himself than to Demaris. He looked exasperatedly at his friend. "Look—do you want me to go to Old Man Sullivan and tell him one of his employees disapproves of his business methods, and would like an hour's time to tell him so?"

"I disapprove of being put in an unnecessarily dangerous position!" Demaris corrected him. "Suppose Genis had decided to pick off the opposition first? That ninny, Holtz, would never have issued instructions to kidnap, instead of kill. What am I—a tin soldier for Sullivan to move about as he pleases?"

"Have you read your contract lately?"

Demaris looked across the desk. "So that's the policy, is it?"

Kaempfert did not drop his eyes. "The policy is to execute each operation with no avoidable casualties to Agency personnel. This was a toughie. You were warned of that from the beginning. One of these three-way switches is always precarious."

"Precarious? Is that the word?" Demaris looked around at the other supervisors in the room, leaned forward, and lowered his voice. "Bill, I've already decided you couldn't refuse to ship me out into that squeeze-play. That's understandable. What it does to our friendship, neither of us can say as yet. Nothing, I hope. But that's beside the point. Look—this has been nagging at me.

You know, and I know, that the Agency started a long time ago. We know it was somehow illegal in nature then, though nobody knows precisely how. We both know what Earth government's like. But, look—is there a chance, any chance, no matter how slim, that it's gradually drifted over and become a secret government arm? I could understand this sort of thing, then."

Kaempfert looked at him silently for a minute. His eyes were weighing something, and at the same time they were aware of all the things Demaris had said, that night before he was shipped out. Then he shook his head slowly. "No. No chance at all."

Demaris sighed and sat back in his chair for a moment. Then the anger returned to his face. "Well, then—"

"Thad," Kaempfert said, "I want to show you something." He got up from his desk. "Come on." He squeezed between his desk and the next, and walked out into the front office with Demaris following him. He fumbled in his pocket and took out a key ring.

Demaris watching him, frowning, as he unlocked a door.

"Come on in," Kaempfert said. Demaris walked through the door. They were in an empty closet. Kaempfert selected a new key, moved a section of molding, and unlocked the concealed door at the back of the closet.

Demaris stepped through the door. He was in a small, bare office. There was no window. Kaempfert turned on the light.

The office was stale and musty. Dust lay thick and furry on the desk, the chair behind it, and the floor.

Demaris spent a minute looking at it. Then he turned to Kaempfert. "So. There is no Old Man Sullivan."

Kaempfert shook his head. "Not any more—not for fifteen years. That's when I quit being an operative. I'm the guy you mean when you talk about Sullivan."

"I don't get it—"

"Sullivan was everything you've called him," Kaempfert interrupted. "And the Agency never was, and is not now, constituted to be anything but a private, money-making enterprise. I run it."

Demaris shook his head and looked at Kaempfert without a trace of recognition. He began to speak, but Kaempfert cut him off again.

"You'll get your chance. Now you tell me what the Agency does."

"I don't follow you."

"The Agency," Kaempfert explained patiently, "supplies Earthmen to do the military planning for all those races which can be reached by us. Right?"

"Yes—"

"What's our military record?"

"Perfect."

Kaempfert smiled wanly. "Not quite. But close enough. All right, next question: What has the Agency done for you?"

"Given me a job."

"All right, it's given you a job. It's also provided an outlet for all the drives and irascibilities that make life on Earth a chancy proposition for you. You're antisocial. You don't fit. The Agency puts you where you *do* fit."

"Sure. I've admitted that. But—"

"You're one of hundreds. We located you—which isn't hard, considering that all you misfits, myself included, kick up such a row. We trained you, we put you in the best kind of Agency jobs for your personality, and we shipped you out. Right?"

"Admitted. But that doesn't give you the right to make our lives more dangerous than necessary!"

"I could argue about necessities, but I won't. I gather that what you want is a private hunting preserve."

"*No!* Look, I'm no killer. If I can change something with my brain instead of my gun, I damn well will!"

"O.K. Then mull this over in your brain: *With* our 'perfect' military record, and *with* Sullivan's efficient system, which I don't dare monkey with—how much have the other races in the universe progressed?"

"Plenty! Stain's a major power, just because of you."

"Oh, yeah? And next year, is it still going to be?

What about Farla, that inherited the Vilk empire? Charging back and forth isn't progress. Small but steady forward motion is. You don't fight wars in space—not big, slam-bang fleet actions, you don't. But you do infiltrate, and you do sabotage. And next year, the guy you skunked sabotages *you*. How far do you get, working that way?

"Thad, you've been griping about Earth government not moving out of the Solar System. Even if their motives are bad, they're right, in a way.

"Except that you, and I, and hundreds of others can't take it. So we're all in the Agency, with new ones joining up every day. And now you tell me—what do you call an outfit that pushes forward when the government wants to stay home? What do you call an organization that operates beyond the accepted frontier, that has its force of fighting men, its politicians, and its board of directors? What do you call an organization set up to penetrate foreign territory, to indulge in extranational politics, to support its employees? Well you might call it The British East India Company, or the Hudson's Bay Fur Company, or Mr. Sullivan's Agency. But I call it a private government. And I say this is the one kind of government that's set up to clear the road for the day Earth—all of Earth, under its own government—steps out into the stars again."

Demaris had been trying to interrupt at Kaempfert's every pause for breath. Now he realized that he was out of breath himself—and that he suddenly had no real points to argue. The Agency was a business. It ran for profit, and the system was designed for profit only.

He looked around the office again. With a little cleaning up, it wouldn't be half-bad—

No. The head of an outfit like this was too used to, and too much in need of, protective coloration.

"Well," he said. "Well, Bill, let's lock it up and see if we can find me some desk space out in Assignments."

> "So, we are the Agency's boy
>   scouts—
> We do our good deeds every day.

*Remember our names to our kids,
     my boys,
When we have drifted away.
And teach 'em that crime doesn't
     pay, my boys,
Except every thirtieth day, my boys,
And hold out for raises in pay."*

EDITOR'S INTRODUCTION TO:

THE STAR PLUNDERER
Poul Anderson

Can there be barbarians in an interstellar civilization? Many of the best science fiction writers have thought so. H. Beam Piper postulated several ways that planets could "decivilize." Isaac Asimov's *Foundation* series was built on the premise.

Even so, at first thought the notion is absurd. Star travel requires high technology and complex equipment; how could ignorant savages have all that?

But of course the savages need not *invent* high technology, nor even be able to build or maintain it; it is enough that they could obtain it and make it work. One needs no understanding of electronics to operate a television or video cassette recorder; one need not understand very large scale integrated circuits to use a computer; few automobile drivers can explain the theory of internal combustion engines, fuel injection, or even Kettering ignition.

Indeed, we can think of contemporary examples. Consider terrorists, whether ideological or religious fanatics. All seem perfectly capable of obtaining and using high technology. Perhaps the notion of "space barbarians" is not quite so silly as we thought.

For that matter, those who do understand technology may not much care for other aspects of civilized behavior. "When I hear the word 'culture' I reach for my revolver," said Reichsmarshal Goering; yet Goering was an air ace, successor to von Richthofen as commander of the Flying Circus, and quite at home with what was then quite advanced technology. Nor were his education and background any bar to his amassing as large a collection of pure loot as has any human in history.

One should not forget: the sailing ships of the Napoleonic era were highly complex, considerably more difficult to operate properly than most modern ships. It would be easier to learn how to operate a space station than a 100-gun ship of the line. Obsolete doesn't mean *simple*.

Finally, of course, new designs continue to make really complex equipment easier to use without understanding. Artificial intelligence and computer systems may well make it possible for savages to operate star ships.

Poul Anderson majored in physics; but he has long been an avid student of history. This story was written before *sputnik*; long before the first men went to space; decades before computers. It's surprising just how well Poul's technology holds together. It's not a story about technology anyway.

Communications change. Weapons change. The nature of man may not keep pace. Here a tale of the founding of empire.

THE STAR PLUNDERER
Poul Anderson

The following is a part, modernized but otherwise authentic, of that curious book found by excavators of the ruins of Sol City, Terra—the Memoirs of Rear Admiral John Henry Reeves, Imperial Solar Navy. Whether or not the script, obviously never published or intended for publication, is a genuine record left by a man with a taste for dramatized reporting, or whether it is pure fiction, remains an open question; but it was undoubtedly written in the early period of the First Empire and as such gives a remarkable picture of the times and especially of the Founder. Actual events may or may not have been exactly as Reeves described, but we cannot doubt that in any case they were closely similar. Read this fifth chapter of the Memoirs as historical fiction if you will, but remember that the author must himself have lived through that great and tragic and triumphant age and that he must have been trying throughout the book to give a true picture of the man who even in his own time had become a legend.

Donvar Ayeghen,
President of the Galactic Archeological Society

* * *

They were closing in now. The leader was a gray bulk filling my sight scope, and every time I glanced over the wall a spanging sleet of bullets brought my head jerking down again. I had some shelter from behind which to shoot in a fragment of wall looming higher than the rest, like a single tooth left in a dead man's jaw, but I had to squeeze the trigger and then duck fast. Once in a while one of their slugs would burst on my helmet and the gas would be sickly-sweet in my nostrils. I felt ill and dizzy with it.

Kathryn was reloading her own rifle, I heard her swearing as the cartridge clip jammed in the rusty old weapon. I'd have given her my own, except that it wasn't much better. It's no fun fighting with arms that are likely to blow up in your face but it was all we had—all that poor devastated Terra had after the Baldics had sacked her twice in fifteen years.

I fired a burst and saw the big gray barbarian spin on his heels, stagger, and scream with all four hands clutching his belly, and sink slowly to his knees. The creatures behind him howled, but he only let out a deep-throated curse. He'd be a long time dying. I'd blown a hole clear through him, but those Gorzuni were tough.

The slugs wailed around us as I got myself down under the wall, hugging the long grass which had grown up around the shattered fragments of the house. There was a fresh wind blowing, rustling the grass and the big war-scarred trees, sailing clouds across a sunny summer sky, so the gas concentration was never enough to put us out. But Jonsson and Hokusai were sprawled like corpses there against the broken wall. They'd taken direct hits and they'd sleep for hours.

Kathryn knelt beside me, the ragged, dirty coverall like a queen's robe on her tall young form, a few dark curls falling from under her helmet for the wind to play with. "If we get them mad enough," she said, "they'll call for the artillery or send a boat overhead to blow us to the Black Planet."

"Maybe," I grunted. "Though they're usually pretty eager for slaves."

"John—" She crouched there a moment, the tiny frown I knew so well darkening her blue eyes. I watched the way leaf-shadows played across her thin brown face. There was a grease smudge on the snub nose, hiding the freckles. But she still looked good, really good, she and green Terra and life and freedom and all that I'd never have again!

"John," she said at last, "maybe we should save them the trouble. Maybe we should make our own exit."

"It's a thought," I muttered, risking a glance above the wall.

The Gorzuni were more cautious now, creeping through the gardens toward the shattered outbuilding we defended. Behind them, the main estate, last knot of our unit's resistance, lay smashed and burning. Gorzuni were swarming around it, dragging out such humans as survived and looting whatever treasure was left. I was tempted to shoot at those big furry bodies but I had to save ammunition for the detail closing in on us.

"I don't fancy life as the slave of a barbarian outworlder," I said. "Though humans with technical training are much in demand and usually fairly well treated. But for a woman—" The words trailed off. I couldn't say them.

"I might trade on my own mechanical knowledge," she said. "And then again I might not. Is it worth the risk, John, my dearest?"

We were both conditioned against suicide, of course. Everyone in the broken Commonwealth navy was, except bearers of secret information. The idea was to sell our lives or liberty as exorbitantly as possible, fighting to the last moment. It was a stupid policy, typical of the blundering leadership that had helped lose us our wars. A human slave with knowledge of science and machinery was worth more to the barbarians than the few extra soldiers he could kill out of their hordes by staying alive till captured.

But the implanted inhibition could be broken by a person of strong will. I looked at Kathryn for a moment, there in the tumbled ruins of the house, and her eyes met mine and rested, deep-blue and grave with a tremble of tears behind the long smoky lashes.

"Well—" I said helplessly, and then I kissed her.

It was our big mistake. The Gorzuni had worked closer than I realized and in Terra's gravity—about half of their home planet's—they could move like a sunbound comet. One of them came soaring over the wall behind me, landing on his clawed splay feet with a crash that shivered in the ground. His wild "Whoo-oo-oo-oo!" was hardly out of his mouth before I'd blown the horned, flat-faced head off his shoulders. But there was a gray mass swarming behind him, and Kathryn yelled and fired into the thick of another attack from our rear.

Something stung me, a bright sharp pain and then a bomb exploding in my head and a long sick spiral down into blackness. The last thing I saw was Kathryn, caught in the four arms of a soldier. He was half again as tall as she, he'd twisted the barrel off her gun as he wrenched it from her hands, but she was giving him a good fight. A hell of a good fight. Then I didn't see anything else for some time.

They herded us aboard a tender after dark. It was like a scene from some ancient hell—night overhead and around, lit by a score of burning houses like uneasy furnaces out there in the dark, and the long, long line of humans stumbling toward the boat with kicks and blows from the guards to hurry them along.

A house was aflame not far off, soaring red and yellow fire glancing off the metal of the ship, picking a haggard face from shadow, glimmering in human tears and in steely unhuman eyes. The shadows wove in and out, hiding us from each other save when a gust of wind blew up the fire. Then we felt a puff of heat and looked away from each other's misery.

Kathryn was not to be seen in that weaving line. I groped along with my wrists tied behind me, now and then jarred by a gun-butt as one of the looming figures grew impatient. I could hear the sobbing of women and the groaning of men in the dark, before me, behind me, around me as they forced us into the boat.

"Jimmy. Where are you, Jimmy?"

"They killed him. He's lying there dead in the ruins."

"O God, what have we done?"

"My baby. Has anyone seen my baby? I had a baby and they took him away from me."

"Help, help, help, help help—"

A mumbled and bitter curse, a scream, a whine, a rattling gasp of breath, and always the slow shuffle of feet and the sobbing of the women and the children.

We were the conquered. They had scattered our armies. They had ravaged our cities. They had hunted us through the streets and the hills and the great deeps of space, and we could only snarl and snap at them and hope that the remnants of our navy might pull a miracle. But miracles are hard to come by.

So far the Baldic League had actually occupied only the outer planets. The inner worlds were nominally under Commonwealth rule but the government was hiding or nonexistent. Only fragments of the navy fought on without authority or plan or hope, and Terra was the happy hunting ground of looters and slave raiders. Before long, I supposed bitterly, the outworlders would come in force, break the last resistance, and incorporate all the Solar System into their savage empire. Then the only free humans would be the extrasolar colonists, and a lot of them were barbaric themselves and had joined the Baldic League against the mother world.

The captives were herded into cells aboard the tender, crammed together till there was barely room to stand. Kathryn wasn't in my cell either. I lapsed into dull apathy.

When everyone was aboard, the deckplates quivered under our feet and acceleration jammed us cruelly against each other. Several humans died in that press. I had all I could do to keep the surging mass from crushing in my chest but of course the Gorzuni didn't care. There were plenty more where we came from.

The boat was an antiquated and rust-eaten wreck, with half its archaic gadgetry broken and useless. They weren't technicians, those Baldics. They were barbarians who had learned too soon how to build and handle spaceships and firearms, and a score of their planets united by a military genius had gone forth to overrun the civilized Commonwealth.

But their knowledge was usually by rote; I have known many a Baldic "engineer" who made sacrifices to his converter, many a general who depended on astrologers or haruspices for major decision. So trained humans were in demand as slaves. Having a degree in nuclear engineering myself, I could look for a halfway decent berth, though of course there was always the possibility of my being sold to someone who would flay me or blind me or let me break my heart in his mines.

Untrained humans hadn't much chance. They were just flesh-and-blood machines doing work that the barbarians didn't have automatics for, rarely surviving ten years of slavery. Women were the luxury trade, sold at high prices to the human renegades and rebels. I groaned at that thought and tried desperately to assure myself that Kathryn's technical knowledge would keep her in the possession of a nonhuman.

We were taken up to a ship orbiting just above the atmosphere. Airlocks were joined, so I didn't get a look at her from outside, but as soon as we entered I saw that she was a big interstellar transport of the Thurnogan class used primarily for carrying troops to Sol and slaves back, but armed for war. A formidable fighting ship when properly handled.

There were guards leaning on their rifles, all of Gorzuni race, their harness worn any way they pleased and no formality between officers and men. the barbarian armies' sloppy discipline had blinded our spit-and-polish command to their reckless courage and their savage gunnery. Now the fine-feathered Commonwealth navy was a ragged handful of hunted, desperate men and the despised outworlders were harrying them through the Galaxy.

This ship was worse than usual, though. I saw rust and mold on the unpainted plates. The fluoros were dim and in some places burned out. There was a sickening pulse in the gravity generators. The cabins had long ago been stripped of equipment and refurnished with skins, stolen household goods, cooking pots, and weapons. The Gorzuni were all as dirty and unkempt as their ship. They lounged about gnawing on chunks of meat, drinking, dicing, and glancing up now and then to grin at us.

A barbarian who spoke some Anglic bellowed at us to strip. Those who hesitated were cuffed so the teeth rattled in their heads. We threw the clothes in a heap and moved forward slowly past a table where a drunken Gorzuni and a very sober human sat. Medical inspection.

The barbarian "doctor" gave each of us the most cursory glance. Most were waved on. Now and then he would look closer, blearily, at someone.

"Sickly," he grunted. "Never make the trip alive. Kill."

The man or woman or child would scream as he picked up a sword and chopped off the head with one expert sweep.

The human sat halfway on the desk, swinging one leg and whistling softly. Now and again the Gorzuni medic would glance at him in doubt over some slave. The human would look closer. Usually he shoved them on. One or two he tapped for killing.

I got a close look at him as I went by. He was below medium height, strongly built, dark and heavy-faced and beak-nosed, but his eyes were large and blue-gray, the coldest eyes I have ever seen on a human. He wore a loose colorful shirt and trousers, rich material probably stolen from some Terran villa.

"You filthy bastard," I muttered.

He shrugged, indicating the iron slave-collar welded about his neck. "I only work here, Lieutenant," he said mildly. He must have noticed my uniform before I shucked it.

Beyond the desk, a Gorzuni played a hose on us, washing off blood and grime, and then we were herded down the long corridors and by way of wooden ladders (the drop-shafts and elevators weren't working it seemed) to the cells. Here they separated men and women. We went into adjoining compartments, huge echoing caverns of metal with bunks tiered along the walls, food troughs, and sanitary facilities the only furnishing.

Dust was thick on the corroded floor, and the air was cold and had a metallic reek. There must have been about five hundred men swarming hopelessly around after the barred door clanged shut on us.

There were windows between the two great cells. We made a rush for them, crying out, pushing and crowding and snarling at each other for first chance to see if our women still lived.

I was large and strong. I shouldered my way through the mob up to the nearest window. A man was there already, flattened against the wall by the sweating bodies behind, reaching through the bars to the three hundred women who swarmed on the other side.

"Agnes!" he shrieked. "Agnes, are you there? Are you alive?"

I grabbed his shoulder and pulled him away. He turned with a curse, and I fed him a mouthful of knuckles and sent him lurching back into the uneasy press of men. "Kathryn!" I howled.

The echoes rolled and boomed in the hollow metal caves, crying voices, prayers and curses and sobs of despair thrown back by the sardonic echoes till our heads shivered with it. "Kathryn! Kathryn!"

Somehow she found me. She came to me and the kiss through those bars dissolved ship and slavery and all the world for that moment. "Oh, John, John, John, you're alive, you're here. Oh, my darling—"

And then she looked around the metal-gleaming dimness and said quickly, urgently: "We'll have a riot on our hands, John, if these people don't calm down. See what you can do with the men. I'll tackle the women."

It was like her. She was the most gallant soul that ever walked under Terran skies, and she had a mind which flashed in an instant to that which must be done. I wondered myself what point there was in stopping a murderous panic. Those who were killed would be better off, wouldn't they? But Kathryn never surrendered so I couldn't either.

We turned back into our crowds, and shouted and pummeled and bullied, and slowly others came to our aid until there was a sobbing quiet in the belly of the slave ship. Then we organized turns at the windows. Kathryn and I both looked away from those reunions, or from the people who found no one. It isn't decent to look at a naked soul.

The engines began to thrum. Under way, outward bound to the ice mountains of Gorzun, no more to see blue skies and green grass, no clean salt smell of ocean and roar of wind in tall trees. Now we were slaves and there was nothing to do but wait.

II

There was no time aboard the ship. The few dim fluoros kept our hold forever in its uneasy twilight. The Gorzuni swilled us at such irregular intervals as they thought of it, and we heard only the throb of the engines and the asthmatic sigh of the ventilators. The twice-normal gravity kept most of us too weary even to talk much. But I think it was about forty-eight hours after leaving Terra, when the ship had gone into secondary drive and was leaving the Solar System altogether, that the man with the iron collar came down to us.

He entered with an escort of armed and wary Gorzuni who kept their rifles lifted. We looked up with dull eyes at the short stocky figure. His voice was almost lost in the booming vastness of the hold.

"I'm here to classify you. Come up one at a time and tell me your name and training, if any. I warn you that the penalty for claiming training you haven't got is torture, and you'll be tested if you do make such claims."

We shuffled past. A Gorzuni, the drunken doctor, had a tattoo needle set up and scribbled a number on the palm of each man. This went into the human's notebook, together with name, age, and profession. Those without technical skills, by far the majority, were shoved roughly back. The fifty or so who claimed valuable education went over into a corner.

The needle burned my palm and I sucked the breath

between my teeth. The impersonal voice was dim in my ears: "Name?"

"John Henry Reeves, age twenty-five, lieutenant in the Commonwealth navy and nuclear engineer before the wars." I snapped the answers out, my throat harsh and a bitter taste in my mouth. The taste of defeat.

"Hmmm." I grew aware that the pale chill eyes were resting on me with an odd regard. Suddenly the man's thick lips twisted in a smile. It was a strangely charming smile, it lit his whole dark face with a brief radiance of merriment. "Oh, yes, I remember you, Lieutenant Reeves. You called me, I believe, a filthy bastard."

"I did," I almost snarled. My hand throbbed and stung, I was unwashed and naked and sick with my own helplessness.

"You may be right at that," he nodded. "But I'm in bad need of a couple of assistants. This ship is a wreck. She may never make Gorzun without someone to nurse the engines. Care to help me?"

"No," I said.

"Be reasonable. By refusing you only get yourself locked in the special cell we're keeping for trained slaves. It'll be a long voyage, the monotony will do more to break your spirit than any number of lashings. As my assistant you'll have proper quarters and a chance to move around and use your hands."

I stood thinking. "Did you say you needed two assistants?" I asked.

"Yes. Two who can do something with this ruin of a ship."

"I'll be one," I said, "if I can name the other."

He scowled. "Getting pretty big for the britches you don't have, aren't you?"

"Take it or leave it," I shrugged. "But this person is a hell of a good technician."

"Well, nominate him, then, and I'll see."

"It's a her. My fiancee, Kathryn O'Donnell."

"No." He shook his dark curly head. "No woman."

"No man, then." I grinned at him without mirth.

Anger flamed coldly in his eyes. "I can't have a woman around my neck like another millstone."

"She'll carry her own weight and more. She was a j.g. in my own ship, and she fought right there beside me till the end."

The temper was gone without leaving a ripple. Not a stir of expression in the strong, ugly, olive-skinned face that looked up at me. His voice was as flat. "Why didn't you say so before? All right, then, Lieutenant. But the gods help you if you aren't both as advertised!"

It was hard to believe it about clothes—the difference they made after being just another penned and naked animal. And a meal of stew and coffee, however ill prepared, scrounged at the galley after the warriors had messed, surged in veins and bellies which had grown used to swilling from a pig trough.

I realized bleakly that the man in the iron collar was right. Not many humans could have remained free of soul on the long, heart-cracking voyage to Gorzun. Add the eternal weariness of double weight, the chill dark grimness of our destination planet, utter remoteness from home, blank hopelessness, perhaps a touch of the whip and branding iron, and men became tamed animals trudging meekly at the heels of their masters.

"How long have you been a slave?" I asked our new boss.

He strode beside us as arrogantly as if the ship were his. He was not a tall man for even Kathryn topped him by perhaps five centimeters and his round-skulled head barely reached my shoulder. But he had thick muscular arms, a gorilla breadth of chest, and the gravity didn't seem to bother him at all.

"Going on four years," he replied shortly. "My name, by the way, is Manuel Argos, and we might as well be on first-name terms from the start."

A couple of Gorzuni came stalking down the corridor, clanking with metal. We stood aside for the giants, of course, but there was no cringing in Manuel's attitude. His strange eyes followed them speculatively.

We had a cabin near the stern, a tiny cubbyhole with four bunks, bleak and bare, but its scrubbed cleanliness was like a breath of home after the filth of the cell.

Wordlessly, Manuel took one of the sleazy blankets and hung it across a bed as a sort of curtain. "It's the best privacy I can offer you, Kathryn," he said.

"Thank you," she whispered.

He sat down on his own bunk and looked up at us. I loomed over him, a blond giant against his squatness. My family had been old and cultured and wealthy before the wars, and he was the nameless sweepings of a hundred slums and spaceports, but from the first there was never any doubt of who was the leader.

"Here's the story," he said in his curt way. "I knew enough practical engineering in spite of having no formal education to get myself a fairly decent master in whose factories I learned more. Two years ago he sold me to the captain of this ship. I got rid of the so-called chief engineer they had then. It wasn't hard to stir up a murderous quarrel between him and a jealous subordinate. But his successor is a drunken bum one generation removed from the forests.

"In effect, I'm the engineer of this ship. I've also managed to introduce my master, Captain Venjain, to marijuana. It hits a Gorzuni harder than it does a human, and he's a hopeless addict by now. It's partly responsible for the condition of this ship and the laxness among the crew. Poor leadership, poor organization. That's a truism."

I stared at him with a sudden chill along my spine. But it was Kathryn who whispered the question: "Why?"

"Waiting my chance," he snapped. "I'm the one who made junk out of the engines and equipment. I tell them it's old and poorly designed. They think that only my constant work holds the ship together at all but I could have her humming in a week if I cared to. I can't wait too much longer. Sooner or later someone else is going to look at that machinery and tell them it's been deliberately haywired. So I've been waiting for a couple of assistants with technical training and a will to fight. I hope you two fit the bill. If not—" he shrugged—"Go ahead and tell on me. It won't free you. But if you want to risk lives that won't be very long or pleasant on Gorzun, you can help me to take over the ship!"

I stood for some time looking at him. It was uncanny, the way he had sized us up from a glance and a word. Certainly the prospect was frightening. I could feel sweat on my face. My hands were cold. But I'd follow him. Before God, I'd follow him!

Still—"Three of us?" I jeered. "Three of us against a couple of hundred warriors?"

"There'll be more on our side," he said impassively. After a moment's silence he went on: "Naturally, we'll have to watch ourselves. Only two or three of them know Anglic. I'll point them out to you. And of course our work is under surveillance. But the watchers are ignorant. I think you have the brains to fool them."

"I—" Kathryn stood reaching for words. "I can't believe it," she said at last. "A naval vessel in this condition—"

"Things were better under the old Baldic conquerors," admitted Manuel. "The kings who forged the League. But even they succeeded only because there was no real opposition. The Commonwealth society was rotten, corrupt, torn apart by civil wars, its leadership a petrified bureaucracy, its military forces scattered over a thousand restless planets, its people ready to buy peace rather than fight. No wonder the League drove everything before it!

"But after the first sack of Terra fifteen years ago, the barbarians split up. The forceful early rulers were dead, and their sons were warring over an inheritance they didn't know how to rule. The League is divided into two hostile regions now and I don't know how many splinter groups. Their old organization is shot to hell.

"Sol didn't rally in time. It was still under the decadent Commonwealth government. So one branch of the Baldics has now managed to conquer our big planets. But the fact that they've been content to raid and loot the inner worlds instead of occupying them and administering them decently shows the decay of their own society. Given the leadership, we could still throw them out of the Solar System and go on to over-run their home territories. Only the leadership hasn't been forthcoming."

It was a harsh, angry lecture, and I winced and felt resentment within myself. "Damn it, we've fought," I said.

"And been driven back and scattered." His heavy mouth lifted in a sneer. "Because there hasn't been a chief who understood strategy and organization, and who could put heart into his men."

"I suppose," I said sarcastically, "that you're that chief."

His answer was flat and calm and utterly assured. "Yes."

In the days that followed I got to know more about Manuel Argos. He was never loath to talk about himself.

His race, I suppose, was primarily Mediterranean-Anatolian, with more than a hint of negro and oriental, but I think there must have been some forgotten nordic ancestor who looked out of those ice-blue eyes. A blend of all humanity, such as was not uncommon these days.

His mother had been a day laborer on Mars. His father, though he was never sure, had been a space prospector who died young and never saw his child. When he was thirteen he shipped out for Sirius and had not been in the Solar System since. Now, at forty, he had been spaceman, miner, dock walloper, soldier in the civil wars and against the Baldics, small-time politician on the colony planets, hunter, machinist, and a number of darker things.

Somewhere along the line, he had found time to do an astonishing amount of varied reading, but his reliance was always more on his own senses and reason and intuition than on books. He had been captured four years ago in a Gorzuni raid on Alpha Centauri, and had set himself to study his captors as cold-bloodedly as he had studied his own race.

Yes, I learned a good deal about him but nothing of him. I don't think any living creature ever did. He was not one to open his heart. He went wrapped in loneliness and dreams all his days. Whether the chill of his manner went into his soul, and the rare warmth was only a mask, or whether he was indeed a yearning tenderness sheathed in armor of indifference, no one will ever be sure. And he made a weapon out of that uncertainty, a man never knew what to await from him and was thus forever strained in his presence, open to his will.

"He's a strange sort," said Kathryn once, when we were alone. "I haven't decided whether he's crazy or a genius."

"Maybe both, darling," I suggested, a little irritably. I didn't like to be dominated.

"Maybe. But what is sanity, then?" She shivered and crept close to me. "I don't want to talk about it."

The ship wallowed on her way, through a bleak glory of stars, alone in light-years of emptiness with her cargo of hate and fear and misery and dreams. We worked, and waited, and the slow days passed.

The laboring old engines had to be fixed. Some show had to be made for the gray-furred giants who watched us in the flickering gloom of the power chambers. We wired and welded and bolted, tested and tore down and rebuilt, sweltering in the heat of bursting atoms that rolled from the anti-radiation shields, deafened by the whine of generators and thud of misadjusted turbines and deep uneven drone of the great converters. We fixed Manuel's sabotage until the ship ran almost smoothly. Later we would on some pretext throw the whole thing out of kilter again. "Penelope's tapestry," said Manuel, and I wondered that a space tramp could make the classical allusion.

"What are we waiting for?" I asked him once. The din of the generator we were overhauling smothered our words. "When do we start our mutiny?"

He glanced up at me. The light of his trouble lamp gleamed off the sweat on his ugly pockmarked face. "At the proper time," he said coldly. "For one thing, it'll be when the captain goes on his next dope jag."

Meanwhile two of the slaves had tried a revolt of their own. When an incautious guard came too near the door of the men's cell one of them reached out and snatched his gun from the holster and shot him down. Then he tried to blast the lock of the bars. When the

Gorzuni came down to gas him, his fellow battled them with fists and teeth till the rebels were knocked out. Both were flayed living in the presence of the other captives.

Kathryn couldn't help crying when we were back in our cabin. She buried her face against my breast and wept till I thought she would never stop weeping. I held her close and mumbled whatever foolish words came to me.

"They had it coming," said Manuel. There was contempt in his voice. "The fools. The blind stupid fools! They could at least have held the guard as a hostage and tried to bargain. No, they had to be heroes. They had to shoot him down. Now the example has frightened all the others. Those men deserved being skinned."

After a moment, he added thoughtfully: "Still, if the fear-emotion aroused in the slaves can be turned to hate it may prove useful. The shock has at least jarred them from their apathy."

"You're a heartless bastard," I said tonelessly.

"I have to be, seeing that everyone else chooses to be brainless. These aren't times for the tender-minded, you. This is an age of dissolution and chaos, such as has often happened in history, and only a person who first accepts the realities of the situation can hope to do much about them. We don't live in a cosmos where perfection is possible or even desirable. We have to make our compromises and settle for the goals we have some chance of attaining." To Kathryn, sharply: "Now stop that snuffling. I have to think."

She gave him a wide-eyed tear-blurred look.

"It gives you a hell of an appearance." He grinned nastily. "Nose red, face swollen, a bad case of hiccoughs. Nothing pretty about crying, you."

She drew a shuddering breath and there was anger flushing her cheeks. Gulping back the sobs, she drew away from me and turned her back on him.

"But I stopped her," whispered Manuel to me with a brief impishness.

III

The endless, meaningless days had worn into a time-lessness where I wondered if this ship were not the Flying Dutchman, outward bound forever with a crew of devils and the damned. It was no use trying to hurry Manuel, I gave that up and slipped into the round of work and waiting. Now I think that part of his delay was on purpose, that he wanted to grind the last hope out of the slaves and leave only a hollow yearning for vengeance. They'd fight better that way.

There wasn't much chance to be alone with Kathryn. A brief stolen kiss, a whispered word in the dimness of the engine room, eyes and hands touching lightly across a rusty, greasy machine. That was all. When we returned to our cabin we were too tired, generally, to do much except sleep.

I did once notice Manuel exchange a few words in the slave pen with Ensign Hokusai, who had been captured with Kathryn and myself. Someone had to lead the humans, and Hokusai was the best man for that job. But how had Manuel known? It was part of his genius for understanding.

The end came suddenly. Manuel shook me awake. I blinked wearily at the hated walls around me, feeling the irregular throb of the gravity field that was misbehaving again. More work for us. "All right, all right," I grumbled. "I'm coming."

When he flicked the curtain from Kathryn's bunk and aroused her, I protested. "We can handle it. Let her rest."

"Not now!" he answered. Teeth gleamed white in the darkness of his face. "The captain's off in never-never land. I heard two of the Gorzuni talking about it."

That brought me bolt awake, sitting up with a chill along my spine. "Now—?"

"Take it easy," said Manuel. "Lots of time."

We threw on our clothes and went down the long corridors. The ship was still. Under the heavy shuddering drone of the engines, there was only the whisper of our shoes and the harsh rasp of the breath in my lungs.

Kathryn was white-faced, her eyes enormous in the gloom. But she didn't huddle against me. She walked between the two of us and there was a remoteness over her that I couldn't quite understand. Now and then we passed a Gorzuni warrior on some errand of his own, and shrank aside as became slaves. But I saw the bitter triumph in Manuel's gaze as he looked after the titans.

Into the power chambers where the machines loomed in a flickering red twilight like heathen gods there were three Gorzuni standing there, armed engineers who snarled at us. One of them tried to cuff Manuel. He dodged without seeming to notice and bent over the gravity generator and signaled me to help him lift the cover.

I could see that there was a short circuit in one of the field coils, inducing a harmonic that imposed a flutter on the space-warping current. It wouldn't have taken long to fix. But Manuel scratched his head, and glanced back at the ignorant giants who loomed over our shoulders. He began tracing wires with elaborate puzzlement.

He said to me: "We'll work up to the auxiliary atom-converter. I've fixed that to do what I want."

I knew the Gorzuni couldn't understand us, and that human expressions were meaningless to them, but an uncontrollable shiver ran along my nerves.

Slowly we fumbled to the squat engine which was the power source for the ship's internal machinerey. Manuel hooked in an oscilloscope and studied the trace as if it meant something. "Ah-hah!" he said.

We unbolted the antiradiation shield, exposing the outlet valve. I knew that the angry, blood-red light streaming from it was harmless, that baffles cut off most of the radioactivity, but I couldn't help shrinking from it. When a converter is flushed through the valve, you wear armor.

Manuel went over to a workbench and took a gadget from it which he'd made. I knew it was of no use for repair but he'd pretended to make a tool of it in previous jobs. It was a lead-plated flexible hose springing from a magnetronic pump, with a lot of meters and switches haywired on for pure effect. "Give me a hand, John," he said quietly.

We fixed the pump over the outlet valve and hooked up the two or three controls that really meant something. I heard Kathryn gasp behind me, and the dreadful realization burst into my own brain and numbed my hands. There wasn't even a gasket—

The Gorzuni engineer strode up to us, rumbling a question in his harsh language, his fellows behind him. Manuel answered readily, not taking his gaze off the wildly swinging fake meters.

He turned to me, and I saw the dark laughter in his eyes. "I told them the converter is overdue for a flushing out of waste products," he said in Anglic. "As a matter of fact, the whole ship is."

He took the hose in one hand and the other rested on a switch of the engine. "Don't look, Kathryn," he said tonelessly. Then he threw the switch.

I heard the baffle plates clank down. Manuel had shorted out the automatic safety controls which kept them up when the atoms were burning. I threw a hand over my own eyes and crouched.

The flame that sprang forth was like a bit of the sun. It sheeted from the hose and across the room. I felt my skin shriveling from incandescence and heard the roar of cloven air. In less than a second, Manuel had thrown the baffles back into place but his improvised blaster had torn away the heads of the three Gorzuni and melted the farther wall. Metal glowed white as I looked again, and the angry thunders boomed and echoed and shivered deep in my bones till my skull rang with it.

Dropping the hose, Manuel stepped over to the dead giants and yanked the guns from their holsters. "One for each of us," he said.

Turning to Kathryn: "Get on a suit of armor and wait down here. The radioactivity is bad, but I don't think it'll prove harmful in the time we need. Shoot anyone who comes in."

"I—" Her voice was faint and thin under the rolling echoes, "I don't want to hide—"

"Damn it, you'll be our guard. We can't let those monsters recapture the engine room. Now, null gravity!" And Manuel switched off the generator.

Free fall yanked me with a hideous nausea. I fought down my outraged stomach and grabbed a post to get myself back down to the deck. Down—no. There was no up and down now. We are floating free. Manuel had nullified the gravity advantage of the Gorzuni.

"All right, John, let's go!" he snapped.

I had time only to clasp Kathryn's hand. Then we were pushing off and soaring out the door and into the corridor beyond. Praise all gods, the Commonwealth navy had at least given its personnel free-fall training. But I wondered how many of the slaves would know how to handle themselves.

The ship roared around us. Two Gorzuni burst from a side cabin, guns in hands. Manuel burned them as they appeared, snatched their weapons, and swung on toward the slave pens.

The lights went out. I swam in a thick darkness alive with the rage of the enemy. "What the hell—" I gasped.

Manuel's answer came dryly out of blackness: "Kathryn knows what to do. I told her a few days ago."

At the moment I had no time to realize the emptiness within me from knowing that those two had been talking without me. There was too much else to do. The Gorzuni were firing blind. Blaster bolts crashed lividly down the halls. Riot was breaking loose. Twice a lightning flash sizzled within centimeters of me. Manuel fired back at isolated giants, killing them and collecting their guns. Shielded by the dark, we groped our way to the slave pens.

No guards were there. When Manuel began to melt down the locks with low-power blasting I could dimly see the tangle of free-floating naked bodies churning and screaming in the vast gloom. A scene from an ancient hell. The fall of the rebel angels. Man, child of God, had stormed the Stars and been condemned to Hell for it.

And now he was going to burst out!

Hokusai's flat eager face pressed against the bars. "Get us out," he muttered fiercely.

"How many can you trust?" asked Manuel.

"About a hundred. They're keeping their heads, see them waiting over there? And maybe fifty of the women."

"All right. Bring out your followers. Let the rest riot for a while. We can't do anything to help them."

The men came out, grimly and silently, hung there while I opened the females' cage. Manuel passed out such few guns as we had. His voice lifted in the pulsing dark.

"All right. We hold the engine room. I want six with guns to go there now and help Kathryn O'Donnell keep it for us. Otherwise the Gorzuni will recapture it. The rest of us will make for the arsenal."

"How about the bridge?" I asked.

"It'll keep. Right now the Gorzuni are panicked. It's part of their nature. They're worse than humans when it comes to mass stampedes. But it won't last and we have to take advantage of it. Come on!"

Hokusai led the engine room party—his naval training told him where the chamber would be—and I followed Manuel, leading the others out. There were only three or four guns between us but at least we knew where we were going. And by now few of the humans expected to live or cared about much of anything except killing Gorzuni. Manuel had timed it right.

We fumbled through a livid darkness, exchanging shots with warriors who prowled the ship firing at everything that moved. We lost men but we gained weapons. Now and again we found dead aliens, killed in the rioting, and stripped them too. We stopped briefly to release the technicians from their special cage and then shoved violently for the arsenal.

The Gorzuni all had private arms, but the ship's collection was not small. A group of sentries remained at the door, defending it against all comers. They had a portable shield against blaster bolts. I saw our flames splatter off it and saw men die as their fire raked back at us.

"We need a direct charge to draw their attention,

while a few of us use the zero gravity to soar 'over-head' and come down on them from 'above,' " said Manuel's cold voice. It was clear, even in that wild lightning-cloven gloom. "John, lead the main attack."

"Like hell!" I gasped. It would be murder. We'd be hewed down as a woodman hews saplings. And there was Kathryn waiting—Then I swallowed rage and fear and lifted a shout to the men. I'm no braver than anyone else but there is an exaltation in battle, and Manuel used it as calculatingly as he used everything else.

We poured against them in a wall of flesh, a wall that they ripped apart and sent lurching back in tattered fragments. It was only an instant of flame and thunder, then Manuel's flying attack was on the defenders, burning them down, and it was over. I realized vaguely that I had a seared patch on my leg. It didn't hurt just then, and I wondered at the minor miracle which had kept me alive.

Manuel fused the door and the remnants of us swarmed in and fell on the racked weapons with a terrible fierceness. Before we had them all loaded a Gorzuni party charged us but we beat them off.

There were flashlights, too. We had illumination in the seething dark. Manuel's face leaped out of that night as he gave his crisp, swift orders. A gargoyle face, heavy and powerful and ugly, but men jumped at his bidding. A party was assigned to go back to the slave pens and pass out weapons to the other humans and bring them back here.

Reinforcements were sent to the engine room. Mortars and small antigrav cannon were assembled and loaded. The Gorzuni were calming, too. Someone had taken charge and was rallying them. We'd have a fight on our hands.

We did!

I don't remember much of those fire-shot hours. We lost heavily in spite of having superior armament. Some three hundred humans survived the battle. But many of them were badly wounded. But we took the ship. We hunted down the last Gorzuni and flamed those who tried to surrender. There was no mercy in us. The Gorzuni had beaten it out, and now they faced the monster they had created. When the lights went on again three hundred weary humans lived and held the ship.

IV

There was a conference in the largest room we could find. Everyone was there, packed together in sweaty silence and staring at the man who had freed them. Theoretically it was a democratic assembly called to decide our next move. In practice Manuel Argos gave his orders.

"First, of course," he said, his soft voice somehow carrying through the whole great chamber, "we have to make repairs, both of battle damage and of the deliberately mishandled machinery. It'll take a week, I imagine, but then we'll have us a sweet ship. By that time, too, you'll have shaken down into a crew. Lieutenant Reeves and Ensign Hokusai will give combat instruction. We're not through fighting yet."

"You mean—" A man stood up in the crowd. "You mean, sir, that we'll have opposition on our return to Sol? I should think we could just sneak in. A planet's too big for blockade, you know, even if the Baldics cared to try."

"I mean," said Manuel calmly, "that we're going on to Gorzun."

It would have meant a riot if everyone hadn't been so tired. As it was, the murmur that ran through the assembly was ominous.

"Look, you," said Manuel patiently, "we'll have us a first-class fighting ship by the time we get there, which none of the enemy has. We'll be an expected vessel, one of their own, and in no case do they expect a raid on their home planet. It's a chance to give them a body blow. The Gorzuni don't name their ships, so I propose we christen ours now—the Revenge."

It was sheer oratory. His voice was like an organ. His words were those of a wrathful angel. He argued and pleaded and bullied and threatened and then blew the trumpets for us. At the end they stood up and cheered for him. Even my own heart lifted, and Kathryn's eyes were wide and shining. Oh, he was cold and harsh and overbearing, but he made us proud to be human.

In the end, it was agreed, and the Solar ship *Revenge*, Captain Manuel Argos, First Mate John Henry Reeves, resumed her way to Gorzun.

In the days and weeks that followed, Manuel talked much of his plans. A devastating raid on Gorzun would shake the barbarian confidence and bring many of their outworld ships swarming back to defend the mother world. Probably the rival half of the Baldic League would seize its chance and fall on a suddenly weakened enemy. The *Revenge* would return to Sol, by that time possessed of the best crew in the known universe, and rally mankind's scattered forces. The war would go on until the System was cleared—

"—and then, of course, continue till all the barbarians have been conquered," said Manuel.

"Why?" I demanded. "Interstellar imperialism can't be made to pay. It does for the barbarians because they haven't the technical facilties to produce at home what they can steal elsewhere. But Sol would only be taking on a burden."

"For defense," said Manuel. "You don't think I'd let a defeated enemy go off to lick his wounds and prepare a new attack, do you? No, everyone but Sol must be disarmed, and the only way to enforce such a peace is for Sol to be the unquestioned ruler.' He added thoughtfully: 'Oh, the empire won't have to expand forever. Just till it's big enough to defend itself against all comers. And a bit of economic readjustment could make it a paying proposition, too. We could collect tribute, you know."

"An empire—?" asked Kathryn. "But the Commonwealth is democratic—"

"Was democratic!" he snapped. "Now it's rotted away. Too bad, but you can't revive the dead. This is an age in history such as has often occurred before when the enforced peace of Caesarism is the only solution. Maybe not a good solution but better than the devastation we're suffering now. When there's been a long enough period of peace and unity it may be time to think of reinstating the old republicanism. But that time is many centuries in the future, if it ever comes. Just now the socio-economic conditions aren't right for it."

He took a restless turn about the bridge. A million stars of space in the viewport blazed like a chill crown over his head. "It'll be an empire in fact," he said, "and therefore it should be an empire in name. People will fight and sacrifice and die for a gaudy symbol when the demands of reality don't touch them. We need a hereditary aristocracy to put on a good show. It's always effective, and the archaism is especially valuable to Sol just now. It'll recall the good old glamorous days before space travel. It'll be even more of a symbol now than it was in its own age. Yes, an empire, Kathryn, the Empire of Sol. Peace, ye underlings!"

"Aristocracies decay," I argued. "Despotism is all right as long as you have an able despot but sooner or later a meathead will be born—"

"Not if the dynasty starts with strong men and women, and continues to choose good breeding stock, and raises the sons in the same hard school as the fathers. Then it can last for centuries. Especially in these days of gerontology and hundred-year active lifespans."

I laughed at him. "One ship, and you're planning an empire in the Galaxy!" I jeered. "And you yourself, I suppose, will be the first emperor?"

His eyes were expressionless. "Yes," he said. "Unless I find a better man, which I doubt."

Kathryn bit her lip. "I don't like it," she said. "It's —cruel."

"This is a cruel age, my dear," he said gently.

Gorzun rolled black and huge against a wilderness of stars. The redly illuminated hemisphere was like a sickle of blood as we swept out of secondary drive and rode our gravbeams down toward the night side.

Once only were we challenged. A harsh gabble of words came over the transonic communicator. Manuel answered smoothly in the native language, explaining that our vision set was out of order, and gave the recognition signals contained in the codebook. The warship let us pass.

Down and down and down, the darkened surface swelling beneath us, mountains reaching hungry peaks to rip the vessel's belly out, snow and glaciers and a churning sea lit by three hurtling moons. Blackness and cold and desolation.

Manuel's voice rolled over the intercom: "Look below, men of Sol. Look out the viewports. This is where they were taking us!"

A snarl of pure hatred answered him. That crew would have died to the last human if they could drag Gorzun to oblivion with them. God help me, I felt that way myself.

It had been a long, hard voyage even after our liberation, and the weariness in me was only lifted by the prospect of battle. I'd been working around the clock, training men, organizing the hundred units a modern warcraft needs. Manuel, with Kathryn for secretary and general assistant, had been driving himself even more fiercely, but I hadn't seen much of either of them. We'd all been too busy.

Now the three of us sat on the bridge watching Gorzun shrieking up to meet us. Kathryn was white and still, the hand that rested on mine was cold. I felt a tension within myself that thrummed near the breaking point. My orders to my gun crews were strained. Manuel alone seemed as chill and unruffled as always. There was steel in him. I sometimes wondered if he really was human.

Atmosphere screamed and thundered behind us. We roared over the sea, racing the dawn, and under its cold colorless streaks of light we saw Gorzun's capital city rise from the edge of the world.

I had a dizzying glimpse of squat stone towers, narrow canyons of streets, and the gigantic loom of spaceships on the rim of the city. Then Manuel nodded and I gave my firing orders.

Flame and ruin exploded beneath us. Spaceships burst

open and toppled to crush buildings under their huge mass. Stone and metal fused, ran in lava between crumbling walls. The ground opened and swallowed half the town. A blue-white hell of atomic fire winked through the sudden roil of smoke. And the city died.

We slewed skyward, every girder protesting, and raced for the next great spaceport. There was a ship riding above it. Perhaps they had been alarmed already. We never knew. We opened up, and she fired back, and while we maneuvered in the heavens the *Revenge* dropped her bombs. We took a pounding, but our force-screens held and theirs didn't. The burning ship smashed half the city when it fell.

On to the next site shown by our captured maps. This time we met a cloud of space interceptors. Ground missiles went arcing up against us. The *Revenge* shuddered under the blows. I could almost see our gravity generator smoking as it tried to compensate for our crazy spins and twists and lurchings. We fought them, like a bear fighting a dog pack, and scattered them and laid the base waste.

"All right," said Manuel. "Let's get out of here."

Space became a blazing night around us as we climbed above the atmosphere. Warships would be thundering on their way now to smash us. But how could we locate a single ship in the enormousness between the worlds? We went into secondary drive, a tricky thing to do so near a sun, but we'd tightened the engines and trained the crew well. In minutes we were at the next planet, also habitable. There were only three colonies there. We smashed them all.

The men were cheering. It was more like the yelp of a wolf pack. The snarl died from my own face and I felt a little sick with all the ruin. Our enemies, yes. But there were many dead. Kathryn wept, slow silent tears running down her face, shoulders shaking.

Manuel reached over and took her hand. "It's done, Kathryn," he said quietly. "We can go home now."

He added after a moment, as if to himself: "Hate is a useful means to an end but damned dangerous. We'll have to get the racist complex out of mankind. We can't conquer anyone, even the Gorzuni, and keep them as inferiors and hope to have a stable empire. All races must be equal." He rubbed his strong square chin. "I think I'll borrow a leaf from the old Romans. All worthy individuals, of any race, can become terrestrial citizens. It'll be a stabilizing factor."

"You," I said, with a harshness in my throat, "are a megalomaniac." But I wasn't sure any longer.

It was winter in Earth's northern hemisphere when the *Revenge* came home. I walked out into snow that crunched under my feet and watched my breath smoking white against the clear pale blue of the sky. A few others had come out with me. They fell on their knees in the snow and kissed it. They were a wild-looking gang, clad in whatever tatters of garment they could find, the men bearded and long-haired, but they were the finest, deadliest fighting crew in the Galaxy now. They stood there looking at the gentle sweep of hills, at blue sky and ice-flashing trees and a single crow hovering far overhead, and tears froze in their beards.

Home.

We had signalled other units of the Navy. There would be some along to pick us up soon and guide us to the secret base on Mercury, and there the fight would go on. But now, just now in this eternal instant, we were home.

I felt weariness like an ache in my bones. I wanted to crawl bear-like into some cave by a murmuring river, under the dear tall trees of Earth, and sleep till spring woke up the world again. But as I stood there with the thin winter wind like a cleansing bath around me, the tiredness dropped off. My body responded to the world which two billion years of evolution had shaped it for and I laughed aloud with the joy of it.

We couldn't fail. We were the freemen of Terra fighting for our own hearthfires and the deep ancient strength of the planet was in us. Victory and the stars lay in our hands, even now, even now.

I turned and saw Kathryn coming down the airlock gangway. My heart stumbled and then began to race. It had been so long, so terribly long. We'd had so little time but now we were home, and she was here and I was here and all the world was singing.

Her face was grave as she approached me. There was something remote about her and a strange blending of pain with the joy that must be in her too. The frost crackled in her dark unbound hair, and when she took my hands her own were cold.

"Kathryn, we're home," I whispered. "We're home, and free, and alive. O Kathryn, I love you!"

She said nothing, but stood looking at me forever and forever until Manuel Argos came to join us. The little stocky man seemed embarrassed—the first and only time I ever saw him quail, even faintly.

"John," he said, "I've got to tell you something."

"It'll keep," I answered. "You're the captain of the ship. You have authority to perform marriages. I want you to marry Kathryn and me, here, now, on Earth."

She looked at me unwaveringly, but her eyes were blind with tears. "That's it, John," she said, so low I could barely hear her. "It won't be. I'm going to marry Manuel."

I stood there, not saying anything, not even feeling it yet.

"It happened on the voyage," she said, tonelessly. "I tried to fight myself, I couldn't. I love him, John. I love him even more than I love you, and I didn't think that was possible."

"She will be the mother of kings," said Manuel, but his arrogant words were almost defensive. "I couldn't have made a better choice."

"Do you love her too," I asked slowly, "or do you consider her good breeding stock?" Then: "Never mind. Your answer would only be the most expedient. We'll never know the truth."

It was instinct, I thought with a great resurgence of weariness. A strong and vital woman would pick the most suitable mate. She couldn't help herself. It was the race within her and there was nothing I could do about it.

"Bless you, my children," I said.

They walked away after awhile, hand in hand under the high trees that glittered with ice and sun. I stood watching them until they were out of sight. Even then, with a long and desperate struggle yet to come, I think I knew that those were the parents of the Empire and the glorious Argolid dynasty, that they carried the future within them.

And I didn't give a damn.

EDITOR'S INTRODUCTION TO:

TWO EDITORIALS
John W. Campbell

It is customary to call the period when John W. Campbell was editor of *Astounding* (later *Analog*) *Science Fiction* the Golden Age of science fiction. Perhaps to some, but to the writers it was more an age of iron. Few writers made a living at science fiction, and nearly all those did so by writing a very great many stories. In those days the magazine rates were low, but they had to do: very little science fiction was published as books.

Astounding paid the best rates; moreover, Campbell paid *promptly*. This was incentive enough to write for him. In fact, though, there was a more compelling reason to work with Campbell. The man was a fountain of ideas. He would discuss story ideas with authors; suggest story themes; edit the work and suggest changes and thematic expansions; and in general work very closely with the stable of writers he considered "his."

He also wrote editorials. He wrote them almost every month, for more than twenty years; a *lot* of editorials. They excited. They enlightened. They enraged. None were dull. Nearly all were controversial. One doubts that Campbell believed more than half of what he said in those editorials—indeed some of them contradicted others—but he was willing to defend the notions he had put forth. You could win an argument with Campbell, but you would have no easy time of it.

Some of his notions were one-shot; ideas thrown to the winds to see what, if anything, they might inspire: letters, certainly. Stories, often enough, since writers read those editorials and rushed to write stories illustrating Campbell's pet new notions. And once in a while he might inspire a young reader and change lives forever. He certainly did with me. I began reading Campbell's editorials in high school: and "inspired" is too gentle a word for what they did.

It wasn't that Campbell persuaded me to his specific views. It was that he truly believed in rational discourse; in the power of human reason; in the vast future of humankind. Those beliefs permeated everything he wrote. Campbell could be, sometimes tragically was, *wrong;* but he was not wrong for bad reasons. Even when he was most in error he inspired and instructed. Moreover: when I thought him wrong, I could write to him and say so; and he would *answer*. Not only answer, but argue. Not only argue, but admit that he could be wrong. It was a heady experience.

Some themes he put forth and abandoned. To some he returned again and again. Although he had no formal training in social sciences, he truly believed that a scientific sociology was possible. You could, from a study of both history and contemporary events, deduce real truths; which could then be tested as any scientific hypothesis might be tested.

Campbell believed it possible to discover axioms of human action. Moreover, he believed that science fiction—good science fiction, the kind of science fiction he liked to buy and publish—could illustrate such axioms; that science fiction could be and indeed would be significant in the advancement of a true science of history and humanity. I've believed that ever since; which is one reason for these books.

Campbell had a background in engineering. He liked to describe himself as a "nuclear physicist." In fact he never had any formal training in that subject; but then as now the self education of many science fiction people was more valuable than much of what passes for university education. Science fiction writers often have considerable insight into not one but many exotic fields. It's unlikely that Campbell ever could have made real contributions to nuclear science, but he did attempt to follow the literature. In fact, he followed the literature of a dozen sciences, and knew more of their interactions than most scientists ever would; and he encouraged his writers, students, and readers to do likewise.

The result was a remarkable influence over a generation. My own case will serve well enough as an example. Before reading Campbell I had not the least notion of what my future would be. After reading *Astounding* I knew: not the details, certainly, but I knew that I would be part of designing and creating the future: and that the future would be a great deal more than any reasonable projection of the past. Campbell, both in editorials and in the stories he bought, told us to question authority, question our assumptions, question what we thought we knew best: but at the same time to have faith in the power of reason, and thought, and human action.

I wasn't alone. Many in my generation who became scientists and engineers were persuaded to do so by science fiction in general, and John W. Campbell in particular. Many of us went on actually to work on projects that Campbell and "his" authors only dreamed of. I will not soon forget his sheer joy when he discovered that he had not one, but many fans involved with Project Mercury.

I don't recall John ever calling himself a teacher, but that is what he was. He taught science fiction writers: taught them to create the kind of science fiction he wanted to read. In doing so he created the Golden Age. But he did more: he taught apprentice scientists; and if they have not yet gone out to create a Golden Age in the real world, we have made a start, and there is yet time. . . .

Herewith a pair of John W. Campbell's most famous editorials.

TRIBESMAN, BARBARIAN, AND CITIZEN
John W. Campbell

In studying history, there are three general, and quite distinguishable levels of culture we can identify. Our own we naturally call "civilized" or "civilization," with the implication of "completely matured and fully developed." It happens to be as far as cultures on this planet have gone; what the fourth, fifth, nth levels of culture may be we can't guess, of course. But judging from history, we can make one pretty high-probability guess—the next stage of development will yield a cultural system that will appear, to us, utterly abhorrent—a system founded on Evil and practicing degradation and repellent immoralities.

That's the characteristic of every level so far . . . as seen from the immediately preceding level.

To define what I mean by the three so-far known levels, I distinguish Tribal, Barbarian, and Civil cultures; the natives of the three we call Tribesmen, Barbarians, and Citizens. Preceding all three is the pre-organized-culture level of the "primate horde"—the sort of quasi-organized group found among baboons and monkeys, in the present time.

The Tribal culture—in its never-actually-existent the-oretical pure state—is a system of pure ritual and taboo. "Everything that is not forbidden is compulsory." The objectively observable system stems from an un-stated philosophy—which is unstated because the Tribes-man doesn't know philosophy exists, any more than a dog knows logic exists, or a fish knows that biochemis-try exists. The philosophy is, essentially precisely that of the Absolute Totalitarian state . . . minus the familiar dictator. That is, in the Tribe, the *individual exists for the service of the state*. The individual has no value whatever, save as a replaceable plug-in unit in the immortal, ever-existent machinery-organism of the Tribe. No individual exists as an individual—neither Tribal king nor Tribal slave; each is a unit plugged in— temporarily, for all these units wear out and are dis-carded in a score or two of years—to the eternal Traditional System of the Tribe. The cells in a living organism wear out and are discarded; the organism is, relatively speaking, immortal. So, in the Tribe, the individual is nothing; the Tribe is eternal,

In return for a practically absolute loss of self-identity, the Tribesman is rewarded with security and peace of mind. The Tribal Traditions have The Answers to all possible real problems; nothing can happen that the Tribal Traditions, in their ancient and time-tested wis-dom, have not already solved. There are no doubts; there are answers which involve "these tribesmen must die," but Death is not intolerable. Uncertainty—Doubt— these are the Terrors that live in the Unknown. And against those horrors, the ancient wisdom of the Tribal Traditions stand a strong, sure defense.

The Tribesman has an exact, clear-cut, and perfectly understandable definition of Evil. Evil is Change. Any Change whatever is Evil. The correlation is absolute— perfect one-to-one.

The Barbarian represents the Ultimate Horror from the viewpoint of the Tribesman; he is the Pure Individ-ual. The Barbarian does not put his faith, his sense of security, in the ancient wisdom of the Traditions—but in the wisdom and strength of a Hero, a living demi-god-man, a Leader who solves all problems.

Barbarism, in other words, is the Dictator, without the Totalitarian State. There is a Hero, who is a strong, and unusually clever leader—an individual who stands out above the men around him.

Tribalism is "a government of laws, not of men," with the minor change that "traditions" replace "laws."

Barbarism becomes a government of Men, not of traditions.

It is the first development of human culture which recognizes the value of the individual. It is *not* true that only civilized people respect the dignity of the individual; any Barbarian will assure you that Citizens have no dignity, that Civilization does not respect the individual. That only Barbarians understand what it means to be an individual.

The Barbarian, in essence, "has too much Ego in his Cosmos."

It's perfectly true that all men seek security—but necessarily, that means they seek *what they believe* is security. A superstitious Tribesman, fleeing a ghost, would happily climb a 100,000 volt power-line tower because he knows that ghosts can't climb.

The Tribesman's security is his conviction that the Tribal Traditions have sure answers to all real problems.

The Barbarian's security is in his absolute conviction that *he* can handle any problem—and if he can't, why, of course his Leader-Hero can, and will.

While the Barbarian leader-hero corresponds with what we think of as a Dictator, the implication we attach is entirely wrong; the Barbarian's leader-hero is followed out of conviction, not out of fear. Oh, there's always the Fear of the Outer Darkness—the fear of the Unknown and Unknowable—but the Barbarian follows the Hero because he admires, respects, and adulates, not because he fears the power of the Hero.

When Barbarism first arises in any area, Tribalism is doomed. The two are mutually exclusive, and there is no possible "peaceful coexistence" between them. To the Tribesman, the Barbarian is Evil Incarnate; the Barbarian has utterly rejected all Good, Moral, and Ethical values. He has rejected the Sacred Traditions, and glories in his absolute defiance of them. He blasphemes not casually, but as a way of life.

To the Barbarians, the Tribesman is a slave, a spineless, gutless coward, a disgrace to human shape. He has no self-respect, no courage to take a risk, no faith in himself. He doesn't respect himself, or any man. He won't fight for any reward, no matter how great and shining! He's a stupid, lazy slug, a disgrace to humanity.

The Tribesman won't fight for reward, he won't take a risk for great gain—because that is not in the Traditions. A Tribesman can't fight an enemy tribe for that enemy tribe's *land;* his tribal traditions refer to *his tribe's* land. If he did take the neighboring tribe's land . . . there would be no traditions to tell what to do with it. It would, in fact, be a Change, and therefore Evil.

The "battles" between two ritual-taboo tribes, anthropologists have long since observed, are practically pure rituals, and actually have a vanishingly small casualty rate. Not greatly different—for all the use of spears! —than in modern college football clashes. The spears are hurled while at a range so extreme that it's sheer accident if someone gets hurt.

When Barbarism appears—that situation changes in a hurry. The Barbarian army isn't going through a ritual; they're out for blood and loot. They don't have traditions as guides, nor as limiting fences about them.

When Genghis Khan appeared, the Mongols, who had been ritual-taboo nomads were converted to Barbarians—and it was only the sheer overwhelming mass of geography that finally stopped them.

Barbarism is one of the great breakthroughs in cultural evolution; for the first time, it establishes that the individual has great value, that the individual must be respected. That it is *not* true that all men are interchangeable plug-in units.

Barbarism introduces the idea that Man can, and should, *make* his fate, rather than accept it. That Man can accomplish, that Change comes in two varieties,

Good and Bad, and that the correlation Evil-Change: Change-Evil is *not* a one-to-one system.

Of course, it horribly complicates the problems of life; where before it was only necessary to show that X was a Change to prove conclusively that X was Evil, it now became necessary to decide whether X was Progress or Degeneracy.

Like most fundamentally sound and necessary ideas, the importance of the individual, which Barbarism first discovered, was very promptly overdone. The Barbarian respects *only* the individual; his respect for self becomes the only effective respect he has. He does not respect Gods, Demons, or other men. He will swear a mighty vow that will endure "so long as the sun shines, the rivers flow, and the grass grows," but which will, in fact, endure until his personal inclinations veer, and he decides he was tricked into the vow.

A democratic vote means nothing whatever to a Barbarian, in consequence. He is a Free Soul, and he spits on sniveling cowards who allow themselves to be compelled to do what they don't want to. Crawling slaves!

So, of course, to accept a vote that goes contrary to his own ideas is impossible; only a whimpering slave lets other people determine what he shall do!

When the Barbarian encounters Civilization, therefore, he is going to be enormously confused and baffled. The Barbarians of North Europe, meeting the Citizens of the Roman Republic, were meeting men who allowed others to order them about, to tell them what to do and when to do it. Who obeyed commands they didn't, themselves, agree with. Obviously, a pack of servile slaves!

But these cowardly Roman Legionnaires, for some incomprehensible reason, did not collapse in battle. These Legionnaires, who had no self-respect, who did not fight man-to-man, but used short swords so that no one of them could say, when he returned home, "I killed Urhtoth!" but only, "I am a member of the Fourth Legion,"—these Romans strangely didn't flee before the fiercest Barbarian charges.

To the Barbarians, the Citizen shows the symptoms

of all the things the Barbarian rejects as vile and degrading—the essence of cowardice. The Citizen yields his will to the demands of others. He allows himself to be limited, and allows himself to be compelled against his own desires.

To the Barbarian, the Citizen shows the same loathsome abnegation that the Tribesman does.

Which makes it all the more incomprehensible that these sniveling Citizens win battle after battle. They who have sacrificed their Manhood, have given up their right to individual dignity, somehow prove able to fight like maddened demons!

At each stage of cultural evolution, the preceding stage appears loathsome . . . and the succeeding stage appears to partake of those same loathsome characteristics.

As a rough guess, it's highly probable that the next stage of cultural evolution will appear, to us, to be Barbarism, and be a horrible, degenerate, loathsome system indeed.

Just as the Civil system appears, to the Barbarian, to be the Tribal system, in which the individual has no dignity, and a man is not a Man, for he lacks the courage to express his individual worth and will.

In a previous editorial, I discussed the effect of the cultural system of the local natives on the type of relationship that grows up between colonists and natives.

Notice that the root philosophy of the ritual-taboo tribesman is such that it is inherently impossible to cooperate with him in establishing a colony. So long as the natives are true Tribesmen, Change is Evil—and the colonists are introducing change. There is no such thing as "a good change" in a pure-tradition system: "Change is Evil; Evil is Change."

More immediately, the Tribesman's sense of security stems entirely from having a sure source of Answers. The Tribesman has no answers himself, and has no sense that he can be a source of answers. His sense of security, his defense against the Unknown, is a Source of Answers. He expects to be told what to do, when, and how; if his Tribal Traditions don't do so, then some other source of Answers must. He has no expectation or desire to be responsible for his own acts; that way lies the terror of the Unknown.

If some colonist comes in and overthrows the Tribal Traditions—then the Colonist must be the Source of Answers. The Tribesman *cannot* cooperate on a man-to-man basis with the colonist, no matter how the colonist may seek to establish such a system. The Tribesman doesn't know he's a man; he knows only that he's a Unit of the System—that he has to be a unit of *some* system.

You can lead a horse to water, but you can't make him drink. And you can lead a Tribesman to Liberty . . . but you can't make him free.

If the colonists move in to an area where there are Barbarian natives . . . again, cooperation is strictly impossible. Barbarians can't cooperate among themselves; they do not operate as a cross-linked, integrated team in any operation, but as individuals heading toward the same goal, and hence incidentally traveling parallel paths. Like the pellets from a shotgun charge, they produce a net group effect, but not by reason of being in a cooperating system.

The colonists, seeking to set up a civilized colony, are presenting the Barbarians with an irresistible challenge; the colonists are showing the weakness, the spineless cowardice, the slave mentality, of allowing themselves to be pushed around by their masters. And they're demanding that the Barbarians give up their self-respect and crawl among them!

He'd rather die in honorable battle, than knuckle under, than crawl before masters, like that!

Of course, if the natives have already reached the Civil level of culture themselves, cooperation is not only possible, but practically inevitable. When there are free men who can and will work, slaves invariably prove too expensive.

The Citizen can be enslaved; on that, the Barbarian is right. The Barbarian cannot be enslaved; he'll either kill himself trying to rebel, or die of psychosomatic illnesses brought on by hopelessness if rebellion is impossible. He loses the will to live, if he cannot live as a Free Barbarian.

A Citizen can be enslaved, because, with him, freedom is not an absolute thing, as it is with the Barbarian. But such men are more efficiently productive as free men than as slaves—and they will, therefore, wind up free-in-fact, whether slaves-in-name or not.

If the natives in an area being opened for colonization by a civilized people are themselves civilized—the result will be a hybrid civilization, with mutual respect between natives and colonists.

If the natives are Barbarians, they cannot be enslaved, and it is impossible to cooperate with them, or establish any form of peaceful co-existence. But the Barbarian is only a short step from civilization himself. After those "sniveling, cowardly slaves" of Citizens have repeatedly defied all the certainties of Barbarian ideas by shellacking every Barbarian attack, the Barbarian—who is *not* stupid!—starts re-evaluating his ideas.

At this point, cooperation may set in—because the Barbarians have ceased to be Barbarians.

The Spanish Conquistadors represent a very unusual sort of "Colonization"; they were, actually, typical Barbarians themselves! Like the Barbarian, each of them was a force unto himself. He may not have thought that he was, himself, God, but he definitely acted on the basis that he was God's Chosen Instrument. They had unlimited faith in themselves—right up to the instant of death. Nothing had ever been able to kill them; they were invulnerable! Death and disaster was something that happened to others.

The resultant personality made possible a level of achievement that was, quite clearly, far beyond any reasonable man's level. Their self-will and self-importance absolutely dominated anything else.

They came from a Civil system, and had many aspects of the Civil system—but they were, individually, Barbarians.

The Barbarian is not a worker; he's a looter. He's a high-risk gambler. He will never develop a land; he will only loot it. For him, vast, rich farm lands, just waiting for an industrious population to develop them, are of no value whatever.

The Spanish Conquistadors never achieved anything whatever in the United States area; all the natives in this area were Barbarian-level themselves—and nothing is less profitable to a Barbarian than getting into a clawing match with other Barbarians.

The Conquistadors did just fine in Mexico and in the Inca empire; there, the natives had recently developed a civilization—they were very-late-Barbarian early—Civilization. They could be enslaved . . . and were.

Spain never established a foothold anywhere where there were no enslaveable natives.

Wherever the enslaveable natives were early-civilization level people . . . the slavery lasted just long enough for the natives to learn the higher-order techniques of mid-civilization. Whereupon the now-educated natives dumped the conquerors: the result is a hybrid civilization.

It's interesting to wonder what would have happened if the British, instead of the Spanish, had been first into those areas. In the areas where British colonists met natives of early-Civilized level—the Polynesians in New Zealand and Hawaii, for example—hybrid cultures grew up from the start.

It's also interesting to wonder what will happen if we go in to some planet, and find what seems to be a Barbarian culture . . . which isn't. It would certainly be baffling, and almost certainly be disastrous in a way we cannot dimly imagine.

It would mean the destruction of our very souls. Just as Civilization, by merely contacting Barbarians repeatedly, brings about the corruption and degradation of their dignity, their self-respect—their very souls. And turns them into cowardly, weakened, crawling things that actually cooperate with another human being.

We can't, of course, guess just what form of loathsome corruption of our selves, our dignity, looms before us.

It doesn't really matter; we're going to get it anyway,

whether from outside, or from our own unwanted, yet inescapable, evolution.

But we won't like it. Any more than a Tribesman likes becoming that essence of corruption and evil, a Barbarian. Or a Barbarian likes becoming that sniveling thing, a Citizen.

THE BARBARIANS FROM WITHIN
John W. Campbell

When the Lion shall lie down with the Lamb—the Lion is going to be in serious trouble. The Lamb, of course, can baaaaah happily as it goes gamboling off through its breakfast, lunch, and dinner supply—but the Lion's in a different spot. He can't live on grass. His digestive system is intrinsically incapable of extracting nourishment from herbal food supplies. It's no good trying to persuade him to learn a new way of life, and be happy eating grass, fruits, and twigs; he can't.

During the hot summer nights last year, race riots broke out in various cities in the Northeast. New York—Rochester—Jersey City—Chicago—Paterson—and other towns had their riots or near-riots as emotions boiled over.

These were undoubtedly true race riots—but I want to suggest that *they were not Negro-vs-White riots.* They only had that surface appearance.

For one thing, remember that only about 0.05% of the Negroes of Harlem, for instance, participated in the rioting. Moreover, while the New York City riots were essentially 100% Negro, this was *not* the pattern in Rochester, Chicago, and other places. There white juveniles did their rioting, looting, and destroying, too. Once the riots got started, it was a happy orgy of looting, destruction, and outlawry in which all interested were joining the party.

They were race riots, all right—but the races involved were Barbarians vs. Citizens—and neither skin-color, religion, or home-background had anything whatever to do with it.

Dr. Kenneth Clark, Harlem's Negro psychologist, of course maintains that it's the poor home environment of the Harlem Negro youths that leads to such behavior—the frustrations and tensions of rejection, poor education, and slovenly home environment.

That's open to argument, of course, since it's proper to ask "Who makes the slovenly home environments?" But skip that problem for a moment, and recognize that full-fledged Juvenile Delinquents come from fine homes, with excellent economic, educational, and social backgrounds.

The Barbarian type is a *genetic* type—he's born that way. True, he can be influenced to some degree—but he's *inherently* a Barbarian, and he'll be a Barbarian no matter what his economic, educational, or social background may be.

First off, let's stop pretending that "all men are born equal"; they aren't, never were, and never will be. They're born with vastly different potentials, and vastly different inherent motivations. It's currently fashionable to say that it's lack of educational opportunities, economic opportunities, et cetera, that keeps the poor man poor and hopeless. This is utter nonsense, as history proves in any number of instances you want. Abraham Lincoln, maybe, had excellent educational, economic, and social background? Or what's your particular choice of field of accomplishment? Science? Then how about Michael Faraday? Or try another type of handicap; how about Charles P. Steinmetz? And, on the other side, every millionaire's son become's a genius in his own right because of his educational, economic, and social advantages?

The men of great personal accomplishment aren't necessarily beneficial to the race, of course. But to see that the much-discussed educational, economic, and social advantages don't seem to matter much—consider Adolph Hitler and Genghis Khan.

Those advantages are helpful—to individuals with the

right kind of potential. But *the individual must have the potential as a genetic gift*.

It's currently popular to hold that Nurture is Everything, and Nature is an unimportant accident of no real importance. The argument is usually advanced on behalf of the poor, down-trodden, dispossessed, rejected slob who never did anything useful for himself or anyone else.

O.K.—try applying it to the millionaire's sons. By the nature of the argument, it follows that every millionaire's son should prove to be a genius. Since they quite obviously don't, despite having every possible advantage (except inherent nature!) it's essential for the social-liberal who claims it's lack of such advantages that makes the poor man poor, to explain why the rich man's son so frequently turns out to be simply a rich slob. The social-liberal is always quick to hold that the rich man's son *is* a selfish, egotistical, useless parasite; is that the effect of every educational and economic advantage? Is that what he wants for the poor man's son?

Of course, there are rich men's sons who have turned out to be fully as brilliantly constructive and creative as their sires—but that's not surprising. There are also poor men's sons who've turned out brilliantly constructive, too. More poor men's sons turn up as great benefactors than rich men's sons, for that matter—which is not too surprising, in view of the fact that there are about 100,000,000 poor men having sons for every rich man having a son.

In any case, the social-liberal who is constantly insisting that it's educational, economic, and social advantages, *and only that*, that makes the vast difference must—loathe the idea however much he may—explain why the millionaire's sons aren't consistently brilliant, creative, constructive, and highly civilized individuals.

Because, quite clearly, despite all those advantages, they aren't consistently what the social-liberal insists good opportunities would make of everyone!

No—there's Nature in there, as well as Nurture. And genetics plays a role that education simply cannot do anything about. There's one very simple fundamental that constitutes an absolute block on the possibilities of education: *You can not teach an organism how to learn.*

The ability-to-learn *must* be genetically endowed; if the ability-to-learn is not already present, then all efforts to teach must necessarily be futile.

Now a chimpanzee can be taught many things—more, and more complex behavior patterns than, for example, a dog. But it can *not* be taught to understand and use word-symbols. It lacks the ability-to-learn speech-symbology. No amount of patient effort can teach what the chimpanzee's mind lacks the ability to learn.

How long must one expose a piece of film coated with a sodium chloride-gelatine emulsion to get a picture? A silver-chloride-gelatine emulsion will record a picture in a millionth of a second—but sodium chloride lacks the ability-to-respond-to-light. No amount of exposure will ever produce the desired recording.

Dogs have been selectively bred by Man for about 200,000 years—say 100,000 generations. The modern Border Collie, like other true working dogs, can learn a quite extensive vocabulary of true sound-symbols; they do learn to understand speech. They are not as intelligent as the chimpanzee—but they have one specific ability-to-learn that the chimpanzee simply lacks.

Point: The existence of a high degree of intelligence has no correlation whatever with *specific* learning abilities.

The chief statistician for one of America's greatest public utilities once took a series of aptitude tests, to aid psychologists who were trying to calibrate their tests in terms of aptitudes-shown vs. success in fields of work. That is, what aptitudes does an individual who succeeds as an engineer show? A banker? A research chemist? Or, in the case under test, a statistician.

One aptitude he lacked with almost incredible completeness was any sense of spatial geometry. Given a wooden cube, which had been sawed up into nine wiggly, irregular blocks, and asked to assemble the scattered pieces—after forty-five minutes of futile trying, they gave up. Most people need about three minutes;

mechanical engineers usually succeed in about forty-five seconds.

Both the psychologists and the statistician were fascinated by this remarkable lack of solid-geometry insight, and agreed to try a teaching program. Over the course of a week or so, the statistician laboriously practiced assembling the wiggly blocks, until he finally was able to do it in about five minutes.

Then they gave him an exactly similar collection of wiggly blocks, but only one-half the size he'd practiced with.

At the end of thirty unsuccessful minutes, he went back to being one of the country's greatest statisticians, and they went back to aptitude testing.

Intelligence has nothing whatever to do with *specific* learning ability.

A specific learning ability can be bred into a genetic line, given time enough, selective breeding, and a reasonable mutability of the organisms being bred. (That's why dogs now understand speech-symbols.)

Some human individuals can't learn to be civilized. Genetics being a statistical thing, the son of five generations of highly civilized men may happen to miss the gene-pattern required, while the son of twenty generations of barbarian warriors shows up with it.

The essence of a learning-ability is, it seems to me, a built-in genetic ability to *enjoy* a specific activity. The Lamb can *enjoy* eating grass—and, incidentally, gets nourished thereby. If we could somehow make a Lion *enjoy* eating grass, he would happily chew away at grass, worried only by the extremely inefficient job his carnivore-style teeth did on chewing the stuff. (He would starve to death, of course, but he'd starve happily.)

The scholar *enjoys* studying. The athlete *enjoys* physical acitivity. The two are mutually exclusive only to the extent that both require time, so we find both scholarly athletes, scholarly nonathletes, and athletic nonscholars.

The trouble with the Barbarian is that he specifically enjoys fighting, and specifically hates working for a living. To him, working for a living is dishonorable, unmanly, slavery—anathema. He can enjoy fighting, though he is fully aware that it has a high probability of killing him. (Remember that a nuclear physicist deeply enjoys working with materials that he is acutely aware can kill him. The chemist continues to do research on materials that he knows are extremely explosive, enormously poisonous, or viciously corrosive. Risk stops neither the citizen nor the barbarian.)

The Barbarian can fight for a living, in any variant of the concept of "fight." These include actual paid-mercenary action, fight-and-loot—which he prefers, of course—or through stealing, swindling, blackmailing, extortion, et cetera. He would, by reason of that general mechanism, rather rape a woman than earn her love, rather seduce her by false promises than marry her—because the latter is a form of slavery, in his opinion. He could not *enjoy* her love—but would delight in his conquest of her. (And don't pity the Barbarian woman; she agrees in full!)

Now history has some six thousand years of records showing the essential pattern of Barbarian behavior. It's quite consistent, whether you study pre-Hellenistic Greek Barbarians as seen by more nearly civilized early Egypt, Mongols as seen by civilized Chinese a thousand years ago, or the problem in central Africa today.

The Barbarian is born with the characteristic that he *can not work for a living.* He *can't* lie down with the Citizen, and cooperate in a constructive, cooperative, eight-hours-a-day building operation. He *can't*—no more than the Lion can live if he lies down with the Lamb.

After the Harlem riots, one Negro rioter said to a newspaper reporter, "They're killing us psychologically, damn it! They're killing us slow! If they're going to kill me, I'd rather they did it with a bullet!"

He was speaking the exact truth. The city-culture is killing them—the Barbarians—psychologically. It must; it cannot live with them, and they cannot live with it. And the Barbarian would rather die by a bullet; he doesn't mind the risk of fighting, any more than the dedicated scientist minds the risk of riding a rocket into orbit.

That rioter who'd rather die by a bullet wasn't saying that because he was a Negro; he was speaking for all the Barbarian rioters, black and white, Jew, Christian, Mohammedan, or Buddhist, in all civilized lands everywhere. He *thought* he was talking about Negroes, when he said "They're killing *us* . . ."—but remember that only a minute percentage of Negroes were actually involved in the rioting, while very considerable numbers of whites joined in the spree of Barbarian-style looting, fighting, and destruction.

I have a little parlor game I like to play on people; you can try it yourself, if you don't mind losing a few friends. It's called "You be Dictator." It's quite simple; you simply say to your victim, "You've just been appointed Absolute Tyrant Dictator of the Earth. Now tell me—what do you do about this problem . . ." and name the problem he's sure he knows the answer to.

Like, "Now you're Dictator—*you* solve the problem of what to do with the Barbarians in our city-civilized culture!"

The thing that makes it so deadly a problem is that some of those Barbarians the city-culture *must* kill either psychologically or physically, will be the sons—and daughters—of your own officers and administrators.

The trouble of the Barbarian in the city-culture stems from the fact that they are a race-within-any-and-every-race.

One of the major reasons the Negro people are having so much trouble gaining acceptance is, simply, that the Negroes are not doing an adequate job of disciplining their own people, themselves.

There are three possible forms of discipline in the Universe; any individual or group has a choice of which of the three he will choose—but there is absolutely no escape from the necessity of choosing. Discipline you will get, whether you like it or not; your choice is which form of discipline you want, not whether you'll accept it or not.

There's Universe Discipline. If Baby sticks his hand in the boiling water—that's what he gets. Or, if he crawls out the fifth-story window. Or, if an African tribesman, convinced that his magic charm makes rifle bullets turn to water—he gets Universe Discipline.

Then there's Other-People Discipline. That's what Baby gets when Mama slaps its hand away as it reaches for the boiling water, or grabs Baby as he starts out the window. Or what the tribesman gets if he's arrested and jailed before he gets a chance to charge the machine gun.

Then there's Self-Discipline. Which is what you use when you get tired of getting your hand burned by the scalding water, and also get tired of having people slap it away from what you want to reach. It's what you achieve when you recognize that the magical charms won't work, and charging machine guns won't give you even a chance of surviving the fighting, and, somehow, learn to enjoy working your way up to having your own machine guns.

The disappointing part about Self-Discipline is that, when you finally achieve what you set out for, you find your wants have changed, and your achievement is, somehow, unimportant. Like the kid who, at age ten, promised himself that, when he grew up and had all the money in his pocket that adults had, he was going to have an ice cream soda and a bag of popcorn every time he wanted one, by gosh.

Well . . . in a sense, he does. He just doesn't seem to want five sodas and fifteen bags of popcorn a day now that he's grown up.

So by the time the African tribesmen grow up to the Self-Disciplined civilization level of producing their own precision machine tools to produce precision machine guns, and the high-level chemical industry necessary to produce the metals and the explosives required to earn their own machine guns . . . they'll be disappointed. They'll be all equipped with a high-level military technology—and no desire, any more, to use it. They'll be citizens, and citizens, unlike Barbarians, just don't enjoy fighting.

The Barbarian's inevitable and highly suicidal error is to think that, because the citizen obviously hates fighting, the citizen must be unable to fight well.

So . . . there you are, Absolute Tyrant Dictator of the world.

How are you going to make the Barbarians in your city-cultures learn to enjoy discipline—and choose Self-Discipline?

But remember—the true Barbarian *can't* learn that—any more than the Lion can learn to lie down with the Lamb.

Oh, by the way—heroin and cocaine may be very useful to your program. They'll keep a Barbarian happy with delusions and illusions. If you just see to it he has an ample supply, he will cause you very little trouble. It has the advantage, moreover, of killing him both psychologically and physically, without arousing any protest on his part.

But you're the Dictator!

What's your brilliant solution to the problem of the born Barbarian in your own family . . . ?

(A reader replies:)

Dear Mr. Campbell:

I agree with your January editorial, but it won't do the people it's aimed at any good.

Since you contend that the Barbarian is a genetic type, it must also be true that the "social-liberal" is a genetic type—he *enjoys* fooling with Barbarians, just as physicists and chemists enjoy fooling with dangerous materials. The Barbarian can't learn to like working constructively, and the "social-liberal" can't learn that the Barbarian is a hopeless case.

Therefore the "social-liberal" will keep banging his head against the brick wall of the Barbarian's character until something gives—either the liberal's skull, or society's patience with the Barbarian.

When society becomes sufficiently impatient with the Barbarian for his brutality toward the citizen-social-liberal, the Barbarian will simply have to go—whether through spontaneous actions of mass emotion, or through the passage of new laws, written or unwritten, making it a crime to be a Barbarian.

R.H.R
Atlanta, Georgia

That isn't the way history has answered that problem. What has happened—Roman Empire for example—is that the Barbarians take over the civilization, squander the accumulated wealth for a few generations, then amuse themselves fighting among the ruins. This kills off the soft-headed Citizen type that produces the social-liberals, a large percentage of the pure barbarians, and the hard-headed citizen types that—as post-graduate barbarians—can out-fight, out-organize, and out-think the barbarians regain control and start rebuilding.

That full cycle, in its pure form, doesn't often get a chance to manifest itself; usually citizen-dominated surrounding cultures step in when the barbarian induced anarchy disintegrates the culture. Rome demonstrated the full cycle, because there weren't any rival nearby citizen-cultures extant at that time.

The fully developed Citizen actually seems to be every bit as hard-headed, ruthless, and dangerous a fighter as any barbarian—he just uses his ruthless determination wisely instead of egocentrically.

EDITOR'S INTRODUCTION TO:

HYMN OF BREAKING STRAIN
Rudyard Kipling

I write this a month after *Challenger* went down. It is still no easy thing to write about. One thing is plain: no one knew better than the Seven that exploring new frontiers can never be risk-free; and if you had asked them, on that cold January morning, whether we should cancel the manned space program in the event that *Challenger* was lost with all hands, they would have thought you mad. They of all understood that we must continue.

HYMN OF BREAKING STRAIN
Rudyard Kipling

The careful text books measure
   (Let all who build beware!)
The load, the shock, the pressure
   Material can bear.
So, when the buckled girder
   Lets down the grinding span,
The blame of loss, or murder,
   Is laid upon the man.
Not on the Stuff—the Man!

But in our daily dealing
   With stone and steel, we find
The Gods have no such feeling
   Of justice toward mankind.
To no set gauge they make us,—
   For no laid course prepare—
And presently o'ertake us
   With loads we cannot bear.
Too merciless to bear.

The prudent text-books give it
 In tables at the end—
The stress that shears a rivet
 Or makes a tie-bar bend—
What traffic wrecks macadam—
 What concrete should endure—
But we, poor Sons of Adam,
 Have no such literature,
To warn us or make sure!

We hold all Earth to plunder—
 All Time and Space as well—
Too wonder-stale to wonder
 At each new miracle;
Till, in the mid-illusion
 Of Godhead 'neath our hand,
Falls multiple confusion
 On all we did or planned.
The mighty works we planned.

We only of Creation
 (Oh, luckier bridge and rail!)
Abide the twin-damnation—
 To fail and know we fail.
Yet we—by which sole token
 We know we once were Gods—
Take shame in being broken
 However great the odds—
The Burden or the Odds.

Oh, veiled and secret Power
 Whose paths we seek in vain,
Be with us in our hour
 Of overthrow and pain;
That we—by which sure token
 We know thy ways are true—
Inspite of being broken,
 Because of being broken,
May rise and build anew.
Stand up and build anew!

EDITOR'S INTRODUCTION TO:

THE MIRACLE OF GOVERNMENT
James Burnham

Like many in this century, James Burnham came to the serious study of man and government by way of Communism: he became a true believer, suffered disillusion, and cast about for something new. What he found was profound enough. His *The Managerial Revolution* was one of the most influential books of this age. In one sense it was *too* influential: it's no longer read, because nearly everything in it has become accepted.

His *The Machiavellians*, written in 1943 and revised twenty years later, is also long out of print, which is a great pity: in that work Burnham examines a number of political theorists, summarizes their work, and presents his own view of political science. As he says in its preface: "Having come to know something of the gigantic ideology of Bolshevism, I knew that I was not going to be able to settle for the pygmy ideologies of Liberalism, social democracy, refurbished laissez-faire, or the inverted cut-rate Bolshevism called 'fascism.'" Any serious student of politics would do well to locate a copy and read it very carefully; for Burnham was far from being a dry academic. Scholarly enough, he never trotted out scholarship without very good reasons.

Government, Burnham says, is a wonderful thing; so wonderful that our ancestors (who were, we must continue to remind ourselves, every whit as smart as we) hastened to ascribe this wonderful thing to actions of gods and demi-gods. In this short essay Burnham lays bare a dread secret; and tells us why there may yet be empire in mankind's future.

THE MIRACLE OF GOVERNMENT
James Burnham

In ancient times, before the illusions of science had
corrupted traditional wisdom, the founders of Cities
were known to be gods or demigods. Minos, author of
the Cretan constitution and of the navy through which
Crete ruled the Aegean world, was the son of Zeus and
Europa, and husband of the moon goddess, Pasiphaë.
On his death he was made one of the three judges of
the underworld, at the entrance to which—in Dante's
description—he sits "horrific, and grins; examines the
crimes upon the entrance; judges, and sends" each soul
to its due punishment.

The half human, half dragon Cecrops, first king of
Athens, who numbered its tribes, established its laws of
marriage, property and worship, and taught it writing,
was reputed to be the secret husband of Athena, whom
he chose as guardian of his City. Minos, doubting
whether Theseus, who was later to bring the rest of
Attica under Athenian command, was indeed the son of
Poseidon, flung a ring into the sea, and was answered
when Theseus, plunging into his father's realm, brought
back not only the ring but the golden crown of Amphitrite.

It was the pious Aeneas, son of Venus, who led to Italy those Trojans whose descendants were to transform a village into a world empire. The local king, Evander, told him of the old days:

> These woods were first the seat of sylvan pow'rs,
> Of Nymphs and Fauns, and savage men, who took
> Their birth from trunks of trees and stubborn oak
> Nor laws they knew, nor manners, nor the care
> Of lab'ring oxen, or the shining share,
> Nor arts of gain, nor what they gain'd to spare.
> Their exercise the chase; the running flood
> Supplied their thirst, the trees supplied their food.
> Then Saturn came, who fled the pow'r of Jove,
> Robb'd of his realms, and banish'd from above.
> The men, dispers'd on hills, to towns he brought,
> And laws ordain'd, and civil customs taught,
> And Latium call'd the land where safe he lay
> From his unduteous son, and his usurping sway.
>
> *The Aeneid*, Book VIII

The seven hills were linked as one city through the exploits of the child of Mars, Romulus, suckled by a wolf and fed by a woodpecker, metamorphosed after death into the god, Quirinus.

Our own John Adams, in spite of his distaste for such modes of explanation, recognized that "it was the general opinion of ancient nations that the Divinity alone was adequate to the important office of giving laws to men. . . . The laws of Lacedaemon were communicated by Apollo to Lycurgus; and, lest the meaning of the deity should not have been perfectly comprehended or correctly expressed, they were afterwards confirmed by his oracle at Delphos. Among the Romans Numa was indebted for those laws which procured the prosperity of his country to his conversations with [the fountain nymph] Egeria. . . . Woden and Thor were divinities too; and their posterity ruled a thousand years in the north. . . . Manco Capac was the child of the sun, the visible deity of the Peruvians, and transmitted his divinity, as well as his earthly dignity and authority, through a line of Incas. . . . There is nothing in which mankind have been more unanimous."

The great principles upon which our own civilization is founded are traced to the commands issued on a mountain top by God Himself to the man who was at once His prophet and His people's chief, to be confirmed and amplified by His Son.

John Adams—though destined to become himself almost a demigod—was inclined to our modern agreement that these old tales are "prejudice," "popular delusion" and "superstitious chimeras." He suggested also one of the favored scientific explanations of their persistent recurrence:

Is it that obedience to the laws can be obtained from mankind in no other manner? Are the jealousy of power and the envy of superiority so strong in all men that no considerations of public or private utility are sufficient to engage their submission to rules for their own happiness? Or is the disposition to imposture so prevalent in men of experience that their private views of ambition and avarice can be accomplished only by artifice?

John Adams—*A Defense of the Constitution*

Or, rephrased as statement instead of question: A superstitious belief in the superhuman origin of government is foisted by rulers on their subjects as one of the devices by which the subjects are kept in line.

A rival and also widespread scientific account stresses a kind of imaginative play rather than political deceit as source of the superstitions. As example, the *Encyclopaedia Britannica* in comment on the story of Romulus:

The whole story [of Romulus and Remus] . . . is artificial and shows strong Greek influence. The birth, exposure, rescue, and subsequent adventures of the twins are a Greek tale of familiar type. Mars and his sacred beast, the wolf, are introduced on account of the great importance of this cult. The localities described are ancient sacred places; the Lupercal, near the *ficus ruminalis*, was naturally explained as the she-wolf's den. . . . Another Greek touch is the deification of an eponymous [name-giving] hero. The rape of the Sabine women is clearly aetiological, invented to account for the custom of simulated capture in marriage; these women and also Titus Tatius represent the Sabine element in the Roman population. The name Romulus (= *Romanus*) means simply "Roman."

In short: the story of the founding of the City is a set of poetic variations on the City's name.

2

There is no need to reject such explanations by modern science, viewed in their own frame, in order to suggest from another perspective that the ancient peoples, who were not notably more foolish than we, were perhaps also communicating truths by their accounts of the origin of Cities, though admittedly they used a rhetorical system quite other than that of the *Encyclopaedia Britannica*.

The central truth is the insight that there is no adequate rational explanation for the existence and effective working of government, much less for good or fairly good government. (I rule out of the definition of "government" a dominion exercised directly and exclusively by physical strength—a social form which by the nature of the case cannot exist in a group that contains more than three or four human beings.) The universality of this insight is really attested by the scientific writers on society as much as by the ancients. Without exception they too introduce a myth in order to explain the origin of the City. The only difference is that post-Renaissance scientists use a less picturesque language. Instead of Cecrops or Minos or Romulus, they write of a "state of nature" (benign or horrific), an isolated Island with first one and then more than one resident, "primitive communism," the Dialectic, "challenge and response," the Zeitgeist, and a host of other mythic entities that have no substantial reality outside of the scientists' own lively but shamefaced imaginations.

Moreover, apart from a few gross and almost self-evident cases, no one has found a purely rational theory to explain why some governments, though very different from each other, do well, whereas others, though closely similar, do badly. When you drop scientist ideology, it becomes clear that you cannot explain the success of some and the failure of other governments without including a non-rational factor that we call, according to our metaphysical habits, chance, luck, accident, magic, or Providence.

Government is then in part, though only in part, non-rational. Neither the source nor the justification of government can be put in wholly rational terms. This is and must be so because the problem of government is, strictly speaking, insoluble; and yet it is solved. The double fact, though real and part of historical life, is a paradox.

Consider the problem of government from the point of view of the reflective individual. I, as an individual, do in fact submit myself (at least within certain limits) to the rule of another—to government. But suppose that I ask myself: *why* should I do so? why should I submit to the rule of another? *what* justifies his rule? To these questions there are no objectively convincing answers in rational terms alone.

Is he physically stronger than I? Granted that his strength might enable him actually to rule me (though I might of course outsmart him), does it give him the *right* to do so? Is he taller, fairer, swifter than I? Is one or the other of these a political credential? He is more intelligent? Very well; but in government may not character or experience or faith be more relevant than brains? And who decides the degree of his possession of any of these fluid qualities? He is rich? But do not riches corrupt? He is poor, then. If so, will he not be tempted the more?

Nature hath made men so equal in the faculties of the body, and mind; as that though there be found one man sometimes manifestly stronger in body, or of quicker mind than another; yet when all is reckoned together, the difference between man, and man, is not so considerable, as that one man can thereupon claim to himself any benefit, to which another may not pretend, as well as he. For as to the strength of body, the weakest has strength enough to kill the strongest, either by secret machinations, or by confederacy with others. . . . And as to the faculties of the mind . . . . prudence is but experience; which equal time equally bestows on all men, in those things they equally apply themselves unto. That which may perhaps make such equality incredible, is but a vain conceit of one's own wisdom, which almost all men think they have in a greater degree, than the vulgar; that is, than all men but themselves, and a few others, whom by fame, or for concurring with themselves, they approve.

Thomas Hobbes, *Leviathan*

Is there a sign that the gods have chosen this man as ruler? Is he the first-born of a certain father? or *named* ruler by the voice of one-half plus one of the adults, or a designated class of the adults, of the City? We begin to reach, it will seem, arguments of more weight. "Arguments?" Axioms or sentiments, rather, which can indeed settle the problem of rule, if by an act of prior faith we share them: one of them, that is, and reject the others, because believing simultaneously in more than one might plunge us into contradiction. These are what Gugliemo Ferrero called "principles of legitimacy," belief in which can "legitimize" rule or government: the theocratic principle, the hereditary principle, and the democratic principle are respectively implicit in the three questions at the start of this paragraph. These principles are the Guardians of the City, which make it possible, when one of them is accepted by the community, for government to be something other than mere brute force.

But why should I accept the hereditary or democratic or any other principle of legitimacy? Why should such a principle justify the rule of that man over me? Does it prove him better than I because he had his father instead of my father, his color skin in place of mine, because his arts can win more votes than mine? I accept the principle, well . . . because I do, because that is the way it is and has been. This may be a sufficient and proper argument, but it is certainly not a rational one.

Ferrero's countryman, Gaetano Mosca, used the term "political formula" for "principle of legitimacy," and explained in this way:

According to the level of civilization in the peoples among whom they are current, the various political formulas may be based either upon supernatural beliefs or upon concepts which, if they do not correspond to positive realities, at least appear to be rational. We shall not say that they correspond in either case to scientific truths. A conscientious observer would be obliged to confess that, if no one has ever seen the authentic document by which the Lord empowered certain privileged persons or families to rule his people on his behalf, neither can it be maintained that a popular election, however liberal the suffrage may be, is ordinarily the expression of the will of a people, or even of the will of the majority of a people.

And yet that does not mean that political formulas are mere quackeries aptly invented to trick the masses into obedience. Anyone who viewed them in that light would fall into grave error. The truth is that they answer a real need in man's social nature; and this need, so universally felt, of governing and knowing that one is governed not on the basis of mere material or intellectual force, but on the basis of moral principle, has beyond any doubt a practical and real importance.

Gaetano Mosca, *The Ruling Class*

A familiar sophistry is often brought up to close the logical breach. By rational argument I can prove it desirable that there should be government in human society. I can in fact prove that government is essential for the satisfying of human interests and values that are all but universal. And if government is necessary, then there must be someone, or some group, to govern. Therefore. . . . Well, therefore just what? My rational argument is non-specific, and thus non-historical. I establish the rational necessity of government in general, in the abstract; I prove that there must be governors, rulers. But I have proved nothing whatever about this particular government here and now, nor that this particular man—myself or another—should be the one who rules.

This impasse is not mere theory. In historical fact we find that groups which do not accept a principle of legitimacy derived from tradition, custom, or faith always undergo a crisis in trying to solve the problem of succession, no matter how rational their pretensions. When the leader of such a group dies (normally by assassination), either the group disintegrates or a new leader must establish his position by unadorned force.

The death of Stalin provoked a grandiose recent test of this general law. The Soviet Empire is a revolutionary and nihilist society, which in establishing its own existence abandoned all the principles that had formerly legitimized the governments of Russia and the ancillary nations. The new regime has not, however, replaced these principles with any other. First the Bolshevik Party and then Stalin gained de facto rule simply by force, direct and roundabout; nor, with power consolidated, did they succeed—or even seriously attempt—to construct a new political formula. At Stalin's death in 1953, which was probably hastened by his colleagues, the Soviet regime faced the logical impasse sketched above.

The members of the Soviet elite have studied the problems of power more seriously than any other men have ever done. Each communist in the leading stratum understood that the Soviet governmental structure was built as a pyramid with a single leader at the apex, and that its stability depended on installing an accepted replacement for the dead chief. Delay in finding a successor was bound to lead—and in the event did lead—to mounting conflicts and a weakening of the entire Soviet system.

The need for a successor and the damaging consequences of the failure to name one were rationally demonstrable. None of the principal communists (the members of the Presidium, for example) doubted the demonstration. But this did not at all solve the specific historical problem. Granted that there must be an accepted successor, a new No. 1, who is it to be, who is the man? Do not I (Beria, Malenkov, Khrushchev, . . . Suslov) have as good a claim as any other? To the specific question there was no rational answer; and there was no shared faith in a non-rational principle (inheritance, election under prescribed rules, drawing lots or whatever) that would have jumped the logical gap. Therefore the answer, if they were ever to find it, could only be obtained from the ultimate non-rational test of force.

Let me restate the argument of this section, so that it will not seem to say more than I intend.

Both the theory and the practice of government are incomplete without the introduction of a non-rational element. Without some allowance for magic, luck, or divine favor, we cannot give convincing explanations why this government does so much better than that, why this one succeeds and endures, and that one fails. Without acceptance by habit, tradition, or faith of a principle which completes the justification for government, government dissolves, or falls back wholly on force—which is itself, of course, non-rational.

3

I have been referring without definition to "good," "worse," and "better" governments, to governments that "work" or "fail." What, then, is a "good government"? How do we recognize that a government is functioning properly? What is badness or evil in government?

Amercians are fortunate in knowing the purposes of government, from which knowledge we may judge the quality of a particular government's performance. We know these purposes because they are stated as the preamble to the charter through which our government came into formal existence: ". . . to form a more perfect Union, establish Justice, insure domestic Tranquility, provide for the common defence, promote the general Welfare, and secure the Blessings of Liberty to ourselves and our Posterity . . ."

The wording of this preamble is not so casual as might seem from the fact that it was prepared at the last moment, without instruction or explanation, by the committee on style and arrangement of the Philadelphia Convention, and adopted without debate as part of the final (September 14) draft of the Constitution. The absence of discussion meant that the Fathers were unanimously agreed to what the preamble said, and took also for granted that there would be no significant disagreement outside the Convention. The same doctrine had been often repeated in their previous writings, and in constitutions of the several States. The Massachusetts Constitution and Bill of Rights, for example, adopted in 1780 in a text largely by John Adams, affirmed:

The end of the institution, maintenance, and administration of government, is to secure the existence of the body-politic, to protect it, and to furnish the individuals who compose it with the power of enjoying in safety and tranquillity their natural rights, and the blessings of life. . . .

At Philadelphia James Madison asserted even more summarily (on May 31) that "he should shrink from nothing which should be found essential to such a form of government as would provide for the safety, liberty and happiness of the community."

In order to fulfill these purposes, a government must be possessed of two distinguishable qualities. If it is to "provide for the common defence" and "insure domestic Tranquility," then a government must be *strong*. If it is to "establish Justice, . . . promote the general Welfare, and secure the Blessings of Liberty," then a government must be *just*. In briefest definition, then, a "good" government is a strong and just government.

What is the relation between these two qualities, strength and justice? Does one have priority over the other in defining the "goodness" of a government? To avoid confusion in the answer, one more distinction must be carefully made.

In their relation to goodness or excellence in government, strength has a causal priority; justice, an ethical priority. Unless it is sufficiently strong, a government cannot exist at all, and therefore cannot be good. It must be strong enough to defend the organized society (the nation) which it directs from enemies both external and domestic. Otherwise the nation will be destroyed or dissolved. In the causal order, therefore, a government must first be strong, must be strong in order to be. From this there follow consequences that are not always accepted by those who do not like to check ideas by fact.

We might set up the following ratio: strength is to a government as food is to an individual human organism. Causally, food has a priority over intelligence and beauty, say, in a human being, because without food a human being cannot exist at all. And as a human organism can have too much food (too much for its own goodness, that is), so can a government have too much power.

Strength is causally prior to justice in constituting the goodness of a government, but few persons assign much positive value to strength, or power, in and of itself. Ethically, justice takes hardly questioned priority over strength. To exist, a government must be strong (strong enough to survive); to be good, it must be just.

But the relationship between strength and justice in government is more subtle, as we may see if we ask, not what is good or the best government, but what government is worst? Now the worst government is the one that in relation to its own citizens is absolutely weak *or* absolutely strong, no-government or all-government: that is, an anarchic or a totalitarian society. The well-being of the organism is destroyed by either starvation or gluttony.

The evil of total government has been thoroughly annotated in our day, when the theoretic limit of totalitarianism has been closely approached by Nazism and communism. There is still some dispute as to whether the same effects must follow from the same causes: whether the indefinite extension of the internal power of government will invariably bring elsewhere the same kind of evil human consequences that came in Germany and the Soviet Empire. But even socialists have tempered their orthodox call for the governmental absorption of political, economic, and social activities.

There is no longer much dispute outside communist circles about the evil of all-government, but there are still many, of otherwise diverse views, who cling to an ideal of no-government, who believe that anarchy is the best form of society. In principle, this is the doctrine of communists, in spite of their contradictory current practice. Communists contend that the dictatorship of the proletariat, which they advocate and exercise, is only a transitional social form that will evolve into a classless, non-violent society in which the state will have withered entirely away. This ultimate communist society is the same in descriptive outline as the society proposed by the anarchists proper. Right wing and conservative "libertarians," moreover, like the late Albert Jay Nock and his *laisser faire* successor, Frank Chodorov, project from a very different starting point an ironically similar vision.

In the abstract—divorced, that is, from an existential context in history—the anarchist ideal of no-government has always been attractive. Human beings voluntarily associated together, freely cooperating in the accomplishment of shared goals, uncoerced by law, police, or army . . . The picture is so idyllic as to seem almost inevitably the goal of mankind. If we inspect the canvas more carefully, we may still feel the picture to be charming, but we will see that it has nothing to do with men.

Anarchism's departure from the real world is symbolized by the myths in which the anarchic ideal is usually expressed. Rousseau's serene anarchic savages, on whom the chains of society have not yet been fastened, live in a Golden Age that Rousseau well knew to be outside of history. The anarchic Paradise of Adam and Eve was also, and markedly, before true history, which could not begin until sin had come to the world. Both Marxism's prehistoric "primitive communism" and his posthistoric "ideal communism" are products of sociological fantasy unhampered by fact. The anarchic world of the avowed anarchists like Prince Kropotkin, wherein each, shorn of selfishness, envy, and the will to power, willingly finds his own happiness in loving cooperation with all, becomes moderately credible only because angels instead of men are tacitly assumed to be its inhabitants. "If men were angels," wrote James Madison, "no government would be necessary"; and only, he made clear, in that event.

Remote from our world as is this ideal image, we have had practical experience of anarchy—of absence of government; and frequently enough to learn what in fact it is like. Anarchy is found under two fairly common circumstances: in remote, scantly populated frontiers; and in the catastrophic stages of massive military defeat, revolution, and inflation.

The remote frontier is beyond the reach of government. There are no officials, courts, police, army, or jails. Instead there are gunmen, lynch gangs, brigands, the noose, knives, and assassins. The picturesque anarchy of the frontier is first-rate material for movies and romances of adventure. One may even add that for certain sorts of men—physically strong, egocentric, emotionally self-sufficient—it offers a good, even the best life. But the joys of the frontier are limited to trappers, explorers, prospectors, hunters and gatherers, bandits. For most men and all women the cost in narrowness and insecurity is too high. The frontier, by its definition, excludes civilization and all of the cultivated arts.

Every man is enemy to every man. . . . There is no place to industry; because the fruit thereof is uncertain: and consequently no culture of the earth; no navigation, nor use of the commodities that may be imported by sea; no commodious building; no instruments of moving, and removing, such things as require much force;

no knowledge of the face of the earth; no account of time; no arts; no letters, no society; and which is worst of all, continual fear, and danger of violent death; and the life of man, solitary, poor, nasty, brutish, and short.

Thomas Hobbes, *Leviathan*

Hobbes wrote this famous passage as a deduction from his principles rather than as a generalization from empirical data, but it is accurate enough as a description of the anarchic society of the remote frontier, and its grim tone is appropriate to the anarchic plunge into which society is often pushed by military defeat, revolution, or unbridled inflation. Family, home, Church, possessions, art, morality are consumed in the wild flames of shifting mass passions. With the inevitability of a physical law, the disintegration of government coincides with the spread of insecurity, immorality, and terror.

The specialty of rule hath been neglected: . . .
The unworthiest shows fairly in the mask . . .
What plagues, and what portents, what mutiny,
What raging of the sea, shaking of the earth,
Commotion in the winds, frights, changes, horrors,
Divert and crack, rend and deracinate
The unity and married calm of states . . .
And, hark! what discord follows: each thing meets
In mere oppugnancy: the bounded waters
Should lift their bosoms higher than the shores,
And make a sop of all this solid globe:
Strength should be lord of imbecility,
And the rude son should strike his father dead:
Force should be right; or rather, right and wrong—
Between whose endless jar justice resides—
Should lose their names, and so should justice too.
Then every thing includes itself in power,
Power into will, will into appetite;
And appetite, a universal wolf,
So doubly seconded with will and power,
Must make perforce a universal prey,
And last eat up himself.

"Troilus and Cressida," Act I scene iii

Anarchy's charm and romance are located in literature only, not in history. Perhaps there are times when the correction of abuses grown intolerable under established government justifies the period of anarchy that is normally part of a mass revolution. A moral man, to choose so black a means, will make very sure of the excellence—and the possibility—of his end, and of the exclusion of every other road.

EDITOR'S INTRODUCTION TO:

TO A DIFFERENT DRUM
Reginald Bretnor

David Hume may have given us the most important statement in political science.

"As force is always on the side of the governed, the governors have nothing to support them but opinion. 'Tis therefore on opinion only that government is founded; and this maxim extends to the most despotic and military governments, as well as the most free and popular. The soldan of Egypt, or the emperor of Rome, might drive his harmless subjects like brute beasts, against their sentiments and inclination; but he must at least have led his *mamalukes* or praetorian bands like men, by their opinion."

In a word, one may rule through force and fear; but there must still be some way to convince the police and other agents of power.

Now true: this century has brought us refinements the old tyrants never heard of. The Soviet Union, having learned from the Czars, sets all against all, so that no one knows who is an agent of State Security; and to this they added the innovation of consigning sane people to madhouses in order to cure them of their rebellion. Still, a government based on no more than fear is a government ready for collapse. Arthur Koestler, who had every reason to know, said that the necessary and sufficient condition for the collapse of the Soviet system was the free circulation of ideas within it; hence the Soviet dedication to keeping their subjects ignorant of true conditions and attitudes in the West.

Of course in the far future we will have remedied all that. Government will be rational, and command universal respect.

Perhaps.

TO A DIFFERENT DRUM
Reginald Bretnor

The name of the ship was *Lapis Lazuli*, and in sunlight, in normal space, she gleamed like the gem she had been named after. She appeared, silently and instantaneously—like all Gilpin ships then or a thousand years earlier. She gleamed there, in the middle of a green wasteland of low mounds, bordered by forest on one side and a rushing river on the other.

That was on the Fourth Planet of a star named Goldenrod.

Lapis Lazuli's mission, like the mission of her innumerable sisters sent out from Old Earth was, if possible, to find the far-scattered descendants of that great diaspora Saul Gilpin had set off by giving war-threatened Earth his cheap, simple, almost do-it-yourself star drive. Her crew were the New People of Old Earth, for only the unshakably sane had survived the last and most hideous of Earth's wars, and during the succeeding centuries they had bred a new race, an amalgam of all previous races, but one which—perhaps because only those who carried the necessary genes had survived—had sloughed off the least appealing traits of their predecessors. They were a beautiful people, as Greek gods and goddesses were beautiful, or the noble Buddhist statues of Japan's Nara Period. And among themselves, especially within families, they were telepathic, consciously so, and able to shut their minds completely— even to those screamed agonies and horrors of unknown and unknowable beings which, from the beginning, had barred Gilpin's Space to most men, and which only the strange Far Outers had been able to traverse willingly.

It had been those Far Outers who, reporting throughout the inhabited Galaxy and beyond, had finally ended Old Earth's post-war quarantine, and it was from them and from the records of long-dead governments and religious sects and merchant venturers that the New People had gathered their data regarding the dispersed. A few had built new civilizations; many had barely maintained their cultural levels; some had reverted to desperate savagery; some had vanished without a trace.

Around the star named Goldenrod, seven planets circled, and there were records of two having been settled, almost simultaneously, only a few years after the Gilpin Drive's introduction. One had been chosen by a consortium of several thousand men and women of different nationalities, all chosen for their scientific and technological sophistication. They had the wealth to purchase the most advanced equipment then available. Everything was computerized. Everything was automated. All Old Earth's learning, all its literature and music, were at their fingertips. Their eighteen ships had reached the most hospitable of the two habitable planets, passing safely enough through Gilpin's Space thanks to their careful choice of passengers.

It was a beautiful, verdant world.

Three decades passed before a Far Outer ship came calling on them. From Gilpin's Space, the Far Outer saw their entire fleet, arrayed in ordered ranks on the broad green plain where it had first landed. It came down next to them, but no one greeted it. The only human being they saw was a sickly, scrawny thing— man or woman?—who fled shrieking out of a ship at their approach. They investigated the ship, and found it strangely intact, and even more strangely ravished. Everything in it that could conceivably have been associated with man's employment of electro-magnetic forces had been dulled, abraded, and somehow, they knew, rendered forever incapable of performing its designed function. And every nuke-pak on the vessel was dead, totally inert. They didn't tarry to investigate the forests, the reed-jungles, the caves of the high hills. They didn't even bother to go near the Sixth Planet. They went away, and passed the word along.

Goldenrod Four remained unvisited until *Lapis Lazuli*'s arrival. She came, and like her predecessor so long before, found the abandoned fleet. Now there was much less left, a thousand years of wind and rain and dust had built mounds and ant-heaps where ruined ships had lain. *Lapis Lazuli*'s people searched carefully. They found nothing, nobody. Finally, in a cave high on the savage face of a mountain where they had spied the remnants of a no-longer-identifiable artifact, they came upon a grinning, dessicated corpse, half mummified, half eaten. It had built fires there before it died. With it lay a cooking vessel of still bright stainless steel, a broken knife, a belt buckle. Sometime before its death, it had scrawled its despair, scrawled on the smooth gray cave-wall. The message was in ancient French:

Ah Dieu! What's happened? Nothing, nothing works. Nothing turns on, not even solar panels. The ship's dead. Everything's dead. Even lasers don't work. Only guns work—guns, guns to kill with. They work. Hirath has gone out—how long? Oh God, days ago, days! What's happen . . .

It ended in insane repetitions, incoherences.

Molane, who would in an earlier age have been called *Lapis Lazuli*'s captain, gazed at the sad remains. "They had *everything*—everything then obtainable. Like every other Gilpin ship, even in those days, they were equipped to conquer any disease; cures could be synthesized in minutes. With them, according to the records, they had foetuses and the sperm and ova of every useful animal on Earth, every prized food fish, and the seeds of every valued plant and flower. And then—"

He paused, trying to shake off the persisting aura of dead despair, and Lahaisa, his golden counterpart, finished the sentence for him. "And then," she said, "there was an *event*. Something came. Or something happened. And it sucked every nuke-pak dry. So everything went dead, every piece of sophisticated equipment, destroying even the unborn life that equipment guarded. And they thought they were prepared for everything."

"For anything but the *event*," said Molane. "Well, perhaps we can find out what it was. Could you—" He used an ancient word, "—could you skry what happened."

"I'd much rather not," she said, "but yes, I will."

She lowered herself to the cave's floor, assuming the lotus posture, and he placed the bright cooking pot in front of her. There was a long silence as he sat beside her, lending her his strength.

Finally, she gasped. She blinked away sudden tears. "Something came, happened—I don't know which. I feel it was alive, from incredibly far away. It was one of the sensate things that scream in the Far Reaches of Gilpin's Space. It was in pain, and it hungered for—for its sustenance, energy, pure energy. Blindly it entered, penetrating every route by which energy might travel, everything that could create energy, convert energy. No, it did not invade any living thing, at least not intentionally, though I feel that there was terrible agony with its passing, partly because of its effect on nervous systems, partly because of sheer shock. Oh, Molane, it was *vast*, incredibly vast! It descended almost but not quite invisibly. Still it was in agony, but now it had fed; it was recharged. It vanished as abruptly as it came, off for a destination even we can't imagine. And it left behind it—" She sat there, weeping silently, and now he held her to him for a time. "It had killed everything they depended on, and they had no way of depending on themselves. They blamed each other, and after they had exhausted their supplies they tried to live on native plants and animals. They blamed each other, group against maddened group. They began to kill each other, senselessly—"

She stopped. "Molane, do you remember that ancient story, 'The Machine Stops?' Mankind had become totally dependent on a machine. It housed them, fed them, suckled them as infants."

Telepathically, he had shared what she had scried. "And when it stopped," he said, "almost instantly they became savages. So it was here. All the knowledge that made them civilized had been destroyed, all their instruments rendered useless. They were utterly alone with each other, with fear, with themselves."

They stood. "Molane," she said, "after this, is there any use our going on to that Sixth Planet? According to the record, the people who went to settle it weren't well equipped either technically or intellectually. Their leader had proclaimed publicly that they were using Old Earth's science only to escape to some world where they could live simply, close to earth and sea, to other living things, to the forests and the fresh winds blowing through them. But still they were dependent on technology; then it would have been inescapable. Even if their data-banks held only a tiny fraction of what was ruined here, what could they have done without them? After that *thing* had passed they would have had nothing but their memories. Besides, the Sixth Planet is by no means as welcoming as this one. Its extremes of climate, its storms, its ice-toothed mountains and its dreadful jungles—all these were reported by the Far Outers who discovered it."

"But that didn't dissuade the men and women who went there," Molane replied. "Granted, what chance did they have? But still, Lahaisa, we must make absolutely certain, mustn't we?"

Once more aboard *Lapis Lazuli*, and with Goldenrod Four still visible as a Gilpin-ghost—as stars and planets always were from that strange Space—they took counsel with the others of their Eight: Lahaisa's parents, a cousin, an uncle and an aunt, and their own seven-year-old son, Kolali. Among the New People, children always were permitted to be present when affairs of importance were discussed; that was part of the process of growing up. They all agreed that, regardless of how hopeless it might seem, they should not by-pass the Sixth Planet.

Through Gilpin's Space, the traverse would have been a matter of minutes only, but they chose to linger a full Earth-day, partly to compose themselves after the trauma of finding only death and desolation, and partly to learn all that was known of the Sixth Planet and its settlers. After they had supped, they spent an hour or so "listening" to the mind-music of Arilé, Lahaisa's mother, her fantasies weaving and interweaving the voices of all known instruments and many another that never existed except in her mind. They seldom wore any clothing aboard ship, for clothing among people who are truly beautiful, people who retain their beauty even as they age, is never really necessary except to defend against vagaries of climate. So they relaxed, listening to Arilé, sometimes when she made it clear that they should do so adding the music of their minds to hers— all of them except Kolali, who always found it oddly difficult. Gradually the impact of the Fourth Planet was softened; gradually it ebbed. Finally Molane spoke to the ship.

"*Lapis Lazuli*," he said, "tell us all you know about Goldenrod's Sixth Planet, all you know about those people who fled Earth to settle here."

"I shall, Molane." The ship's voice was very soft and very beautiful, synthesized now to caress their minds. "Look!"

Instantly a hologram appeared between them, half sunlit, half in darkness, gleaming with the blue-green of its seas, its browns and umbres, its greens dark and pale, the light tan of its deserts, its white polar caps; and *Lapis Lazuli* told them what the Far Outers had recorded of its continents, its storms, its tectonic upheavals, its infinite variety of living things, its beauties and mysteries and its perils. And they realized it was indeed a far less friendly world than the Fourth Planet. Around the hologram, three small moons circled, one pallid, one dull red, one mirror-bright, and Molane wondered whether that last could perhaps once have been a spaceship.

Lapis Lazuli caught the thought. "No," she told him, "it's a true moon, but of almost solid ice. When all three are in the sky together at night they can provide some very curious shadow-play."

The Far Outers had found no intelligent autochthones, though there had been mammals and pseudo-mammals whose evolution had paralleled that of more or less similar creatures on Old Earth. They had found one outstanding difference. Archaic reptiles still lived whose counterparts had long since died out on Earth. These they had called dragons.

At that, Kolali spoke up excitedly. *"Dragons?"* he cried out. *"Real* dragons?"

"Very possibly," Molane answered with a smile, "but I doubt that they breathe fire, which real dragons are supposed to do."

"You never can tell," said *Lapis Lazuli*, with a gentle smile in her voice. "And now shall I tell you about the people?"

"Please," Lahaisa answered.

"As you know, Saul Gilpin's star drive came at a time of suspicion and tension and pervading terror, a time when men and women fearful for themselves and for their families would follow any prophet who offered what they hungered for subconsciously, sometimes a nonexistent Eden, sometimes cruel dominion over their fellows, sometimes simply death. It was one of these cults that sought out this planet, taking second choice because they knew a much more powerful expedition had picked the Fourth. They were not a wicked cult. Their leader, Gurat Singh, had started out as a devout Sikh, but had then split off, preaching simplicity, non-aggression, and a deep distrust of high technology. He converted thousands, first in the English-speaking countries, then in South America and along the rim of Asia, Hongkong, Singapore, Malaysia, Thailand, Taiwan, and finally in his native India. Nearly three thousand fled Earth with him. Few of them were rich, and the ships that carried them were all they could afford. Like all Gilpin ships in those early days, they were converted submarines, mostly huge old tankers with rough accomodations, not only for the people, but also for the beasts Gurat Singh insisted they take with them. Taking embryos would have entailed too much of the high technology he despised. It was only reluctantly, and because he could not reverse what had become common practice, that he accepted the sensors and synthesizers aboard every Gilpin ship, the data storage that had virtually replaced the printed word, the navigational computers, even all those small devices used to keep individual records and solve petty mathematical problems. Their ships were few, and space was terribly limited, so possessions were strictly limited. We can assume that, whether Gurat Singh approved or not, they were as dependent on their electronics as those others. That is all we really know. Because the Far Outers who last touched down on Four decided to bypass Six, we don't even know how many of them made it through Gilpin's Space."

"What do you think of their chances?" Molane asked.

"Just of getting there? They were good. They were not hostile people. Instead they were fleeing hostility. Such people were much less likely to come apart when the space-voices started to scream their agonies and insanities into their minds while they were asleep."

They spent an hour or two discussing possibilities, quite sure that the Sixth Planet had been hit by whatever it was that had ravaged Four, and saddened now by the seeming certainty of what they would find there.

But Arilé cheered them again with mind-music, letting it sing of the myriad calm, settled, burgeoning worlds that swam the seas of space.

Their approach was, of course, through Gilpin's Space, so that the planet's ghost-shape swelled suddenly in their view-ports, tenuous and uncanny in the non-light. It grew, and *Lapis Lazuli* told them that besides its three moons it had two moonlets, but that there was no sign of artificial satellites. They slowed, coming in from the night side. They watched, all of them.

And then they saw that the Sixth Planet was not dead, not as the Fourth had been, for lights were shining in the night, tiny elfin ghost-glows clustered here and there.

"They live!" cried big Orano, Molane's uncle. "Praise the Guardians! There are cities there."

They made a first careful survey from Gilpin's Space. One continent, the northernmost, was ribbed and girdled with ferocious mountains, snowclad, seeming to dwarf even Nix Olympica. They surrounded an immense rolling taiga cut by mighty rivers, and itself broken by more gentle grassy plains. There were four true continents, not contiguous, and a number of large islands—Ceylons, Tasmanias, Madagascars. These lay between and around the two central continents, one of which was an enormous fantasy of mountains, jungles, deserts. The southernmost continent began as verdant prairie, climbed up, up, range by hilly range, and finished as a veritable Antarctica of glaciers.

They followed the moving line of daylight, shuttling north and south as the land was lighted, knowing that *Lapis Lazuli* would be counting settlements and cities. Roads crossed the continents, and railroads. Ships plied the seas and the great rivers. Over the cities, there were no palls of smoke, no winding-sheets of smog.

The largest cities were not on the continents but on the great islands, and most were seaports. The Eight looked at them in wonder, descending in the ghost-light to barely a stone's-throw above their towers. Each city's structures were hauntingly, tantalizingly familiar. In the streets, self-powered vehicles moving; in the far-flung fields, self-powered machines were harvesting. The clothing worn by the men and women whom they saw was, again, familiar and yet, looked at more closely, totally new and strange.

From island to island, the architecture varied. On one, it was as if they were flying over Europe, but a Europe with vast sections of its history surgically removed. Over another, Lahaisa exclaimed that it was like looking down on the ruins of Singapore, Shanghai, Madras, long before they had fallen into ruin. And there were others which, echoing old Europe, were even more removed: echoing what? the mixed cultures of old South America?

There were fewer communities on the continents— mountain scarps crowned by settlements; towns in the heart of jungles surrounded by defensive works: against intelligent, hostile natives? against whatever dangerous brutes the planet nurtured?

They asked *Lapis Lazuli*, who repeated that the first discoverers had found no sign of indigenous intelligence.

They scanned each of the continents, each of the great islands. "Could you estimate the population?" Molane asked.

"Give or take ten percent," she answered, "about two hundred million, with perhaps seventy percent on the great islands."

"Look at what they've accomplished!" marvelled Arilé. "Could they possibly have been hit by whatever it was on Four?"

"Well, there's only one way to find out," Molane said. "We'll have to monitor their radiation spectrum from normal space. If their ship's nuke-paks haven't been utterly drained, there'll still be some indication. Also we'll have to check their communications media, find out what kind of languages they're speaking, and see if we can get in contact."

Landing on an inhabited world with an advanced culture without first getting permission from one authority or another was something they never did.

"Where do you want to make the shift?" the ship asked.

"I think on their closest moon, in its dark sector."

Moments later, Goldenrod Six was receding, shrinking. The closest moon, perhaps half the size of Earth's was getting larger, the details of its rough face were becoming visible. They touched down on a worn crater's rim, and shifted into normal space immediately.

"What do you get?" Molane asked after a few moments.

"Nothing, absolutely nothing," the ship replied. "There

simply are no nuclear devices on that planet. Whatever they had with them has been sucked dry. And I detect no video signals of any sort—just radio, and very sparingly. There's nowhere near the noise you'd normally expect, and I've scanned every band. Another thing—there's no music, just talk. Apparently they don't use radio for entertainment."

"That's understandable, isn't it?" Arilé said. "After what happened to them, they're probably still scared of another visitation. What language are they speaking?"

"Listen!"

Suddenly a man's voice filled the ship's wardroom, clipped, oddly accented, but still recognizable as English, antique and changed, but changed far less than might have been expected.

"I wonder if English has become their universal language?" commented Orano, of them all the most competent with ancient tongues. "When a language has no real competition, it evolves more slowly, like Old Norse on Earth which hardly differed from Icelandic a thousand years later. We'll be able to understand each other. Shall I make the first approach?"

"Do that. *Lapis Lazuli*, please send a signal on their busiest band—and put all the power you can into it."

"Done," said *Lapis Lazuli*. "You're on the air."

Orano spoke, his voice deep and melodious, each word slowly enunciated, precisely carved. "We are eight people from Old Earth, man's birthplace. We have come to you through Gilpin's Space, as your ancestors came. Much has changed on Earth. Even man has changed. We now make it our mission to seek out all men everywhere. Our vessel rests on your nearest moon, waiting. Will you speak with us?"

They listened, and at first there was no change. The voices on their frequency kept on, talking about the weather, matters economic, news incomprehensible out of context.

Orano repeated his message once again.

And again there was no reaction.

He spoke a third time—and abruptly the voices stilled.

Minutes passed. Then Orano spoke once more, and this time an answer came.

"We have heard you," a man's voice said. "Please be patient. Arrangements must be made for someone with adequate authority to speak with you. You are the first visitors we have ever had except—except the Eater."

"We shall wait eagerly," answered Orano.

Half an hour went by. Finally,

"I am Lord Burlow Erris," a new voice declared, "First Secretary to His Majesty's Government—"

Lord? thought Molane. *His Majesty?* He and Orano exchanged glances.

"—His Majesty and the Privy Council have told me what to say to you. If you are really from Old Earth, we do not want you here. Our Own Gilpin ships brought the Eater, the living terror that destroyed everything electrical and electronic, and even though we no longer are so vulnerable, we fear this."

"Lord Erris, our Gilpin ship today is undetectable. We can not endanger you. We want only to tell you what we have learned, on Earth. We want to help you if we can. Did not your own *sant*, Gurat Singh, declare that all mankind is One?"

"When the Eater came," Lord Erris answered, "all that was changed—even Gurat Singh, blessed be his name! We know that even if you do not bring the Eater, you will bring us back all those uncontrolled evils from which we fled."

"No, Lord Erris, we will not. We too have changed. Old Earth has suffered much, and in that suffering all our age-old passions, all our fury to destroy, which you so justly fear, have been bred out of us. You must believe me."

"*Must* I?" There was more than disbelief in Lord Erris' voice—there was contempt. "And if you have, what then? Here we have learned to live with those same passions, to master them. But enough. I gather you would like to walk among us, and see what's to be seen, and breathe our air. Therefore I must again consult my master, the King-Emperor. Will you wait?"

They waited patiently, speculating on what quirk of

fate had placed a King-Emperor and his Privy Council and a peerage here so many centuries after all these had been dead on Earth. Four hours later, the invitation came.

"I am honored," said Lord Erris, "to announce that His Majesty King Edward, the Eleventh of his name on this world, has consented to your visit. Because you have a Gilpin ship, and we have not forgotten their capabilities, it really wouldn't matter where you first come down, but under present circumstances we prefer to show you precisely where. We are at war with the Holy Roman Empire, and—"

"You are *what?*" exclaimed Molane.

"We are at *war.* Surely you, from Old Earth, are familiar with the term? In any case, the war will not inconvenience you, for it is being fought far from Great Britain, on the Asian Continent. Besides, your permission will be limited. His Majesty wishes to look at you himself, and otherwise make certain you pose no danger to us."

"We understand. Where do you want us to come down?"

"Are you equipped to pinpoint a radio signal's origin?"

"Certainly." Molane signed to *Lapis Lazuli,* and the hologram of Goldenrod Six appeared instantly.

"Great Britain is the larger of our two most central islands, and London, our capital, is its greatest city. I am speaking from Hampton Court Palace, in its outskirts. You may land in the great meadow between the Palace and the park. You will have no trouble locating it from Gilpin's Space, for we will have a pavilion there for His Majesty. We shall expect you in two hours, roughly at mid-morning."

On the island's eastern shore, a brilliant spot of light appeared. *Lapis Lazuli* had pinpointed the transmitter.

"Thank you, Lord Erris," said Orano. "We will be there."

The contact ended. The hologram disappeared.

Molane looked at the others. "A British Empire? A Holy Roman Empire? And are they actually at war? What next?"

"They have *dragons!*" cried the boy Kolali. "*Real* dragons!"

London, like its Old Earth ancestor, was built along a great river and near the sea. It had its miles of docks, its bridges, and even from Gilpin's Space it seemed at once utterly strange and yet curiously familiar. Here and there, spires and steeples of its churches stood out from their surrounding buildings, a massive dome which could have been St. Paul's lording it over them. The Palace was not hard to find, for the grassland between it and its vast park held a small crowd, kept from a clearly defined landing area by orderly ranks of men in uniform. Beside that area, a pavilion stood. There, Molane judged, the King would be awaiting them.

"We'll have to dress for the occasion," he said. "Their women all wear skirts and dresses; their men either are in trousers or what look like jodhpur breeches, with a variety of upper garments. I'd suggest we come as close to these as possible."

He put on a pair of trousers, and over them a long jacket much like a soutane, and the others followed suit. Lahaisa donned a silver gown that left one shoulder bare. The colors all were muted, pale blues and greens, soft yellows with complicated knots of gold embroidery. The ship touched down. At Molane's signal, she shifted into normal space, and through the ports they could see the crowd's startlement.

Molane was first out. As soon as the port opened, he stepped onto the gangplank, halted there, one hand raised in greeting, serenely smiling. He was an impressive figure, all six foot six of him, black haired, golden skinned, gray eyed, wide shouldered. He waited for Lahaisa to come out to him. She took his arm. Together they walked to the pavilion.

After the pallid ghosts of Gilpin's Space, the sight before their eyes was dazzling. Brilliant banners and pennants whipped in the breeze. Everyone at the pavilion, the uniformed guard of honor, the King and Queen on their two thrones, everyone in the breathless crowd, all displayed an Elizabethan passion for color, for finery, for scintillating gems.

Four tabarded heralds blew three flourishes on crested golden trumpets, and King Edward stood, a man in his fifties, almost as tall as Molane and quite as straight. For moments, he looked penetratingly at his visitors, searching first Molane's eyes, then Lahaisa's. Obviously, he liked what he saw. He stepped forward, held out his hand.

"This is an Old Earth custom we have not forgotten," he declared. "Stranger, I am Edward the King."

They shook hands. "Come," the King said, and led them into the pavilion, the others of their Eight following after them. They stood while Molane introduced them one by one. They stood while the King himself introduced his Queen. Then he called to Lord Erris, proud, portly, diamonded, and he in turn introduced two Archbishops, of York and Canterbury, the Prime Minister and other civil dignitaries, a First Lord of the Admiralty and a Field Marshal, and a towering, turbanned Sikh, Sir Partab Singh, Viceroy of India. Molane felt that he was swimming in a sea of titles.

They were seated by uniformed equerries, and as Molane sat down Lord Erris whispered in his ear. "His Majesty," he said, "has decided there is no danger from you, and in this he is *never* wrong."

"He can see into the minds of men?"

"Infallibly. He cannot read your thoughts. It is simply that he can detect the slightest evil there."

Lord Erris sat down next to him. "First, before we converse, we shall be served refreshments. That is our custom. Your lady presently shall sit beside the Queen, and you beside His Majesty. Some of our food will doubtless be unpalatable to you. Do not hesitate to say so. You will give no offense."

Footmen appeared with small tables, table silver, napery. Swiftly, efficiently, they made ready for the food their fellows now were bringing: flagons of cool white wine, trays of small roasted birds, more trays of thin sandwiches on a variety of breads, salvers of steaming sea-crustaceans like nothing on Old Earth. Molane, watching them, felt a wave almost of *déja vu;* their liveries, like everything around him, were at once so uncannily familiar and, seen more closely, so alien.

They ate, slowly and with relish, realizing that whatever this culture lacked it was not the fine art of cookery, and finally there were toasts, from silver vessels like champagne flutes filled with a sparkling brandy. The first, proposed by the King-Emperor, was to his guests. The second, by Molane, to his gracious hosts, Their Majesties. The third, offered by the Archbishop of Canterbury, was to Gurat Singh, "Blessed be his Name!"

Then Molane and Lahaisa were escorted to sit beside King and Queen, who smiled at them.

"Your Majesty," Molane said, "shall I tell you what has happened on Old Earth since your ancestors went off so long ago?"

Instantly, the King's face was grave. "Molane," he answered, "I must tell you *no*. We want to hear nothing of the happenings on Old Earth. It is your world, and this world is ours, and here we not only have all we need, but we feel we are fulfilling a great purpose. After we tell you our own history since the landing and the coming of the Eater, you will understand why this must be so. We will remember you with pleasure, but we do not want you to come again. We have our own ways, our own beliefs, our own arts and sciences, all developed because the Eater came and destroyed, and forced us to build anew. This we could not have done had we not had The Book."

"The Book, Your Majesty?"

"Yes, Molane, The Book that Providence decreed Gurat Singh would bring with him. Before you leave, we will show it to you." Again he smiled. "But I feel that there are many things we do that you would like to change. For instance, you were shocked to learn that we still fight wars?"

"I was, Your Majesty."

"Very well, we fight them because The Book informs us that they are part of man's heritage, that wise men never tried to abolish them completely, but instead did their best to ritualize and ameliorate them. In the Twentieth Century, according to the memories written by our ancestors, there was a change. Instead of trying to limit war, the world tried to outlaw it—and the result was war after more terrible war, culminating in that awful fear from which Saul Gilpin saved us. Besides, war has its challenges—like dangerous, strenuous sports it can bring out the very best in men. What do they fight for? Honor and glory, and this we share with them."

Molane smiled sadly and shook his head, but he remained silent, and the King pointed at a uniformed equerry. "Look at Captain Harrion there," he said. "He has served in two wars, one against the Chinese Empire, another against the Europeans. He has killed more of the beasts whom those first Far Outers called dragons than any other man, with a spear, either on horseback or from a shooting-cycle. They are saurians, very savage, and very hard to kill. Yet he is a courteous, kindly, gentle man."

Out of the corner of his eye, Molane saw his son staring in awe at Captain Harrion, at his polished boots, his spurs, his braided uniform in gold and green, at the jeweled insignia on his epaulettes and the panoply of decorations on his chest.

More toasts followed, then a parade of troops, first cavalry with a mounted band, then infantry with its own music, then artillery, some drawn by horses, some by sleek, silent, self-propelled vehicles. Aircraft, silent except for the sound of their propellers, flew overhead, and all was done with brilliance, to perfection. When the final band had passed, and its disturbingly reminiscent music had died away, King Edward turned back to Molane. "And now," he said, "His Grace of Canterbury, who is best qualified to do so, will tell you what happened to our ancestors and what we have accomplished since.

The Archbishop, a square, solid man in black and saffron, wearing a stiff white collar and a large pectoral cross, smiled at them, but with no real warmth.

"In those days," he began, "Earth, as you know, was on the verge of suicide. It was a grace and a mercy that when our ancestors fled into space they had as their leader our *sant*, Gurat Singh—blessed be his Name! —who embraced all religions within his teaching, showing them how to live together, and we might live like men with man's heritage. But I proceed too quickly. Our ancestors landed in what the Far Outers' report had stated was the most fruitful valley on this island. And they gave thanks that our *sant* had led them there, for our sensors, which were then still working, corroborated what the Far Outers had reported—nothing growing here, neither trees nor grasses, flowers nor beasts nor insects, was seriously inimical to man."

He and the Royal couple and his fellow Archbishop momentarily bowed their heads.

"Then, on the third day, the Eater came. Our nukepaks were drained in an instant. Every channel along which force might flow was ruined. Every microchip became totally useless. We no longer had our libraries. We no longer had the music or legends or scientific textbooks of Old Earth. Our ancestors were not rich men, so all our ships were crowded, with medical supplies, with food, and with all those living creatures our *sant* had told us we could not leave behind, our horses and our cattle, our sheep and cats and dogs—the beasts themselves, and not their frozen seed. For lack of space, every work of reference, every personal note, even the works of Gurat Singh himself had been recorded electronically.

"We lost all, everything, even our small devotionals, which we then used to carry everywhere.

"Only one thing remained—The Book. The Book that Gurat Singh himself had brought. And it was then, when we were in despair, that for the first time he brought it forth and showed it to us. '*Listen!*' he said. 'You say all is lost. Even the words of Gurat Singh are lost. That last is true. But everything is not lost, for in this Book is recorded all that was best in the history of Old Earth. And there is recorded also much of what was worst. But the very worst is not recorded, for it occurred after The Book was written. It is with this Book, my children, that you build the civilization of your new world.'

"Those first decades were hard indeed, but this island is not only richer and more clement than the others, it has none of the ferocious creatures that still infest so many areas of our continents. Our winters here are severe but endurable, our summers are seldom really hot. Even so, I do not know what we would have done had Gurat Singh not planned for us. From the start, everything was methodical. We began harvesting native fruits and grains and wild vegetables, herbivorous native mammals, and fish from our waters; and we successfully established the animals we had brought with us. Nor was that all. Everyone with a skill, everyone with special knowledge of any kind, was required to contribute to books of memories, and printing and papermaking were among the first of our simple industries, for it was absolutely essential that every section of The Book was reproduced as soon as possible.

"Gurat Singh lived more than forty years after we arrived, dying when he had almost reached his hundredth year, and when he died he left his Testament, a document which has guided us ever since. First, from The Book, he told us that only one form of governance on Old Earth had ever had stability and permanence and a high measure of security for peoples, and that was empire. 'So,' he said, 'you must prepare, for in two more centuries you will be ready. On Earth, the greatest empires were the Chinese, the Roman, and the British. I enjoin you to rebuild them here. This island we shall call Great Britain, and those of you who came from England, America, Australia, shall consider it your motherland. The second of our middle islands we shall name Austro-Italy, and there shall be the center of the new Roman Empire. Its capital shall be Vienna, and there shall be a Pope in Rome. Finally, on our largest island, the Chinese Empire will once again come into being, ruled by a new Son of Heaven from Peking. Why do I thus counsel you? Because it would not be well for one Empire to rule the world. As for the island we shall call India, it will be included in the British Empire, for under British rule India was united and ruled by law, and as soon as Britain left it fell again into virtual anarchy, ethnic group against ethnic group, sect against sect. As for your laws, The Book will teach you all you need to know, The Book and your compiled memories. You will have three great Empires, but you shall have one language, that in which The Book is written. Your other languages may be learned and spoken, but English shall be the language of education and diplomacy, science and the arts, for I can foresee the day when you will recreate your sciences, and then a confusion of tongues would only hold you back.' "

The King thanked him. "Our ancestors worked long and hard," he said, "and when the Empires were established, we adopted the practice, which we have followed ever since, of the three reigning Emperors or Empresses, for we have had both, holding council thrice a year with the leaders of the great religions and with the *sant's* Successor in New Delhi. This we do whether we are at war or not, and always we abide by the decision of this Imperial Council, for we recognize that it is the decision of Gurat Singh himself. Before you landed, I communicated with my fellow Emperors, and they agreed that three days should be the duration of your visit. Tomorrow you shall visit their Imperial capitals, their island nations. Next day you will be shown our vast continents, their settlements, their wildlife and, if you wish, the war zone. Then, before you leave, you will be allowed to see The Book."

"You Majesty is gracious," Molane said. "I gather that you want us to travel in our own vessel?"

"Certainly, Molane. Our aircraft, while they serve our purposes, are slow and primitive by comparison."

"And will Your Majesty come with us?"

The King shook his head. "That would be improper. As King-Emperor, I cannot permit myself to be con—" He hesitated, and Molane knew he had almost said 'contaminated.' "—being *in*fluenced by Old Earth, even so indirectly. However, you shall have Lord and Lady Erris as your guides, and Captain Harrion and his lady too. For the remainder of today, you shall tour this city and see something of our industries, our schools and universities and libraries, and how our people live."

He stood. The heralds blew three flourishes. The interview was over. Then Lord Erris also stood. "May I escort you to your ship?" he said. "You may want to freshen up before the cars arrive and we begin our tour."

"*Lapis Lazuli*, you've been recording everything?" Molane asked as soon as they were aboard again.

"Of course."

"Good. We probably have twenty or so minutes. Can you get us views of London in Saul Gilpin's time? Views and perhaps a general plan? First over-all, from the air or space—it was an enormous city. Then the heart of it, the most important parts, and one especially— Hampton Court Palace, if there was such a place."

At once, a screen came into being, covering an entire wardroom wall, and they were looking down on London, its great grayness cut by the Thames. Then they were zooming down, and *Lapis Lazuli* was delineating the City proper, showing them the Tower, and building after famous building, site after historic site.

"My choice has been pretty arbitrary," she told them, "but here's your Hampton Court Palace, which was about fifteen miles from the city's center."

They looked. Here, in general outline, was the same building, but at a second glance, a third, the differences appeared, as though its reincarnation on this planet had been evoked from sketches and memories of the edifice Cardinal Woolsey had built for his private pleasure. Its surroundings, too, were different, and yet, even here, there was an echo, a vague resemblance.

Then *Lapis Lazuli* took them into the city's streets, showed them the hurrying crowds, the streams of traffic, the double-decked busses, tube stations, lorries.

"It was a mighty city in its day," she said. "I wonder how this one will compare."

The cars had come for them, and Captain Harrion was waiting as they filed out. These were nothing like most of the cars that filled the streets of ancient London. They were tall, majestic, built with no thought for such frivolities as wind-resistance. They might have been the lineal descendants of old Queen Mary's Daimlers. They had four wheels, pneumatic tires, but no hood that might conceal a motor. The driver's compartment, where two liveried servants sat, was separated from the passengers' by a pane of glass, as in any 20th Century limousine; and inside, as they approached, Molane saw comfortable seats for five or six, three or four facing forward, two facing aft. Servants held the doors open, and Harrion showed Molane and Lahaisa to the second car.

"You will ride with Lord and Lady Erris," he informed them. "Your parents and your son will ride with me in the first car. The others in your company will be with my own wife in the third. That is as protocol requires it."

Greeted by Lord Erris, Molane and Lahaisa got in, and Molane was not surprised to see fresh flowers in crystal vases at their elbows.

"Ordinarily," Lord Erris said, "we do not ride in these seats, facing backward. But His Majesty asked us to on this occasion, so we could better show the city to you."

"We are honored," said Molane gravely.

The cars moved out. They were completely soundless, odorless, vibrationless, and the traffic on the streets moved like a stately pageant. Nobody seemed to hurry, and here again Molane observed the lust for color characteristic of these new Londoners, not only in their clothing, but in a multitude of flags and banners, and even in such things as roofs and window frames, and building bricks in hues no brick ever had on Earth. These did much to counteract the overwhelming grayness of the great stone edifices that dominated everywhere.

During the entire afternoon, they toured the city and its environs while Lord and Lady Erris pointed out places of historic interest and importance: Trafalgar Square with its Nelson Column, the Bank of England

and the British Museum, the Houses of Parliament. As their car ghosted through the streets and avenues and great squares, he told his guests how Gurat Singh had planned their progress.

"Our ancestors," he said, "were blessed with a world which, for all its perils and rigors, was far more bountiful than Old Earth in their time. Neither its minerals nor its forests had been depleted, neither its vegetation nor its wildlife had been destroyed by slaughter, by erosion, by senseless pollution; and Gurat Singh—blessed be his Name!—was determined that they would never be. From the very first, he ordained that education and research would have absolute priority, and he laid out a general plan for each, with The Book as its foundation, his Testament and the Books of Memories our ancestors compiled as its building stones. One law he laid down which we shall always keep; it forbids any technology that could result in highly concentrated energy sources, such as those that brought the Eater. Another was that we must never again allow ourselves to become dependent on machines to do our thinking and remember for us. That is why electronics was the last of our technologies to be developed, and why we have never attempted to build new Gilpin ships—and never will."

Molane thought of *Lapis Lazuli*, of how her kind had been evolved, and how she was regarded in their new animism, but he did not comment.

Erris went on to tell them of the gradual rebirth of the sciences; how the first three centuries passed in bridging the gap between what The Book contained and what their ancestors remembered in bits and pieces and half-understood terminologies.

"By that time," he said, "we had developed steam power to a degree never achieved on Old Earth. We have entire genera of plants here, growing like weeds, that produce abundant fuel alcohols, so abundant that we use them to run almost everything, our vehicles, our aircraft, our electric generators. We now have wind power and water power and solar power, but still most of us prefer to rely on our individual power-plants—in many areas every household has one."

They drove through residential districts crowded with houses and apartments, and through business districts with an unusual number of small shops and minor industries. The signs, always small and restrained, told them that here there was a tremendous reliance on fine handwork: gun and violin making, tailoring and cabinet-making, gem-cutting and book-binding and bootmaking. The marquées announced plays, operas, concerts—all live performances, and Molane commented on this.

"Do you have holovision?" he asked.

"We do *not*," Lady Erris answered. "No, nor television. We want our children to grow up in a *real* world. We want them to learn to *do*, instead of watching. We simply have no spectator sports here, unless we count horse-racing, because of the betting, and of course the wars. This isn't a safe world. We do not want it to be, and we don't pretend it is. There are enough dangers on the continents, where almost all our young people spend a few years at least, to satisfy anyone's desire for excitement."

"Do you mean," Lahaisa asked, "that people are allowed to go and watch the fighting? People who take no part?"

"Indeed yes. At their own risk, of course, and with proper permits. Our wars, even controlled as they are by our Council of Emperors, still show them how things were on Old Earth, and how fortunate they are to be here. If you wish, Captain Harrion can arrange for you to view the one now in progress on the Asiatic Continent."

They stopped occasionally. They entered shops and workshops, and invariably they were amazed at the courtesy that prevailed, with no servility on the one side, no arrogance on the other. They were shown libraries and colleges, hospitals and factories. They were driven to a district Lord Erris referred to as Soho, where everything and everyone looked alien: East Indian, Southern European, Chinese. It, more than any other area, had the look of having been contrived.

They dined at Erris House, sumptuously, then were

taken to see a recreation of Shakespeare's *Julius Caesar*. It was an eerie experience, for Molane especially because he had the original practically by heart. Costumes, dialogue, everything would at one moment seem totally unreal, at the next almost too real, as *deja vu* usually is.

They returned to *Lapis Lazuli* with the promise that their escorts would come again next morning; and after they went to bed, Lahaisa said thoughtfully, "Molane, think what happened on both planets. Consider all these people have accomplished. Whatever could that Book have been?"

"A Book that provided the basis for rebuilding everything they lost? I can't imagine. But much they have is now on a par with ours, their medicine, their plant and animal genetics, their careful conversation of their new environment."

She was silent for a moment. "Yes," she finally said, "but they're so *strange*."

"Their society progresses, dear, but still in some ways it is completely static, more so than the Roman Empire, far more so than the British, more so even than the Chinese—which is perhaps why Gurat Singh chose those as his models. The Eater apparently convinced them that the rest of the Universe is off-limits to them. At any rate, they're civilized compared to most cultures, even if they do fight wars—there seems to be no poverty, and consider their emphasis on all the arts, on beauty, on good manners. Lahaisa, they march to a different drum, one which we— mercifully—have not heard for centuries, and now would never listen to."

"Well, they have been kind and courteous to us, their unwanted guests, but still—" She paused, frowning. "Still, I am uneasy."

Next morning, ceremoniously, Lord and Lady Erris and the captain and his lady were received aboard the ship, and somewhat against their will they allowed themselves to be shown the wardroom and the control tower. As they shifted into Gilpin's Space, Lady Erris surreptitiously crossed herself, but they rigid-controlled any amazement they may have felt at the swiftness of the ship or the uncanniness of the reality perceived from the control tower's ports. When explanations were offered them, they took pains to display neither curiosity nor interest.

Their first stop, after a flight over the ocean, over fanged continental mountain ranges that towered in frozen silence over jungles and forests unbelievably enormous, was a great island Lord Erris announced as China, and a huge city named Peking. Here again they made their landing outside a palace—or more properly a complex of palaces behind a frowning wall—and in a flowering courtyard beside a lake on which multi-colored swan-like birds were sailing. Here again, too, stood a pavilion, with an Emperor and an Empress on lacquered thrones, surrounded by dignitaries uniformed and costumed very much as their counterparts had been the day before, except that the clergy were robed in saffron faced with black and wore white scarves, and their heads were shaven. The majority of those present looked definitely Asian, but only vaguely so; on Old Earth, in Saul Gilpin's day, one would have been hard put to classify them more definitely. As for the architecture, Lahaisa's father, Jerlan, who knew more about the subject than any of them, at once decided that it was based on data much more tenuous than that of the new England.

He thought the thought "aloud," and their answers echoed their agreement.

Here, again, the Emperor stood and strode toward them. He and his Empress alone were robed, in yellow silks embroidered with great dragons. He and she alone wore jeweled headdresses.

He strode forward and greeted Molane in English, and again there was the long eye-searching which yesterday had preceded their interview with the King and Queen. After that, everything followed almost exactly the same pattern, with the same attitude toward Old Earth, the same guarded less-then-friendliness, and virtually the same hospitality. Only the food was different. Whether it was indeed Chinese, they did not know.

An hour, and it was over. They were dismissed, and

at their next stop, Vienna on the island named Austro-Italy, they followed a similar routine. Here the palace was rococo, ornate and enormous, surrounded by pools and fountains and endless statuary. Here the Emperor, fiercely moustached, was a Caucasian, as were his Empress and their entourage, most of them slightly darker than Lord Erris' countrymen. And here, once again, the pattern was followed in every detail, the eye-searching, the conversation, the introduction of important personages, beginning with cardinals in red-and saffron robes, and continuing with ministers of state and ranking officers. There was one difference only: only wines and liqueurs were served, doubtless because every visit had been carefully orchestrated.

Everyone had spoken English, and there had been little or no difference in their accents. Now, as they went again into Gilpin's Space, Molane asked Lord Erris if other languages had indeed survived.

"Oh, they've been preserved—" Lord Erris smiled, "—by scholars in the universities and to some extent in the churches—Latin and that sort of thing. We are Anglicans; the Holy Roman Empire is Roman Catholic; the Chinese are Buddhists. The old languages add something to them. But all religions are embraced within the teachings of our *sant*—blessed be his Name! When you meet the Successor, you may understand."

They hovered for a short time over Rome, built on a site carefully chosen for its seven hills, and Erris pointed out the Vatican. Then they headed halfway round the planet to a somewhat smaller island, far more tropical, which they were told was India.

They landed at New Delhi, a European city with overtones of a remembered East, echoing Benares, perhaps Amritsar, perhaps the Taj Mahal. Lord Erris guided them to an empty quadrangle in which a domed building stood, all white and gold, but much smaller than they would have expected. No one was there to greet them.

"The Successor," said Erris, "does not come to visitors. We must go to him."

They walked a hundred yards to the building's steps. Everything was white marble, beautifully proportioned, owing nothing to any discernible tradition on Old Earth. Two huge doors stood open. They entered, followed a wide corridor. They emerged into a hall. There were no attendants, no servitors, but on a marble dais stood a single golden chair.

In it, the Successor sat, all white except for his brown face, his bare brown feet: white robe, white turban, white beard, all pure white.

Arilé caught her breath. *He—he's beautiful!* she thought.

And instantly the thought came back to her, *Thank you, my child.*

She made no effort to hide astonishment, and caught his unvoiced chuckle.

Then Lord Erris presented them, and the Successor acknowledged each with an inclination of his head, a smile. His voice, when finally he spoke, was soft and very powerful.

"I know why you have come," he said, "and my Emperors tell me you are without guile, without intent to change us. They have also told you that our destiny was decreed when the Eater came. So you are being shown our world and what we have accomplished. You will see one of the wars we still fight. You will even be allowed to see The Book that shaped us. Go with my blessing. Perhaps someday in the future our destiny will bring us to you." Again he inclined his head. "Farewell," he said.

Bowing, they said goodbye. Then, once more aboard *Lapis Lazuli*, where they could converse mind to mind, Arilé said, *I sang him seven bars of mind-music when we left, and he was pleased.*

He's a full telepath, Lahaisa answered. *The Emperors are partially telepathic, and probably many others are, too. Perhaps that's how they keep everything so—well, so stable.*

It would help, Molane said. *I'm sure the Successor has a goal in mind, one that unites them all. But does even he know what it is?*

I still fear them. Lahaisa looked at her small son. *Not personally, no. But I feel something in the offing, something ominous.*

I think that old man was wonderful! said Kolali.

The balance of the day consisted of brief touchdowns at various islands and cities, glimpses of industries some unbelievably sophisticated, at modes of transportation almost invariably sacrificing speed to a maximum of comfort and of scenery. It is impossible to swallow a whole world in an afternoon, but they learned that there were other religions besides the major three, that many of the planet's animals had been domesticated but that mankind's pets were still those brought from Earth, that except for the three capitals no city had been allowed to grow to more than one hundred thousand, and that the economic pressures which, on Old Earth, had dictated a sometimes deadly overcrowding in a few artificially maintained centers here simply did not exist.

Once more, they dined at Erris House, and when they left, "Tomorrow," Lord Erris said, "Captain Harrion and his lady will accompany you, for he is much more competent to show you the wild regions and their dangers than I would be, and in the war zone you'll be much safer in his hands."

"Don't worry," the captain told them. "Headquarters'll be expecting us, and anyhow you can watch most of the action from Gilpin's Space—" He sounded disappointed. "—Though of course it'll scarcely be the same."

"But we'll *really* see the dragons, won't we?" pleaded Kolali.

"Yes, really," the captain promised.

Just before she went to sleep, Lahaisa once more mentioned her nagging apprehension. "But it's not only that," she said. "I'm troubled about Kolali. His mind has not been open to me."

"Kids get that way," Molane reassured her. "He's just thinking about those dragons he has his heart set on, probably."

Next morning, the captain and his lady arrived immediately after breakfast, and from there on it was just one quick touchdown after another, this time on the continents. They perched on mountain peaks that made Everest seem a foothill; vast black birds of prey with cruel serrated beaks soared among them, swooping down like bullets on their unknown victims. In the heart of the continent called Africa, they saw hairy rhinoceroids, wandering at the foot of glaciers, fall victim to a veritable army of small gleaming serpents moving as army ants move. They were shown precipices plunging down into impenetrable jungles—and a river far mightier than the Amazon dropping half a mile down one of them. In America, there were more mountains, forests, deserts, enormous rivers running through jungle-marshes where raw hunger lived. And Captain Harrion named every place and every creature, and told them how difficult it was to climb, to penetrate, to kill or capture. His eyes shone as he told it, and—to Lahaisa's astonishment—so did his lady's.

The continent of Asia was as varied as the other two had been, and quite as perilous; and on each continent they saw settlements, roads, and railroads, fighting the wilderness, signs of husbandry and cultivation and development, but at none of these did they pause.

"On each continent," explained the captain, "each Empire has its sphere of influence, as you know, and—men being men—when these clash we sometimes go to war. It's very exciting, and a very satisfactory way of settling things."

He pointed down at the War Zone, a great rift valley a hundred miles or so from the Asian coast, stretching perhaps forty miles between rain-forest on the one side and sodden bogs on the other.

Landing at Headquarters, they were introduced to the Commanding General and his staff, who were coldly polite to them. Suddenly, as they spoke, the general pointed at the sky. Three swept-wing silver aircraft floated down from a single gray-white cloud directly at them.

Instantly, weapons spoke. Puffs of smoke appeared. And suddenly the lead plane erupted in a gout of flame, lurched, collided with its partner on the left, crippling it. Both lost headway. Both suddenly were falling, while the third turned tail.

"Good shooting!" cried the general.

Molane and Lahaisa exchanged glances. "Thank you, general," Molane said, still watching the falling funeral pyre and its crippled mate. "You have been very kind, but we've taken too much of your time, and we need see nothing more here on the ground. The rest we can see from Gilpin's Space."

The general shook his head in puzzlement; Captain Harrion again looked disappointed, but he escorted them back into the ship, and from Gilpin's Space he explained the disposition of the two armies, where an advantage had been gained or lost, and where they might expect an action to be taking place. Finally, far to the right, he pointed out a regiment of self-propelled vehicles, more armored cars than tanks, advancing flanked by cavalry, lancers most of them, and followed by infantry. Artillery was vigorously in action. An occasional vehicle was staggering out of column or bursting into flame; horses were falling, others, riderless, galloping aimlessly away; men who had been marching suddenly were lying still.

Abruptly, then, a similar force appeared from a woods directly ahead of the attackers, and at the captain's signal Molane dropped *Lapis Lazuli* down to fifty feet over their heads just as they clashed.

Even from Gilpin's Space, they could see the expression on the faces of the soldiers as they killed, were wounded, died.

Sadly, they exchanged one unspoken thought. "Captain, it is enough," Molane said softly. "Let us go. It's time, I think, for my son to have his dragons."

The captain's momentary annoyance vanished. "My own regiment," he said, "the Fourth Hussars, the King-Emperor's Own, have a camp right in the best dragon country. They'll be expecting us, with a horse ready for me."

"Why a horse, captain?" Orano asked.

"Sir, you don't think I'd miss a chance to kill a dragon while we're here, do you? Otherwise, I'd have to wait

for special leave. This is something the boy will really
have to see. You don't mind, do you?"

The best dragon country, it turned out, was several
hundred miles further down the Asian coast, in a British enclave, and the dragons were true saurians, with
tough skins armored in hard scales. Fully grown, they
were from ten to twelve feet long from savage jaw to tip
of powerful tail, enormously strong hind legs that ena-
bled them to leap frighteningly when attacking, and
much smaller front legs equipped with tearing claws.
The only sporting way to kill them, the captain said,
was with a lance, on horseback. Carniverous, they could
always be relied on to attack. Then it was just a matter
of nerve and skill. At the right instant, you thrust your
lance up through the roof of the hideous mouth into the
brain—and then, just as instantly, whirled aside and
away. If you didn't—he laughed—either those front
legs would get you, or the tail would, or the beast
would fall over on you.

They landed at the camp, a palisaded ring of wooden
bungalows; were introduced to one or two different
officers; waited for a corporal to bring up a saddled
horse, a great bay with the conformation of a Lippizan
and the fiery eye of a medieval charger.

Harrion asked one of his brother officers to accompany the party in *Lapis Lazuli*, and for a moment they
talked about the most likely place. Then he shed his
blouse, rolled up his sleeves, took the long lance the
corporal handed him—a good two feet longer than those
used by lancers in the 19th Century, with a three foot
steel head—and mounted up.

The officer detailed to guide them, introduced as a
Captain Swinney, entered the ship a little apprehen-
sively, then pulled himself together and told Molane
that, while the dragons ranged far and wide in their
insatiable search for meat, their lairs were almost always in an area a mile or two away.

"It's eroded into all sorts of little cliffs," he said.
"We'll give old Harrion a few minutes to get there, then
follow up. When we see he's spotted one, you can set

down, but be sure not too close. We wouldn't want to spook it."

Fifteen minutes later, they spotted Harrion in the rough country he had just entered. He had slowed to a walk, and was reconnoitering—a Gilpin-ghost of a horseman, Molane thought, seeking a ghostly dragon.

Suddenly, they saw him rein in, point with his lance. A dragon had just emerged from a cliff-cave. It stood there for a moment, eyeing its approaching meal. Then it moved forward, all business.

Molane set the ship down about a hundred yards away, shifted into normal space. The dragon, as though he knew ships were inedible, paid them no heed. First he strode, then hopped, then ran directly at the captain. His low-ridged head was nearly two feet long, and most of it was open mouth and teeth. His color was a yellowish green.

Captain and horse stood stock-still, motionless. The dragon closed the distance rapidly. They saw him tensing for the final leap—

The lance was pointed forward, but scarcely raised.

The dragon leaped. The horse, perfectly trained, sat back on his hocks, braced his front legs, the lance point flashing upward— and an instant later, horse and man had whirled aside, the captain still clinging to the embedded lance, the saurian writhing, thrashing, twisting, flat on the ground. The lance point pulled free, and horse and man were turning off—

The captain's lady screamed. "God, Swinney!" she cried out. "*Look!*"

From behind a hummock scarcely feet away, a second dragon had appeared, one just as large and just as hungry as the first.

The horse heard it first, whirled without command. The captain held his seat, lifted his bloody lance. In seconds, it was over. Neither man nor horse lost his nerve. The lance point found the second dragon's brain, and they whirled away, the tail missing them by inches.

"Lord!" exclaimed Swinney. "*Two!* Lizveth," he told Harrion's wife, "that's damned well a record. I can't remember *anyone* ever getting two like that before!

You have a man really to be proud of." He turned to Molane. "It'll take those brutes a while to die," he said. "We might as well get back and send some people out to measure them before their relatives come out and eat them up."

And Harrion's wife stood there, her fear forgotten, proud indeed.

Within minutes after his return, Captain Harrion was again immaculate, obviously well pleased and basking in his lady's admiration.

"Well," he declared, "now all we have to do is get you back to Hampton Court so you can see The Book and bid His Majesty goodbye. This has been a splendid day for me! You've really brought me luck, and I thank you for it."

In front of Hampton Court Palace, this time only Lord and Lady Erris were waiting, with an equerry. The ship landed. The Harrions said goodbye to them.

Lord Erris greeted them. "Come," he said, "the Palace isn't far, and it'll be a pleasant walk. How did your day go?"

"You have a fantastic world," Molane answered. "Everything's on a grander scale than on Old Earth."

"So I understand," said Erris. "So I have gathered from The Book. And we intend to keep it that way. There shall be no ruined forests, no dessicated hillsides washing to the sea. Not here."

It was a criticism no man from Earth could answer, not even the New People. Molane gave a brief account of what they had been shown, and Kolali finished with a highly dramatized recital of Harrion's dragon-slaying.

At the Palace door, a tall man in clerical was awaiting them, and Erris introduced him as the Librarian Royal. The Librarian said simply, "Follow me," and led them through corridors hung with paintings.

Here is the Library," he announced, throwing open two massive doors. They opened on an enormous hall lined with shelves and glassed book-presses, and filled with scholars' carrels. A surrounding balcony, beautifully panelled, led to more shelves; and they were told that this was only one of many rooms.

They walked through it to a final door, panelled also but giving access to a great fireproof vault. The door, inches thick, swung open. The Librarian stood aside for them to enter. In the vault's very center, in a case of gold and crystal, stood The Book.

There were twenty-nine volumes of it, rebound in vellum and stamped in gold.

"The last one," the Librarian said, "is the Index. I shall show you Volume I, but I cannot allow you to handle it."

Very reverently, he unlocked the case, took out the first volume, opened it to the fly-leaf. There was a name written there: *Gurat Singh, Balliol College*, and a bookseller's label: *Basil Blackwood, Oxford*.

"Our *sant*," said the Librarian, "bought it when he was a student, blessed be his Name!"

He turned to the title page, holding the book out so all could see:

THE
ENCYCLOPAEDIA BRITANNICA
A
DICTIONARY
OF
ARTS, SCIENCE, LITERATURE AND GENERAL
INFORMATION
ELEVENTH EDITION

Cambridge:
at the University Press
1910

"You see," the Librarian told them, "it was published during the very year of King Edward VII's death when the old British Empire was at the height of its power and glory, before the horrible wars of the Twentieth Century had brought chaos and destruction to Old Earth."

He replaced the volume, locked the case, and indicated to Lord Erris that he could take over. Then Erris led them off to a small throne-room, where the King-Emperor and his Queen said goodbye to them and wished them a pleasant trip home.

Only Lord Erris walked back with them to *Lapis Lazuli*, and he too bade them only a brief farewell.

Molane ordered the port closed, and they followed him into the wardroom. Lahaisa caught his momentary thought: *No, we accomplished nothing, but thank the Guardians that we at least are immune to the excitements of these people and their barbarism!*

"Lapis Lazuli," he said, "in your data banks do you have any information on an early Twentieth Century work called *The Encyclopaedia Britannica*, the Eleventh Edition?"

In seconds, she replied that, yes, she did.

"Scan it," said Molane, "and tell us if in your opinion a civilization such as the one we have just seen could possibly have been founded on it and on the largely untutored recollections of those disciples of Gurat Singh's who landed here?"

More seconds passed, and then the ship replied. "Yes, Molane, I think it could. Let me give you one example. That work of course says nothing about Einstein, but it has a great deal to say about James Clerk Maxwell, upon whose work much of Einstein's was based, and it gives certain of his basic equations. Does this make the point clear?"

"And what of the society that produced it?"

"It was a very proud society, Molane—in many, many ways justly proud. It had a great heritage."

There was a silence. *Lapis Lazuli* had, of course, recorded everything, and there would be plenty of time to discuss it.

It was Lahaisa who broke the silence. "*Kolali!*" she cried aloud. "Child, what's *wrong* with you? You're *crying?*"

"*Kolali, Kolali!* You shouldn't cry—don't you understand? We're going *home.*"

He responded to the pain in her voice, but he did not run to her. Nor did his mind open to her anxious invitation.

"G-going *home?*" he choked. "I—I don't *want* to go home. I want to stay here, right *here*—and kill dragons—and—and be a soldier!"

EDITOR'S INTRODUCTION TO:

THE WHIRLIGIG OF TIME
Vernor Vinge

Government is miracle; but when the miracle goes wrong, what can be done? Government, Ben Franklin said, is like fire: a dangerous servant and a fearful master.

Still: one must, finally, rule through opinion.

Ortega y Gasset said it well:

"Even the man who attempts to rule through janissaries depends on their opinion and the opinion the rest of the inhabitants have of them.

"But the truth is, there is no ruling with janissaries. As Talleyrand said to Napoleon, 'You can do anything with bayonets, Sire, except sit on them.' Rule is not so much a matter of an iron hand, but a firm seat."

Orders are carried out because someone wants to carry them out. No matter how many are enslaved, some will remain free; and opportunity eventually comes to all.

THE WHIRLIGIG OF TIME
Vernor Vinge

The defense station high in the Laguna Mountains had been on alert since dawn. The clear fall day had passed without event, and now the dark was closing in over the pine-covered hills. A cool, dry wind blew among the trees, nudged at the deep layers of pine needles and slid around the defense station's armored cupolas. Overhead, between the dark silhouettes of the pines, the stars were out, brighter and more numerous than they could ever seem in a city's sky.

To the west, limning the dark Pacific, a narrow band of greenish yellow was all that was left of day, and the city was a fine thin dusting of light spread inward from the ocean. From the Laguna Mountains, eighty kilometers inland, the city seemed a surrealistic carpet of tiny glowing gems—the most precious of the treasures this station had been constructed to protect.

This was the last moment of comfortable tranquillity that this land would know for many, many centuries.

The life in the forest—the birds asleep in the trees, the squirrels in their holes—heard and felt nothing; but deep within the station men looked out into space with microwave eyes, saw the tiny specks rising beyond the polar horizon, plotted their trajectories and predicted that hell would burn in heaven and on earth this night.

On the surface, concrete and steel cowlings whirred open to reveal the lasers and ABM's now tracking the enemies falling out of space. The birds fluttered nervously about their trees now, disturbed by the noises below, and a faint red light shone up from the holes in the ground. Yet from the next ridgeline over, the night would still have seemed silent, and the starlit pine forest undisturbed.

Halfway up in the northern sky, three new stars lit, so bright that a blue-white day shone on the forest, still silent. Their glare faded swiftly through orange to red and guttered out, leaving a play of pale green and gold to spread through the sky. Those pastel colors were the only visible sign of the immense fog of charged particles the explosions had set between ground radars and the missiles that were yet to come. The men in the station held their fire. The explosions had not completely blinded them— they still had a proxy view of part of the battle space from a synchronous satellite—but the distance to their targets was far too great.

In the skies to the north and east more miniature stars were visible—mostly defensive fires. The unnatural aurora spread from horizon to horizon, yet in the west the lights of the city glowed as placidly, as beautifully as before the end began.

Now the defenders' radars could pick up the enemy warheads falling out of the ionospheric fog that had concealed them. But not one of the incoming missiles was targeted on the city to the west—all were falling in toward the defense station and the ICBM bases in the desert to the east. The defenders noticed this but had no time to puzzle over it. Their own destruction was seconds away unless they acted. The station's main laser fired, and the pines and the hills flashed red by its reflected light. The ten-centimeter beam was a hundred-kilometer-tall thread of fire, disappearing only at the top of the sensible atmosphere where there was no more air to be ionized. Its sound, the sound of whole tons of air being turned into plasma, was a bone-shattering crack that echoed off the distant hills to sweep back and forth across the land.

Now there was nothing left asleep in the forest.

And when the beam itself was gone, there—high in the sky—hung a pale blue thread, with a nob of faintly glowing yellow and gold at one end. The first target, at least, had been destroyed; the beam was so energetic it created its own miniature aurora as it passed through the ionosphere, and the knob at the end of it marked a vaporized target.

Then the other lasers began firing, and the sky was crisscrossed by strange red lightning. The ABM's streaking from the hillside contributed their own peculiar roar to this local armageddon. The tiny rockets were like flecks of molten metal spewed up on rays of fire and smoke. Their success or failure was determined in the scant five seconds of their powered flight—five seconds in which they climbed more than thirty kilometers into the sky. The spaces above the hills were filled with bright new stars, and the more frequent—yet less impressive—glows that marked successful laser interceptions.

For seventy-five seconds the battle in the spaces over the defense station continued. During that time the men could do little but sit and watch their machines—the defense demanded microsecond reflexes, and only the machines could provide that. In those seventy-five million microseconds, the station destroyed dozens of enemy missiles. Only ten of the attacking bombs got through; bright blue flashes on the eastern horizon marked the end of the ICBM bases there. Yet even those ten might have been intercepted, if only the station had not held back its reserve, waiting for the attack that must sooner or later come upon the great city to the west.

Seventy-five seconds—and the city they waited to protect still lay glowing beneath the yellow-green sky.

And then, from the middle of the gleaming carpet that was the city, one more new star was born. In an astronomical sense, it was a very small star; but to itself and to what lay nearby, it was an expanding, gaseous hell of fission-fusion products, neutrons and x-rays.

In seconds the city ceased to be, and the defenders in the mountains realized why all the enemy missiles had been targeted on military installations, realized what must be happening to the larger cities all across the land, realized how much easier it had been for the enemy to smuggle his bombs into the nation's cities than to drop them in along ballistic trajectories.

From where the yacht floated, a million kilometers above the ecliptic and six million behind the Earth in its orbit, the home planet was a marbled bluish ball, nearly as bright as a full moon yet only a quarter the size. The moon itself, a couple of degrees further out from the sun, shone twice as bright as Venus. The rest of heaven seemed infinitely far away, misty sweeps at the bottom of an endless well.

By the blue-white sunlight, the yacht was a three-hundred-meter silver crescent, devoid of fins and aerials and ports. In fact, the only visible marking was the Imperial escutcheon—a scarlet wreath and a five-pointed star—just short of the nose.

But from within, a larger part of that hull was not opaque. Arching over the main deck it was as clear, as transparent as the air of a desert night; and the lords and ladies attending the Prince's birthday party could see the Earth-Moon system hanging just above the artificial horizon created by the intersection of deck and hull. The scene was lost on most of them. Only a few ever bothered to look up into the strange sky. They were the fifteenth generation of an aristocracy that regarded the entire universe as its just due. They would have been just as bored—or just as amused—on Luna or back at the Avstralijan Riviera on Earth.

In all the two-million-ton bulk of the yacht, perhaps only four or five people were really aware of the surrounding emptiness:

Vanja Biladze floated near the center of the yacht's tiny control cabin—he liked to keep it at zero gee—steadying himself with one hand draped negligently around a wall strap. His three-man crew sat belted down to control saddles before the computer inputs and the holoscreens. Biladze gestured at the gray-white cone that tumbled slowly across the central screen. "Do you have any idea what it is, Boblanson?" he asked the fifth man in the control cabin.

The little man called Boblanson had just entered the cabin from the kennels below decks, and he still looked a bit green about the gills. His rickets-bent hands held tightly to the wall straps as his balding head bobbed about in an attempt to focus on the screen. The three crewmen seemed as intrigued by this twisted dwarf as by what the long-range scope was throwing on their screen. The men were new to the Imperial yacht, and Biladze guessed they had never before seen a non-Citizen in person. Outside of the Preserves, about the only place one could be found was in the Emperor's menageries.

Boblanson's nearsighted eyes squinted for a long moment at the screen. The ship's computer had superimposed a reticle on the image, indicating the cone was about a meter wide and perhaps three meters long. Ranging figures printed below the reticle showed the object was more than two hundred kilometers away. Even at that range the synthetic aperture scope resolved a lot of detail. The cone was not a smooth, uniform gray but was scored with hundreds of fine lines drawn parallel to its axis. There were no aerials or solar panels protruding from the cone. Every fifteen seconds the base of the object rotated into view, a dark uninformative hole.

The little man licked his lips nervously. If it had been possible to grovel in zero gee, Biladze was sure that Boblanson would have done so. "It is marvelous, Your Eminence. An artifact, to be sure."

One of the crewmen rolled his eyes. "We know that, you idiot. The question is, would the Prince be interested in it? We were told you are his expert on pre-Imperial spacecraft."

Boblanson bobbed his head emphatically, and the rest of his body bobbed in sympathy. "Yes, Emimence.

I was born in the Prince's Kalifornija Preserve. For all these centuries, my tribes have passed from father to son the lore of the Great Enemy. Many times the Prince has sent me to explore the glowing ruins within the Preserves. I have learned all I can of the past."

The crewman opened his mouth—no doubt to give his acid opinion of illiterate savages who pose as archeologists—but Biladze broke in before the other could speak. The crewman was new to the Court, but not so new that he could get away with insulting the Prince's judgment. Biladze knew that every word spoken in the control cabin was monitored by Safety Committee agents hidden elsewhere in the ship, and every maneuver the crew undertook was analyzed by the Safety Committee's computers. Citizens of the Empire were used to surveillance, but few realized just how pervasive the eavesdropping could be until they entered the Imperial Service. "Let me rephrase Kolja's question," said Biladze. "As you know, we're tracking back along Earth's orbit. Eventually—in another fifteen hours, if we hadn't stopped for this thing—we will be far enough back to encounter objects in trojan orbits. Now there is some reason to believe that at least a few of the probes launched into Earthlike orbits eventually wound up near Earth's trojan points—"

"Yes, Eminence, I suggested the idea," said Boblanson. *So there is spirit in you after all,* thought Biladze with surprise; perhaps the little man knew that the Prince's pets sometimes counted for more than an Imperial Citizen. And the fellow's education obviously went beyond the folk tales his tribe passed from generation to generation. The idea of looking for artifacts near the trojan points was clever, though Biladze guessed that careful analysis would show it to be unpractical for at least two different reasons. But the Prince rarely bothered with careful analysis.

"In any case," continued Vanja Biladze, "we've found something, but it's nowhere near our destination. Perhaps the Prince will not be interested. After all, the chief reason for his excursion is to celebrate his birthday. We are not sure if the Emperor and the Prince and all the gentle people attending will really be too happy if we interrupt them with this matter. But we know that you have the special confidence of the Prince when it comes to his collection of pre-Imperial space probes. We hoped—"

We hoped you'd take us off the hook, fellow, thought Biladze. His predecessor at this job had been executed by the teen-age prince. His crime: interrupting the boy at dinner. For the thousandth time, Biladze wished he were back in the old-time Navy—where research had been disguised as maneuvers—or even back on Earth in some Gruzijan lab. The closer a Citizen came to the Centers of power, the more of a madhouse the universe became.

"I understand, Eminence," said Boblanson, sounding as if he *really* did. He glanced once more at the screen, then back at Biladze. "And I assure you that the Prince would hate to pass this up. His collection is immense, you know. Of course it contains all the moon landers ever launched. They are rather easy to find, given your Navy's maps. He even has a couple of Martian probes— one Republican and one launched by the Great Enemy. And the surviving near-Earth satellites are generally quiet easy to find, too. But the solar and outer planet probes—those are extremely difficult to recover, since they are no longer associated with any celestial body but roam through an immense volume of space. He has only two solar probes in his entire collection, and both were launched by the Republic. I've never seen anything like this," he motioned jerkily at the tumbling white cone on the screen. "Even if it were launched by your ancestors in the days of the Republic, it would still be a find. But if it belonged to the Great Enemy, it would be one of the Prince's favorite acquisitions, without doubt." Boblanson lowered his voice. "And frankly, I think it's conceivable that this spacecraft was not launched by either the Republic or the Great Enemy."

"*What!*" The exclamation came simultaneously from four throats.

The little man still seemed nervous and half-nauseated, but for the first time Biladze saw an almost hypnotic quality about him. The fellow was diseased, half-crippled. After all, he had been raised in a poisoned and desolate land, and since coming to the Imperial Service he had apparently been used to explore the radioactive ruins of the Great Enemy's cities. Yet with all that physical abuse, the mind within was still powerful, persuasive. Biladze wondered whether the Emperor realized that his son's pet was five times the man the Prince was.

"Yes, it would be fantastic," said Boblanson. "Mankind has found no evidence of life—much less intelligent life—anywhere else in the universe. But I know . . . I know the Navy once listened for signals from interstellar space. The possibility is still alive. And this object is so strange. For example, there is no communication equipment sticking through its hull. I know that you of the Empire don't use exterior aerials—but in the time of the Republic, all spacecraft did. And, too, there are no solar panels, though perhaps the craft had an isotopic power source. But the pattern of rays along its hull is the strangest thing of all. Those grooves are what you might expect on a meterorite or a space probe—after it had come down through a planetary atmosphere. But there is simply no explanation for finding such an ablated hull out in interplanetary space."

That certainly decides the question, thought Biladze. Everything the non-Citizen had said was on tape somewhere, and if it ever came out that Vanja Biladze had passed up an opportunity to obtain an extraterrestrial artifact for the Prince's collection, there would be need for a new pilot on the Imperial yacht. "Kolja, get on the printer, and tell the Lord Chamberlain what Boblanson has discovered here." Perhaps that phrasing would protect him and the crew if the whirling gray cone did not interest the Prince.

Kolja began typing the message on the intraship printer. Theoretically, a Citizen could talk directly to the Lord Chamberlain, since that officer was a bridge of sorts between the Imperial Court and its servants. In fact, however, the protocol for speaking with any member of the aristocracy was so complex that it was safest to deal with such men in writing. And occasionally, the written record could be used to cover your behind later on—if the nobleman you dealt with was in a rational mood. Biladze carefully read the message as it appeared on the readout above the printer, then signaled Kolja to send it. The word ACKNOWLEDGED flashed on the screen. Now the message was stored in the Chamberlain's commbox on the main deck. When its priority number came up, the message would appear on the screen there, and if the Lord Chamberlain were not too busy supervising the entertainment, there might be a reply.

Vanja Biladze tried to relax. Even without Boblanson's harangue he would have given an arm and a leg to close with the object. But he was far too experienced, far too cautious, to let such feelings show. Biladze had spent three decades in the Navy—whole years at a time in deep space so far from Earth-Luna and the pervasive influence of the Safety Committee that the home world might as well not have existed. Then the Emperor began his crackdown on the Navy, drawing them back into near-Earth space, subjecting them to the scrutiny accorded his other Citizens and outlawing what research they had been able to get away with before. And with the new space drive, no point in the solar system was more than hours from Earth, so such close supervision was practical. For many officers, the change had been a fatal one. They had grown up in space, away from the Empire, and they had forgotten—or else never learned—how to mask their feelings and behave with appropriate humility. But Biladze remembered well. He had been born at Suhumi in Gruzija, a favorite resort of the nobility. For all the perfection of Suhumi's blindingly white beaches and palm dotted parks, death had been waiting every moment for the disrespectful Citizen. And when he had moved east to Tiflis, to the technical schools, life was no less precarious. For in Tiflis there were occasional cases of systematically disloyal thoughts, thoughts which upset the Safety Committee far more than accidental disrespect.

If that had been the sum of his experience on Earth, Biladze, like his comrades, might have forgotten how to live with the Safety Committee. But in Tiflis, in the spring of his last year at the Hydromechanical Institute, he met Klaśa. Brilliant, beautiful Klaśa. She was majoring in heroic architecture, one of the few engineering research fields the Emperors had ever tolerated on Earth. (After all, statues like the one astride Gibraltar would have been impossible without the techniques discovered by Klaśa's predecessors.) So while his fellow officers managed to stay in space for whole decades at a time, Vanja Biladze had returned to Tiflis, to Klaśa, again and again.

And he never forgot how to survive within the Imperial system.

Abruptly, Biladze's attention returned to the white-walled control room. Boblanson was eyeing him with a calculating stare, as if making some careful judgment. For a long moment, Biladze returned the gaze. He had seen only four or five non-Citizens in the flesh, though he had been piloting the Imperial yacht for more than a year. The creatures were always stunted, most often mindless—simple freaks kept for the amusement of the noblemen with access to the vast Amerikan Preserves. This Boblanson was the only clever one Biladze had ever seen. Still, he found it hard to believe that the frail man's ancestors had been the Great Enemy, had struggled with the Republic for control of Earth. Very little was known about those times, and Biladze had never been encouraged to study the era, but he did know that the Enemy had been intelligent and resourceful, that they had never been totally defeated until they finally launched a sneak attack upon the Republic. The enraged Republic beat back the attack, then razed the Enemy's cities, burned its forests and left its entire continent a radioactive wasteland. Even after five centuries, the only people living in that ruin were the pitiful non-Citizens, the final victims of their own ancestor's treachery.

And the victorious Republic had gone on to become the world Empire.

That was the story, anyway. Biladze could doubt or disbelieve parts of it, but he knew that Boblanson was the ultimate descendant of a people who had opposed the establishment of the Empire. Vanja briefly wondered what version of history had been passed down the years to Boblanson.

Still no answer on the printer readout. Apparently the Lord Chamberlain was too busy to be bothered.

He said to Boblanson, "You are from the Kalifornija Preserve?"

The other bobbed his head. "Yes, Eminence."

"Of course I've never been there, but I've seen most of the Preserves from low orbit. Kalifornija is the most terrible wasteland of them all, isn't it?" Biladze was breaking one of the first principles of survival within the Empire: he was displaying curiosity. That had always been his most dangerous failing, though he rationalized things by telling himself that he knew how to ask safe questions. There was nothing really secret about the non-Citizens—they were simply a small minority living in areas too desolate to be settled. The Emperor was fond of parading the poor creatures on the holo, as if to say to his Citizens: "See what becomes of my opponents." Certainly it would do no harm to talk to this fellow, as long as he sounded appropriately impressed by the Enemy's great defeat and yet greater treachery.

Boblanson gave another of his frenetic nods. "Yes, Eminence. I regret that some of my people's greatest and most infamous fortresses were in the southern part of Kalifornija. It is even more to my regret that my particular tribe is descended from the subhumans who directed the attack on the Republic. Many nights around our campfires—when we could find enough wood to make a fire—the Oldest Ones would tell us the legends. I see now that they were talking of reaction-drive missiles and pumped lasers. Those were primitive weapons by the Empire's present standards, but they were probably the best that either side possessed in those days. I can only thank your ancestors' courage that the Republic and justice prevailed.

"But I still feel the shame, and my dress is a penance for my ancestry—it is a replica of the uniform worn by the damned creatures who inspired the Final Conflict."

He pulled fretfully at the blue material, and for the first time Biladze really noticed the other's clothing. It wasn't that Boblanson's dress was inconspicuous. As a matter of fact, the blue uniform—with its twin silver bars on each shoulder—was ludicrous. In the zero gee of the control cabin, the pants were continually floating up, revealing Boblanson's bent, thin legs. Before, Biladze had thought it was just another of the crazy costumes the Imperial family decreed for the creatures in the menagerie, but now he saw that the sadism went deeper. It must have amused the Prince greatly to take this scarecrow and dress him as one of the Enemy, then have him grovel and scuttle about. The Imperial family never forgot its opponents, no matter how far removed they were in time or space.

Then he looked back in the little man's eyes and realized with a chill that he had seen only half the picture. No doubt the Prince had ordered Boblanson to wear the uniform, but in fact the non-Citizen was the one who was amused—if there was any room for humor behind those pale blue eyes. It was even possible, Biladze guessed, that the man had maneuvered the Prince into ordering that he be dressed in this way. So now Boblanson, descendant of the Great Enemy, wore that people's full uniform at the Court of the Emperor. Biladze shivered within himself, and for the first time put some real credit in the myths about the Enemy's subtlety, their ability to deceive and to betray. This man still remembered whatever had happened in those ancient times—and with greater feeling than any member of the Imperial family.

The word ACKNOWLEDGED vanished from the screen over the printer and was replaced by the Lord Chamberlain's jowly face. The crew bowed their heads briefly, tried to appear self-composed. The Chamberlain was usually content to communicate by printer, so apparently their message—when it finally got his attention—was of interest.

"Pilot Biladze, your deviation from the flight plan is excused, as is your use of the Prince's pet." He spoke ponderously, the wattles swaying beneath his chin.

Biladze hoped that old Rostov's implied criticism was *pro forma*. The Lord Chamberlain couldn't afford to be as fickle as most nobles, but he was a hard man, willing to execute his patrons' smallest whim. "You will send the creature Boblanson up here. You will maintain your present position relative to the unidentified object. I am keeping this circuit open so that you will respond directly to the Emperor's wishes." He stepped out of pickup range, ending the conversation as abruptly as if he had been talking to a computer. At least Biladze and his crew had been spared the trouble of framing a properly respectful response.

Biladze punched HATCH OPEN, and Boblanson's keepers entered the cabin. "He's supposed to go to the main deck," Biladze said. Boblanson glanced briefly at the main screen, at the enigma that was still slowly turning there, then let his keepers bind him with an ornamental leg chain and take him into the hallway beyond. The hatch slid shut behind the trio, and the crew turned back to the holographic image above the printer.

The camera sending that picture hadn't moved, but Rostov's obese hulk was no longer blocking the view and there was a lot to see. The yacht had been given to the Prince by the Emperor on the boy's tenth birthday. As with any Imperial gift, the thing was huge. The main deck—with its crystal ceiling-wall open to all heaven—could hold nearly two thousand people. At least that many were up there now, for this party—the whole twenty hour outing—celebrated the Prince's eighteenth birthday.

Many of the lords and ladies wore scarlet, though some had costumes of translucent and transparent pastels. The calculated nudity was not limited to the women. The lights on the main deck had been dimmed, and the star clouds, crowned by Earth-Luna, hung bright above the revelers—an incongruous backdrop to the festivities. That these people should be the ones to rule those worlds . . .

Scattered through the crowd, he caught patches of gray and brown—the uniforms of the traybearers, doing work any sensible culture would reserve to machines.

The servants scuttled about, forever alert to their betters' wishes, forever abjectly respectful. That respect must have been mainly for the benefit of Safety Committee observers, since most of the partygoers were so high on thorn-apple or even more exotic drugs that they wouldn't have known it if someone spit in their eye. The proceedings were about three-quarters of the way to being a full-blown orgy. Biladze shrugged to himself. It was nothing new—this orgy would simply be bigger than usual.

Then the tiny figures of Boblanson and his keepers came in from the right side of the holoscreen. The two Citizens walked carefully, their shoulders down, their eyes on the floor. Boblanson seemed to carry himself much the same, but after a moment Biladze noticed that the little man shot glances out to the right and left, watching everything that went on. It was amazing. No Citizen could have gotten away with such brazen arrogance. But Boblanson was not a Citizen. He was an animal, a favored pet. You kill an animal if it displeases you, but you don't put the same social constraints on it that you would upon a human. No doubt even the Safety Committee passed over the fellow with only the most cursory inspection.

As the figures walked off to the left, Biladze leaned to the right to follow them in the holo and saw the Emperor and his son. Paśa III was seated on his mobile throne, his costume a cascade of scarlet and jewels. Paśa's face was narrow, ascetic, harsh. In another time such a man might have created an empire rather than inherited one. As it was, Paśa had consolidated the autocracy, taking control of all state functions—even and especially research—and turning them to the crackpot search for reincarnators.

On only one issue could Paśa be considered soft: his son was just eighteen today, yet the boy had already consumed the resources and the pleasures of a thousand adolescences. Saśa X, dressed in skintight red breeches and diamond-encrusted belt, stood next to his father's throne. The brunette leaning against him had a figure that was incredibly smooth and full, yet the

Prince's hand slid along her body as negligently as if he were stroking a baluster.

The keepers prostrated themselves before the throne and were recognized by the Emperor. Biladze bit back a curse. The damn microphone wasn't picking up their conversation! How would he know what Paśa or his son wanted if he couldn't hear what was going on? All he was getting were music and laughter—plus a couple of indecent conversations close by the mike. This was the type of bungle that made the position of Chief Yacht Pilot a short-lived one, no matter how careful a man was.

One of his crew fiddled with the screen controls, but nothing could really be done at this end. They would see and hear only what the Lord Chamberlain was kind enough to let them see and hear. Biladze leaned toward the screen and tried to pick out from the general party noises the conversation passing between Boblanson and the Prince.

The two keepers were still prostrate at Paśa's feet. They had not been given permission to rise. Boblanson remained standing, though his posture was cringing and timid. Servants insinuated themselves through the larger crowd to distribute drinks and candies to the Imperial party.

The Emperor and his son seemed totally unaware of this bustle of cringing figures about them. It was strange to see two men set so far above the common herd. And it all brought back a very old memory. It had been the summer of his last year at Tiflis, when he had found both Klaśa and the freedom of the Navy. Many times during that summer, he and Klaśa had flown into the Kavkaz to spend the afternoon alone in the alpine meadows. There they could speak their own minds, however timidly, without fear of being overheard. (Or so they thought. In later years, Biladze realized how terribly mistaken they had been. It was blind luck they were not discovered.) On those secret picnics, Klaśa told him things that were never intended to go beyond her classes. The architecture students were taught the old forms and the meaning of the inscriptions to be found upon

them. So Klaśa was one of the few people in all the
Empire with any knowledge of history and archaic languages, however indirect and fragmentary. It was dangerous knowledge, yet in many ways fascinating: In the
days of the Republic, Klaśa asserted, the word "Emperor" had meant something like "Primary secretary,"
that is, an elected official—just as on some isolated
Navy posts, the men elect a secretary to handle unit
funds. It was an amazing evolution—to go from elected
equal to near godling. Biladze often wondered what
other meanings and truths had been twisted by time
and by the kind of men he was watching on the
holoscreen.

"—Father. I think it could be exactly what my creature says." The audio came loud and abrupt as the
picture turned to center on the Prince and his father.
Apparently Rostov had realized his mistake. The Chamberlain had almost as much to lose as Biladze if the
Emperor's wishes were not instantly gratified.

Biladze breathed a sigh of relief as he picked up the
thread of the conversation. Saśa's high-pitched voice
was animated: "Didn't I tell you this would be a worthwhile outing, Father? Here we've already run across
something entirely new, perhaps from beyond the Solar
System. It will be the greatest find in my collection.
Oh, Father, we must pick it up." His voice rose
fractionally.

Paśa grimaced, and said something about Saśa's "worth-
less hobbies." Then he gave in—as he almost always
did—to the wishes of his son. "Oh very well, pick the
damned thing up. I only hope it's half as interesting as
your creature here," he waved a gem-filthy arm at
Boblanson, "says it is."

The non-Citizen shivered within his blue uniform,
and his voice became a supplicating whine. "Oh, dear
Great Majesty, this trembling animal promises you with
all his heart that the artifact is perfectly fit to all the
greatness of your Empire."

Even before Boblanson got the tongue-twisting promise out of his mouth, Biladze had turned from the holo
and was talking to his men. "Okay. Close with the

object." As one of the crew tapped the control board, Biladze turned to Kolja and continued. "We'll pick it up with the thirdbay waldoes. Once we get it inside, I want to check the thing over. I remember reading somewhere that the Ancients used reaction jets for attitude control and thrust— they never did catch on to inertial drive. There just might be some propellant left in the object's tanks after all these years. I don't want that thing blowing up in anybody's face."

"Right," said Kolja, turning to his own board.

Biladze kept an ear on the talk coming from the main deck—just in case somebody up there changed his mind. But the conversation had retreated from the specifics of this discovery to a general discussion of the boy's satellite collection. Boblanson's blue figure was still standing before the throne, and every now and then the little man interjected something in support of Saśa's descriptions.

Vanja pushed himself off the wall to inspect the approach program his crewman had written. The yacht was equipped with the new drive and could easily attain objective accelerations of a thousand gravities. But their target was only a couple hundred kilometers away and a more delicate approach was in order: Biladze pressed the PROGRAM INITIATE, and the ship's display showed that they were moving toward the artifact at a leisurely two gravities. It should take nearly two hundred seconds to arrive, but that was probably within Saśa's span of attention.

One hundred twenty seconds to contact. For the first time since he had called Boblanson into the control cabin ten minutes earlier, Biladze had a moment to ponder the object for himself. The cone was an artifact; it was much too regular to be anything else. Yet he doubted that it was of extraterrestrial origin, no matter what Boblanson thought. Its orbit had the same period and eccentricity as Earth's, and right now it wasn't much over seven million kilometers from Earth-Luna. Orbits like that just aren't stable over long periods of time. Eventually such an object must be captured by Earth-Luna or be perturbed into an eccentric orbit.

The cone couldn't be much older than man's exploration of space. Biladze wondered briefly how much could be learned by tracing the orbit back through some kind of dynamical analysis. Probably not much.

Right now the only difference between its orbit and Earth's was the inclination: about three degrees. That might mean it had been launched from Earth at barely more than escape velocity, along a departure asymptote pointing due north. Now what conceivable use could there be for such a trajectory?

Ninety seconds to contact. The image of the slowly tumbling cone was much sharper now. Besides the faint scoring along its hull, he could see that the dull white surface was glazed. It really did look as if it had passed through a planet's atmosphere. He had seen such effects only once or twice before, since with any inertial drive it was a simple matter to decelerate before entering an atmosphere. But Biladze could imagine that the Ancients, having to depend on rockets for propulsion, might have used aerodynamic braking to save fuel. Perhaps this was a returning space probe that had entered Earth's atmosphere at too shallow an angle and skipped back into space, lost forever to the Ancients' primitive technology. But that still didn't explain its narrow, pointed shape. A good aerodynamic brake would be a blunt body. This thing looked as if it had been designed expressly to minimize drag.

Sixty seconds to contact. He could see now that the black hole at its base was actually the pinched nozzle of a reaction jet—added proof that this was an Earth-launched probe from before the Final Conflict. Biladze glanced at the holoscreen above the printer. The Emperor and his son seemed really taken with what they were seeing on the screen set before the throne. Behind them stood Boblanson, his poor nearsighted eyes squinting at the screen. The man seemed even stranger than before. His jaws were clenched and a periodic tic cut across his face. Biladze looked back at the main screen; the little man knew more than he had revealed about that mysterious cone. If he had not been beneath their notice, the Safety Committee would have long since noticed this, too.

Thirty seconds. What was Boblanson's secret? Biladze tried to connect the centuries-deep hatred he had seen in Boblanson with what they knew about the tumbling white cone: It had been launched around the time of the Final Conflict on a trajectory that might have pointed northwards. But the object hadn't been intended as a space probe since it had evidently acquired most of its speed while still within Earth's atmosphere. No sensible vehicle would move so fast within the atmosphere . . .

. . . *unless it was a weapon.*

The thought brought a sudden numbness to the pit of Biladze's stomach. The Final Conflict had been fought with rocket bombs fired back and forth over the North Pole. One possible defense against such weapons would be high acceleration antimissile missiles. If one such missed its target, it might very well escape Earth-Luna—to orbit the sun, forever armed, forever waiting.

Then why hadn't his instruments detected a null bomb within it? The question almost made him reject his whole theory, until he remembered that quite powerful explosions could be produced with nuclear fission and fusion. Only physicists knew such quaint facts, since null bombs were much easier to construct once you had the trick of them. But had the Ancients known that trick?

Biladze casually folded his arms, kept his position by hooking one foot through a wall strap. Somewhere inside himself a voice was screaming: *Abort the approach, abort the approach!* Yet if he were right and if the bomb in that cone were still operable, then the Emperor and the three highest tiers of the nobility would be wiped from the face of the universe.

It was an opportunity no man or group of men had had since the Final Conflict.

But it's not worth dying for! screamed the tiny, frightened voice.

Biladze looked into the holoscreen at the hedonistic drones whose only talent lay in managing the security apparatus that had suppressed men and men's ideas for so long. With the Emperor and the top people in the Safety Committee gone, political power would fall to the technicians—ordinary Citizens from Tiflis, Luna City, Eastguard. Biladze had no illusions: ordinary people have their own share of villains. There would be strife, perhaps even civil war. But in the end, men would be free to go to the stars, from where no earthly tyranny could ever recall them.

Behind the Emperor and the nobles, Boblanson cringed no more. A look of triumph and hatred had come into his face, and Biladze remembered that he had said this would be a gift fit for the Empire.

And so your people will be revenged after all these centuries, thought Biladze. As vengeance it was certainly appropriate, but that had nothing to do with why he, Vanja Biladze, floated motionless in the control cabin and made no effort to slow their approach on the tumbling cone. He was scared as hell. Mere vengeance was not worth this price. Perhaps the future would be.

They were within a couple thousand meters of the object now. It filled the screen, as if it whirled just beyond the yacht's hull. Biladze's instruments registered some mild radioactivity in the object's direction.

Good-bye, Klaśa.

Seven million kilometers from Earth, a new star was born. In an astronomical sense, it was a very small star, but to itself and what lay nearby it was an expanding, plasmatic hell of fission-fusion products, neutrons and gamma rays.

EDITOR'S INTRODUCTION TO:

NIGHTMARE, WITH ANGELS
Stephen Vincent Benet

Like many another, my first encounter with Stephen Vincent Benet was "The Devil and Daniel Webster"; which delightful story directed me to an early Pocket Book of his short stories (alas, my copy was read until it fell apart, and the book is out of print). "Paul's Case," "The Last of the Legions," "Old Doc Carter and the Pearly Gates"; a flood of stories, all different all readable; all heady stuff indeed to one not yet in high school.

I found his poetry only in libraries, and again it's mostly out of print. Benet, like many poets who wrote during the turmoil between the world wars, could see great storms ahead; and though he was basically an optimist, he had nightmares.

Like this one.

NIGHTMARE, WITH ANGELS
Stephen Vincent Benet

An angel came to me and stood by my bedside,
Remarking in a professional-historical-economic and ir-
ritated voice,
"If the Romans had only invented a decent explosion-
engine!
Not even the best, not even a Ford V-8
But, say, a Model T or even an early Napier,
They'd have built good enough roads for it (they knew
how to build roads)
From Cape Wrath to Cape St. Vincent, Susa, Babylon
and Moscow,
And the motorized legions never would have fallen,
And peace, in the shape of a giant eagle, would brood
over the entire Western World!"
He changed his expression, looking now like a combina-
tion of Gilbert Murray, Hilaire Belloc, and a dozen
other scientists, writers, and prophets,
And continued, in angelic tones,
"If the Greeks had known how to cooperate, if there'd
never been a Reformation,

If Sparta had not been Sparta, and the Church had
    been the Church of the saints,
The Argive peace like a free-blooming olive-tree, the
    peace of Christ (who loved peace) like a great, beautiful
    vine enwrapping the spinning earth!
Take it nearer home," he said.
"Take these Mayans and their star-clocks, their carvings
    and their great cities.
Who sacked them out of their cities, drowned the cities
    with a green jungle?
A plague? A change of climate? A queer migration?
Certainly they were skillful, certainly they created.
And, in Tenochtitlan, the dark obsidian knife and the
    smoking heart on the stone but a fair city,
And the Incas had it worked out beautifully till Pizarro
    smashed them.
The collectivist state was there, and the ladies very
    agreeable.
They lacked steel, alphabet and gunpowder and they
    had to get married when the government said so.
They also lacked unemployment and overproduction.
For that matter," he said, "take the Cro-Magnons,
The fellows with the big skulls, the handsome folk, the
    excellent scribers of mammoths,
Physical gods and yet with sensitive brain (they drew
    the fine, running reindeer).
What stopped them? What kept us all from being Apollos
    and Aphrodites
Only with a new taste to the nectar,
The laughing gods, not the cruel, the gods of song, not
    of war?
Supposing Aurelius, Confucius, Napoleon, Plato, Gau-
    tama, Alexander—
Just to take half a dozen—
Had ever realized and stabilized the full dream?
How long, O Lord God in the highest? How long, what
    now, perturbed spirit?"

He turned blue at the wingtips and disappeared as
    another angel approached me.

This one was quietly but appropriately dressed in cello-
    phane, synthetic rubber and stainless steel,
But his mask was the blind mask of Ares, snouted for
    gasmasks.
He was neither soldier, sailor, farmer, dictator, nor
    munitions-manufacturer.
Nor did he have much conversation, except to say,
"You will not be saved by General Motors or the pre-
    fabricated house.
You will not be saved by dialectic materialism or the
    Lambeth Conference.
You will not be saved by Vitamin D or the expanding
    universe.
In fact, you will not be saved."
Then he showed his hand:
In his hand was a woven, wire basket, full of seeds,
    small metallic and shining like the seeds of portulaca;
Where he sowed them, the green vine withered, and
    the smoke and the armies sprang up.

EDITOR'S INTRODUCTION TO:

THE ARISTOCRAT
Chan Davis

It is well known that I uphold a radically aristocratic interpretation of history. Radically, because I
have never said that human society *ought* to be
aristocratic, but a great deal more than that. What I
have said, and still believe with ever-increasing conviction, is that human society *is* always, whether it
will or no, aristocratic by its very essence, to the
extreme that it is a society in the measure that it is
aristocratic, and ceases to be such when it ceases to
be aristocratic. Of course I am speaking now of society
and not the State.

> Jose Ortega y Gasset, *The Revolt of the
> Masses*

Aristocracy literally means "rule of the best." Plato
and Aristotle classed states as "aristocratic" if the most
powerful offices were elective and unpaid. There was a
considerable "aristocratic" element in the governments of
the original founding states of the U.S.; it is only in very
recent times that all property, educational, and literacy
requirements were removed from electoral qualification.

A poll tax is "aristocratic" in that it imposes a duty and burden on those who wish to vote. Poll taxes were used as a means of excluding blacks from voting in the old south, and have thus acquired a terrible reputation; but anything can be abused. I have often wondered: just what *is* so horrified about charging, say, fifty dollars a year for the privilege of voting? And why *shouldn't* literacy, and residence in the community be required? For that matter, is it so evil that only taxpayers be allowed to vote in property tax elections?

John Stuart Mill certainly thought that no recipient of unearned public funds should be allowed the franchise. Republics, we are told, last until the voters realize they can vote themselves largesse from the public treasury; after which the many despoil the few; the indolent plunder the industrious; and the state begins to dissolve.

Indeed: that kind of dissolution very often generates an emperor. Those who come after generally long for the older days of aristocracy and republic. It is easy enough to idealize aristocracy. After all: don't we *want* the best to rule? And certainly the achievements of aristocratic states have been great indeed.

The Roman Republic was nakedly an aristocracy long after all offices were thrown open to patrician and plebian alike. Most public offices were not paid; and to hold the highest office, one had to enter the "cursus honorum," a series of positions which had the effect of allowing only the experienced in the highest positions of the state—but allowed only those who had private means to get that experience.

C. Northcote Parkinson tells us:

"Viewed as a structure or mechanism, the Roman constitution seems complex, confused, and unworkable. It had, to all appearances, too many legislatures, too many independent officials, too many elections, and too many rules. No distinction was ever made between legislative, executive, and judicial functions, nor even between military and civil. It worked, nevertheless, to some purpose. Rome was governed, in effect, by a class of men of similar birth, similar training, similar experience, and (one might add) similar limitations. They all understood each other very well and probably reached agreement privately before Senate even met. The magistrates could have nullified the powers of Senate. But why should they? They were magistrates only for a time, and thereafter Senators for life. The Senators might have obstructed the work of those in office. But why should they? They had all been in office themselves. Senators might have become dangerously divorced from the people at large. But it was not altogether closed to talent, not entirely insensitive to upper middle class opinion. The people, finally, might have found some means to demand a share in government. But the Roman ruling class was a true aristocracy. Its members were respected for their courage and ability, not merely envied for their wealth. Of the aristocrats, every one had served in the field without disgrace, every one had legal and administrative training, every one had served as executive and judge. They affected, moreover, a Spartan simplicity in dress and manner, resting their influence merely on birth, reputation, and known achievement. They were able, between them, to conquer the known world (*The Evolution of Political Thought*, Viking Press, 1964).

The Roman model has been consciously copied: in Britain during the period of the Napoleonic wars; and to a lesser extent in the infant United States.

That is one remembered aristocracy. We have, buried within western history, another: the memory of Arthur and the Round table; Charlemagne and his palladins; the valiant fight of civilization against a long night of barbarism and decay.

Rank Hath Its Privileges; but how great should those privileges be? What price aristocracy?

I first read this story in high school. It disturbed me a lot, for it presents the clash of two valid ideas. I have remembered this story for thirty years; certainly reason enough to include it here.

THE ARISTOCRAT
By Chan Davis

I.

It was an hour or so after sunset on a heavy September night. I was sitting alone in the high-ceilinged main room of the temple, reading by the light of a five-foot candelabrum. The corners of the room were dark as always; the white tree trunks outside the window seemed to catch more of the light than the piles of books which lined the walls.

The silence was broken by a loud but patient knocking at the door.

"Who would enter?" I called.

"Jim Jenkins. See the Elder Stevan."

I laid down my book. "Enter, Jim Jenkins." He came in and stood just a few yards inside the door, blinking at the candlelight. Jenkins was in his late forties, graying, but still one of the best farmers in the Village. Like all the Folk he had a round and almost chinless face, and just now its gray-shot eyebrows were drawn together in uncertainty. He stood just at the limit of the candles' light and shifted from one foot to another.

"What would you ask the Elder Stevan?"

"Elder Stevan," he said, "Paul Pomroy wants to marry my daughter."

"Your daughter—"

"Grace Jenkins."

I searched my memory. I had not seen the girl since she last came to the Temple, several years before. "Bring me the Record, Jim Jenkins."

With clumsy respect, he crossed the room, got the high, thin book and, holding it in both hands, brought it to me. "She's young," I said, after a moment.

Jim Jenkins looked troubled. "Paul Pomroy wants to marry my daughter," he repeated.

I considered. He sounded pretty insistent, and it behooved me as a priest of Truth to recognize a fact, preferably in advance. Besides, there was definitely a percentage in my doing Jenkins a favor at this point. I spoke, sternly. "You have room for Pomroy and Grace in your house?"

"Yes."

"Jim Jenkins, they may marry, but because Grace is young they live and work with you for one year."

"Yes, Elder Stevan." He turned, thinking the interview was over.

But it wasn't. There was my very necessary percentage to collect—very necessary indeed, at this particular time. And I couldn't have asked for a better one to collect it from than him. "Jim Jenkins! You know Old Red has gone to the west with Buddy Hoey and others to forage. How long have they been gone?"

"Ten days, more."

"Thirteen days. You know they went against the word of the Elder?"

He half-whispered, "Yes."

"Do you expect the Elder will punish them when they come back?"

He frowned a little, apparently suspecting a trick. "Yes, Elder Stevan."

"The others in the Village—do they expect it also?"

"Some do."

"Do they wish it?"

"The Word of the Elder—" He bowed as my parents had taught him.

"The Word of the Elder will be given when Old Red comes back. But those who do not wish to see Old Red punished, Jim Jenkins?"

He stood a moment, absently scratching one hairy forearm against his hip, then answered, "The other day two of the Folk said something against the Elder, for Old Red. Tony Shelton heard. I told Tony Shelton and Paul Pomroy and Tim Marvic to beat them up. They beat them up."

"Why didn't the Elder hear of this?"

"The two didn't tell the Elder. They knew Tony Shelton heard them. They said something against the Elder."

"But why didn't *you* tell the Elder? You did wrong, Jim Jenkins. You should not beat up men like those two. You should tell the Elder."

"Yes. I hear other Folk say something the same, I tell the Elder Stevan."

I let him go without asking him the names of the two dissidents. I was more than satisfied. It couldn't have worked out better if I'd planned it. Jenkins was one of the Folk whom I could trust, and now that I could count on him and his friends to form the beginnings of a spy system I felt easier about the situation.

A spy system in the Village was something new, but so was Old Red's action in leaving on a foraging party without my sanction. That was new, and unpleasant. I was alone, the only Elder, and now that the routine of obedience to the Word had been broken I was none too sure of what to expect.

I entered the information of Grace Jenkins' wedding in the Record, then stood up and slowly walked to the window. The chalky white trunks of the long-dead oak grove stood motionless between me and the night. As a child, here in the Temple, I had once thought of them as guards protecting the Elders' home; now I found myself wishing, whimsically, that each of them had at least a bow and arrows in its hand.

*   *   *

The foraging party returned several nights later. The first thing I noticed when the leaders of the party were brought to me was not Old Red, or Buddy Hoey, or anything connected with them. The first thing I noticed was the girl.

She was a prisoner who had been taken on the expedition. She was dressed in a cloak of animal skins of some sort, quite different from the rough woven clothes of the Villagers. But that was not the only difference. There was her firm-jawed oval face, with its arched brows—it took me a moment to place the nature of the difference.

She was human. She was the first human I'd seen since my father's death years before. Human—not Folk!

I addressed Old Red. "Tell of the people you found."

"To west and north, near the river. Had no houses, not much clothes, only deerskins, other skins. Had beards. Meat, but no leather, had no cows to keep. Many dogs."

"About how many people were there in the tribe?"

"Twenty, thirty, more." He frowned and shrugged. "We caught them."

"You surprised them—at night?"

"Yes. But dogs barked, they got away. They thought we were more than them, they ran away. We killed some. None of us killed. We took meat and—her." He indicated the tall, black-haired girl beside him. "Tried to take dogs. Good dogs."

Then I asked the question that was uppermost in my mind. "Were all the people like the Folk?"

"Didn't see faces of all of them."

"But of those you saw—?"

Again he nodded at the prisoner. "She was the only one like the Elders." (*Like the Elders,* I thought. *Well, he was the first to say it.*) "The others like us."

"Was she a prisoner from some other tribe?"

The girl herself answered. "I child of Chief. Name Barbi."

She was part of this Folk tribe, then. That was something to puzzle over later. But something else was brought home to me by her words. They were spoken in English, of course, but they were spoken so exactly with the intonation of the Village that I realized suddenly where the Chief and his tribe must have come from. During the time when my parents were Elders, shortly after the Folk had been taught the use of the bow and arrow, a number of Folk had left on hunting trips and never returned. They must now be the "Chief" and his men. Let's see—if this Barbi had been born soon after they left the Village, that would make her eighteen now; about right.

I put it up to Old Red. "These people may be those who left the Village in the Elder David's time. Did you see any faces of men you knew?"

Obviously the idea was new to him, for he was taken off guard and made one of his rare slips. "Yes, Elder Stevan," he said. "I thought it were the same. We punished them for going from the Elder—"

I laughed harshly. The laugh was well done. He stopped.

I questioned him further. It seemed he and Hoey really knew very little more about the tribe. For the rest, they had found few houses along the way, but there was one large cache of canned goods; they had not made many attempts at hunting; there had been considerable woodland in the territory they covered, but mostly prairie; enough water.

My questions were over. I stared at Old Red and Buddy Hoey. Hoey dropped his eyes, preferring the sight of his unshod toes to my face. The two Folk guards and Barbi watched curiously. Except for the sputtering of one of the thick bayberry candles beside me, the room was still.

I had to name the transgressors' penalty. It couldn't be as stiff as I'd planned, because the party had been too successful; at the same time I couldn't go too easy in punishing a disobedience of the Word of the Elder. I improvised, and hoped the four Folks wouldn't notice my scanning their faces. "Until harvest next year, those of the foraging party will clean the barn." That, they would not like. "And each of them gets forty lashes; in public, next rest day. Fifty for Old Red, and Buddy

Hoey." That was enough. "You did very wrong, and the forfeit is small. Another time it will be much more.

"Later this summer another party will go out, to bring back the food you discovered. It will be led by Jim Jenkins." Buddy Hoey didn't like that, either; the idea of Jenkins, the farmer, in charge of such an expedition rubbed him the wrong way. Let it rub.

One of the guards, Tim Marvic, moved as if preparing to leave, but the other told him by a nudge that I had more to say. And I had. Something as important as all the rest.

"Barbi is not any more Old Red's prisoner." As I spoke I glanced at her; she returned the look with unwavering calm. I hoped the trembling I felt didn't sound in my voice. "Nor is she any longer the prisoner of the Village. This night she is freed. She lives at the temple, and her name is the Elder Barbi."

The two young guards turned toward each other, startled; even the imperturbable Old Red bit his lip behind his carroty beard. The girl looked alertly at them and at me, taking the situation in.

"The Word of the Elder," said Tim Marvic hoarsely.

I motioned to the guards to leave with the two raiders, and they shuffled out through the blackness of the door, leaving me with the unknown stranger who was the Elder Barbi.

"You know you are different, don't you, Barbi?"

"Different, yes. Was child of Chief, now Elder Barbi—Elder Barbi." She smiled.

"You know that's not what I meant."

"Yes."

She was sitting on the floor, restlessly I thought, in the direct sunlight from the paneless window. I watched her lazily from the Elders' chair, between its rude candelabra. Barbi's black hair shone blue-white in the sun. She shifted, sitting upright and clasping her knees in her arms, and the hair fell liquidly around her shoulders.

"How are you different? Tell me."

"Look different. Father told me I look different, told me I look—"

"Like the Elders?"

"Don't know. Heard the word—" She stopped to frame the sentence. "I know I heard the word 'Elder' before I came here. I think my father told me that."

I mused, wondering what the results would be of my precipitate action in taking the girl into the Temple. There was one big result already—I had Barbi. That was, so far, a decidedly pleasant result.

But what I had was a half-savage Barbi, illiterate and ignorant as any of the Folks, in spite of her alertness and her obvious human intelligence. Not an Elder. She accepted completely her position and title as my wife, but she was not yet an Elder. I smiled, then wondered why.

"Barbi, did you ever ask your father why you looked different?"

"Yes."

"What did he say?"

"Didn't know. You know," she stated, turning toward me.

"Yes, partly. Shall I tell you?"

"Yes."

"Well, long ago, more than a hundred years ago, there were many more people here than there are now. They had large houses and many other things; this house and all the other large houses in the Village were built in that time. And all the people were like you and me."

"None like the Folk?"

"Not as far as I know. The books"—I waved toward the hundreds of volumes piled on the floor along the room's walls— "have many pictures of men, and none are Folk."

She jumped up, crossed in front of me, and leafed through a few of the books on top of the piles, as she had done several times before in the two days she had been at the Temple. "Yes," she said. "Father didn't say that."

"He doesn't know it. From what you've told me,

your parents came from the Village, and no one in the Village knows what I'm telling you."

"Why not!"

"Only the Elders know."

She said nothing.

I took a deep breath. "You have seen the City?"

"The City?"

"Let's go and take a look at it."

I lifted myself to my feet and led the way out the back door of the Temple and up the small knoll to the east. It was hot, I realized. The sun's constant yellow speared down on the bare hill, the sun's blue hung in a haze around us. From the threshing floor far behind us, in the Village, came the sound of a new Folk singing.

I spoke as we walked. "These people long ago had many things we don't have. For instance, they had ways of killing other people much stronger than our bows and arrows. They could kill more with one blow than there are in the whole Village."

"How?"

I smiled. "Don't worry: *I* can't do it. But when people fought then, more would die in a single night than you can count." We had reached the top of the hill, and I was out of breath. "I'm getting old," I said, offhand.

She looked at me, aslant. "How old are you?"

"Thirty-five. Same as Buddy Hoey."

She seemed incredulous. Well, *that* was one of the things I'd have to explain, too.

I pointed ahead of us, where the hill sloped down to a broad level valley. "There's the City." I tried to speak matter-of-factly; it did no good to be bitter after a hundred years. "See that ring of peculiar brown and gray things, like rocks? They used to be houses, some much larger than the Temple. See that space in the middle, on the river, where the very green grass is? There were houses there, too, and people."

Her face showed awe, or perhaps just bafflement. Still she did not move, but stood beside me, independently.

"People died there, Barbi. And horses, and dogs, and rats, and birds . . . everything died. More people in a single night than you can count. Other places there were other cities, and everyone there died, too.

"And after that there was the radiation—you can learn from the books what that is. Those people who were still alive were poisoned, they grew weak and sick, they died in one way or another."

"Not all of them."

"I hope . . . I don't know. There may not be anyone alive anywhere except right here. Here, a strange thing happened. One of the people near the City, or perhaps more than one, were changed when the City was destroyed, so their children were Folk, and their children's children." And what a fantastic accident that had been! But there was no point in trying to get Barbi to appreciate the extent of the coincidence, or the luck it must have taken for the first Folk to survive. "The Folk were different. The radiation hurt them hardly at all. They weren't sick and weak, like all of my grandfather's people."

"But—"

"I know, you don't understand. You can learn from the books. Here's what happened. The Folk lived near the City for many years; my grandfather's people lived out behind this hill, where the Village is now. My grandfather and the rest had the sickness and were dying off; on the other hand the Folk didn't have the knowledge that the people, before, had had. Living so close to the City, the parents of the first Folk and the other survivors from before the War must not have lived long enough to teach the Folk much. I suppose all of them must have been gone within ten years; and the last of their children—those that weren't Folk— must have died within the next twenty years after that. Leaving the Folk, who knew how to open the cans of food they found in the ruins but didn't know much more. They could speak hardly at all, I understand."

"Yes, and later the Folk came here and the Elders taught them and had them work on farms. You told me about that already, a little. And the Village, and the Elder David and the Elder Carmela, and you— But Stevan, what you said before isn't right. I'm not like you said. The other childs . . . the other children in the tribe never—"

She must have seen the way I was looking at her, for she broke off. In a strained voice, I said: "Let's see you run down to the Temple and back."

For just a fraction of a second she hesitated, a questioning look in her black eyes. Then she was off, and by the time I'd turned my head to follow her she was going all out. And I mean all out! "Scamper" isn't the word; "fly" isn't the word either. She simply and matter-of-factly covered ground. It was just that she covered an awful lot of it. A little way down the slope she stooped, hardly breaking stride, and snatched off the leather moccasins I had given her; barefoot she went faster if anything.

I walked down toward where she'd dropped the moccasins. I still stared at the distant Barbi, her long golden legs flashing in the sunlight, but my thoughts were on my older sister Beth. Beth had died, at about Barbi's present age, of a tumor—radiation again. My picture of her was of a slight, heavy-eyed girl who moved quietly about the Temple, avoiding the patches of direct sunlight from the windows. There were no clocks still operating in the Village, but I didn't need to time Barbi's dash to the Temple to draw quite a clear comparison between her and Beth. Or between her and me.

So. Either Barbi was nearly immune to radiation, like the Folk, or else her health had been spared so far by her living farther away from the City. And the second possibility didn't count for much—this long after the War, the radioactivity was pretty much universal, I was sure, though of course weaker in intensity.

I stood waiting for Barbi. She was racing uphill toward me, at the same rate she'd gone down. She was beautiful to watch, as long as I didn't think about it.

When she got to me she was smiling. Just a gentle, unassuming smile, reflecting the fact that she had made her point in the discussion. I smiled too, shaking my head ruefully, and handed her the moccasins, which she put on again without objection.

It was just as well the discussion had to wait a few moments for Barbi to catch her breath. I wanted time to think. Just at that point I was a little afraid of Barbi.

"That makes it more difficult," I remarked finally, as we stepped through the door into the sudden darkness of the Temple's interior.

"What's 'difficult'?"

"Oh . . . it means 'hard to understand', in this case. You remember what we were talking about before we went up to see the City?"

"Why we're different. But you told me why." She added, "Partly."

"What I've told you partly is why *I* am different. As for you—" I sat down, wearily; Barbi stood in front of me, arms folded. "Your parents were both Folk—unless the Chief captured you from another tribe."

"He never said that."

"No . . . I suppose he was your father, all right. You see, Barbi, the child is usually like its parents. The cattle on the plains—you have seen the high-shoulders and the short legs?"

"Yes."

"Do two short legs ever have a calf that grows as tall as a man?"

"Don't know."

"Oh. Well, it almost never happens. Sometimes the big cattle have short-leg calves. The Folk have seen them running with the herds. If you have a high-shoulder bull and cow, and know what calves their parents and grandparents had, you can say whether it's possible they will have short-leg calves, and you will be almost sure to be right."

"You haven't tried it."

"No."

"It's in the books."

"That's right."

"Then why don't— Oh no. The books don't say about Folk and Elders because there weren't Folk then. But there were two kinds of cattle then?"

"I don't even know whether there were or not."

"What!"

There was a frown of puzzlement on her impassive face for the first time. I laughed apologetically. How could Barbi be expected to grasp what I'd been driving at: that there were general principles of genetics? The only "general principles" she'd ever have run into would be of the sort that you don't need to state explicitly, or the sort you can state in terms of familiar objects. And here I was trying to tell her about dominant and recessive genes! About the problem of whether Folk differed from human in more than one gene: about the strong reasons for thinking it was only one; about the evidence her existence gave—the highly confusing evidence, now that she'd proved she was not altogether human.

If I'd thought a little further, I'd have realized she'd showed pretty acute intelligence, just now, in seeing that she *didn't* understand what I was driving at. I'd have been a little more afraid of her than I was.

But she was my wife, and the Elder Barbi, and I'd already decided I was going to teach her. I said: "Many things in the books are still true, even though so much is changed now. By reading them you can figure out a lot of things you couldn't otherwise."

" 'Reading'—that means finding out what the books say."

"That's right. It's hard to learn how, though. Shall I teach you?"

Apparently her curiosity had been aroused by the disjointed conversation; she answered, "Yes," without hesitation.

So I began the job of teaching Barbi to read.

Not that that was the only thing I had to occupy my time that fall. After harvesting and threshing were done there was the storing of grain, seed, and silage. Later on three cows were slaughtered, at intervals, and their hides hung up to cure. The— rather tough—meat I found welcome, as did the Folks, but it reminded me again how much better it would be to have a larger herd of cattle and an adequate refrigeration system. All in good time.

When Jenkins and the other farmers would come to me to ask about the routine affairs of the Village, or to discuss the building of two new houses planned for next year, Barbi would usually put down the book she was struggling with at the time and turn to listen. She never said anything; just sat there on the floor beside me, her arms crossed on her raised knees, one thumb holding her place in her book, her dark eyes alert and thoughtful.

She always listened when Jenkins came alone to report in his capacity as unofficial head of the secret service. The first few times Jenkins had been visibly uncomfortable about speaking before her, but after all she was an Elder. These reports of Jenkins' were generally encouraging. I hadn't expected them to be. As a matter of fact I had rather expected it might occur to Old Red and some of the others who felt chronically cooped up and bored in the Village that the Chief had the right idea. However, none of the Folk left the Village, and Jim Jenkins reported only two or three remarks tending to this direction.

Which may have been because winter was coming on, the best season to be in the Village, or because the dissidents among the Folk had learned who not to talk to!

In any case, the dissatisfaction was still there. Wherever it was possible without losing face, I made concessions. At the same time I was more careful than ever about not losing face.

The principal concession was in allowing an Elder-sanctioned party to go out to bring back the canned goods Old Red had found previously. Among those who went were several of Old Red's adherents. At the same time I saw to it that these were outnumbered by Folk I could count on—people who would just as soon have stayed at home. The expedition was successful and caused no more friction than was to be expected; a large store of prewar canned goods was brought back and added to our winter provisions.

In the face-preserving line, I kept a Temple Guard on duty all the time, as my parents had done. The Guards chosen were Tony Shelton, Tim Marvic, and Jane Anderson. All three enjoyed the job for its prestige, and got a kick out of the rigamarole I prescribed for Villagers who came to see the Elder. It was a new game, just complicated enough not to pall quickly, and they carried it off with considerable dignity.

There was one more worry—the Chief. Old Red had routed him once, but that didn't mean much. Hunters who made their livelihood from the bow and arrow could be expected to use the weapon better than the Folk here. They were a danger. On the other hand, they had the whole continent for their hunting ground, probably with no human competition anywhere, so there wasn't too much reason for them to turn this way. I was more concerned about dangers close to home.

I remember it was in November, after the first woodchopping parties had left, that it became definite that Barbi was pregnant. The fact seemed neither to inconvenience her nor excite her. In fact it was only shortly after that she began to attack the Temple's library with remarkable single-mindedness.

Reading came astonishingly easily to her; in fact the principal hurdle seemed to be accustoming her eyes to focusing at the same distance, and such a short distance, after a life spent outdoors. From December on she got along without tutoring. The dictionary got plenty of use, but she had also a special skill for scanning a half-understood passage and extracting the meat.

By this time, of course, the Temple's glassless windows had been shuttered for the winter; so, on all but the coldest days, Barbi would save candles by reading outside. With her cloak of pieced-together rabbit pelts pulled around her and over her ears, with her feet drawn up on and edge of the cloak to keep them out of the snow, she would sit there in the lee of the house for hours, glancing up occasionally to rest her eyes, but never once coming inside to thaw out. I made no attempt to duplicate her performance.

Or else the two of us would sit and talk in the half-light of the boarded-up Temple—about her life in the tribe, about some prewar subject or other which it was hard to get from the books, or about the Village. Barbi rarely expressed an opinion, but I was more than eager to know what she was thinking, on that last subject particularly. There was just once when I got a hint.

We were in the Temple's main room, and the candles had been lighted in honor of the talk I was giving her on cell structure, which required diagrams. When I came to a stopping place, she got up and began to pace the floor.

"You've always been here and been boss?"

"Yes. Well, my parents were—"

"I know. But you were always boss after them and never did work."

"I couldn't do much work with my hands and back if I tried. Too bad, but there it is."

"Would you if you could?"

"Well—maybe not. Once the Elders were Elders, it wasn't too good an idea to be working with the others."

"Dignity of the Elders," she said, smiling a little. "Like the Lords in that book—can't soil your hands. Aristocrats."

"*Aristo*crats," I corrected, "Yes, that's it exactly."

"You never had any wife?"

"No. My mother said it was all right, but my father told me no. Said I shouldn't have a wife from the Folk till I was sure I couldn't find one of my own race."

"If you got a Folk wife, that'd make you too much like the rest."

"That's right."

"Can't be like the rest, can't do work. *Aristo*crats. Different from the Chief," she added suddenly.

"Not entirely," I said. "If people hadn't been willing to obey your father, they could have got a new Chief. Somebody could have fought your father for it. But from what you've told me, nobody ever did."

She stopped her pacing, sat down on the floor. A heavy lock of black hair fell across one cheek, shadowing her face. "You're right," she answered, turning her face up into the candlelight again. "Nobody really thought of changing things. He was a good Chief."

I leaned forward, elbows on knees. "Same with us. We're the Elders—'Elders' with a capital 'E', even though the Folk can't write—the Folk don't think of changing things. And we're good Elders. We earn our food. We know things they don't, we can figure out things they can't, we can rule them best for their own good."

"For *your* own good."

"For our good and theirs." I didn't mention how completely the Folk were left out of my mental picture of the world two hundred years from now. Better to give her the picture of myself as benevolent despot.

"Why can't they go hunting all the time the way my people—the Chief's people do?"

"It may seem to you the Folks are being held back. I suppose that's true, in a way. But how are we going to build up the civilization people had before the War if we don't have something like the Village and the Elders? Start from nothing? Without the Elders it would have taken the Folk many thousand years to get where they are now. If they all scattered in bands of hunters now, the Temple library wouldn't have anyone to read it, and people would forget the ways of getting food from wheat, vegetables, and tame cattle. The Folk would suffer in the long run from forgetting all this."

"And you'd suffer. Even if they didn't forget you'd suffer."

"That, too. But they'd forget."

"I'll think about it."

And I knew she would.

II.

Barbi's son was born in July, almost two weeks premature.

The fact that he was premature was fortunate in one way at least. It saved me a lot of worrying. As it was, the whole thing broke quite unexpectedly. Barbi announced, calmly as ever but quite positively, that things were about to happen: the Temple Guard went to the Village to fetch a midwife; the midwife retired upstairs to Barbi's bed; and I was left alone downstairs to catch up on the worrying which normally would have been begun some time before the event.

There was enough to worry about. Even objectively, this was a darned important child that was being born. And subjectively I was nervous as all get out.

I waited, in silence. After a time, there were conclusive sounds from upstairs; I still waited. Crickets shrilled through the warm night.

Finally I could go up. The midwife met me at the door of the room. "Boy, Elder Stevan." She stood aside to let me in. Barbi lay on the old, rusted bedstead in the corner. Her covers looked oppressive in the heat; sweat was standing on my own face. Hers was streaked, but unlined. I stroked her cheek, and she smiled— not a brave smile, but a perfectly spontaneous one; there was nothing to be brave about.

The midwife came up with the child in her arms, wrapped in a single piece of rough linen cloth. I turned to look at him.

Now any newborn child has a disconcerting similarity to a young pig; that I knew from the picture in the books, which—believe me!—I had studied. And I understand that a newborn chimp looks practically human. None the less, the distinction can be made, and you'd have to be pretty short-sighted to hesitate in making it. What's more, racial characteristics if pronounced enough, even sometimes family resemblances, can be distinguished in the walnut-wrinkled faces of the newborn. I had no difficulty at all in perceiving that Barbi's son was Folk.

Did the midwife know? Probably not. But Barbi— Well, she'd never seen a young human, but she could look at the books' pictures as well as I could. If she didn't suspect, she would, and soon.

I said nothing about it to either of them, but fought the problem out with myself.

The father—Elder Stevan—human. The mother— Elder Barbi—human. The child: Folk. High-shoulder and short leg—

All right then. There must be at least one gene in which I was distinguished from the Folk. Were there more than one?

My grandfather had thought not. Since the Folk strain had been unknown before the War, it must have originated at the time of the City's bombing, so my grandfather assumed. Now the percentage of mutations which are able to live at all is so extremely low that it's stretching probabilities too far to assume that more than one gene was changed—whether in the same or in different children. This one gene might be one which appeared in several different forms among humans, of course; but among the Folk there was only the one allele at this particular point on this particular chromosome—the mutated form.

On the other hand, my grandfather hadn't known about Barbi. Suppose there were actually two genes wherein the two races differed. Suppose Barbi had the human gene in one case—so that she looked like me— but didn't have the other human gene, which would have made her susceptible to radiation poisoning. Then consider only the first gene, in which Barbi and I agreed. Then in order for us to have a child which, as regards this gene, was Folk—let's see. The Folk gene would have to be recessive, for if it were dominant one of the parents would have to be Folk in appearance. But if the Folk gene was recessive, then both parents must be heterozygous! There must be Folk in my ancestry as well as in Barbi's.

There were other difficulties in the theory, when I thought it over; but at least it held promise that our next child would probably—seventy-five percent probability— be human.

Anyhow, the theory was not true. There was another birth in the Village only a week later—Paul and Grace Pomroy had their first child, a daughter.

She was human.

I made no attempt to conceal my agitation from Jim Jenkins, the child's grandfather, when he brought me the news. "Are you sure?" I asked unsteadily.

"I saw the Elder Stevan when he was a child. Think I know—"

"Are you sure!"

"Yes."

"Has this ever happened before, Jim Jenkins?"

His heavy pepper-and-salt eyebrows drew together in thought. It wasn't just the effort of remembering, I was sure. His answer was, "Yes, Elder Stevan."

"When?"

He bit his lip. "My sister, she named Grace, too."

"Yes, Tim Marvic's mother."

"Yes. Her second child looked like Elders. They killed it."

"*What?* Why didn't they tell the Elder?"

"Elder Stevan, before Elders came there were childs like that, Folk had childs like that. My grandmother told me. All childs like that died anyway, so Folk killed them. My grandmother told me.

"I told my sister shouldn't kill child, should ask Elder. She said Elder not like child that kind, Elder kill *her*. So I didn't tell Elder either."

"Hm-m-m. It was long ago, so there is no punishment, but she did very wrong. Tell her that. No killing in the Village, ever."

"I'll tell her."

"Jim Jenkins, was your sister's husband any relation to Paul Pomroy? Or to you, or to the Elder Barbi's parents?"

The lines between his heavy eyebrows deepened.

"Bring the Record," I said.

"No, I remember, Elder Stevan. Mother of Elder Barbi's father was sister of . . . sister of grandmother of Paul Pomroy."

That was enough for now. Some other time I could get a list of any other human births in the Village and study the suddenly important genealogy of the Folk. Right now I had to see Barbi.

When I got to Barbi's room I was puffing and flushed. I sank onto a chair; she looked up from her bed and smiled.

"Barbi, two of the Folk have a child, a girl, which is—like us! You know our child is—Folk."

She feigned mild astonishment at this last. "Oh?"

"Yes," impatiently. "You can tell by pictures of human babies in the books."

"Human? My baby looks human to me."

"Human—all right, human. But different from us."

Calmly, "Never noticed." She smiled disconcertingly.

Then, propping her head on one arm and staring at me, "Dignity of the Elders again? Yes, I see your point. Well, what did you have on your mind when you came running up here in such a hurry? It wasn't just to give me the news. No, don't tell me, I'll guess. You wanted to switch the two babies." She glared—there's no other word for it.

There was no point in admitting her guess was right. "Not exactly. I think the Pomroy girl should be brought up here, though."

"Her poor mother!"

"Grace Pomroy can come to nurse," I added hastily, "and wean the girl soon to go back to her husband."

Pause. Barbi lay on the bed, starting a train of groans in its decrepit joints. She said: "Why is it so important the girl comes here?"

"Barbi, the Folk are all very well now—they can live with the radiation, which none of us have been able to do except you. But against the time when the radiation dies down, we must have as large a group as possible for people like us, and we must keep the group pure." My voice died out on the last words. The idea was one I'd accepted for years, but *now*— Keep the group pure, indeed!

"You've said something like this before. Why must this be?"

"Why must we keep our group alive? Because when the radiation dies down we'll be the stronger race. We have more intelligence and initiative. We're more—"

"*Maybe*." The word was pronounced in an intense half-whisper which seemed to project it direct to my brain, bypassing sound. I looked at Barbi, jolted.

"Maybe," she repeated. "The books tell of many

aristocrats who have thought themselves superior. Remember?"

I started to answer: she forestalled me with a lifted hand, but said nothing. We exchanged a long, ambiguous stare—which was interrupted by the baby's waking.

Barbi sat up quickly, with a little laugh, and I left. But the conversation had not been finished. I finished it with myself as I walked slowly down the stairs.

Yes. The aristocrat had denied the slave education, and called him stupid; had given him routine jobs with no hope of advancement, and called him lazy; had refused him his share in civilization, and called him a savage. All without justification. Barbi was right.

But surely the Folk were different from me, less intelligent, less—I could hear Barbi's answer: *Maybe.*

As I'd suggested, Grace Pomroy came to the temple with her girl, Terry. Barbi accepted the idea, accepted it cheerfully in fact. When the babies slept, Barbi and Grace would take turns keeping an ear on them; when the babies were awake, they'd take care of them together. It was hardly any time at all before the two women were like sisters. This situation may have bothered Grace a little; to me it was definitely disquieting.

My peace of mind during those weeks was practically nonexistent anyhow. Jim Jenkins came to the temple often—too often—and it wasn't just to see his daughter and grandchild. I did not enjoy the things he had to tell me. First, there were the jokes circulating among the Folk about Fritz and Terry. I found these stories anything but amusing, but what could I do?

Then there was Paul Pomroy's request, apologetically forwarded to me by Jenkins. Pomroy didn't like Terry's staying at the Temple; she was his girl and he wanted to keep her. I wondered: Had someone put him up to this? Hard to guess. My answer was obvious—no.

These things were just the minor symptoms of dislocation. Pomroy's Terry and our Fritz—two still-unexplained mysteries of genetics; they were causing a lot of trouble, considering that neither had reached the age of one month.

They weren't causing *all* the trouble, though. Jenkins reported several times that various Villagers were discussing leaving the Village. Summer had come around again, and here it was again, the problem of Folk who thought hunting would be a better living than sweating on the farms. Well—I appealed to Jenkins. "How many want to go?"

The familiar half-frown. "Twenty, thirty."

"How many are you sure you can trust? How many will do whatever the Elder says?"

The frown deepened. "Twenty, thirty."

That was a shock, and not just because thirty plus thirty failed to add to the population of the Village. I called in the Temple Guard, Tony Shelton, and got about the same answer from him.

There it was. I couldn't afford a showdown, because all Old Red's men had to do was clear out, head for the hills, and I would have lost! The Village had to be held together. As for keeping the dissidents here as prisoners, that would require more loyal supporters than I had, and even if it could be carried off it might be merely postponing the issue. I'd lost too much face recently to try appealing to Word-of-the-Elder hocus pocus; which about exhausted the possible courses of action.

"Jim Jenkins," I said the next time he appeared, "can you say things so the Folk will think the Elder will let them go hunting? Not say you *know* what the Elder will do, but make the Folk *think*—"

"Yes, Elder Stevan."

It was the best I could do. If I couldn't prevent the group from leaving, I'd have to persuade them to allow their leaving to be sanctioned! That was the only way there was a good chance of their coming back. Still, even if they did leave with permission, there was a good chance they'd go the way the Chief had gone. Maybe, I thought, the party when it goes should be loaded with loyal Folk. Even with that idea, though, there were all sorts of difficulties. There might be fighting in the party once it got out of the Elder's shadow;

the ringers I included might find they liked farming less once they'd had a taste of something different—

I *said* my mind wasn't exactly at ease.

The answer to this particular problem was simple, although I would never have thought of it. It was Barbi who made the suggestion: A foraging party should go out, and *she* should accompany it. I was startled by the idea of her going off and leaving Fritz, but she assured me that the women of the Chief's tribe frequently took part in long treks carrying their infant children on their backs; she would take Fritz with her. And really, the plan was perfect. If anybody could keep Old Red and the others in line it was Barbi: she knew as much about hunting and camping as any of them; and, to go with that, she had the name of Elder and as much prestige as still went with the title.

I agreed to the plan quickly. Two days later the party left, with Fritz incredibly asleep in the linen pouch on his mother's back; and that night I slept peacefully again.

It was not new to me, sitting alone, weak and inactive, sitting in the Temple with the problems of the farms and with my books. It had never bothered me before. Perhaps now it was the thought of my wife and son out there to the west with the foragers which gradually made me restive. *They* were not weak. They were where the adventure was. They could live under the sky while I was imprisoned here by my own feebleness.

It was this very mood of dicouragement which led me to an adventure of my own. The phenomenon of Fritz's Folk-ness recurred to me oftener and oftener, until finally it reminded me of a long-forgotten fact which had never held any great interest to me, but which suddenly offered hope of an explanation. What was the book? Babcock and Clausen's "Genetics for Students of Agriculture." It turned up near the bottom of a heavy pile in a corner of the main room; in my impatience I worried it out of the stack myself, rather than wait to call Grace, who could have done it easily. And after a session of leafing through the dried, brown-edged pages I had what I wanted.

The term was "incomplete penetrance"; the way it works is this. Suppose you have a dominant and a corresponding recessive gene, call them A and B—say, high-shoulder and short-leg cattle. Then an individual having one A paired with a B will have the characteristics that go with the A—almost always. Pure-bred high-shoulder bull and pure-bred short-leg cow will have calves resembling the father—almost always. It's that "almost" which I'd only now remembered. The recessive characteristics *can* show up. A hybrid bull *might*, for example, stand as tall as the high-shoulders but have the down-turned horns of the short leg.

Whether that particular type of bull ever lived, I didn't know. I thought I knew rather intimately a much more important example of incomplete penetrance.

Barbi.

I ran rapidly over the other theories which had occurred to me. There was, I verified, some fatal weakness in each of them. I was left with this new theory, which checked perfectly.

The Folk strain—the mutant strain—had to be dominant. Dominant mutations are rare, but the conclusion was inescapable. The Folk gene—and one mutant Gene was all I had to suppose existed—was the A, the corresponding "normal" gene was the B.

The first Folk would have had to mate with one of the City's few human survivors; so originally the Village's ancestors would have been at least half human. A good many of the children in each generation would have been BB; but those paired human genes would have meant human characteristics and, in the radiation-drenched City, an early death. After awhile, the Folk killed human children at birth, by custom, so Jenkins had told me.

Still, the AB type could survive, being no more radiation-susceptible than the AA, the pure-bred Folk. And sometimes a child of two AB's could be—well, could be like little Terry, who already showed symptoms of feebleness dangerously like my own.

Then Grace and Paul Pomroy must have the same geno type, AB; as did my son. Barbi, too, was AB, but she was the anomaly, incomplete penetrance. She showed some characteristics of the recessive human strain she carried. But in the matter of resistance to radiation she ran true to form.

Genetically, my wife and son were as much Folk as Grace Pomroy. What was it I'd said to Barbi? "We must keep the group pure." A praiseworthy project indeed, I thought bitterly.

The morning after Barbi's return I awoke before dawn. Outside, rain was falling, the slow rain we get sometimes at night—but never by day in summer. I could hear the small sound of the water running down the valley in the roof; immediately above me there was a steady drip on the attic floor; around these intimate noises there was the hushed murmur of the sodden grass. It would have been pleasant to forget everything but the statistical patter of the rain, and go back to sleep.

But whatever had waked me kept me awake. What was it? Not the rain. Some night sound—some thought that had recurred to me in my sleep.

Getting up, I pulled my coat around me and crossed to the window. And suddenly I knew what had been on my mind.

The Chief. Before the foraging party's return, Tony Shelton had seen outside the Village two men with deer skins across the shoulders—a costume unknown among the Folk here. Yet Barbi's party had not reported meeting the Chief, or seeing any sign of his camp sites. Strange, to say the least.

Barbi's whole account of the expedition, after we got back to the Temple, had been strange. She was far more articulate than Old Red, yet her account was hardly less sketchy than his would have been. I questioned her, and she answered openly enough; but most of the answers were negative and all were just the minimum required. There was no complaint I could make—but the thing puzzled me.

Then I told her of the discovery I'd made while she was away. She listened calmly, and when I was done she lighted a few extra candles, got the genetics book out, and read over the passages I showed her.

At the end, she looked up and smiled. "Good work," she said. " 'Incomplete penetrance.' Nice phrase.

"Now," she went on, "what does this mean for the Elders?"

"Go on," I said, on my guard.

"All right. In the first place, there won't be any keeping the line of the Elders pure. Any children we have later will be likely to be like Fritz. Fifty percent probability, to be exact. And then—what are the probabilities for 'human' births among the Folk, do you think?"

"Two percent," I hazarded.

"Two percent—all of that. There's one consolation for you, Stevan. Even if the direct line of Elders dies out, the 'human strain' you worry about will still be around."

"Among the Folk."

"Yes."

I stood and began walking nervously about the room. "That doesn't console me much. There's something in one of the books about population sizes. The smaller a population is, the more likely it is for a strain to die out completely among the population—just by accident. Maybe it just so happens that all the AB-type Folk are out on a hunting party that gets trampled by a herd of cattle. Maybe something less spectacular. There's no safety except in numbers; if the Village were a hundred times as large as it is, the human strain would be reasonably sure of surviving, even if it wasn't present in any greater proportion than it is."

"I see, yes. And beside that—"

"Beside that, it's *not random*." I crossed in front of her. It was funny for me to be pacing the floor while she sat there, relaxed. "The BB's—the human proper— wouldn't have an even chance of survival, not for another hundred years. They'd be sickly—"

"That's true. And your strain absolutely must be given a chance, mustn't it?"

*   *   *

Now, standing at the window and staring at the gray oak trunks against the blank darkness, I mulled over that last question. A threat? Or just a taunt? I didn't like it. And there had been plenty on Barbi's mind that night that I hadn't been let in on.

A new sound cut though the monotonous sluicing of the rain water. Though I couldn't identify it exactly, it told me Barbi was awake. I stood rigidly in the solid silence.

Behind me, "Can't sleep, Stevan?"

"No; no. I just woke up."

"Worried?"

"About what?"

"You should be worried, Stevan."

"Oh?"

"I wasn't going to talk to you about it again, but I will. Stevan, you haven't got the right answer."

"What do you mean?" But I thought I knew.

"Let's see what your excuses are for this 'Elder' business." I swallowed hard, stood stockstill at the window. Her voice came clear and brisk from the shadows behind me and fell weirdly on my tired brain. "You want to save time, right? You don't want civilization to have to start at the beginning again, you want to save time by keeping hold of the knowledge from before the War. But this isn't the way to do it—keeping the Folk here as your slaves."

Weakly, "The Folk aren't slaves."

"Some of them want to stay here," she conceded. "But some of those would be dissatisfied if they thought they had alternatives. Look. You know what a civilized world's like, you want to see one built. Well, if it's done it'll be done by the people. You can't just decide what it'd be nice to have happen. The men who are going to do it have to *want* to do it."

Her earnestness frightened me; so I tried to sound amused and academic. "You seem pretty confident of your theory of history."

That stopped her. She'd learned a lot in the last year, but she realized how much there was she didn't know. "O.K.," she said, "I'll be specific. You might like the idea of a race of farmers, sticking peacefully to one place. But if there's an easy living to be made by hunting somebody's going to take to the idea. If there's an easy living to be made by raiding villages, somebody'll take to that, too. Your books won't stop them."

"You're worried about the Chief, too."

"No," I turned at that, but she was in darkness and I couldn't see her face. "I'm not worried, I just admit he exists. You don't, so you can't have the right answer."

An abrupt weakness came over me. My limbs felt as if they were loose in their sockets. I clutched at the window frame, half surprised that my hands would still move. "Yes," I brought out, "I've got the *only* answer."

"I think not, Stevan."

My head fell forward. The red lightning erased everything then; it did not stop when I shut my eyes.

Barbi was watching me. Holding my breath and balancing carefully, I made it back to the bed without falling.

III.

"Elder Stevan."

The voice was gentle, but insistent. "Elder Stevan," it repeated. There was an urgency in it which carried it through to my sleep-drugged consciousness. I rolled over and sat up.

The first thing I noticed was that the first trace of light was just now showing in the sky. Then, that Barbi was not in the room.

The next thing was that Jim Jenkins was at the door. Seeing that I was aware of him, he spoke. "My daughter is at my house. Grace Pomroy. She has the two childs with her. Paul Pomroy isn't anywhere; can't find him."

"Well?"

"Grace has brought the two childs from the Temple to my house."

The strangeness of the report hit me then. "What? Why did she do that?"

"She says the Elder Barbi told her to do it, told her not to tell anybody, but I saw her there and—"

"Yes," I rose, passed Jenkins, and called from the door. "Barbi!"

The echo spent itself. There was no one in the Temple.

"You came here, in this part of the Temple where the Folk do not go, and just to tell me— Well, you did right," I decided, keeping my voice carefully under control. "Do you know where the Elder Barbi is?"

"No."

We started downstairs, Jenkins trailing. "Do you know of anything else unusual's happening, Jim Jenkins?"

His answer was negative, but a positive answer arrived soon enough.

We made our way into the great unlighted cavern that was the Temple's main room. Jenkins was still in the process of lighting candles when we heard footsteps outside, someone running. Tim Marvic, the Guard, called, "Tony Shelton would see the Elder."

"Enter, Tony Shelton."

He burst in, followed by an identical shadow on the book-lined wall. "Elder Stevan . . . oh, Jim Jenkins."

Jenkins nodded, lighted another candle.

After a moment's pause to catch his breath, Shelton announced explosively: "Lookouts saw men at five different places. To south, and over hill toward river, and off there to west. Not men of Village. All five seen just now, this night."

"So soon," I said, sinking into a chair.

The Chief! It might be no coincidence he came now; he could have seen Barbi's party, followed it here. No, not that, he wouldn't have needed the expedition to lead him to the Village, for he had been born here. *Was* it coincidence, then?

"Coincidence, heck!" I said to myself angrily. Everything pointed to one simple and unpleasant explanation, and I might as well face it. Jim Jenkins' spy system had failed completely. That expedition to the west had been a council of war with the Chief, against me, and neither Jenkins nor I had realized it.

But *why?* Why would Barbi do it?

"Elder Stevan." Shelton had more to report. "All gone from Buddy Hoey's house. No one there."

That clinched it. I said rapidly: "There may be a fight. The Chief hasn't surrounded the Village without a reason. Just the same, we shouldn't start sending arrows after the first of the Chief's men we see. If there is a fight, it will be because they start it."

"Yes, Elder Stevan."

"We aren't sure how many of the Folk will be with us. Do you have any idea, Jim Jenkins?"

Jenkins was conscious of his recent failure, and didn't offer a guess. Shelton said: "Twenty, more." That might mean almost anything; I wasn't sure how far Shelton could count.

For a long half-minute I sat desperately trying to think what to say next, realizing that I wasn't completely awake yet. "Tony Shelton, how many lookouts are there now?"

"Six."

"Good. Bring them all here to the Temple . . . no, send one of them to Marvic's house and houses near there, to wake the Folk. Jim Jenkins, you get the Folk in the rest of the Village. Have them bring bows and arrows."

"All come to the Temple?"

"Yes."

"But then the Chief—" Jenkins floundered, and Shelton took over. "Chief can take food, all things from the Village. We're at the Temple then we can't stop him."

"Yes—" But there was Barbi. Barbi was almost certainly among the attackers. Without knowing why, I was quite sure there would be a fight at the Temple," I repeated. "Go now, and, Jim Jenkins, take Tim Marvic with you."

"No Temple Guard?"

"No, don't leave any Temple Guard. You have to hurry."

So the three of them went: I watched their gray shirts flickering away into the darkness.

The instant I was left alone I realized guiltily that the

candles should never have been lighted. I put them out at once before returning to my chair. It was too late to do any good, of course. The enemy, if there was an enemy, would have seen the lights before now, and deduced that the Village was preparing.

If there was an enemy! What were Barbi's motives, after all? She had spoken earlier this same night about letting the Folk leave the Village as hunters. Maybe that was it. Maybe there would be no fight; Barbi would simply carry off a prearranged plan to smuggle Old Red's partisans off to the Chief's tribe, where they'd feel more at home.

But Barbi had also spoken of allowing the Folk to raid the Village. Sometimes her present sophistication made me forget that the first eighteen years of her life had been lived in near-savagery.

So, while the night slowly thinned outside the windows, I sat there, wide awake now, staring at the high ceiling, where the shadows still hung black as midnight. It was some time before it occurred to me that my life was in danger.

Immediate danger! I got to my feet with a start. I was alone here, and if the Temple should be attacked *now* I was defenseless.

No, not quite. With a surge of relief I remembered the rifles. There had been quite a number of the venerable weapons here in my grandfather's time. When the Folk had come and it became clear they could not be fought off, my grandfather had buried all the remaining ammunition, assuring the Folk there was none left and the rifles were useless. I knew where the ammunition was hidden, and the rifles were in the cabinet in the kitchen. I smiled gleefully to myself. Not many prewar battles had been won by secret weapons, but the battle coming up now might be.

As I was crossing the room to the kitchen door I heard footsteps outside. I hesitated. If these were not friends, nothing would help now. I reversed my steps, opened the front door. They were friends.

Tim Marvic, Jane Anderson, and about twenty others burst chaotically into the Temple, breathing hard from the haste of their coming. Then, as abruptly, their motion stopped and they stood bewildered in the darkness.

I gave rapid instructions. The windows of the Temple had to be boarded up, leaving only a narrow slit at the side of each, through which a bowman could fire. The job had to be done in darkness. The board ordinarily used for covering the windows in winter could be trimmed to size for the purpose; they were already fitted with dowel-holes. I would help the Folk match the shutters to the windows—quite a necessary job, in order that the dowel-holes come in alignment. I'd have given a lot for a hundred prewar nails!

So everyone fell to work. I said nothing about the hidden cartridges. They had been kept secret from the Folk for excellent reasons, and I didn't plan to use them as long as there was a chance of winning without them.

Shortly afterward, Tony Shelton and the lookouts arrived, and on their heels the group from the southern part of the Village. Where was Jenkins? Well, there was no time to worry about it. When the windows on the ground floor had been boarded up I stationed a line of bowmen at each slit, with instructions that in case of a charge on the Temple the first in line should loose an arrow quickly and drop out of the way of the second. I took the new arrivals upstairs to take care of barricading the windows there.

I was standing at a window on the west side of the Temple when Shelton whispered over my shoulder, "Look! Men leave Lavery's house. Two I saw."

"I missed it."

"On this side."

"Jenkins and the rest must have stayed there because they thought it was too dangerous to come on to the Temple. If you saw two leave, they're probably all leaving."

"Yes."

Then I saw the reason.

At first it was only one of the windows gleaming redly. It stared for a moment, as if the flames had been frozen in place. Then a stream of fire spilled out and poured up the roof of the house.

"They use fire," said Shelton quietly.

Between us and the blaze ran a silhouetted man with his stubby shadow. At this distance he was tiny; even in the firelight he'd have been invisible except that he moved. Astonishingly, he ran all the way across into darkness without falling. When he had passed, two more followed, then there were only the flames; it was as if there were no one left in the Village to care about the loss of the house. The fire unfolded out of the window and leisurely spread its orange palm over the roof.

"We'll be safe from that in the Temple," I said, "because we can keep watch on all four sides."

"Except—"

"Except that Jenkins' men may not make it here. Tony Shelton, you'd better take ten men out and hide in the corn at the bottom of the hill on this side of the Temple—to cover Jenkins when he comes."

Shelton left. Moments later, he and his men were scattered down the gray hillside, filtering between the gaunt tree trunks and unobtrusively as smoke. When one reached the edge of the corn, he would drop to the ground and disappear. Once there was a sudden commotion in the corn, over toward the right, and out of it erupted two men, locked together, struggling grimly. The fight was terrible, but brief. A third figure rose out of the ground beside them and grasped a head in both arms, savagely; at once all three figures dropped into the sea of corn and there was only the burning house off in the distance to remind my eyes of danger.

So some of the rebels *were* hiding around the Temple. Yet they hadn't attacked; perhaps they would when Jenkins got here.

I started downstairs. Before I'd reached the main room I heard a suppressed shout from the bowmen at the windows there. I hurried in.

"Men by the threshing floor, Elder Stevan," a woman said. "Running this way."

"The Chief's men?"

"Yes. Chase the Folk." She didn't sound too certain of this; I looked out. There were two groups. The more distant was running in a body; the nearer—now fairly close—was dispersed, zigzagging to avoid arrows from behind. Although the dawn was coming faster now, it was impossible to make out faces; still the woman's guess was obviously right.

The nearer group reached the cornfield. Now, I thought, they would be ambushed by the rebels hiding down there, and the killing would begin. I waited; and it didn't! The men raced up the rows of corn. There was an occasional, quickly-ended scuffle, and then Jenkins' and Shelton's men scampered up through the oak grove to the Temple.

As far as I knew, not a single arrow had left its bow. It had been too simple.

It had been too simple.

A crowd of the Folk stood in the center of the main room, bewildered, panting from their run. The lines of the bowmen at the windows fidgeted. No one knew what came next.

The Folk were a crowd of shadows against the timid grayness of the windows. I picked my way among them, searching their faces. Finally I found the Temple Guards, Shelton and Marvic, squatting in the pitch blackness under the stairs. Shelton had a dark bruise, five inches long and the width of a thumb, running from his ear down across his throat.

I crouched beside them, and they greeted me quietly. "How did you get the bruise, Tony Shelton?" I asked.

"Out there, when I first went into the corn. Man right near me, hiding: I stopped. He knew I saw him, so we fought." He gripped his bow more tightly.

"I saw it, but I didn't know it was you."

"Did you see the other's face?"

"No."

"Paul Pomroy. I think his neck's broke." Shelton and Marvic both looked me squarely in the face. Less than a year before Pomroy had been their best friend.

"Others will be killed, too," I said. "Too many. It is not good."

They relaxed. That was what they'd wanted to hear, though they wouldn't have said it themselves.

"All these people here," I said, "they must be ready to fight. When the Chief charges—"

"Yes," said Shelton, "but maybe the Chief doesn't charge. He can keep his men all around the Temple. We don't have food. He can wait to charge."

"That's true," I answered thoughtfully, appalled that I had never thought of a siege. "Do you think he'll do that?"

"Don't know."

I stood up, glanced out the nearest window. "It's getting lighter. If he does charge, he'll have to do it right away."

We waited, and the rest of the room waited.

Now and then the enemy would be sighted—always beyond bowshot, and always only a small group. One of the watchers at the windows would report the fact, calmly. Very calmly.

"It's getting pretty light outside for them to charge," I said. Then I thought: Why had the Chief not attacked earlier in the night? Why had Jenkins' men been allowed to reach the Temple? Why had the enemy's only offensive action been to force the Folk in Lavery's house to leave it for the Temple? Barbi was with the other side, I was sure, and while she'd have difficulty giving orders to the Chief and Old Red she might have got them to accept her plan. And Barbi would have thought of a siege.

There was only one answer.

"After you've fired," I said rapidly to the small group around me, "pull back this knob and flip it to the side. The next round—the next cartridge goes in here, and then you go through the same thing again." I handed the rifle to Shelton; he went through the procedure and passed the weapon on to the others. "Remember, you don't have to aim above your target; I've fixed the sights so you just look straight down them, the way I told you."

I left them to discuss it among themselves, and crossed to where the lone semiautomatic was lying. It was too bad we hadn't been able to clean the guns better after their long interment. Too bad the ammunition, which was supposed to be used within five years of manufacture, was going to be used after a hundred plus years, and too bad there were only four guns for which there was any ammunition at all. Too bad also that I was going to use the semiauto, which would have fared better by the stronger, sharper-eyed Shelton; but it was easier and quicker to do the job myself than to go through explaining another loading and firing procedure. I sighed, reread a page of the manual I'd been referring to, and slammed the book shut.

The riflemen followed me upstairs. We looked in turn from each of the attic windows, picking out the enemy in the fields around the hill—beyond range, they thought. It wasn't too far before sunrise now, and you could see them clearly. I recognized a few.

The four of us who were armed chose our targets and took up our stations, each of us with an attendant carrying ammunition. I had the south side, where targets were most numerous. Closest was a campfire, with five men beside it, apparently asleep. It lay in a cleared space in a wheat field. What they were burning I couldn't guess. For that matter, why had they started the campfire at all?

Farther from me two groups were sitting or squatting, staring this way; also I was quite sure Marvic's house was occupied, and not by friends.

"Ready!" I called. From the other rooms came acknowledging echoes. I reminded the bowmen to stand by too, then raised my rifle and yelled, "Go to it!" And fired.

The shock almost knocked me over. It can't have been only the kick. As much as that, it was the shattering noise. I took a step backward; my hearing cleared.

The others' shots were a slow, irregular crackling. I tried again. No, the kick wasn't so bad, but the gun was heavier than I'd realized. I got a chair, experimented till I found a comfortable position; then began in earnest.

In the directionless light of dawn, a group of men crouching in a lane between fields of wheat. Only their heads were visible to me; but their bodies, though hidden, were better targets. I aimed low. Two of the men had jumped up at the first shot, but I stuck to the stationary targets. I fired more rapidly, getting the feel of the weapon. My whole body shuddered in phase with the explosions. The sights seemed to be set wrong; I raised the barrel a little. Three of the targets fell. I shifted to the others, now running toward Marvic's house. Shock! Shock! against my shoulder. Got one of them.

As I inserted a new clip of ammunition the stock trembled against my hand, silence poured shouting into my ears. Raised the barrel again, blinked away the green dizziness.

Death, my brain reminded me. Blink that away, too. This wasn't killing. This was a contest against the weakness in my left forearm, the wrenching ache in all my ribs. Besides, *we had to win.*

Sweep the barrel to follow the running men, my elbow pivoting on the bruise on my knee. Rake the walls of Marvic's house. Shock! Shock! Viselike around my chest—

A figure darted from the house. Even as I sighted on it, I was suddenly filled with *joy*, the foreign irrelevant joy of remembering what came before the rifle and the shooting. The target was Barbi. I pulled the trigger— once, before I stopped myself.

I sat back then in a cool haze of relief; for now I had to stop shooting. The jolting agony could stop for a moment.

I didn't know whether I'd hit Barbi or not.

The voice was Shelton's: "You got many."

"Yes." I opened my eyes. "You through shooting?"

"Bruise here hurt too much." He fingered his throat carefully. "Jane Anderson took my place." He was behind me, peering over my shoulder through the window slit. "Look, Elder Stevan," he interjected now, "the men by the fire."

"I can't see, this powder smoke gets in my eyes— Oh! They're burning their arrows."

"Not burning—"

"No! They're lighting them, going to shoot them at the Temple." To send it the way of Lavery's house. The Temple! They couldn't get close enough to set a torch to it, so they were using burning arrows. The Chief had a secret weapon to match ours.

"Stop them—"

Before I had my aim the first of the arrows had left the bow. I dropped the archer immediately. The others knew better than to stand up as he had. They fired lying flat on their backs; not easy targets. The rifle jumped in my hands as I swung the sights in an arc around the campfire. Still the bowmen's needles drew the threads of scarlet flame across the sky, toward the Temple.

Shelton: "They hit! They hit!"

"What?"

"Arrow on the roof!"

Desperately, "How do you know?"

"I heard, right above us."

"Shelton, get . . . no, get water . . . get rugs, get many Folk to help."

"Rugs?"

Shock! Shock! And, "Yes, cover flames with them— dip rugs in water first—" but he was gone.

I had to stop to reload. I looked up at the bare boards of the slanting ceiling. No charred boards, no sign— yet. Had the arrow put itself out as it hit? The room might still be damp from the rain, mightn't it?

From the next room, "Fire! Look, there, fire!"

Before I knew it I had to run to the source of the shouting. But it was not what I'd feared. At one of the room's two windows Jane Anderson stood calmly, rifle raised. At the other was a cluster of Folk, jostling, staring out. "Elder Stevan, another campfire out there."

From which would come more of the deadly arrows.

The dizziness again. Back to my own window, into my chair. The dizziness again.

I look around me helplessly, and my eyes can't quite focus on the bright mouth that has opened in the ceiling over me. The slitted mouth of red and black, widening into a yellow grin.

The sound of my horror is a shrill screaming. Not from me. Maybe not from me. But a terribly screaming, like the powder smell which scalds my lungs.

Take aim again out the window. Can't make out— Why, that's not the campfire, that's the Temple burning. Of course not, it's the campfire. The screaming goes on. My finger keeps pressing the trigger, but I don't think about my aim. Nor about the Folk scrambling about behind me, beating at the flames. Nor about the flames themselves. I think about the screaming. It's shrill and loud, but it's distant. Sometimes there are words to it; can't make them out.

What is the voice saying!

This is important, I must know what it is saying, this terrified voice—of Barbi screaming.

Hands took the rifle from me and carried me through a wave of flames.

Before I opened my eyes I felt the grass under me and the warm sun on my face. That was strange, but it didn't matter because the voice wasn't screaming any more, it was quiet, and it was saying, "Stevan? Are you awake?"

"I'm awake."

"Good. I hope you're all right. We didn't know what was wrong with you. I have to talk to you, Stevan."

I intended to speak, but Barbi began at once on an account of the battle. Most of this I only half-heard, for it was at this point that I opened my eyes and discovered that I couldn't see.

I blinked hard and rolled my head to one side and the other, with very little effect. It must be hemorrhages in my retina, I thought, from the jolting that semiauto gave me; but even a sure explanation wouldn't have comforted me!

The unseen Barbi was still reciting her reckoning of the dead and wounded. I forced myself to listen. When she was done I said, on impulse: "So the Chief takes over. This is what you had in mind ever since you came here, isn't it?"

"What!"

"You've just been waiting your chance to let the Chief into the Village."

"No. You know me better than to think that. When I first came, maybe—but I can hardly remember the way I thought then. I don't think the same now. Know what I mean?"

"I suppose so. I'm sorry, Barbi." I sat up, and as I did so the blood drained from my head and I shouted: "I can see!"

"You can—?"

"When I first opened my eyes I was blind. I can see again now." I exulted in the sight of Barbi standing in the grass in front of me, her feet spread and her hands on her hips.

"That's not good," she said. "You'll have to take it easy for a couple of days till your eyes heal."

"You're not going to kill me, then."

"No, I think you still don't understand what's happened."

"Maybe not. What do you have to show for all this bloodshed? Shelton and Jenkins didn't like the idea of Pomroy's dying, and they won't forget easily."

Sitting down beside me, she plucked a blade of grass and put its stem in her mouth. "In the first place, let's admit that the Village was sure to be attacked, and defeated—maybe not for several generations, but eventually."

"Possibly."

"Certainly. The hunters, with the whole continent to expand into would multiply indefinitely. They'd have recruits from Old Red and his kind, who'd bring them any new weapons the farmers might have. That's one thing you refused to recognize—this had to happen."

"So you precipitated it, instead—"

"Now hold on. By having our . . . our barbarian invasion now, with me leading it, we get several advantages: The hunters come while there's only one weak tribe of them. Also, they come under leaders who know the value of the Village. They may loot, but they leave the Village standing, because they learn that the Village is good for leather, woven cloth, corn, and so forth. This way the Village can continue. The people here, and later in other settlements, will have the highest technology; the hunters may take the golden eggs, but they won't kill the goose. Civilization *will* be rebuilt, Stevan."

"Why didn't you discuss this with me?"

"I did, enough to know you'd never agree! Besides, you had to stop being God." She chewed on her stalk of grass. "I hope you don't think the Folk *liked* asking the Word of the Elder every time they turned around. Why do you think Paul Pomroy was on my side last night? Oh, you'd have had a revolt on your hands eventually, if the hunters didn't raze the Village first. Your 'Elder' religion wouldn't have fooled the Folk forever."

"I had to try to hang on, to save the books."

"Yes, yes! But what's happened was the only thing that *could* save the books. I didn't order those bowmen to set fire to the Temple, you know—"

"The screaming—"

"Oh, yes, before. I was shouting to the Chief's men to stop the fighting so we could put the fire out. It was close."

I looked up at the Temple. It was as if a great bite had been taken out of it; most of the top story was black and open to the sky. But the ground floor, where the books were, still stood.

"Yes," Barbi went on, "we have to keep the books; and the scholars. If the Elders had stayed set apart, learning might have died with the last of them. But now, we can try something else.

"You Elders studied history. You patterned your Village after what you read—a Neolithic town, with yourselves as Shamen; or a feudal manor, with yourselves as lords. Let's take another chapter in the history books. Remember? *In ancient Rome, the teachers were slaves.*"

She rose and stood facing me, smiling. "You see how perfect it is? Some people will always want to be scholars; it's an interesting and useful job. But the stigma attached to it will prevent the scholars from setting up an aristocracy, Elder-style, and that's the big danger in the weird situation the world's in now.

"I think all the 'humans' will be scholars, at first, because they're not good for anything else. And that fits, too. Why shouldn't they be slaves? Such weaklings! Obviously inferior." Again she smiled.

"The teachers are slaves—"

The mighty were fallen. I had lost my kingdom, I had lost my wife; I was a sick man, incurable; now I was a slave. But around me on all sides lay the farms, aswarm with Folk, the freed Folk, and before me Barbi stood strong and confident in the sunlight.

I looked down, tried to think. It was no use. I couldn't concentrate on what she'd said. Barbi had won, the thing was over with—what good did thinking do?

"You're right," I said, quietly. And wondered if she was.

EDITOR'S INTRODUCTION TO:

THE SONS OF MARTHA
Rudyard Kipling

There is more than one kind of aristocracy.

Luke tells the story: Mary and Martha, the sisters of Lazarus, were entertaining Jesus and his disciples. Martha rushed about the kitchen and household, seeing to the cooking, bringing wash basins, changing towels, and doing the other things needful when one's home has been unexpectedly invaded by a celebrity and his entourage.

"Now it came to pass, as they went, that he entered into a certain village: and a certain woman named Martha received him into her house.

"And she had a sister called Mary, which also sat at Jesus' feet, and heard his word.

"But Martha was cumbered about much serving, and came to him, and said, Lord, dost thou not care that my sister hath left me to serve alone? Bid her therefore that she help me.

"And Jesus answered and said unto her, Martha, Martha, thou are careful and troubled about many things:

"But one thing is needful: Mary hath chosen that

good part, which shall not be taken away from her."
(Luke 10:38-42)

Much has happened since then; but as Rudyard Kipling tells us, we sons of Martha have yet to pay the final reckoning.

THE SONS OF MARTHA
Rudyard Kipling
1907

The sons of Mary seldom bother, for they have inherited
that good part;
But the Sons of Martha favour their Mother of the
careful soul and the troubled heart.
And because she lost her temper once, and because she
was rude to the Lord her Guest,
Her Sons must wait upon Mary's Sons, world without
end, reprieve, or rest.
It is their care in all the ages to take the buffet and
cushion the shock.
It is their care that the gear engages; it is their care that
the switches lock.
It is their care that the wheels run truly; it is their care
to embark and entrain,
Tally, transport, and deliver duly the Sons of Mary by
land and main.

They say to mountains, "Be ye removed." They say to
the lesser floods, "Be dry."
Under their rods are the rocks reprovèd—they are not
afraid of that which is high.

Then do the hill-tops shake to the summit—then is the bed of the deep laid bare,

That the Sons of Mary may overcome it, pleasantly sleeping and unaware.

They finger death at their gloves' end where they piece and repiece the living wires.

He rears against the gates they tend: they feed him hungry behind their fires.

Early at dawn, ere men see clear, they stumble into his terrible stall,

And hale him forth a haltered steer, and goad and turn him till evenfall.

To these from birth is Belief forbidden; from these till death is Relief afar.

They are concerned with matters hidden—under the earthline their altars are—

The secret fountains to follow up, waters withdrawn to restore to the mouth,

And gather the floods as in a cup, and pour them again at a city's drouth.

They do not preach that their God will rouse them a little before the nuts work loose.

They do not teach that His Pity allows them to drop their job when they dam'-well choose.

As in the thronged and the lighted ways, so in the dark and the desert they stand,

Wary and watchful all their days that their brethren's days may be long in the land.

Raise ye the stone or cleave the wood to make a path more fair or flat—

Lo, it is black already with blood some Son of Martha spilled for that!

Not as a ladder from earth to Heaven, not as a witness to any creed,

But simple service simply given to his own kind in their common need.

And the Sons of Mary smile and are blessèd—they know the Angels are on their side.

They know in them is the Grace confessèd, and for
    them are the Mercies multiplied.
They sit at the Feet—they hear the Word—they see
    how truly the Promise runs.
They have cast their burden upon the Lord, and—the
    Lord He lays it on Martha's Sons!

EDITOR'S INTRODUCTION TO:

MAIL SUPREMACY
Hayford Peirce

You often hear that something needs no introduction.
This story is one such. It's just too obviously true.

MAIL SUPREMACY
Hayford Peirce

It all seems so inevitable, now that mankind is spreading out through the galaxy. The only question is: Why wasn't it done sooner? Why did the road to the stars have to wait until 1994 when an Anglo-Chinese merchant fell to musing over his correspondence? But perhaps all of mankind's greatest advances, from fire through the wheel from penicillin through hydrogen fusion, seem inevitable only in retrospect.

Who remembers the faceless thousands who unlocked the secret of nuclear energy, the man who dropped the first atomic bomb? Mankind remembered Einstein.

Who remembers the faceless thousands who built the first moonship, the man who first stepped upon an alien world? Mankind remembered Verne and Ley and Campbell.

As mankind remembers Chap Foey Rider.

Chap Foey Rider's main offices were in New York, not far from Grand Central Station. From them he directed an import-export firm that blanketed the globe. On November 8, 1994, a Friday, his secretary brought him the day's mail. It was 11:34 in the morning.

Chap Foey Rider frowned. Nearly noon, and only now was the mail delivered. How many years had it been since there had been two deliveries a day, morning and afternoon? At least twenty-five. Where was the much-vaunted progress of the age of technology?

He remembered his childhood in London, long before the war, when there had been *three* daily deliveries. When his father would post a letter in the morning, asking an associate to tea, and receive a written reply before tea-time. It was enough to make a bloke shake his head.

Chap Foey Rider shook his head and picked up his mail.

There was a bill of lading from his warehouse in Brooklyn, seven miles away. Mailed eight days ago.

There was a portfolio print-out from his investment counselor in Boston, 188 miles away. Mailed seven days ago.

There was an inquiry from his customs broker in Los Angeles, 2,451 miles away. Mailed four days ago.

There was a price list from a pearl merchant in Papeete, Tahiti, 6,447 miles away. Mailed three days ago.

Chap Foey Rider reached for his calculator.

He then called his branch manger in Honolulu. He told him to mail a letter to the branch manager in Capetown, 11,535 miles away.

The Capetown manager called Chap Foey Rider two days later to advise him that the letter from Honolulu had arrived. Although still Sunday in New York, it was early Monday morning in Capetown.

Chap Foley Rider pondered. The length of the equator was 24,901.55 miles. No spot on Earth could be farther than 12,450.78 miles from any other.

He reached for the World Almanac.

Bangkok was 12,244 miles from Lima. He smiled. He had offices in each city.

A letter from Bangkok reached Lima in a single day.

Chap Foey Rider returned to his calculator.

The extrapolation was staggering.

One further test was required to prove his theory. He pursed his lips, then carefully addressed an envelope: *Occupant, 614 Starshine Boulevard, Alpha Centauri IV.* He looked at his watch: good, the post office was open for another hour. He personally pushed the envelope through the Out-of-Town slot and strolled home.

Returning to his office the next morning, he found in his stack of mail the envelope addressed to Alpha Centauri. Frowning, he picked it up. Stamped across the front in purple ink were the words: *Addressee Unknown, Returned to Sender.*

Chap Foey Rider lighted his first cigarette of the day and to conceal his discontent puffed perfect rings toward the ceiling. Was the test actually conclusive? True, the envelope had been returned. But with suspicious speed. He reviewed his chain of logic, then studied the envelope with a magnifying glass. There was, after all, nothing to indicate *which* post office had stamped it.

He ground the cigarette out and reached for a piece of paper. He wrote firmly, without hesitation:

The Rgt. Hon. Chairman
of the Supreme Galactic Council
Sagittarius

Sir: I feel I must draw to your attention certain shortcomings in your General Post Office system. Only yesterday I mailed a letter . . .

Chap Foey Rider awaited the morning's delivery. Eventually it arrived.

There was an envelope-sized piece of thick creamy parchment, folded neatly and held together by a complex red seal. His name appeared on one side, apparently engraved in golden ink.

Expressionless, he broke the seal, unfolded the parchment, and read the contents. It was from the Executive Secretary, Office of the Mandator of the Galactic Confederation:

Dear Sir: In reply to yours of the 14th inst. the Mandator begs me to inform you that as per your speculation the Galactic Confederation does indeed exist as primarily a Postal Union, its purpose being to promote Trade and Commerce between its 27,000 members. Any civilization is invited to join our Confedera-

tion, *the sole qualification of membership being the independent discovery of our faster-than-light Postal Union. His Excellency is pleased to note that you, on behalf of your fellow Terrans, have at long last fulfilled the necessary conditions, and in consequence, as Ambassador-Plenipotentiary from the Galactic Confederation will be arriving on Terra within the next two days. Please accept, Mr. Rider, on behalf of the Mandator, the expression of his most distinguished sentiments.*

". . . to promote Trade and Commerce . . ."

Chap Foey Rider restrained himself from rubbing his hands together in glee. Instead he pushed a buzzer to summon his four sons to conference. The stars were coming to mankind, Rider Factoring, Ltd. would be ready for them; he called the mailroom to tell them to be on the alert for a large package from Sagittarius.

EDITOR'S INTRODUCTION TO:

HERBIG-HARO
Harry Turtledove

Science has a unity about it: invent one branch of technology, and you'll probably discover others. Burke's delightful *Connections* makes that clear. Still, it's not invariable. Technology without science can be sterile. Archeologists tell us that batteries and electroplating were invented in the Levant several thousand years ago; and a very modern-looking calculating machine was found in a ship that went down off the island of Antikythera in Greco-Roman times. Heiro made a working model of a steam engine, and Archimedes did surprising things with winches, levers, and burning glasses. None of this led to anything important.

Harry Turtledove has a doctorate in Byzantine history. There being little formal demand for that skill, he works as an administrator in the Los Angeles County Department of Education— where a knowledge of matters byzantine comes in rather handy at that. One of his duties is to assist teachers in coping with Federal regulations.

John W. Campbell would have loved Turtledove, who has the knack of combining new science with old forms.

HERBIG-HARO
Harry Turtledove

Like all the ships Loki flew, Erasmus Chang's scout *Praise of Folly* was too old. She went into or out of hyperdrive with a jolt that twisted a man's guts, her air recycler wheezed, and she had a 5% waver in her pseudogravity, so Chang's weight went through a seven-kilo cycle every twenty minutes.

The computer was old, too. In a way, that was an advantage: the navigation data programmed in were Terran Confederacy, the most far-reaching set even if it was six hundred years out of date. But after enough time, memory dumps or no, a computer will develop a personality of its own—the current flows get set. Chang did not trust his machine very far. It was as cynically underhanded as he was.

"Well, hero, they're still gaining," it said with what he thought was misplaced amusement.

"I can see that for myself, thanks," he growled. He paced up and down the cabin, a lean, trim man a bit below middle height whose wide, high-cheek-boned face was framed by a thin fringe of black beard.

Pace as he would, though, his eyes kept coming back

to the hyperdrive detector. There was little enough else
to see; with the drive on, none of the normal-space
instruments worked. The four glowing points in the
detector display were Zanat warships. One he might
have challenged. Taking on four was sure suicide, and
he could not afford it. Loki and all the worlds in human
space needed to know about the Zanat.

Unfortunately, they would overtake him long before
he could deliver the news—long before he got out of
the Orion Nebula, for that matter.

He punched for a sandwich, ate it. When he looked
at the FTL display again, the four warships had slid a
little closer.

"I wish I'd chosen a different bar," he said.

"You aren't the only one," the computer told him.

As soon as the shavetail lieutenant had stepped into
the London Pub, Chang knew his leave was doomed.
The youngster was in uniform, which meant he was on
duty, and Chang was the only Service man in the dive.
Just my luck, he thought sourly: run a successful mission and not get the chance to celebrate.

The load of books, cassettes, and floppies he'd snaked
out of the cathedral on Cienfuegos deserved celebrating, too. Old floppies especially were more precious
than gold. Even the Cienfuegans remembered that much;
they'd mounted the discs above the altar, by the statues
of their gods.

The scout pilot was still fuming when the lieutenant
brought him back to Salvage Service Central. B'kila
thought it was very funny. "Where did he find you?
The London Pub or Nadia's?"

"The London Pub," Chang sighed. That his habits
were known did not surprise him; he would have been
surprised had it been otherwise.

B'kila looked him over, cocked a critical eyebrow.
"That's not much of a beard, either."

The scout pilot put a defensive hand to his chin. He
had grown the whiskers on Cienfuegos, to make himself
less conspicuous there, and was proud of them. In spite
of his name, he had enough caucasoid genes to let him

raise a fair crop. "The day you start telling me how to wear my hair, you old harridan, is the day I get out of the Service."

B'kila laughed out loud, a bad sign; things that amused her generally meant trouble for other people. She was a plump black woman with straight, graying hair, the head of what was euphemistically known as the Loki Salvage Service. Loki's few friends called the Service a band of scavengers. Everyone else started with names like pirates, thieves, spies, and went downhill from there.

Having wasted enough time on pointless chatter, B'kila waved Chang to a chair by the big holo tank that took up most of one wall. He sat with the same feeling he had whenever he was in her office—that of being in the center of a spiderweb, watching the spider at work. Being on the same side helped only a little.

"What's gone wrong?" he asked bluntly, sure she would not have recalled him without pressing reason. Operatives got their chance to roister between missions.

She punched a button on her desk. The holo tank sprang to life with a view of that small chunk of the galaxy humans had touched. Stars with planets that were thought from any source, however ancient, to have been settled by men were shown in blue; those about which Loki actually knew something flashed on and off. Red marked the suns of nonhuman species that used the hyperdrive, yellow those of planetbound races. Most others were omitted; the white points here and there were stars with absolute magnitudes bright enough to make them useful nav checks over many light years.

She moved a vernier, touched another control. One of the winking blue points flared brighter for a moment. "Cienfuegos," she said unnecessarily. "I've listened to your report. A good run."

"Thanks." He waited. The compliment was another danger signal. Anything she had to get around to by easy stages was bound to be dicey—not for her, of course. For him.

His suspicion was confirmed when four brilliant orange points sprang to life beyond the glowing mist of the Orion Nebula, which dimmed to show their location more clearly. She said, "As well as I can judge, those spots mark where we've lost ships in the past two years."

"That's impossible," Chang blurted. "There are no human worlds out there." Loki itself was two hundred light-years Terraward from the Nebula, and hardly any blue points lay between it and the great cloud of gas.

"Impossible is not a word used to describe what's already happened," B'kila said in mild reproof, as though to a student who should do better.

"But—" Chang's protest died unspoken. B'kila knew the obvious as well as he. Starships in hyperdrive flew blind, of course; there was always the chance of returning to normal space coincident with solid matter. It was a very long one, though. Aliens might have worked up a trick good enough to snare one ship, he thought, but hardly four, not with the technological lead humans had—and especially humans from a planet like Loki, which still kept most of the skills of the dead Confederacy. That left . . . nothing he could see.

B'kila spoke with seeming irrelevance: "Do you know 'The Road Not Taken,' a poem by a Middle English writer named Frost?"

"Never heard of it."

"You might look up a modern translation when you leave. This Frost person could have been looking a hundred years into his own future."

The galactic map disappeared from the holo tank. A scratchy flat image replaced it: a crowded city scene, with swarms of humans in strange clothes, both civilian and military, milling about at a cautious distance from a starship of a make Chang did not recognize: a pretty crude one, he thought.

"This is Los Angeles—the first Roxolani landing on Terra; it might just as well be Cairo, New York, Moscow, Shanghai, or twenty others. A.D. 2039," B'kila said softly. Seeing that the archaic date meant nothing to Chang, she added, "45 pre-Confederacy."

He whistled. No wonder the video was scratchy—it

was over twelve hundred years old. He wondered how many times it had been rerecorded.

In the picture, the ship's ramp was lowering. "You can imagine the Terrans' anxiety," B'kila said dryly. "They'd been radioing the Roxolani since the fleet came out of the hyperdrive in the solar system." Chang nodded. Naturally, they had gotten no reply.

Out came the Roxolani, a platoon of stout, furry humanoids in high-crowned helmets and steel corselets. They moved with the precision of veteran troups, shaking themselves into a skirmish line. At a shouted command from an officer wearing scarlet ribbons on his arm and fancy plumes, they raised their weapons to their shoulders and fired into the Terrans.

Chang heard the ancient screams. Undoubtedly the man holding the video set ducked for his life, for the picture jerked and twisted, but the scout pilot saw the clouds of black-powder smoke float into the sky.

The Terran soldiers around the star-ship returned fire automatically, opening up with small arms, rocket and grenade launchers, and recoilless shells from the armored fighting vehicle that had somehow squeezed into position close by.

When the video straightened, the starship was holed and all but two of the aliens down. The survivors gaped at their fallen comrades. Neither had made the slightest move to reload his musket. Reading nonhumans' body language was always tricky, but Chang knew stunned horror when he saw it.

" 'The Road Not Taken,' " B'kila murmured. "Back then, on Terra, they *knew* FTL travel was impossible forever. It was a rude shock when they found that a couple of simple experiments could have given them the key to contragrav and the hyperdrive three, four, even five centuries earlier."

"How *did* they miss them?" Chang asked.

"No idea—in hindsight they're obvious enough. What's that race that flew bronze ships because they couldn't smelt iron? And every species we know that reached what the old Terrans would have called a seventeenth-century technological level did what was needed—except us.

"But trying to explain contragrav and the hyperdrive skews an unsophisticated, developing physics out of shape. With attention focused on them, too, work on other things, like electricity and atomics, never gets started. And those have much broader applications—the others are only really good for moving things from here to there in a hurry."

With a chuckle, Chang said, "We must have seemed like angry gods when we finally got the hyperdrive and burst off Terra. Radar, radio, computers, fission and fusion—no wonder we spent the next two hundred years conquering."

"No wonder at all," B'kila agreed soberly. "But the Confederacy grew too fast and got too big to administer, even with all the technology we had. And unity didn't last forever. None of our neighbors could hurt us, but we did a fine job on ourselves. Someone back then wrote that it was only sporting for humans to fight humans; no one else gave any competition."

"And so, the Collapse," Chang said.

"And here we are, on Loki and a few other worlds, picking over the pieces, a scrap from here, fragment from there, and one day we'll have the puzzle together again—or maybe a new shape, better than the one before . . . if we get the time. But those four missing ships frighten me."

That was a word Chang had never heard her use before. "I still don't see how they disappeared. There's no one out there."

"No one we know of," B'kila corrected. "But I keep thinking that a road traveled once might be traveled twice." As he took her meaning, Chang felt the little hairs at the nape of his neck trying to stand up. She finished low and fierce. "Find out what happened. *And come back.*"

"Any other little favors you'd like?" *Praise of Folly*'s computer had demanded when Chang described the mission. "Shall we write the suicide note, too? I won't go, I tell you—I'd end up in the scrapper there just as much as you."

"Shall I shift into override mode?" Chang snapped, in no mood for backtalk.

"No, don't," the computer said with poor grace. "It always leaves me slow and stupid for a couple of days afterwards."

Surly was a better word, the scout pilot thought, but held his peace. The takeoff was as smooth as takeoffs under contragrav always were, the shift into hyperdrive as brutal as the others *Praise of Folly* had been making lately. Chang staggered into the head and threw up. When he came out, he asked plaintively. "Isn't there any way to smooth that out?"

"Of course," the computer said. "Get me the parts and—"

Chang grunted. Loki's own yards turned out decent craft, but some techniques of precision manufacture had yet to be rediscovered. If one of the old Confederacy ships went wrong, repairs weren't likely to do much good.

Despite *Praise of Folly*'s tape library, travel under hyperdrive was dull. The computer played chess at a setting that let Chang win about half the time, until one day he escaped from a trap it thought he shouldn't have seen. Then it trounced him six times running, adding insult to injury by moving the instant he took his finger off a piece. After that it seemed satisfied, and went back to a level mere mortals could match.

From time to time other ships showed on the detector. Most of them never sensed *Praise of Folly*; Confederacy instrumentation handily outranged non-human or post-Collapse gear. Once, though, two vessels made a chase of it. "Damned pirates," Chang growled, and outran them.

He approached his planned emergence-point obliquely, not wanting any observers to track his course back to Loki. The jolt on leaving hyperdrive was not as bad as the one entering it—quite.

"Now what?" the computer said.

The viewscreen showed a totally unfamiliar configuration of stars. Even the Orion Nebula was not as Chang knew it, for he was seeing the side opposite the one it presented to human space. He shrugged. "Make for the nearest main-sequence G or K," he said, and gagged as *Praise of Folly* returned to hyperdrive.

The first yellow-orange sun proved without habitable planets. So did the second and third. A lean region, Chang thought. He was on his way to the fourth when the detector picked up the alien squadron.

Excitement and alarm coursed through him. From the brilliance of the blips on the screen, those were sizable ships. They were making good speed, too, far better than most of the nonhuman craft he knew. He held his course and waited to be noticed.

In short order he was; the strangers had sensitive detectors. Three vessels peeled off from the main group toward him. He took no evasive action; he was looking for contact. "Fool that I am," he said to no one in particular.

The lead ship's drive field touched his; they were both thrown back into normal space. Gulping, Chang wondered whether the aliens were subject to nausea.

The two ships emerged on divergent vectors several thousand kilometers apart. That would have been enough to make it impossible for most of the aliens the scout pilot knew to find him in the vastness of space, but the stranger swiftly altered course and came after him.

"I'm picking up radar," the computer reported.

"Wonderful," Chang said morosely. As usual, B'kila had been right.

The other two ships must have slaved their engines to their detector screens, for they returned to normal space at the same instant as their comrade and *Praise of Folly*. Chang's radar soon found them. They closed rapidly.

"Radio traffic," the computer said. The whistles and growls that came out of the speaker sprang from no human throat.

"Let's give them something to think about." Chang recorded his name and the name of his ship. "Squirt that out on their frequency."

There were several seconds of absolute silence, then a burst of alien noise that sounded much more excited than the previous signals. Chang wondered if the nonhumans had learned English or Low Mandarin from any of the earlier pilots. If so, they were not letting on. The incomprehensible babble continued.

Then alarms hooted and the computer was shouting, "Missile away!" A moment later it reported, "Contragrav job, fairly good velocity, but a clean miss—trajectory far ahead of us."

"Just the one launch?" the scout pilot asked tensely.

"So far." *Praise of Folly* was a confirmed pessimist.

"Might be a shot across our—" A new star bloomed in the forward screen, a supernova burst that went from white through yellow and orange to red and slowly guttered out.

"Fission explosion," the computer said matter-of-factly. "Thirty kilotonne range."

Chang held his head in his hands. Not just electronics, then: the aliens had a grasp of nuclear physics, too. He could not imagine anything worse.

"It lit up these," *Praise of Folly* said. Another screen came on, its images grainy with high magnification. The scout pilot did not recognize the craft displayed, but he knew warships when he saw them. They bristled with launchers and also sported two turrets each: quick-fire guns for close-in work, he guessed.

He weighted his options. Even winning a standup fight would not give him enough information to make B'kila happy. Meekly stopping, though, stuck in his craw. "They may as well be as worried as I am," he decided. "Give the lead ship a peewee at about the same distance they put theirs—but throttle down the missile so theirs seems to out-perform it." He did not intend to show all his cards.

Atomic fire blossomed again, unmistakably brilliant. The gabble of alien noise rose to a roar. Then abrupt silence fell; it must have occurred to one of the nonhumans that Chang might somehow know their language. Cat and mouse, he thought, with neither side sure which was which.

The three alien ships approached one another, though not so close that a single blast could take out more than one. Boats flitted back and forth: a meeting, no doubt. Glad he was a loner, Chang went to sleep. In case of serious attack, the computer would have to defend *Praise of Folly* anyway.

The computer woke him a couple of hours later to report that one of the aliens had gone into hyperdrive. "Which one?" he asked. The smallest of the three appeared onscreen for a moment.

A boat left one of the remaining aliens and moved slowly toward *Praise of Folly*. Unlike its parent craft, it blazed with lights: the equivalent of a flag of truce? Chang could not afford to be trusting. "If it comes inside 2000 kilometers, fire another warning shot," he said. "Chemical explosion this time, not nuclear."

But the boat stopped at more than twice that distance. It retreated to its own ship, leaving behind a small metal canister made conspicuous by a floodlight and radar beacon. "Playing it very cozy, aren't they?" Chang said.

"Probably booby-trapped."

"Probably," he agreed. "Shall we find out? Send the probe over for a look."

The little robot sped toward the canister. The scout pilot wondered what the nonhumans would make of it. It would tell them something of the technology he had, but he hoped to learn more about theirs.

The light on the canister was incandescent, not a plasma tube; the battery pack that powered it was larger than the Terran equivalent. The canister itself looked suspiciously like a wastebasket. A foil cover had been taped across the top; the paper tape was already beginning to come loose as its adhesive dried in vacuum.

At Chang's direction, the probe peeled back the foil. Nothing untoward happened. The camera pickup showed that inside the canister there were only two rectangular sheets of thick, parchment-like paper, one perfect, the other with a ragged edge, as if it had been torn from a book.

The book page had a line of incomprehensible script,

but a black-and-white print took up most of the surface: an irregular pattern of lines and spaces. The scout pilot was used to seeing them in color, but he recognized it at once. "Spectrogram!" He had an inspiration. "Match it against the sun their fleet was heading for."

After a few seconds, the computer said, "It checks." Chang fancied that he heard a note of puzzled respect in the electronic voice. He hid a smile. The computer was smarter than he was, but it did not make intuitive leaps.

The other sheet proved that the aliens were used to contacting other races. A series of skillful cartoons instructed Chang to go into hyperdrive between the two nonhuman ships and let them pace him to the star. They also warned that he would be attacked if he dropped into normal space on his own; he was to let one of the aliens bring him back by cutting across his drive field.

"Sensible enough precautions," he said. "They'll have scrambled every warship in that system to look out for me as I emerge, too. I would, in their shoes."

For *Praise of Folly*, the jump into hyperdrive was smooth. Chang's escorts hovered close, just far enough away to let their fields operate. To his regret, they kept up when he increased speed. Though the rest of their skills seemed a bit behind those of the Terrans, their hyperdrive systems were first-rate.

Shortly before he expected to return to normal space, the scout pilot gritted his teeth and injected himself with several cc's of memory-RNA. For the next ten days to two weeks he would have nearly total recall—and a raging headache.

Like Terrans, the aliens preferred to emerge well away from a system's ecliptic plane, to minimize the risk of encountering sky junk. Chang listened torpidly as radio traffic crackled back and forth between his escort and the ships that, as he had guessed, were standing by awaiting his arrival.

Several formed up in a globe around him. Another message canister showed him that he was to stay in the center of the formation as they approached the system's second planet. "If it weren't for the honor of the thing,

I'd rather walk," he grumbled; reading Frost had gotten him interested in other ancient authors.

The lead ship in the escorting array slowed until it was only a couple of kilometers ahead of *Praise of Folly* and began flashing its lights on and off. After a minute or so, the scout pilot understood. "Folly, if you will."

"So it is," the computer said, but went after the alien in spite of his slip of the tongue.

Spaceports on civilized worlds have a depressing sameness; it is next to impossible to make vast expanses of concrete interesting. The perimeter buildings, though, caught Chang's eye when *Praise of Folly* dipped below the last cloudback; they had the massive look of fortifications.

Atmospheric flyers screamed overhead as *Praise of Folly* touched down near the center of the field. Gun-carrying armored vehicles that reminded Chang of the ones he had seen in B'kila's ancient tape rumbled toward the ship.

There were also footsoldiers running across the concrete. Chang turned up the magnification on his vision screen. The aliens were fairly humanoid, taller and thinner than Terrans, with knees that bent in the opposite direction. They had narrow, foxlike faces, long jaws, and blunt carnivore teeth. Thick reddish-yellow hair covered most of their bodies; they went nude except for boots, belts with bulging pouches, and helmets.

Their hand-weapons gave the scout pilot a momentary start. The guns' curved magazines reminded him of the Kalashnikovs that were still ubiquitous in human space. He quickly saw, though, that it was only coincidence; the rest of the design was not similar at all.

He checked the atmosphere analysis. The air seemed good enough, barring some noxious oxides of nitrogen and sulfides that probably came for the noisy, smoke-belching iron monsters out there. He didn't worry about diseases. Few alien germs found humans tasty, and his broad-spectrum immunity shots left him doubly safe.

After instructing the computer, he strapped on a sidearm and cycled through the airlock. The pistol meant nothing as a weapon against the fire-power out there, but no race with an organized military could fail to grasp what it represented.

The worst moment came as the outer airlock door swung open. If one of the aliens panicked or got trigger-happy, B'kila would have five missing scouts to brief the next pilot about.

Some of the aliens yelled when Chang came into sight. "Officers, it would appear," the computer said into a receiver implanted behind his ear. "Notice the stripes on their helmets." Seeing one of them knock a soldier's gun aside, Chang tentatively identified his first phrase in the alien language: "Hold your fire!"

For a moment he thought his weight was shifting, then realized it was the opposite: like a seaman rolling on land, he had become so used to *Praise of Folly's* pulsing generator that steady gravity felt odd.

After the ship's mechanically pure air, the unidentifiable spicy smells of growing things hit him like wine. He did not even mind the diesel stink mixed with them, though it made him cough.

He paced off a circle of about ten meters around *Praise of Folly*, made pushing motions to show that the troopers should keep their distance. When a squad arrogantly strode inside his perimeter, *Praise of Folly* let go with an ear-splitting siren screech. Machine guns swiveled to bear on the aliens. They scrambled back.

Chang smiled to himself. It would not hurt to have the aliens think the ship still manned. In a way, it was.

One of the nonhumans stepped out of a small group and came forward, ostentatiously stopping at the boundary line Chang had set. The scout pilot caught his musky body odor; who could say what he smelled like to the other?

The alien—an officer of some rank, by the five stripes on his helmet—pointed to himself and said, "Zan." He pointed at one of the soldiers behind him. "Zan." Another. "Zan." A wave that encompassed a dozen or more. "Zanat."

The language lesson went from there. Chang soon decided that the Zanat officer was a trained contact specialist. He went about his business with a calm competence that implied he had undertaken such tasks many times before. Skillfully he gave Chang both vocabulary and grammatical structure. The latter made the scout pilot want to groan, for the Zanat language was highly synthetic. Chang wished for the simpler analytic structure of low Mandarin or English, but he had been on enough worlds that spoke Russian-based tongues to cope. And what he learned, he did not forget.

The contact officer's name was Liosh; that, at least, was as close as Chang could come to it. His own name sounded like "Razmuzjang" in the other's mouth. Liosh undid his belt, tugged off his boots, put his helmet on the tarmac. When completely naked, he pointed to himself, then to *Praise of Folly*'s entry ladder. His mobile ears twitched in what Chang had already come to recognize as the equivalent of a raised eyebrow. "Go there?"

"No." The scout pilot could not make his refusal polite.

Liosh gave a very human shrug. He pointed to one of the blocky structures several hundred meters away. "Go there, then?"

The scout pilot decided to risk it. He had several days' worth of food concentrates in the knapsack on his back, as well as vitamins to supplement alien food and reagents to test for the more common sorts of indigestible proteins and lipids. If the Zanat intended killing him, they had easier ways than poisoning.

He spoke into his handset, telling *Praise of Folly* what he was about and adding, "If I'm lost, get the data home if you can: override command. And another override: destroy yourself to avoid capture."

"Acknowledged," the computer said sulkily, speaking, as Chang had ordered, through both the receiver behind his ear and the handset. He wanted to make sure Liosh understood what that was; the Zanat model was a back-carried unit bigger than his knapsack, and looked to be much heavier.

Liosh, he suspected, was smart enough to draw his own conclusions from that.

After several tries, he conveyed to the Zanat that hell would break loose if he was not allowed to communicate with his ship regularly, or if they tried to seize it while he was gone. Liosh agreed so promptly that Chang was sure the aliens would take their chances when the time came. He shrugged; he had known that already.

Troopers fell in around him and Liosh as they walked toward the port building. When they were nearly there, Chang heard a spatter of small-arms fire: single shots, followed by the harsh *tac-tac-tac* of automatic weapons.

He whirled, but the gunshots had nothing to do with *Praise of Folly*. In fact, several of the armored vehicles were rumbling away from his ship toward the far edge of the spaceport. "What's going on there?" he asked the computer.

"Fighting." Sophisticated as it was, *Praise of Folly* could be annoyingly literal, especially just after an override command. A moment later, though, it added some worthwhile information: "The attackers stay well hidden, but do not seem to be Zanat."

"Interesting," Chang said. He turned to Liosh, used the only interrogative he had. "What?"

The contact officer spread his four-fingered hands in a gesture many races used. "Slayor," he said. "People of the world." He approached that several ways, until he saw that Chang understood. He did not have a high opinion of the Slayor. Pointing at a starship: "Slayor—no." At a fighting vehicle: "Slayor—no."

Local barbarians, the scout pilot translated mentally. Which meant that this is not the Zanat homeworld. He had not really thought it was, but the implications jarred him all the same. The Zanat were plainly here as conquerors, not traders—which argued for an expansive, unified imperialism such as the dead Confederacy had known.

And if they found fragmented humanity unprepared . . . Their technology was not up to the best Terran standards, but not much in human space was either, any more. Chang wanted to run and hide.

Instead he followed Liosh into the port building. The door closed behind them with a thud that told of metal reinforcement. Liosh led him up a couple of flights of stairs and through a tangled set of corridors to a suite of rooms from which troopers were hauling desks, cabinets, and other office furniture. Others were standing by with gear that looked as though it had come from their barracks: a big metal footlocker, a table, a cot amazingly like Loki standard issue, and several peculiar free-standing contraptions that puzzled Chang until he realized they had to be what a race with back-acting knees used for chairs.

Liosh pointed at the gear and the rooms. "Yours," he said. Chang nodded, a gesture with which the Zan was already familiar. The scout pilot noted that, as befit a fortress, the windows were mere firing slits. Nor was he surprised to discover a guard-squad outside his door. He had been a prisoner ever since his ship emerged in this system.

He gained fluency in the Zanat language with a speed that won Liosh's respect. The alien contact officer pushed hard; he did not have the advantage of an artificially unfailing memory, but he owned a good one, and the Zanat seemed to need only about half as much sleep as Terrans. He found Chang's dormancy amusing.

The scout pilot came to like him, not least because he did not take himself too seriously. For all that, the Zan was a clever interrogator, adept at sliding smoothly from one subject to the next. One secret, though, he did not penetrate: the scout pilot was careful always to speak of the Confederacy in the present tense. He was so perfectly consistent that Liosh never thought to doubt him.

Still, it was not an easy time. Liosh extracted a good deal of information, and yielded little in return. Chang started seeing those probing golden eyes, started hearing that guttural voice in his sleep.

He dreamed they were trying to talk during a storm. Thunder boomed; lightning seared the sky. When he woke, for a long moment he was unsure he had. The night was pitch-black, but lurid flashes of light came stabbing into his chamber. The crashes that tore the air were louder and more continuous than those from any tempest.

He heard shouts through the turmoil: the harsh yells of the Zanat and different cries, high thin wails that rose and fell in weird ululation. The wails grew ever louder and ever closer.

The Zanat had not bothered to disarm him. He belted on his pistol, dashed to the window and looked out. Carbon arc lamps on tall poles spread a hellish blue glare over the spaceport tarmac; the shadows of the figures dashing across it were black and sharp as if cut from dies. Most moved with a sinuous grace the Zanat did not possess.

A machine gun chattered from a gun-pit, spitting flame. Running shapes toppled, one after another. A couple, Chang thought, were Zanat. Then the gun stopped—a jammed cartridge? A broken firing pin? The scout pilot had no way of knowing. Some of the graceful runners leaped into the pit. The machine gun stayed silent.

Crump! From the great cloud of smoke that shot up, it was a black-powder explosion, primitive but effective. An arc-light support tottered, swayed, fell with a heavy boom. A moment later another lamp was taken out, and a quarter of the field plunged into twilight.

The Slayor yowled in triumph. Not all of them toted only their native arms. A burst of half a dozen bullets thudded into the wall near Chang's window. He hurriedly pulled away. That had to be a captured gun.

Another explosion was followed by the iron clang of a starship smashing against concrete. Chang's gut clenched with fear. If *Praise of Folly* went down under the locals' attack, he was marooned as inevitably as if the Zanat smote her with a nuclear warhead.

The Zanat inside the spaceport buildings had not been taken entirely by surprise. The sentries were alert, and the species as a whole was not so sunk in sleep of nights as Terrans would have been. Alarms yammered. There were shouted orders in the next room, a tinkle of glass as a window was broken out, and a rattle of rifle fire. "That got a couple of the motherless *fargs!*" a trooper shouted.

But the Slayor must have been building their attack in secret for months, maybe years. They were throwing everything they had at the hated invaders from the stars. Somehow they had even hauled one of their clumsy fieldpieces to the edge of the spaceport to oppose Zanat artillery. Back at his window, Chang saw the muzzleflash and belch of smoke. A solid shot smacked into the building.

The Zanat, though, had built to withstand a lot of that kind of pounding. And when the natives tried to force the stout door through which Chang had entered, they were bloodily repulsed. The Zanat raked their retreat with fire. The scout pilot thought the assault had been wrecked.

But it was only a diversion, to draw the enemy's attention while a squad of Slayor set a charge against the far side of the port building, lit a fuse, and fled.

The blast hurled Chang from his feet. He rolled into a tight protective ball. The floor lurched beneath him. The noise was stunning, a blow at the ears.

He staggered upright, dazed, half-deafened. Faintly, as if through roaring water, he heard injured Zanat screaming. The air was thick with the smell of smoke and blood. There were other screams too, of wild excitement. The Slayor were in the building.

The door burst open. Only wan auxiliary lights burned in the hallway, but they sufficed to show Liosh and a pair of soldiers with rifles. The contact officer was limping; someone had slapped a rough bandage on his lower leg.

"Come on!" Liosh barked at the scout pilot. "We'll get you away. We may not hold here, and you're too precious to leave for the savages to butcher."

Chang agreed with that, though for reasons very different from the Zan's. Yet being taken from the neighborhood of *Praise to Folly* was the last thing he wanted. When he hesitated, one of Liosh's troopers hefted his gun menacingly. He yielded.

Liosh made no concessions to his wound as he hurried through the maze of corridors, picking his way over rubble and corpses. Chang saw his first Slayor, dead, a slim, gray, hairless being still clutching a large musket. Neat bulletholes stitched its chest; the exit wounds chewed its back to red ghastliness.

The contact officer followed his eyes. "They are fools, brave fools but fools. They do not see they will be better off once we pacify them and bring them into our Sphere."

The Romans had sung that song in Gaul, Chang thought, and the British in India, and the Americans in Indochina, and the Confederacy on Epsilon Eridani I. Sometimes they turned out right in the end, sometimes not. Either way, a lot of people got killed finding out.

A live native poked its head round the corner, let out a yell, and charged. It was armed only with a rapier. A burst of fire from the Zanat chopped it down.

Behind them, a gun spoke, the dull report of Slayor powder. One of the troopers with Liosh pitched forward on his face. A squeal of agony said the local had not enjoyed its victory long. Liosh knelt, asked the wounded soldier a question too low for Chang to catch. The answer came in a choked grunt. Liosh drew a knife across the Zan's throat in a quick, practiced motion, touched the ears, eyes, and nose of the body in turn, then straightened and hurried on.

He led the remaining trooper and Chang to a door. "In here." When his companions were through, he dogged it shut behind them. "Now down, all the way." On the spiral stair his injury did trouble him. His thin, dark lips skinned back from his teeth as he forced the pace.

There were no Slayor in the sub basement, not yet. Even the auxiliary lights failed, though, as Chang emerged from the stairwell. Before he could think of escape, the two Zanat had electric torches out.

Liosh went ahead with such confidence that he hardly needed light. At last he came to the door he was seeking. "Escape tunnel," he explained to Chang, "in case of such embarrassments as this. I hope there's a vehicle left at the far end."

The passage was several hundred meters long, with only thin orange beams of light stabbing into the blackness ahead. Then the scout pilot smelled fresh air ahead, night-cool and moist. Liosh swarmed up a metal ladder. "You next," he called. Very conscious of the trooper's rifle at his back, Chang climbed.

A belt of thick, shrubby vegetation had hidden the vehicle park from the spaceport. Two or three pieces of heavy armor still sat there, squat and deadly, but most were already in the fight; their passage had flattened wide swathes of the native plant life.

Liosh ignored the behemoths, heading instead for lighter, swifter transport. A military historian would have called it an armored personnel carrier; Chang had seen similar machines on several human worlds.

The trooper scrambled into the driver's compartment. Liosh and Chang went round to the rear of the vehicle. The contact officer turned to open its double doors—and Chang, at last unwatched for an instant, drew his pistol and sapped the Zan behind the right ear.

Liosh fell bonelessly. The scout pilot raced back to the trooper, who was cursing as he tried to coax the machine's engine to life. The sight of the handgun froze him. "Out," Chang ordered. He clubbed the second alien into unconsciousness.

He paused for a moment over Liosh, pistol in hand. But shouts came echoing up from the mouth of the tunnel—and the Zan, after all, had been trying to save him. He turned and trotted toward the field. The smell of sap from crushed plants filled his nostrils.

He dug his handset from a pocket. "On my way!" he shouted.

"Took you long enough," *Praise of Folly* said tartly. "Things have been lively out here."

That, the scout pilot saw as he emerged from the undergrowth, was putting it mildly. Several armored vehicles blazed on the tarmac; they and the burning port buildings gave all the light there was.

Chang ran past corpses of Zanat and Slayor flung every

which way in death, past wrecked spacecraft. He knew a moment's relief when he realized that *Praise of Folly* had been away from the worst of the fighting. Then a bullet whistled past his ear and another spanged viciously from concrete, and he realized that the greater distance did nothing for *his* safety.

Still, he was only one more shape moving through darkness, not likely to draw much fire and not a good target if he did. *Praise of Folly* stood tall a couple of hundred meters ahead.

He did not spy the Slayor until almost too late. The local slashed at him with a sword—no rapier this, but a great two-handed claymore. The blow went wide. Chang fired at point-blank range, and also missed. He threw his pistol in the native's face. The Slayor went down, keening. Chang did not look back. He flew up *Praise of Folly*'s boarding ladder three rungs at a time.

"Out of here!" he bawled the instant the airlock doors were sealed behind him. "They have more things to worry about now than us."

Praise of Folly outran the missiles that came streaking after her, sped toward free space. Chang whooped and punched for champagne.

His glee proved short-lived, for the Zanat spacecraft in orbital patrol were more alert than the distracted planetary forces. The radio crackled with challenges, which he ignored. Radar and contragrav detector warned of ship-to-ship missiles, faster and more deadly than ground-based weapons.

"Take 'em out," Chang said, adding quickly, "Chemical warheads only. One day soon we'll have to deal with these people, and I don't want to be remembered for screwing up a whole planet with an electromagnetic pulse from our atomics."

But he did not want to be shot out of the sky, either, and did not tell *Praise of Folly* to degrade its counter-missiles' performance. With better sensors and stronger contragravs, they easily destroyed the attackers. Small puffs of red and gold flame blossomed astern.

Far sooner than most pilots would have dared, he went over to hyperdrive. He was so exhilarated that the surge was over before he remembered he should have been sick.

He gunned *Praise of Folly* for all the ship was worth, trying to get out of detector range before his pursuers went FTL. For most of an hour, he thought he'd done it. Then a point of light winked on in the detector display, far behind but indisputably there. He swore and shifted vectors. The enemy followed. He swore again. He had already seen that the Zanat had good FTL instrumentation.

"Just have to run them into the ground, then," he muttered.

But the bogey refused to disappear. After awhile, another crawled onto the edge of the screen, and then two more. All were prominent echoes, warcraft for certain.

He tried to console himself with the truism fallen back on by every captain in trouble since the days of ships on Terran seas: a stern chase is a long chase. But when he looked at the detectors, he saw that it would not be long enough.

It was several days later, ship's time, when he and the computer finished commiserating with each other over his poor choice of drinking establishments. By then his lead, almost a light-year when he set out, had melted to hardly more than half an AU. The Zanat ships were maneuvering into englobement formation: if they surrounded him and touched his drive field with all theirs at once, they and he would be thrown into normal space together, with all the odds in their favor in the ensuing slugging match.

"I'll have to go sublight myself first," he decided unwillingly: the last resort of an outmatched pilot. "Maybe," he added without much belief, "they'll lose me." If the ploy would ever work, the Nebula was the place for it. Gas and dust could play merry hell with gadgetry.

"Any particular thick patches close by?" he asked hopefully.

The computer was silent for nearly a minute while it

searched its memory and added corrections for several centuries of proper motion. At last it said, "As it happens, yes. We're near a Herbig-Haro object."

"New one on me," the scout pilot admitted. "What is it?"

"A luminous nebula with a denser center that—"

"Say no more; that's exactly what we need. They'll have to have their engines linked to their detectors and drop out of hyperdrive the moment we do, or else overshoot and lose me for good. FTL, half an AU is nothing. Set our course so that when we and they break out, they'll be smack in the middle of that denser center." Chang let his optimism run wild. "One of them might even emerge coincident with a rock, and lower the odds. Can we fight three?"

"Not with our store of missiles depleted as it is," the computer answered at once. The scout pilot sighed. *Praise of Folly* went on, "Reconsider your plan. Herbig-Haro objects are—"

Chang was not about to be balked by mechanical mutiny. "Execute, and no chatter," he said harshly. "Override command."

The silence that fell had a reproachful quality to it. *Praise of Folly* changed course. Like hounds after a rabbit, the Zanat ships followed.

Chang's nails bit into his palms. His lead was a bare half-AU now, hardly seventy-five million kilometers. If this Herbig-Haro whatsit didn't show up soon, the Zanat would force him out of hyperdrive and fight on their own terms.

Praise of Folly gave a sudden, sickening lurch. Her normal-space instruments came back to life—and at that same instant, every alarm in the ship went off. Red lights flared, claxons hooted, bells jangled, a commotion to wake the dead.

Chang did not even notice it. His mouth hanging open, he was staring in disbelief at the viewscreens. "What the bleeding hell is a star doing there?" he said in something like a whispered scream.

A star it was, a crimson monster. *Praise of Folly* could hardly have been more than fifteen million kilometers from the edge of its chromosphere. Had Chang been on the surface of a planet at that distance, its great orb would have stretched across almost two-thirds of the sky.

He could peer deep through the tenuous gases of its outer atmosphere, could gauge the temperature of the swirling currents by their colors: here a ruby so deep the eye almost refused to register it, there a coruscating uprush of brighter, molten red. It was like looking down on a stormy ocean of flaming wine.

The sight held Chang fascinated until he absently wiped his hand across his forehead. It came away slick with sweat. As the alarms could not, that reminded him where he was. Another few seconds and he would cook, no matter how well-shielded the ship was. His finger jabbed the hyperdrive switch.

The abused engines groaned, but the wrench that sent *Praise of Folly* FTL was the most welcome thing he had ever felt. The clamor of alarms faded away. Nothing whatever showed on the hyperdrive detector. Chang shivered. "One thing's certain, they never knew what hit 'em." Moths in a blowtorch—

He shivered again as reaction set in. That could have been him emerging in the center of a star . . . a star the computer had not known about. "You almost fried out both!" he howled.

There was no reply. He remembered his last command. "Override lifted," he said. "I want to hear what you have to say for yourself. Why did you think you were diving into a nebula instead of a star?"

"That should be obvious even to you," the computer said, testy as usual after an override. "When my navigation data was compiled, that star did not exist."

"Tell me another one," Chang snorted, "one I'll believe."

"Your ignorance is not my problem, except that it almost destroyed *Praise of Folly*, and you with it. You would not listen to my warning. As long ago as the end of the second century pre-Confederacy, astronomers knew that a Herbig-Haro object was the precursor to a star."

"You really mean it," the scout pilot said in wonder.

"Yes, I really do." The computer seemed determined to gets its own back. "Why do you think a Herbig-Haro object is luminous? The energy emitted by the slowly condensing cloud in the center ionizes the gas around it and makes it glow.

"But when gravitational contraction brings the cloud down to about the size of Sol's system—say, eighty AU's across—something new happens. Some of the energy inside stops going into heating the gas of the cloud and starts breaking up hydrogen molecules and such in the center: things are beginning to get hot in there.

"And when that energy gets diverted, there isn't enough gas pressure left to support the outside of the cloud any more. It falls in on itself over the next half a standard year or so, until it shrinks to a diameter of about eight-tenths of an AU. Then the heat and pressure generated by the collapse restore equilibrium and the new star becomes visible, with a surface temperature of 4,000° K or so."

"Visible! I should say so." Chang would never forget that fierce red glare. "Why hasn't any survey since the old Confederacy come by and noticed it?"

"There isn't much human traffic out this way," *Praise of Folly* said with what sounded like an electronic shrug. "And no one on more traveled routes would have seen the star yet; its light simply hasn't traveled far enough. From its diameter and spectrum, it can hardly have been shining longer than twenty years."

"Twenty years," the scout pilot murmured. As the fear leached out of him, awe began to replace it, the awe of having been present at the biggest birth in recorded history.

"Shape direct course for home," he told *Praise of Folly*. "Now I have something to keep B'kila happy and the astrophysicists, too." His expression suddenly went mercenary. "I wonder how much I can get for the tapes."

*   *   *

The air inside B'kila's sanctum was conditioned to the same temperature as every other part of Salvage Service Central, but always seemed five Celsius colder. "Incompetent," she was saying, "fumbling, harebrained, lucky—lucky twice, which is more than anyone deserves." She sounded annoyed that Chang had come back at all.

He grinned like an impudent schoolboy. "Who is it who teaches that nothing matters like results? And how do you like my results, O mentor mine?"

"I can find flaws there too," she said grimly. "These Zanat of yours will have to be reckoned with. From your tapes, I'd rate their technology at the level of mid-twentieth century Terra: say, 130 pre-Confederacy. There can't be more than a couple of hundred planets in human space that can match them, and no three of those trust a fourth. Loki sadly included. Now a whole united species knows where we are."

"They had a fair notion before I met them," Chang replied. "And we can hope they also have the idea we're a good people to stay away from. They took out our first scouts, yes, but from what Liosh said they had to work for it. Then they sent four good-sized warships after *Praise of Folly*, and lost every one."

"No thanks to you," B'kila said.

"Ah, but they don't know that. What can they think? Either *Praise of Folly* handled all four of their bigger ships by itself, or else everything I told them about the Confederacy was true, and I had reinforcements waiting. Neither prospect can appeal to them."

B'kila smiled thinly. "You didn't make a hash of that," she admitted. "By all odds, it was the best you did out of the whole mission."

"Well, not quite," Chang said. His tapes and records had sent the entire astronomy department of the Collegium of Loki into ecstasies, and fetched even more than he expected. He had plenty for a really first-class spree, to make up for the one B'kila had cheated him out of.

She was not through with him yet, though. "How do you read the Zanat? Do you really believe they'll avoid us, say by fortifying their Sphere to the eyebrows and waiting for trouble to find them, or will they come looking to see what went wrong. Honestly, now."

Chang's smile slowly disappeared. B'kila had a way of piercing to the heart of problems. The scout pilot had to answer, "I'm afraid they'll come looking."

"That was the impression your reports gave me," she nodded, "but firsthand experience and the feel it brings are worth more than all the reports ever recorded. It was important to have your judgement check mine."

B'kila doled out compliments sparingly. Flushed under the effects of this one, Chang ventured, "When Liosh was grilling me, I had the impression that you and he would have worked well together." He brought the notion out hesitantly; it half-pleased and half-disturbed him.

She did not turn a hair. "I think so, too," she replied. "Yes, as a species they're quite a bit like us—altogether too much, as a matter of fact." She sighed and shook her head. "Interesting times, interesting times."

She turned away as if Chang was not there, spoke into her phone box: "Josip, Neelam, are you in place? It'll be plan two." The scout pilot took his leave; B'kila did not stand on ceremony, and often went straight from one piece of business to the next. She paid no attention to his departure.

Just outside Salvage Service Central, though, another of those curseworthy young lieutenants saluted and said, "Excuse me, sir, are you Master Pilot Chang? I'm Josip Broz; I'll be briefing you on your new assignments."

Chang's mind raced. As usual, B'kila was one step ahead of him, but this time he could see where she was going. "Interesting times" translated to "crisis," and he knew only too well what the crisis was. He also knew with sudden dreadful certainty that his leave was about to get canceled again.

Not without a fight, though. "Chang?" he said blandly. "No, he's an older fellow. I did see him in the lobby, if you're looking for him." As Josip Broz trustingly turned his back, the scout pilot bolted.

Lieutenant Neelam Sanjiva Reddy corraled him, of course, before he made a hundred meters.

EDITOR'S INTRODUCTION TO:

THE FIGHTING PHILOSOPHER
E. B. Cole

John W. Campbell believed in science. We do not yet have a rational science of humanity and social action, but he had no doubts: we will, inevitably, evolve one.

Campbell's original blurb for this story serves well enough for an introduction not only to the story, but to his way of thought:

"Archimedes was the philosopher who wouldn't bother to fight the Roman soldier and had his philosophical work terminated permanently. A true philosopher avoids brawls but is a deadly effective fighter for all that."

John believed that. After all, it had not been long since Goebels could say, "The noblest of spirits, the highest of philosophies, can be eliminated if their bearer is beaten to death with a rubber truncheon." Truth is strong, but truth undefended cannot be victorious.

Of course there's more to it than that. If we truly believe in science, then once we have a scientific sociology and scientific penology we will be ready to take our place in the galaxy; for if something goes wrong, we will be able to fix it. That will be our destiny. A manifest destiny.

FIGHTING PHILOSOPHER
E. B. Cole

". . . And this, gentlemen, is what we saw from the *Rilno*."

The three-dimensional screen glowed as a dozen suns sprang into being within it. Light glanced fitfully from a multitude of spheres grouped about their primaries. These were the suns and planets of the Empire of Findur. Near the center of the screen, a number of small sparks dodged swiftly about in the emptiness of interstellar space. One of these seemed to be surrounded. Tiny lines of light swept from the others, causing the central spark to pulsate with a vivid glow.

"Captain Tero called me at this time," announced the voice from the darkness beside the screen. "He requested permission to cut a ten-degree, four-microsecond void, since he was englobed and his screens were in danger of overloading under the Finduran fire." The speaker paused, then continued. "I granted permission, since I could see no other feasible means of pulling him out of the globe. We could have opened fleet fire, but Tero's screens might have gone down before we could control

267

the situation. The *Kleeros* acknowledged, then Tero cut in his space warp."

On the screen, a narrow fan of darkness spread from the englobed spark. The attacking sparks vanished before it. Suddenly, the dark fan widened, vibrated, then swung over a wide angle. As it swung, the brilliant suns went out like candles in a high wind. A black, impenetrable curtain spread over most of the scene. Abruptly, the spark at the origin of the darkness faded and was gone. The scene remained, showing an irregularly shaped, black pocket amongst the stars. It hung there, an empty, opaque, black spot in space, where a few moments before had been suns and planets and embattled ships.

"As you gentlemen know," the voice added tiredly, "before a space warp can be cut in, all screens must be lowered to prevent random secondary effects and permanent damage to the ship. The cut is so phased as to make it virtually impossible for a shear beam or any other force beam to penetrate, but there is one chance in several million of shear-beam penetration while the warp is being set up. The only assumption we could make aboard the *Rilno* was that a beam must have struck Tero's controls while his screens were being phased. He apparently swung out of control for a moment, then disrupted his ship to prevent total destruction of the Sector. Before he could act, however, he had destroyed his attackers and virtually all of the Finduran Empire. Of course, the warp remained on long enough to allow permanent establishment. We have nothing further to base opinions on, since Tero did not take the time to report before disrupting." The scene on the viewer faded and the room lights went on.

The speaker stood revealed as a slender, tall humanoid. His narrow face with its high brows and sharply outlined features gave the impression of continual amusement with the universe and all that was in it, but the slight narrowing of the eyes—the barely perceptible tightening of the mouth—evidenced a certain anxiety. Fine lines on his face indicated that this man had known cares and serious thoughts in the past. Now, he stood at attention, his hands aligned at the sides of his light-gray trousers. Fleet Commander Dalthos A-Riman, of the Seventeenth Border Sector, awaited the pleasure of the Board.

In front of him, the being at the desk nodded at the other members of the Board. "Are there any questions, gentlemen?"

A small, lithe member raised a hand slightly. A-Riman looked toward him. He had met Sector Chief Sesnir before, and knew his sharp, incisive questions.

"You said that Captain Tero was at point, commander," stated Sesnir. "How did he happen to get so far in advance of the rest of the fleet that he could be englobed?"

"You remember, sir," replied A-Riman, "the Findurans had developed a form of polyphase screen which made their ships nearly undetectable when at rest. We could only detect them when they were in action, or when they were within a half parsec. This encounter took place several parsecs outside their normal area of operation." The fleet commander brought a hand to his face, then dropped it. "I was just about to call Tero in to form a slightly more compact grouping when he ran into the middle of their formation."

"You mean they had maneuvered a fleet well inside Federation borders, and had it resting in ambush?" persisted the questioner. "What was wrong with your light scouts?"

"That, sir," A-Riman told him, "was the reason I approached in fleet strength. I had received no scout reports for three days. I knew there was enemy action in the region, but had no intelligence reports."

"You mean," another Board member broke in, "you went charging into an unknown situation in open fleet formation?"

"I felt I had to, sir. I regarded open formation as precautionary, since damage to one ship would be far less serious than involvement of the entire fleet in an ambush. I was sure I had lost several scouts, and was not inclined to lose more. Tero volunteered to draw fire, then planned to take evasive action while the rest of the fleet moved in." A-Riman paused. "Except for superb planning by the Finduran admiral and a million-to-one accident, Tero would have extricated himself easily, and we could have moved in to take police action in accordance with the council's orders."

"I see," commented the questioning member. "Probably would've done the same thing myself."

"Why," demanded Sesnir impatiently, "didn't you simply open up from a safe distance with a ten-microsecond, forty-degree space warp? You'd still have been within your orders, we'd have saved a ship, the Findurans would've given us no more trouble—ever—and we wouldn't have a permanent space fold to worry about in Sector Seventeen."

A-Riman looked at the sector chief. "That, sir," he announced firmly, "is just what I wanted to avoid doing. I felt, and still feel, that complete destruction of suns, planets and youthful cultures, however inimical they may seem to be at the time, is wasteful, dangerous, and in direct violation of the first law of Galactic Ethics."

The president of the Board looked up. "The Ethic refers to Federation members, commander," he said. "Remember?"

"I believe it should be extended to include all intelligent life, sir," A-Riman answered.

"You will find, 'Treat all others as you would wish yourself to be treated in like circumstances,' a very poor defense against a well directed shear beam," commented Sesnir.

A-Riman smiled. "True," he admitted, "but there are possibilities. Why—"

Vandor ka Bensir, Chief of Stellar Guard Operations, rapped on his desk. "Gentlemen," he said dryly, "a discussion of the Galactic Ethics is always very interesting, but I believe it is out of order here. Unless there are more questions or comments pertinent to this inquiry, I will close the Board." He looked about the room. "No comments? Then, as president of this Board of Inquiry, I order the Board closed for deliberation." Again, he rapped on the desk. "Will you please retire,

Commander A-Riman? We will notify you when we have reached our findings and recommendations."

As the door closed, Bensir turned to the other Board members. "The floor is open for discussion," he said. "You're the junior member, Commander Dal Klar. Do you have any comments?"

"Admiral, I have what almost amounts to a short speech." Dal Klar glanced at the chief of operations, then looked slowly about at the rest of his colleagues. "But I hesitate to take up too much of the Board's time."

Ka Bensir smiled gently. "You mean that juniors should be seen and not heard?" he queried.

"Something like that, sir."

"This Board," ruled its president, "has all the time in the Universe. You can think out loud; you can bring up any points you wish; you can come to whatever conclusions you want to. The floor is yours."

Dal Klar took a deep breath. "Well, in that case, here I go: In the first place, I feel that A-Riman acted properly and in accordance with his ethics and those of his civilization. If you gentlemen will remember, A-Riman is from the Celstor Republic, which is one of the older members of the Federation. The Celstorians have been responsible for many of the scientific advances and for a large share of the philosophy of our civilization. A-Riman, himself, has written two notable commentaries on philosophy and ethics, both of which have been well received in the Federation."

Dal Klar glanced toward Sector Chief Sesnir, then continued. "Had the commander destroyed without warning, inflicting utter and complete destruction upon a young and comparatively helpless civilization, he would have been acting in direct contravention to his own stated ethical code. In that case, he would have been deserving of all the censure we could give. As it is, I feel that he acted in accordance with the best traditions of the Guard, and simply met with an unforeseen and unfortunate accident which could have happened to any fleet commander who went on that mission."

Dal Klar paused, cleared his throat, then concluded. "We have heard definite testimony that there was no laxity in drill or maintenance in A-Riman's fleet. On the contrary, some of his officers feel that he is extremely strict about both action drill and maintenance. Certainly, then, we can't say he was negligent."

As Dal Klar stopped, ka Bensir looked at another Board member, who shook his head.

"I might have phrased it a little differently, sir," he commented, "but the commander expressed my views quite well. I have nothing to add."

Two more members declined to comment, then Sector Chief Sesnir wagged his head.

"I seem to be in the minority," he remarked, "but I feel that the coddling of these young, semibarbaric and aggressive cultures is suicidal. Before we could teach them our ways of thinking, they would inflict tremendous damage upon us. They might even subvert some of our own younger members, and set up a rival Federation. Then, we would have real trouble. I have read A-Riman's commentaries on ethics, and I know the history of the 'Fighting Philosopher.' Frankly, I feel that a man with his views should not be in the Combat Arm of the Guard. He is simply too soft."

The Board president nodded. "I'll reserve comment," he decided. "Will you gentlemen please record your findings?"

A few minutes later, the clerk inserted a small file of recordings into the machine in front of him. The viewscreen lit up.

Findings: The Kleeros, a Class A Guard ship, was lost, and a permanent space-fold was set up in Sector Seventeen due to the ill-advised tactics of Fleet Commander Dalthos A-Riman, who risked his fleet against an unscouted force rather than destroy a criminal civilization by means at his hand.

Ka Bensir pointed at Dal Klar, who shook his head. "No," he said decisively. The pointing finger moved to the next member. Again, the answer was a definite "No." Only one member assented to the proposed finding. Ka Bensir nodded to the clerk. "Next recording," he said.

Findings: The Class A Guard ship, Kleeros, was destroyed by its captain to avert major disaster. The cause of failure of the space-warp controls aboard the Kleeros cannot be accurately determined due to the destruction of the ship with all on board and to the lack of communication prior to that destruction. Fleet Commander Dalthos A-Riman was acting within his orders and was using reasonable caution prior to the incident. The failure of the space-warp controls and the permanent space-fold resulting therefrom could not have been foreseen by the fleet commander or by Captain Nalver Tero. Since the use of the space-warp is recognized as a legitimate defensive tactic by single ships of the Federation, no censure will be brought against Captain Tero for requesting permission to use the warp, nor against Commander A-Riman for granting that permission. The disaster was due to circumstances beyond the control of any of its participants.

Again, ka Bensir pointed at Dal Klar, who nodded. "I agree," he said. The next member assented. So did the next, and the next. Finally, ka Bensir rapped on his desk. "The findings are complete, then," he said. "Since we find that no censure will be brought against Commander A-Riman, we need not go into that phase of the matter. Do I hear a verbal motion on a citation for Captain Tero and his crew?"

"Federation Cluster for Tero; Heroic Citations for his crew," rumbled a deep voice. "Second," came a sharp reply.

"All in favor?" An assenting murmur arose. "Unanimous," commented Bensir. "Record it."

Vandor ka Bensir drew his side arm. "Have Fleet Commander Dalthos A-Riman come in," he ordered. He laid the weapon on his desk, its needlelike nose pointing away from the door and toward the screen which still bore the accepted findings of the Board and the posthumous citation for the captain and crew of the *Kleeros.*

A-Riman stepped in. Glancing at the weapon on the

desk, he nodded slightly, then looked at the viewscreen. "Thank you, gentlemen," he acknowledged. "Now that the inquiry is over, I wish to request reassignment to the Criminal Apprehension Corps. I feel that I may be more useful there than in the Combat Arm." He nodded at the screen. "In spite of the recorded findings, it is possible that some of you agree. My real reason, however, for requesting reassignment, is my feeling that I may be able to offer some constructive recommendations which should result in fewer problems for the Combat Arm in the future, and I wish to be in Criminal Apprehension where I can furnish practical proof of the feasibility of those recommendations."

The Tenth Sector Officers' Club wasn't particularly crowded. Commander A-Riman walked into the Senior Officers' dining room. At one of the tables, he saw two old acquaintances. He went toward them.

"Mind if I join you?"

They looked up. "Dalthos," exclaimed one, "where'd you come from? Thought you were over in Seventeen."

A-Riman grabbed a chair, pulling it out. "Just reported for duty, Veldon," he remarked as he sat down. "I'm the new CAC Group Commander."

Veldon Bolsein looked at him quizzically. "Heard you had a little trouble with a runaway warp," he remarked. "What'd they do, damp your beams?"

"No, they decided I wasn't at fault," grinned A-Riman. "I requested transfer to CAC."

Bolsein cocked one eyebrow up and the other down. Then, tilting his head to one side, he looked hard at A-Riman. "My hearing must be going bad," he decided. "I was sure you said you requested transfer."

"I did."

"How barbarous," murmured Fleet Commander Plios Knolu, as he placed his elbows on the table. He leaned forward, cupped his face in his hands, and fixed A-Riman with a pitying stare. "Tell me," he asked, "did they beat your brains out with clubs, or did they use surgery?"

A-Riman leaned back and laughed. "Thought you'd

have lost your touch by now," he remarked. "No, I'm still sane as ever, but—"

"Jets ahead," warned Bolsein softly. He started to rise. A-Riman glanced around to see the sector chief walking into the room. He and Knolu got to their feet.

Sector Chief Dal-Kun took his seat at the head of the table. "Your health, gentlemen," he greeted them. "I see you have already met." He looked over the menu card and dialed a selection. "I've been checking over your records, A-Riman," he continued. "Look good, all of them, up to that space-fold. Board didn't hold you responsible for that, either." He paused as his dishes rose to the table top. Lifting a cover, he examined the contents of a platter. "Food Service is in good condition, I see," he remarked. He transferred a helping to his plate. "Can't understand how you happened to go into Criminal Apprehension, though. No promotion there."

A-Riman smiled. "I was just about to explain to Bolsein and Knolu when you came in, sir." He paused, collecting his thoughts. "I've been doing some thinking on criminology for quite a while, and I've a few theories on preventative work in the new civilizations I'd like to try out. There are several systems in this sector that could stand some investigation, and— "

Dal-Kun laid his utensils down. "Let's not get in too much of a hurry, commander. Suppose you turn in some good, routine work for a couple of cycles or so, then we'll talk about new theories." He picked up his fork again. "We've got a lot of these young, do-nothing Drones roaming about in this sector, getting into scrapes, violating quarantines, creating space hazards. They'll keep you busy for a while." He grunted angrily. "Why, right now, you've got five pickup orders on file, and those people of yours can't seem to get anywhere with them."

"In that case, I'll get to work immediately," said A-Riman. "Can I have Fleet Support where necessary?"

The sector chief grunted again. "Don't see why not. Commander Knolu hasn't done anything but routine patrol for two cycles. Do him good to run around a bit and work off some of his fat." He continued with his meal.

Finally, the chief left the table. Bolsein dialed another glass of *Telon* and leaned back. "Don't worry too much about the boss," he remarked. "He snarls like mad, but he'll back you up all the way, long's you're somewhere near the center of the screen."

"Just what's this big, new idea of yours, A-Riman?" inquired Knolu.

"Either of you ever get a 'cut back, or destroy' order?"

Knolu nodded. "Sure—several of them. Last one was in this sector, not more than ten cycles ago."

"How did you feel about it?"

Knolu shook his head. "How does anyone feel about destruction? I hated it, but the council doesn't put out an order like that unless it has been proved necessary. They hate destruction and waste, too."

"Suppose we could figure out a method of eliminating most of this type of destruction?"

Bolsein narrowed his eyes. "It would take a terrible load off the mind of every combat commander." He sighed, "But what can be done? We contact new civilizations as soon as they achieve space travel, and the negotiators fail with a good share of them. Pretty soon, they're too big for their system. They try to take over the Federation, or part of it, and we're ordered into action."

"Suppose we contacted them long before they came out into space?"

"Unethical. You know that."

"Is guidance and instruction unethical?"

Knolu sat up sharply. "I think I see what you're driving at," he said, "but who's going to spend his time and effort on a primitive planet, living with primitive people, just so he can teach them? What guarantee has he of success?"

A-Riman smiled. "You heard the chief. I've got five pickups in the files. I'll bet, without looking, that three of them at least are for quarantine violations on primitive planets. Now—"

Bolsein interrupted. "All five of 'em are," he grumbled. "We have more trouble in this sector with these foolish Drones violating quarantine than we do with anything else. I even had a minor engagement with a bunch of them last cycle. They'd organized some sort of an eight-way chess game, with the planetary population as pieces." He hesitated. "What a nasty mess that was," he added. "My captains were so disgusted, they didn't pick them up for rehabilitation; they just blasted them out of space. I lost a ship, too, over the deal."

"There," announced A-Riman, "you had quite a few people who were willing to live with primitives on a primitive planet."

"Sure," grunted Bolsein. "Drones, though."

"What is a Drone?"

Knolu leaned back, smiling. "I read the manual once, too, remember?" He folded his arms. " 'A Drone,' " he quoted in a singsong voice, " 'is an entity who prefers not to do anything productive. Having acquired the necessary equipment for subsistence, he devotes his time to the pursuit of pleasure, to the exclusion of all other activity.' " He sat forward again. "I've gotten a few more thoughts on the subject, though. In my opinion, a Drone is an entity which should be picked up for rehabilitation as soon as he shows his characteristics."

He held up a hand as Bolsein started to speak. "Oh, I know, the Ethic says we should not interfere with the chosen course of any citizen so long as he does no harm, commits no unethical act, or interferes with the legitimate good of no other citizen, but this should be an exception. Most Drones tire of normal pleasures in a few cycles. Within a hundred cycles, they turn to exotic pleasures. Finally, they tire even of these, and get into some form of unethical, immoral, or downright criminal activity. Eventually, we have to pick most of them up anyway, so why not pick them up right away?"

"More than a thousand periods ago," commented A-Riman, "long before the Celstorians burst out into space, my planet had a problem like this. To be sure, it was on a much smaller scale, but there were similarities. The governors set up a sort of 'Thought Police,' to combat the evil at its roots. It led to a dictatorship, and the civilization of Celstor was set back a thousand planetary cycles. We almost reverted to barbarism, and the matter wasn't corrected until a planetwide uprising overthrew the Board of Governors and destroyed the Police State. Finally, the Republic was founded, but not until many sterile reversions had been set up and overthrown. No, we don't want to amend or correct the Ethic. We merely need to extend it."

He looked at Knolu. "But to get back to my original query. In my opinion, a Drone is an entity whose original training was somehow less than completely successful. He is an entity who wishes excitement—action, if you will—but is unable to accept the discipline which goes with productive work. At the present civilization level, subsistence is easy to get, on almost any desired scale. Matter converters allow us to live wherever we are, and live well. Subsistence and property then are no incentives. Most of us, who are well oriented, get our pleasure and our reward from a feeling of accomplishment. The Drone, however, has not yet reached that stage of development. It is only when his pursuit of pleasure has led him far out of the normal paths of pleasure that he is a fit subject for rehabilitation. After rehabilitation, he can be a very useful citizen. Many of them are, you know."

"Thus speaks the 'Fighting Philosopher,'" laughed Knolu. "A-Riman ever since you published 'Galactic Ethics, an Extension,' you've been living in a world of your own."

"No," denied A-Riman, "I've been trying to investigate the entire Galactic civilization. I've been trying to solve the problem of those new civilizations, many of which have risen from the ashes of former civilizations which either destroyed themselves or were destroyed by Interstellar conflict anywhere from twenty to several hundred periods ago." He hesitated, then continued. "It takes a long time for a burned-out planet to produce a new civilization. It takes even longer for a damped sun to return to life and to liven its planets. Why, the Finduran Empire, which one of my captains took with him into final oblivion, had its beginnings when my father was a very young schoolboy, still learning primitive manual writing and the basic principles of life. These periods of progress, of learning of life, should not be merely thrown away. They should be conserved."

"How?" Bolsein leaned forward.

"For short times, say ten cycles or so, I can order my CAC agents in to work on primitive worlds. Of course, I must then grant them long leaves, but during those small spaces of time, I plan to prove that an impetus can be given to a primitive civilization, which will cause it to conform to the Galactic Ethic, and will pre-dispose it to desire membership in the Galactic Federation when it becomes aware of the existence of such a body. If this works out, I feel sure that we can find recruits who will be willing to spend even longer stretches of time as educators and guides.

"I may even be able to train certain primitives and enlist their aid on their native planets. If a group of Drones can find amusement on a primitive world, surely productive personnel can stand considerable tours of duty, and can so guide primitive civilizations from their infant, barbaric beginnings that very few if any new civilizations, upon bursting into space, will have a desire to form great empires of their own. They will be willing and even glad to exchange technologies and ideas with the rest of the galaxy, and will become useful and honored members of the Federation."

"So, what do we do?" queried Knolu.

"Easy. I've got five pickups on file. The chief wants 'em cleared immediately if not sooner. I gather he expects me to take a couple of cycles to clean up things. Let me have full cooperation, and then we can go to work."

Bolsein shook his head. "I never thought I'd see the day I'd be following CAC orders," he complained. "What do you want? Do you need both fleets, or will a few hundred scouts satisfy you?"

*   *   *

Unquestionably, Besiro was the most beautiful capital on all the planet. Here was gathered all the talents, all the beauty, all the wit, and most of the wealth of the civilized world. Here, also, were gathered the most clever, the most experienced, the most depraved thieves and criminals of the planet. After dark, the Elegants of the Court, the wealthy idlers, and the solid merchants of the city, took care to have a trusted bodyguard when they ventured abroad. It was strange, then, that on this night, there was a lone pedestrian in the narrow side street which led to the Guest House of the Three Kings.

The man was dressed expensively and well. His ornate, feathered hat was cocked at exactly the fashionable angle, the foam of lace at his shoulders jutted up and out precisely the correct distance, and the jeweled buckles of his shoes and his coat buttons reflected the glow of the occasional street taper like miniature suns. He strode casually along the street, glancing incuriously at the shuttered windows of the houses along the way. Finally, he approached the entrance to an alley. Momentarily, he paused, tilting his head in a listening attitude, then he smiled to himself and continued. He brushed a hand lightly against his belt, then took the hilt of his sword in a firm grasp.

In the alley, "Sailor" Klur was giving his last minute instructions in a low tone.

"Now, One-eye," he said, "soon's he heaves into sight, you dive for his feet. Me'n the Slogger'll finish him off before he gets up." As the footsteps approached, Klur gave One-eye a slight shove.

"Now," he whispered. One-eye dove for the glittering shoe buckles.

At the slight commotion, the pedestrian stopped abruptly, then danced back half a pace. One-eye never realized he had failed in his assignment, for the long, sharp sword in the elegantly ringed hand severed his head before he had time to hit the stones of the street.

Klur's intended victim turned smoothly, meeting the sailor's rush with a well-directed point. Klur dropped his long knife, looked for a moment at the foppish figure before him, then collapsed silently to the pavement. The victor advanced, forcing "Slogger" Marl against the wall, the point of his sword making a dent in the man's clothing. Marl sobbed in terror.

"Please, my master, please, they made me do it. I'm a peace-loving man. I wouldn't do nothing. On my honor, I wouldn't."

The man with the sword smiled engagingly. "I can see that," he agreed. "Drop your club, my man."

The club clattered to the alley.

"Now," said the Elegant, "I'm minded to let you go, for you're such a poor thing beside those two valiants who lie there." He dropped the sword point slightly. "Be off," he ordered. With a gasp of surprised relief, Marl turned to make his way to safer parts.

The sword licked out suddenly, and Marl's sudden protesting cry of surprise and pain became a mere gurgle as the flowing blood stopped his voice.

The killer stepped toward the body, glance disdainfully at its clothing, and shook his head.

"Filthy," he murmured. He walked out to the street, examining the other two. Finally, he decided that Klur's coat was comparatively clean. Leaning down, he carefully wiped his sword blade on the skirt of the coat, then restored the weapon to its sheath, carefully adjusted his hat, and sauntered on his way. Manir Kal, master swordsman, had proved his ability again, and to his own critical satisfaction.

The reports were long and detailed. A-Riman checked them over, rapidly at first, then more slowly, gathering each detail. Occasionally, he nodded his head. Some of these agents were good. Others were very good. He touched a button on his desk. Nothing happened. He frowned and touched another button. Still, nothing happened.

Indignantly, A-Riman glanced down at the call-board and punched two more buttons in quick succession. His viewscreen remained dark, and he punched the button marked "Conference," then sat back to await developments. A minute passed, then a light blinked on the desk. As A-Riman pressed the button below the light, the door opened to admit a captain, who took two paces forward, halted, came to rigid attention, saluted, and announced himself. "Captain Poltar reporting, sir." He remained at attention.

"Relax, captain," ordered A-Riman. "Why didn't you answer my screen?"

The captain was still at attention. "The previous commander wanted personal contact, sir," he said, then, as the order to relax penetrated, he quickly took a more comfortable pose.

"Open the door again, then take a chair. I think we're going to have company," smiled his superior.

A voice drifted through the open door. "Oh, I suppose he wants someone to check the guards on that suspect planet. As though we haven't—" The voice trailed off, as the speaker realized the group commander's door was open. Two highly embarrassed officers entered, announced themselves, stood at attention, and waited for the thunders of wrath to descend about their ears.

"Sit down, gentlemen," ordered A-Riman mildly. "We'll have more company in a minute."

Three more officers filed into the room, took two paces, saluted, and announced themselves. A-Riman waved a hand. "Relax, gentlemen," he told them. He turned to Captain Poltar. "Are there any more officers present?" he inquired.

Poltar glanced at the others present in the room, then shook his head. "No, sir. The rest are off the base, checking or investigating."

"Good." A-Riman nodded. "When they come in, have them report to me one at a time." He turned to face the entire group. "Gentlemen," he began, "this is my first, and very probably my last, staff meeting." He raised a hand. "No, I don't mean it that way. I plan to be here for a good many cycles, but I'm going to see to it that the 'conference' button gets good and corroded." He turned to Captain Poltar again. "What were you doing when I buzzed you?"

"Working out the deci-cyclic report, sir."

"It took you over a minute to get here," stated the commander.

"Yes, sir."

"It'll take you ten or fifteen minutes to get back on your train of thought and start over where you left off?"

"About that, sir."

"So, you will lose at least a quarter of an hour from your work, plus the time we take in this discussion. How long is that?"

"I expect to lose about an hour and a half, sir."

A-Riman glanced about the group. "Anyone here think he'll lose any less than that?" There was silence.

"So," decided the commander, "I push a few buttons and lose nine man-hours of work—more than one day for an officer." He frowned at the row of buttons on his desk. "Mr. Kelnar, you're engineering, I believe. Have these things rewired right away so that when I call someone I am cut into his viewscreen. There'll be no more of this."

An older man, one of the last to report, rose to his feet. "I'm on my way, sir," he announced, and turned to go out of the door.

"Just a minute," ordered A-Riman. "You were in the Combat Arm once. How did you happen to transfer out?"

"Crash landed in a repair ship on a primitive planet, sir. When they got me patched up, a Board decided I was unfit for further combat duty."

"Why didn't you retire?"

"I like it here."

A-Riman waved a dismissal. The senior technician saluted, swung through the door, and was gone. The group commander gazed after him thoughtfully, then returned his attention to the five remaining officers.

"Maybe, gentlemen, we're not wasting so much time, at that," he remarked softly. "Maybe I'd better go into my philosophy of operation. I just came from the Combat Arm, gentlemen. No one forced me into this job—I came here because I was something like Mr. Kelnar. I like it here. From now on, we're going to work. There'll be very little time for two-stepping, reporting, and so on. We've got a job to do, and we're going to concentrate on it. When I call one of you, I expect an immediate answer by viviscreen, or I expect someone in your office to locate you within a very short time. Then, you will call me. If you have any problems, I expect a prompt call. I'll probably be out of my office. I may be at the other end of the sector, but there'll be someone here that'll know how to get in touch with me."

He picked up the tiny recordings of the pickup data. "We have five pickups on Drones who have violated quarantine of Planet Five, Sun Gorgon Three, number four five seven six, Sector Ten. They are still at large and presumably still on the planet. What's wrong?"

"We have guards staked out all around the Sun's system, waiting for them to move, sir. So far, they haven't attempted to leave." Captain Poltar looked a little surprised.

"You're sure they are on the planet?"

"Yes, sir, definitely. We tracked them in shortly after they made planetfall. Since then, not a dust mote could've gotten out. Our people are keeping constant watch on their actions."

"What's your disposition?"

"It's in the report, sir," said another officer. "We have ten two-man scouts englobing the planet, at close range, with detectors full out. If they even move, we know it."

"That's twenty men on full-time duty, just watching a mouse hole," commented A-Riman. "Why not simply send in five of the scouts, hunt up your people on the planet, and bring them back here?"

Captain Poltar looked shocked. "Regulations, sir," he exclaimed.

"Which regulations?"

"Why, I believe it's SGR 344-53-4, sir. I'll have it checked if you wish."

"Don't bother." A-Riman smiled at him wryly. "I

checked. It says, 'Excepting in cases of extreme emergency, no Guard Unit will make planetfall on any primitive world without prior clearance from higher authority.' Have you checked with the sector chief for permission to make planetfall?"

"I haven't, sir. Commander Redendale said 'Higher Authority' in this case meant the council, and he wasn't about to contact the council to cover my people's incompetence. He said they should certainly be able to do a simple thing like bringing the quarry into the open."

The commander grinned. "He told you, of course, how that was to be done?"

"No, sir.'

"And they sent that guy to Combat," mused A-Riman silently, shaking his head. He punched a sequence of buttons on his desk.

The viewscreen lit up, showing a blue haze, then cleared as an alert face appeared, and a voice said crisply, "Admiral's office, Orderly here."

"CAC group commander here," he was told. "Let me talk to the admiral."

"Yes, sir." The orderly reached forward and his image was abruptly blanked out. A few seconds later, Sector Chief Dal-Kun's heavy face appeared. "Yes, commander, what is it?"

"Sir, I would like permission to land ten of my people on a primitive planet."

"Why?"

"I have five pickup orders, sir. The subjects have been located, and I'd like to land agents to bring them in."

"When were they located?"

"Half a cycle ago, sir."

The sector commander's face whitened slightly, then its normal silvery gray became suffused with a pale bluish tint. "Why," he deamnded angrily, "wasn't I contacted for this permission half a cycle ago?"

"I don't know of my own knowledge, admiral," replied A-Riman softly.

"Find out, commander. Call me back with the answer within an hour." The sector chief leaned forward. "Go in and get those Drones—now. I want a report on their apprehension within ten days." The screen became blank.

A-Riman looked up. "Gentlemen, you heard the conversation, so now you know where 'Higher Authority' may be found. The admiral said ten days. I know that doesn't leave much time to comb an entire planet and locate five men," he paused, looking about the group, "but I'm going to make it stiffer. If our people are any good at all, they'll have kept some track of our subjects. I want to see those Drones tomorrow, right after lunch—alive."

The five officers looked at each other. Then, they looked at their new group commander. "Tomorrow, sir?" said one. "Right after lunch?"

A-Riman nodded. "Alive," he emphasized. "I don't care how you do it. If you wish, and if ten men can, you may turn the planet inside out, but bring them in. We'll pick up the pieces and clean up the mess later. Now, let's get at it. You go to work while I explain to the admiral why this wasn't reported to him long ago." He touched the buttons again. "This meeting's adjourned."

Master Search Technician Kembar looked sourly at the communicator.

"Half a cycle, I'm hanging around this planet, watching a bunch of monkeys swagger around. They won't let me touch 'em. I can't just go in, fiddle around for a couple of days, then pick them up. No—I sit here, rigging gadgets to let me watch 'em." He turned to his companion, who merely grinned.

"Go ahead. Grin, you prehistoric Dawn-man. It ain't funny."

Scout Pilot First Class Dayne stretched his long arms. "So, now they tell you to go in. What's wrong with that?"

Kembar wagged his head. "Half a cycle, that's what's wrong. Then, they tell me to bring 'em in for lunch tomorrow." He glanced over the pilot's shoulder at the clock. "Well, set her down just outside of the city, and we'll get on with it. Tell the rest of the section to meet us in that park just outside of town."

Dayne nodded and turned to his controls. "They've got the old style Mohrkan body shields, haven't they?" he asked over his shoulder.

"Yeah," replied Kembar. He opened a locker, pulling out equipment and clothing. "Set up your hideaway projector now."

The Guest House of the Three Kings wasn't a very elaborate place, nor was it in the best section of Besiro. It had become the haunt of some of the capital's Elegants due to some chance whim of one of the leaders of fashion, and an astute proprietor had held this favor by quickly hiring excellent help, and stocking the best wines, while still retaining the casual atmosphere of a small, slightly down-at-the-heels public drinking place.

In the guest room, long wooden benches lined the walls. Before these were the scrubbed wooden tables. The center of the room was normally kept clear, so that the waiters could move more quickly to their customers. Sometimes, the customers used this open area for swordplay, but this was discouraged. Master Korno didn't like bloodstains marring the scrubbed whiteness of his floors.

Outside the Guest Room, in the large hall, Manir Kal met his friends. Balc was teasing one of the waitresses, while Kem-dor looked on with mild amusement.

"Where's Bintar?" queried Kal.

Kem-dor gestured. "Kitchen," he said. "He wanted the roast done just so."

Balc gave the waitress a slight shove. "I'm getting tired of this place," he remarked. "Getting to be a routine. How about finding something else?"

Kal shook his head. "Have to wait a while," he exlained. "Malon says they're still watching. Better not move till they give up." He frowned a little, looking at the bare hallway.

Kem-dor nodded. "I suppose you're right," he agreed, "but there must be something better than these silly gambling games. I'm just turning into a money-making machine, and it's beginning to bore me."

"Try their business houses," suggested Balc. "Might be some interest there."

Kem-dor snorted. "Tried that long ago," he complained. "At first, their elementary tricks were amusing, but—" He waved a jeweled hand.

"I know what you mean," said Kal. "The bravos don't put up much of a fight, either." He started for a door. "Well, let's go in and get a drink, anyway."

As he entered the Guest Room, Manir Kal started for the usual table over in the far corner. There was a large man sitting on the bench. Kal looked him over casually. He was a tall, lean individual—well enough dressed, but not in the precise height of style. Probably some rustic land-owner in for the carnival, decided Kal. He walked over.

"Sorry, fellow," he remarked. "You're in my place."

The man looked up, but made no effort to move. "Plenty more tables," he remarked. "I've been here for quite a while." He gestured at the table next to his. "Here, try this spot."

Kal smiled inwardly. Perhaps this one would provide some sport. "Possibly you didn't understand me," he said evenly. "You are sitting in the place I am accustomed to occupy. I'll thank you to move immediately."

The other picked up his glass and took a casual drink. "As I said," he remarked, setting the glass down again, "I've been here quite a while. I like it here." He looked Manir Kal over carefully. "Surely, you can get used to another table."

Someone at another table laughed.

Manir Kal's face flushed. He swept a hand past his belt, then picked up the stranger's glass and dashed it at the man's face.

The rustic vaulted over the table so rapidly he seemed to float. A hard fist struck Manir Kal in the nose, then, as he staggered back, a backhanded cuff sent him reeling against a table. For an instant, rage flooded through him. He snatched his sword out.

"I'll cut you to ribbons for this," he snarled.

The stranger had a sword, too. "Come and try," he invited.

Korno interposed his fat body between the two disputants. "Now, gentlemen," he protested, "there's a—"

Impatiently, Kal poked him with his sword. "Out of the way, fool," he growled, "before we use your body for a fencing mat."

With a shriek, Korno leaped out of the center of the room, then stood and rubbed his injured posterior as he watched the fight.

The blades slithered against each other as the duelists felt each other out, then Kal tried a quick thrust. It was parried, and the riposte nearly threw Kal out of balance. He felt a surge of enthusiasm. At least, this one could fight. He wove a bewildering net of thrusts and counterthrusts, then moved in with his favorite trick, a disarm he had learned long ago.

Somehow, it didn't work. He found his blade borne down to the floor. Quickly, he swung it up again, closing in to avoid a thrust.

"Have to do better than that," laughed the stranger in Kal's native language. "Much better."

Manir Kal started to answer, then the significance of the sudden language change struck him. "You're—"

With an easy shove, the stranger pushed Kal back, then, beating his blade aside, pierced the swordsman's shoulder with a straight thrust.

"That's right," he admitted, "I am."

"Hey," protested someone. "The Old Man said to bring 'em in alive."

"I know," replied Kal's assailant, sheathing his sword, "but he didn't say anything about cuts and bruises."

For a moment, Manir Kal stood, looking at this man who had so easily brushed aside his swordsmanship, then a haze closed in on him and he slipped to the floor. His three companions started for the door, but were met by several grim looking individuals with small objects in their hands—familiar objects.

"Screens down," ordered one of these. As the three

hesitated in bewilderment, he added, "Don't tempt us, children."

The large duelist hoisted Manir Kal to his shoulder and started for the door.

"All right, fellows," he said, "let's go." Then, he caught sight of Korno. "Oh, yes," he remarked. "We're taking this man to a doctor. His friends are going along with us."

A-Riman sat back in his chair. For the moment, his work was done and nothing remained outside of purely routine matters, which he had no intention of considering. He yawned, then glanced at his watch. It was just about time for someone to come up with a report on those five Drones. He smiled to himself.

"Wonder what activity they've taken so far?" he asked himself. He leaned forward and touched a button. An enlisted man's face showed in the screen for an instant, then blanked out, and Captain Poltar appeared.

"Yes, sir."

"How about those five pickups?"

The captain glanced down at his desk. "They're being interrogated right now, sir," he explained. "We planned to bring them to you after lunch as you ordered."

A-Riman raised his eyebrows. "Who brought them in, and when?"

"Lieutenant Norkal's patrol was on duty, sir. Sergeant Kembar took his section in and made the pickup. He came in early this morning."

"Very good," nodded the commander. "I like operations that come off ahead of schedule." He glanced at his watch again. "I think I can wait a little before lunch. Have the sergeant bring them here." He shut off the screen and sat back, waiting.

The door light flashed, and as A-Riman touched the button, Sergeant Kembar walked in and saluted. He was in a fresh uniform, his insignia gleaming like a new rainbow against the blackness of his clothing. He stepped to the side of the door and drew his sidearm.

"Send 'em in, corporal," he instructed.

Five slightly disheveled individuals filed in, followed

by a pair of neatly uniformed guards, who quickly herded them into a line facing the group commander.

A-Riman looked over the tableau, then laughed. "Fine, useful bunch of citizens," he remarked amusedly. "We have here a real credit to the Galactic Civilization."

Sergeant Kembar looked over the prisoners. "Things like these will happen, sir," he commented expressionlessly.

The group commander's amusement evaporated. "Unfortunately, sergeant," he replied, "they do." He pointed at Manir Kal, who stood facing him defiantly. The former swordsman of Besiro had a fresh bandage on his shoulder. His arm was carried in a sling, but he attempted to carry himself with something of his former swagger.

"What's this one good for?"

Sergeant Kembar smiled slightly. "It picks fights," he stated.

"Has it found anyone it can lick yet?"

The sergeant's smile broadened. "With the help of a body shield, it can conquer almost any primitive swordsman," he answered. "Of course, its knowledge of fighting arts is limited, but it knows which end of the sword is sharp—now." The sergeant glanced pointedly at the bandage.

Manir Kal looked angrily over at the sergeant, started to speak, then looked at his feet.

"Well," prompted A-Riman.

"He had a body shield, too," stated Kal.

A-Riman looked at the sergeant, who grinned. "Naturally, sir. Mine wasn't neutralized, either, but the subject found that out after it got pinked, fainted, and came to on the scout ship. It couldn't direct its blade close enough to me to find my shield during the little tussle." He examined his knuckles reflectively. "It leads with its nose, too," he added.

Manir Kal was stung. "I'm a Galactic Citizen," he stated angrily. "I object to being referred to as an 'it'!"

Dalhos A-Riman looked at him sternly. "You gave up your citizenship when you made planetfall on a primitive world," he commented coldly. "Now, you're simply a subject for rehabilitation. You are regarded as being of insufficient competence to speak for yourself." He waved a hand at Balc. "This one?"

The sergeant made a grimace of disgust. "It runs after females," he growled. He looked down the line of prisoners. "This one eats," he added, pointing. "This one, with the aid of a calculator, can solve elementary permutations and possibilities. It fancies itself as a gambler." The sergeant paused, then pointed again. "Here is the talented one. It can actually land a pleasure cruiser without having a wreck."

Malon looked at him sneeringly. "I managed to evade you," he pointed out.

The sergeant was unperturbed. "The subject ship headed in for planetfall after giving a false course plan," he said. "We could have blasted, but we were ordered not to destroy unless necessary. We have had all five of these subjects under close observation ever since their landing."

A-Riman nodded. "These are typical Drones?" he asked.

"Yes, sir. Some of them engage in other forms of amusement, some show a little more imagination, but these five are typical."

"I see." A-Riman stood up. "Take these things out, tag them, and ship them to Rehabilitation. In the future, simply pick up any criminal Drones, ship them to Aldebaran Base with suitable tags, and make out a report. I've seen enough of them." He started for the door. "I'm going to lunch now, sergeant," he added. "Be ready to report to me with your section when I return."

The sector chief was half way through his lunch when A-Riman walked into the dining room. With a quick, "By your leave, sir," the group commander slid into a chair and consulted the menu. As he dialed his choice, Dal-Kun cleared his throat.

"Hate to spoil your appetite, commander," he said, "but what's being done about those five Drones?"

A-Riman glanced at his watch. "They should be about

ready for shipment to Aldebaran by now, sir," he reported. "The reports are being prepared for submission to your office."

Dal-Kun speared a morsel of food. "Very good, commander," he started. "I'm—" Then, he looked up. "You picked 'em up in less than one day?" he roared. "What's been happening for the last half cycle?"

A-Riman shook his head. "I reported the situation to you, sir. The scouts were forbidden to make planetfall until yesterday afternoon. They had their subjects under extremely close observation and were able to bring them immediately they were granted permission to act."

"I suppose they made a mess on the planet. How long will it take you to clean up and prevent a stir for the planetary historians to pick over?"

"The pickup created very little disturbance," A-Riman frowned thoughtfully, "but I'm not sure yet about the effects of the Drones' stay. It may take as much as two tenths of a cycle for complete cover-up."

Bolsein and Knolu looked up as the sector chief planted both hands on the table.

"Commander," he demanded, "are you giving me a story?" He looked at his subordinate sharply. "Commander Redendale always insisted that it frequently took cycles to cover up a planetary landing by Guard Units."

A-Riman nodded his head. "Sometimes it does," he admitted. "I'd rather not comment on the commander, sir. I inherited some very good people from him." He touched the side of his face. "So good," he added, "that they went into this planet without more than ten people seeing them. They staged a minor barroom brawl, picked up their subjects, and were gone without any contact with the planetary authorities.

"I have ordered the sergeant in charge of the section to report to me this afternoon," he added. "I believe he and his entire section are due for a commendation on the operation. When I get through congratulating them, I'm going to order them back to clear up the rather unsavory mess our subjects left for them."

Dal-Kun grunted. "You didn't inherit anything from

Redendale but trouble," he announced. "Those people of yours either just came in from other sectors or were trained by previous commanders." The admiral glanced down at his plates distastefully, then punched a button for their removal.

"Redendale was here for less than a cycle," he continued. "I had him transferred because I wasn't sure he was the man for the job. Now, I'm almost sorry I didn't hold him for a Board." He leaned back, folding his arms.

"I believe, commander, that you said something about some experiments you wanted to make. As long as you can keep up with your routine like this, and you don't break any regulations, go ahead. Do you need any clearances?"

"Yes, sir." A-Riman told him. "I need planetfall clearance and at least a three-cycle occupation clearance for personnel on a primitive planet."

"For what reason?"

"General rehabilitation, sir. The civilization I have in mind is still in its infancy. Observer reports say that it is not a particularly desirable civilization, and I'd like to try a rehabilitation program.

"I feel that this civilization will either destroy itself in the near future, or force us to destroy it within five periods. I feel that, with proper supervision, it can be rebuilt into a useful, law-abiding culture, and one which will be a valuable addition to the Federation." He placed his hands on the table. "I feel we can do this without changing the basic characteristics of the civilization in question, and I feel that it is our Ethical duty to do so."

Dal-Kun looked at him thoughtfully. "I've read your 'Fighting Philosophy,'" he admitted, "but this is something new, isn't it?" He drummed on the table, then looked down the table. "Where are you going to get the personnel?"

"I can use existing CAC personnel for the first few cycles, sir, and possibly borrow a few men from the Fleets. After that, if the experiment shows promise, I will request additional agents."

"Do you think Operations will hold still for a further personnel requisition? You're a little fat right now."

"I know that, sir, but I hope to be able to show the desirability of my experiment before the ten-cycle survey. I should be able to establish a trend in eight cycles at the most."

"It'll be intensive work." The sector chief shook his head slowly, "About four thousand days to make noticeable changes in a planetary civilization which is at least that many cycles old." He looked at A-Riman searchingly. "Wonder if your people can swing it." Slowly, he nodded his head, then brought a hand down on the table. "Go ahead, commander. Try it. If you can show me convincing trends within six cycles, I'll keep the survey people off your back for another ten and let you build a case." He looked at the three officers for a moment then abruptly got up and left the room.

Veldon Bolsein exhaled explosively. "Brother," he said, "what a bill of goods." He looked at A-Riman, smiling crookedly. "You better make good, Old Philosopher. If you muff this one, your name's not even 'Space Dust.'"

Knolu grinned. "The man's right," he announced. "Slip up, and the Old Man'll feed you to the matter converter in tiny chunks, then he'll re-synthesize you to make a new pair of shoes."

A-Riman nodded. "I know," he told them. "I came here to try this, though, and I'm going to do it." He eyed the other two seriously for a moment. "If I mess this up," he added, "the Old Man'll have to do some delicate filtering to find enough of me to feed the converter with." He started for the door.

"See you," he called back. "I've got me a job of work to do."

Quel-tze, high priest of Gundar, Lord of the Sky, stood at the altar atop the temple of Dolezin. He looked skyward, estimating the time needed for Gundar to mount to his zenith, for it was nearly time for the sacrifice. The bright sun shone out of a cloudless sky on the spectacle. The large altar of white, polished stone reflected the light dazzlingly, causing the under-priests to avert their eyes from its surface. The shadow of the ring atop the pinnacle of the temple slowly approached the altar.

Quel-tze glanced about him at his priests, making a last minute check to see that all was in order. The five were at their proper stations, their regalia in proper order, reflecting the light of Gundar with the proper glory. One of them held the large golden bowl, another, the long sacrificial knife. The others were properly placed to strap the sacrifice into position with a minimum of lost motion. The high priest looked out over the city, where a sea of upturned faces greeted him. Good enough—all the populace were present.

The shadow started to mount the altar and Quel-tze made a sign behind his back, reaching for the knife with his other hand. A sonorous chant started from the level below and before the altar. The walls of this level, cut into a reflector, projected the chant out over the waiting people, and prevented more than a low murmur to reach the priests of the altar. The hymn to the Sun flooded the city of Dolezin to the exclusion of other sounds.

From the shadowed doorway behind the altar, two powerfully built priests came, holding the arms of a feebly protesting girl. Two more priests followed them. As she looked at the waiting altar, the girl's eyes widened, and her mouth opened.

"Silence, my child," instructed Quel-tze. "You are being honored beyond all other women of the city."

"I don't want to be honored," sobbed the girl. "I want to go home."

The high priest smiled thinly. "That cannot be, my daughter," he said.

He nodded to two priests behind the girl, who quickly removed the ceremonial kilt and the heavy breastplates and collar which she wore. They laid these aside, and grasping her ankles, they assisted the two who held her arms as they laid her quickly on the altar. The priests waiting at the altar quickly adjusted the straps to wrists and ankles so that the girl lay helpless on the altar, facing the sky and Gundar. She closed her eyes against the glare and screamed.

Below, the chanting voices harmonized with the scream, the basses weaving a slow, rhythmic pattern with the high, terrorized ululations.

The shadow of the great ring crept slowly along the girl's body, the brilliant disk of light within it approaching the breast.

Quel-tze raised both hands and gazed upward in a gesture of supplication. Below, the chorus chanted, "Grant, O Great Gundar, that our crops be fertile, that our ventures be successful."

The disk of light crept to the breasts. Quel-tze brought the knife down in a swift arc, ending at the center of the disk. Then, he made a rapid incision, the blade making a tearing noise as it progressed. The body of the girl twitched, then lay quietly. Now, the chant softened, and was still.

Reaching down, Quel-tze grasped the still feebly pulsing heart of the Harvest Maiden, cut it free with a few skillful slashes of the knife, and held it aloft for a moment before he handed it to one of the attendant priests. He held his hands up once more.

"The Harvest Maiden has gone to the realm of the Lord of the Sky," he declaimed. "Her pure spirit will assure us of plenty in the year to come."

A sigh arose from the onlookers below. Slowly, they started to disperse to their homes. On the outskirts of the crowd, an elderly man slowly led his obviously heartbroken wife away.

Quel-tze turned and made his way down the stairs to his apartment. As usual, he felt tired—emotionally spent— after the exhilaration of the sacrificial moment. This girl had been of striking beauty, he realized, but there were plenty of these.

He made a gesture of dismissal to his attendant priests and entered his rooms. He closed the door and took a few steps toward his sleeping room.

"Well," commented a voice, "our boy's come to us, all in one piece."

Quel-tze turned to the door, but a man stood before

it. He was a large man, dressed in unrelieved black, from which blazed small insignia. In his hand, he held a small instrument. Somehow, the manner in which he held this unfamiliar object made Quel-tze realize that here was a weapon which could easily prevent any effort of his to approach its holder. He turned again.

Now, where before there had been merely a vacant space, stood another man. This one was dressed in the ceremonial robes of the high priest of Gundar—Quel-tze's robes. He, also, held one of the small objects.

"They can't talk to you here," this man explained, "so I'm going to stand in for you while you become educated and instructed in your duties."

It seemed to Quel-tze that the object in the pseudo high priest's hand glowed for an instant. Then, all became dark.

Slowly, consciousness returned to Quel-tze. First, he was aware of the sounds of conversation about him, then of light, then of the straps which held him in his chair. Angrily, he strained at these bonds.

"You'll suffer for this," he threatened. "When I am missed—"

He was interrupted. A man in black uniform came into his field of vision. "Afraid you're wrong, baby," he said. "First, you won't be missed. Second, your world is far behind us." He stepped aside, waving to a screen, which lit up, showing small points of light in a black void. "That little one over there," he exlpained, pointing, "is your 'Lord of the Sky.' "

He turned again, smiling at Quel-tze. "Third," he added, "your re-education is about to begin." Again, he gestured to the screen.

"Many thousands of cycles ago," said a calm voice, "suns shone on their planets much as they do now. The planets were hardly more than cinders, but on scores of them were the faint stirrings of life."

Quel-tze felt a strong mental compulsion which forced him to look at the screen closely, to become part of it, to take up every bit of the offered information and absorb it into his awareness.

On the screen, the field of view narrowed, to show a single sun, with its planets, then one planet gradually filled the screen, its surface details becoming plain to see.

The lesson continued step by step. Quel-tze saw the beginnings of life. He saw the rising of life forms, then the beginnings of civilization. He was fed. He slept. The lessons continued.

Civilizations rose and flourished. Some declined and fell. The voice pointed out the reasons for their successes and their failures. As Quel-tze watched, a civilization reached peaks of technical and mechanical ability almost beyond his comprehension. The people of the planet traveled into space, reached for the stars, then, turning again to their old, internecine struggles, destroyed the results of centuries of slow development in a few short, blazing weeks. A few dazed survivors sadly picked over the wreckage of their once powerful, luxurious world. Their descendants reverted to savagery, then slowly began the laborious climb to civilization. Quel-tze shuddered—tried to shut the images from his mind—but always at the threshold of his consciousness was the almost inaudible, but powerful command: "Learn, for only by learning will you survive."

On the screen, the civilization was rebuilding, its development accelerating as it progressed. Again, this planet reached to space—successfully, this time. Other solar systems were reached. Interstellar conquest began, and Quel-tze watched the building of an interstellar empire. He also saw destruction, as civilizations crumbled to ruins, then to complete obliteration before the weapons of implacable conquerors.

The tone of the instruction changed. Before, the emphasis had been on the technologies of the subject civilizations. This second phase of his instruction was focused upon the growth of custom, of ethics, and of law. Again, the civilizations were on the march, their legal, ethical, and religious structures laid bare for observation. Cultures were traced, their oscillations—from high, super morality to definite immorality, to high morality again—becoming obvious under the quiet analysis of the teacher. Some of these systems of life led to decline and fall, others to sudden, blazing extinction. Several of them were successful, and were still extant in the galaxy. The basic framework of the Galactic Federation was exposed, and Quel-tze saw how multitudes of worlds, inhabited by varying peoples of widely varying origins, differing physical shapes, bodily chemistry, and mentalities could live in harmony and complete tolerance.

On one world, he saw a quiet, pastoral people, tending to their own business. Here was civilization which was fully cognizant of the high technology surrounding it, but which preferred to pursue its own quiet ways of life. Quel-tze came to the realization that in the eyes of the rest of the Federation, this technically undeveloped civilization was recognized as an equal. In the council, delegates from this world were received with respect when they voiced their opinions. Further, it was pointed out, the people of this world were by no means all indigenous. Numbers of them were natives of worlds far removed in space, and of totally differing original cultural pattern. Quel-tze also noted that in several cases, the ships flitting about in space actually formed cultures of their own. There were Federation members who rarely set foot upon any planet, and then not for long. Yet, these wanderers, too, were regarded as equals. They had their voice in the council, and contributed to the welfare and development of the Galactic Civilization in their own way.

The screen cleared. Again, dead planets circled a brilliant sun. Life stirred. Life forms grew and developed. One of these became predominant and formed a civilization, which slowly grew, rose, and flourished in its way. Quel-tze stirred uneasily. This was a familiar pattern. He examined the ethical structure, realizing that it was very familiar indeed. A religion came into power, superseding the power of state and of the people. The Sun became the "Lord of all Creation." Ceremonies were instituted, and the priesthood of the Sun gradually took over the reins of actual power, though none outside the temple realized what was actually happening. Quel-tze shook his head. He had seen similar patterns in previously analyzed civilizations, and the result had been invariable—decline, failure, fall or destruction.

Quel-tze squirmed in his chair as the account went on. A minor government official was proving to be unexpectedly and annoyingly honest. Despite veiled warnings from visiting priests and from some of his own associates, he refused steadfastly to condone and allow certain lucrative practices. Finally, the Temple acted. The daughter of the annoying officer was chosen for the annual sacrifice.

As the ceremony went on, the analytic voice detailed motives, reasons, probable consequences. Other, similar situations were recalled. Quel-tze shuddered, and as the climax of the ceremony occurred, he strained at his bonds for a moment, then collapsed in the chair.

Two men hurried to his side. One applied a small instrument to his throat, listened for a moment, then nodded.

"Close, sergeant," he remarked, "but he's still with us."

He made an injection in the high priest's arm and stood back.

Again, consciousness slowly returned to Quel-tze. This time, the room was silent. For a moment, madness crept into his eyes, then, he sat back quietly and waited for the screen to light up again. Nothing happened.

"You may continue with my education, gentlemen," remarked Quel-tze calmly. "I am ready again."

The black uniformed psychologist came into his field of vision. He looked closely at the captive, then smiled at him. Bending over him, he loosened the confining straps.

"I think you are, Quel-tze," he answered. "Would you like to meet your fellow-students?"

Quel-tze nodded wordlessly, then stood, flexing his muscles. He looked about the room for a moment, then followed the two guardsmen into the next compartment, where several people waited. One man came forward as the priest entered.

"Quel-tze," he said, holding out his hand. "A few days ago I hated you, but now, I think I can work with you."

Quel-tze raised his own hand. For a moment, the two men stood, hands on each other's shoulders. "I'm sorry, Tal-Quor," said the preist.

"I was at fault, too," the other admitted. "Had it been someone else's daughter, I would have remained undisturbed."

Someone called "Attention." Sector Chief Dal-Kun walked to the front of the room, looked at the twenty officers, then nodded.

"At ease, gentlemen," he ordered. "We seldom have a full staff meeting here, but Commander A-Riman has a report which should be of interest to all of us. I would like to have comments when it is completed. Commander A-Riman."

The CAC Commander faced the group. "As many of you gentlemen know," he began, "CAC has been engaged in an experiment for the past five cycles. The Criminal Apprehension personnel, as well as many of the Combat personnel, have become extremely interested in this experiment, and most of them have worked much more than normal time on it. With the cooperation of the sector comptroller"—A-Riman nodded to an elderly officer—"we have written off a good deal of our time to training. We think this time has not been wasted. I believe you gentlemen will agree after reviewing this report." A-Riman bowed slightly and took a seat.

The lights dimmed and the viewscreen lit up. A solar system appeared as seen from an approaching ship. One planet crept to the center of the screen and grew larger. The voice of an observer came from the speaker.

"This is the seventh planet of Sun Frank Three, number six two nine, Tenth Sector. Life has been in existence here for at least a thousand periods. The age of the present dominant civilization is estimated at seven periods."

The screen closed in, to show details of cities. Conversations between members of the populace were repeated. The thoughts and actions of officials were shown. The growth of cruelty in government, in private life, in the temple, was shown, as was the appearance of immorality and of human sacrifice. Finally, detailed scenes of the Harvest Maiden sacrifice appeared. The voice broke in again.

"As can be seen, this civilization has a high probability of failure. It will stagnate and eventually be eliminated, either by another civilization not yet formed, or by Federation Council orders, if it progresses far enough to warrant that attention." There was a pause. The screen showed an overall view of a large city, its buildings gleaming in the sun. "This is the civilization picked for initial experiment," added the voice.

The abduction of Quel-tze and his companions was shown. Scenes of their training appeared in brief flashes, then their return to their own world was shown. The reforms instituted by these people began to appear, one scene showing Quel-tze as he faced six councilors of the Kelmiran Empire. One of them was speaking.

"This tampering with the time-honored ceremonies of our religion will not be tolerated," he announced.

"I thought I was the high priest," objected Quel-tze mildly.

The councilor looked at him scornfully. "You should know, priest, that your temple has always been the creature of the state. We give the orders—you merely furnish the cloak of sanctity."

"This borders upon sacrilege," remarked the priest.

"This is merely practical government," snorted the councilor. "Now, for the last time, will you accept our nomination for the Harvest Maiden?"

Quel-tze smiled gently. "As I said before," he insisted, "the Harvest Ceremony is being changed to conform with the ceremony of many years ago, before the age of cruelty and immorality. The altar has been removed."

The councilor's mouth tightened. "Then, you force us to act," he growled with a gesture of finality. For a moment, he stood looking at the high priest, then he turned. "Guards," he called, "arrest this man for treason."

A group of armed priests stepped into the room. The councilors looked at them in puzzlement.

"These," explained Quel-tze calmly, "are my guards. Yours are in the temple dungeons, where you will soon join them." He looked at the leader of the priestly warriors. "Take them below, Qual-mar. They will await a Temple Trial for sacrilege."

The six councilors blanched. "The emperor—" one of them quavered.

Again, Quel-tze smiled. "The emperor," he told them, "is receiving a priestly delegation. I might add that it is a much more effective delegation than yours. No threats will be made, no violence will be offered, but tomorrow, the emperor will find it expedient to appoint new councilors."

Further scenes showed the operations of the new Imperial Council. The final scene showed the Harvest Maiden, standing proudly atop the temple at Dolezin. She had reason to be proud, for she had been chosen from all the young girls of the city as the most beautiful, the most talented, of all. By her side, stood a prize draft animal, which would be later used in the Imperial stables. In her hands, she held the best of the year's crop. Below her, the priests chanted. It was the same hymn to the Sun, but now it was slightly muted, and the clear, high voice of the Harvest Maiden could be plainly heard, leading the melody. The voice broke in again.

"Probable success is now indicated for this culture. Considerable supervision must be given for at least a period, but it is believed that the civilization will now progress to become a valued member of the Federation."

The lights brightened. Commander A-Riman stood again. "Gentlemen," he said, "this is the report on the first five cycles of this experiment. You have seen most of the steps taken. Of course, we forced this process somewhat to prove our point in a short space of time. I believe further activity of this type should take place at a more leisurely pace, but we think we have shown a desirable result. Are there any comments?"

Geronor Keldon, the sector comptroller, stood. "Gentlemen," he said, "I will admit that I authorized the utilization of Commander A-Riman's personnel on this experiment with some misgivings. Now that I've seen the results, I have no further objections to continuation."

Several other officers added their remarks. Most of them were laudatory. A few expressed regret that they had not been involved in the operation. Finally, Dal-Kun got to his feet.

"Well," he remarked, looking about the room, "it seems that the report has met with general favor. I would like formal reports of your reactions, and any suggestions as to improvement. I feel that this report, with recommendations should be presented to the Federation Council for consideration." Again, he looked about the room. "This meeting is adjourned."

A-Riman switched off the report as the buzzer sounded. The screen lit up and his secretary's face appeared.

"Who is it?" queried the commander.

"Captain Poltar, sir."

"Put him on."

The captain's face was slightly amused as he appeared on the screen. "The new personnel just came in, sir," he announced. "Do you want to see them now?"

A-Riman dropped the report recordings into their cases. "Send them in," he instructed. "How do they look to you?"

"Pretty good, sir." Again, the expression of secret amusement crossed the captain's face. It annoyed A-Riman slightly.

"What's so funny, captain," he demanded.

"Nothing important, sir. I'll send in the first one now."

"Bring him in personally," growled his superior. "Then, we'll both be able to enjoy the joke." He switched off and waited. There must be something very strange about this new batch of personnel to make Poltar laugh.

A-Riman couldn't remember too many times that officer had even smiled.

He pressed the admittance button at the signal, and the captain walked in. "Here's the first one, sir," he said, stepping aside.

A guardsman entered. He held his head directly to the front, paying no attention to the furnishings of the office. Pacing off the prescribed two paces with mathematical precision, he halted and came to a rigid salute. A-Riman's practiced eyes took in the man's entire appearance at a glance. He was freshly uniformed. No spot of light reflected from the absolute, dead blackness of his clothing, excepting where the iridescent glow of the torches at his collar picked up the light and broke it into a blazing spectrum.

"Junior Search Technician Manir Kal reporting for duty, sir," the man reported. He dropped his hand sharply, standing at perfect attention.

"At ease, guardsman," said A-Riman. "Haven't I seen you before?"

"Yes, sir," the man replied. "I've been here before."

"I remember," commented the group commander dryly. He fixed Captain Poltar with a mildly scornful look. "It's happened before," he remarked. "What's funny?"

"There's more to it, sir," grinned Poltar. He moved to the door and beckoned. Another guardsman entered and stood at salute.

"Junior Psychologist Barc Kor Delthos reporting for duty, sir."

"Well, well," commented A-Riman. "Any more?"

"Three more, sir," said Poltar. "A physicist, a trend analyst, and a pilot."

A-Riman's face broke into a grin, then he sat back and laughed. "All right," he admitted. "You've scored. Bring 'em in and send for Sergeant Kembar."

Three more men filed in, reported, and stepped to the side. A-Riman looked at them severely. "Now," he inquired, "just who dreamed up this idea?"

Manir Kal raised a hand. "I'm afraid I did, sir," he

admitted. "Of course, Senior Rehabilitation Technician Kwybold had something to do with it, too."

A-Riman nodded. "I thought I recognized his delicate touch," he commented. "How was rehabilitation?"

Manir Kal grimaced. "I spent a good share of it in the hospital, sir." He rubbed his chest reflectively. "I can name at least twenty guardsmen who can beat me at swordplay. They all tried it." He paused for a moment. "I learned plenty, though," he added. "I've an idea I could give Sergeant Kembar a hard time now."

"Want the opportunity?" A-Riman smiled at him.

Manir Kal shook his head. "Thank you, sir, no," he said decidedly. "Next time I unsheath a sword, it'll be in line of duty. It's part of my business now, and I'm not giving out any free samples of my swordsmanship."

Sergeant Kembar came into the office. A-Riman caught him on the first pace. "At ease, sergeant." He waved a hand. "Here are five more men for you."

"Thank you, sir. I'm a little shorthanded right now." Kembar looked toward the five guardsmen. "I'll get their—" He looked again, then stared directly at Manir Kal. "I've met you before," he stated positively. Then, he looked at the others.

"This one picks fights," stated Manir Kal expressionlessly.

"It runs after females," announced Barc.

"I'm the talented one," boasted Malon.

Kembar placed his hands on his hips, and shook his head helplessly. "All right," he chuckled, "so I know Rehabilitation, too. How do you think a lot of us got into this business?"

A-Riman coughed. "I've got news for you, sergeant," he said.

Master Search Technician Kembar snapped to attention. "Yes, sir."

"I know Mr. Kwybold, too," A-Riman told him. "A few thousand cycles ago, I led a revolution against the Federation Council."

* * *

Kilar Mar-Li arose slowly from his chair. As the senior delegate from Celstor, he realized that his word carried weight. He also realized that this report and proposal was from a compatriot and protégé of his. He thought, however, that the report still warranted comment.

"Fellow members," he began, "we have just seen an interim report, and heard a proposal." He noticed smiles on the faces of several members and decided against too dignified an approach. He smiled, too. "Terrible introduction, I'll admit," he added, "but the fact remains that for the past four Galactic Standard Hours, we've been watching a report from Sector Ten. A new experiment has been tried, and I think it's worth following up. I would like to move that the council issue special authorization to Commander A-Riman to continue his operations."

A delegate from the comparatively new Paldorian Empire arose. "I would like to propose an amendment," he said, "to the effect that a motion be entered for the consideration of the delegate from the seventh planet, Sun Frank Three, number six two nine, Tenth Sector, for the establishment of a new corps in the Stellar Guard, this corps to be devoted to the education and, where necessary, the rehabilitation, of new cultures over the entire galaxy."

The chairman laughed. "I might remind the delegate," he commented, "that it may be a couple of thousand Standard Cycles before that still unborn gentleman takes his seat."

Mar-Li arose again. "I accept the amendment," he remarked. "The Federation has waited for more than a thousand periods for this experiment to begin. We can wait for two or three more periods to see its results. I predict that many of us here will be present to welcome the new delegate to his seat."

Marzold Quonzar, first delegate to the Federation Council from the newly admitted Gundarian Association, blinked his eyes as the lights came on.

"So that's the true story," he mused. For a few minutes he sat thinking, then he called his secretary.

"Write a motion for consideration of the Federation Council. Title it 'A proposal for the formation of a new corps in the Stellar Guard.' You can word most of it, of course." He paused. "Let me see," he reflected. "That Commander was nicknamed 'The Fighting Philosopher.'" He nodded his head. "We will recommend as a name for this new organization, 'The Philosophical Corps.'"

EDITOR'S INTRODUCTION TO:

THE VOODOO SCIENCES
J. E. Pournelle, Ph.D.

Every now and then I recall that I'm supposed to be a scholar. You can blame it all on my early exposure to science fiction; and to John W. Campbell's unfailing devotion to reason and science as ways to solve all human problems.

Science fiction stories are by definition fiction. A truism, of course; but consider what it means. We can, in science fiction, postulate a faster-than-light drive, or anti-gravity, or collapsed metal. We can postulate new sources of cheap energy. We then work out what the world might be like if we had those things.

We can do that in the social sciences. During the Golden Age there were a lot of whacking good stories based on the notion of rational social sciences: and in nearly every one of them there was a scientific penology. Rehabilitation worked; and of course it was better to rehabilitate than punish.

You just read such a story, and you'll read many others, and that's fine—so long as you remember that they're stories. Because there are places where they truly believe they have a science of history: and thus it's a good idea to put dissidents into madhouses. Rebels must be crazy. Sakharov is perhaps the best known of those; but there are thousands of others in the Soviet Union.

After all, it's logical, isn't it? If you assume that Marxism-Leninism is a true science of history, then to rebel against the rule of Marxist-Leninist social engineers is irrational; and you don't want to be irrational. Best cure you of your delusions. Orwell saw it coming. By the end of *1984* Winston loved Big Brother. . . .

Herewith two essays on social science. They were originally columns in *Analog Science Fiction*; and although they were written some time ago, I see no need to revise either. One predicts drastic consequences of our neglect of the space program; predictions that came true well before the *Challenger* disaster made it clear to everyone that something was fundamentally wrong. I fear it still isn't clear enough. The long-term consequences of our failure to invest in the future may return to make our children curse our memory.

These essays are polemical; but I do mean what I say. I may have overstated the case against the so-called social sciences, but not by much.

Both essays are mostly concerned with economics, simply because economics is supposed to be the most advanced of the social sciences. We have, by law, a Council of Economic Advisors, and they give Nobel Prizes in economics. God help us.

THE VOODOO SCIENCES
Jerry Pournelle

Part One: The Gamblers

This 1982 meeting of the American Association for the Advancement of Science featured as keynote speaker Dr. George A. Keyworth, Science Advisor to the President.

Much of what Dr. Keyworth said made sense. We must, he said, cut back; be selective. The days of "As long as you're up, get me a grant" are over. We shall rigorously pursue excellence—

I'd have been more impressed if he hadn't, in the same speech, made it pretty clear that they're cutting back the planetary exploration program. If you want excellence, what's better?

He did announce that they've no intention of saving money by turning off the Deep Space Net; they'll be listening to *Voyager* when he gets to Uranus. The rest of the planetary program, however, is in trouble.

So is space investment. The Citizen's Advisory Council (The Citizen's Advisory Council on National Space Policy: J. E. Pournelle, Ph.D., Chairman; a civilian advisory group privileged to make reports to the President) has shown that every year for a decade we have seriously underestimated the requirements for capability to put payloads in orbit. This includes *all* requirements: civil, scientific, environmental (such as weather and pollution monitoring), and communications. If we lose one Shuttle—something not at all impossible—we are in *real* trouble. Yet, with all the evidence staring them in the face, the administration has not made any commitment to great expansion of our space access capability.

That's the space front. We're not doing so much on the rest of the high technology front, either. Why?

One problem, I think, is that we have so many economists pretending they know something. Perhaps one or two do. Perhaps. But no two of them seem to make the same recommendations, and most of them ignore what seems so obvious that I suppose you have to get a Ph.D. before you can't see it.

I once heard John Kenneth Galbraith and Arthur Laffer, respectively champions of liberal and conservative economics, debate for a full two hours on the subject of why the 60's were so good and the 70's so bad; and in all that time, neither mentioned the words "research", "development", "space", or "technology."

Yet it seems clear: if you've got to spend more than you make, you'd better do some investing, and fast. You might also want to gamble.

If a family can see that over the next five years they've no choice but to spend money that won't be coming in, they've got some decisions to make. Perhaps a second job, or a new source of income; but suppose there aren't any?

Sell something? But if there's nothing to sell? Cut expenses? Perhaps, although if the expenses are *taxes* that's not going to work either. And governments, it seems, *can't* cut expenses. Reagan's "cuts" were only a slowdown of increases; the 1983 budget is considerably larger (in real dollars) than was the 1982 budget. So while we talk of budget cuts, we dont' mean it, and I don't suppose we ever will.

Then what's left? In the case of a family, it's obvious.

Speculative investments. If you're going to go broke anyway, take a high flyer and the worst that happens is you're bankrupt sooner; at best you make enough to keep going.

Return now to the US: we have an aging work force. It is absolutely predictable that in a few years there are going to be more people retired, and fewer able to work; and somebody's got to support the retired. They're voters, you know, and they'll be organized.

Project this scenario ahead twenty years, and you can scare yourself; yet I think of no single institution, none whatever, that can and will do anything about it. All parts of our government operate on a much shorter time frame. If we had one hereditary house in Congress— heresy as it is to say—we'd at least have an institution that worried about the next decade, since its members would know they'd still be there to face the problems. They might also be concerned about their children. But we have no such institution in government, and now that the family has become relatively unimportant we don't have many private ones to look that far ahead either.

Does this mean we're doomed?

I don't know. It's sure a hell of a challenge.

How, then, can we prevent our children from cursing our memory?

The best way, it seems to me, is investment; to do what Keyworth said the administration wants to do; but do it in a big way. Look: we're facing bankruptcy. They keep projecting federal deficits larger than the whole budget was during the Johnson administration. The remedy, some say, is to raise taxes, but we all know that's asinine. All higher taxes do is stimulate people to spend effort on tax avoidance rather than wealth creation. Right now we have teams of the brightest people in the nation working for the IRS, and other equally competent teams working for their victims; the vectorial sum of their activity is zero. How is the Republic well served by this?

No: if we're headed for bankruptcy, we'd as well be

hung for sheep as lambs. You're going to have deficits? Pity; but if so, take some of it and invest. Back long shots. Like space industries. Lunar colonies. Heave money at the universities. Change tax laws to provide really heavy incentives for industry to do basic R&D.

What you're praying for is a breakthrough; some way to change the very rules of the game. That's happened often enough in history, although seldom in response to deliberate stimulation; but what the hell, we're desperate, or should be.

And I mean that: we should be in a state of near panic just now. How can you look into the future and be anything but scared? The work force gets older. Our machines get older. Our taxes get higher, and our savings get lower. More and more people become concerned with "survival", the underground economy is the only thing that's booming (and what a marvelous thing that is! We get surgeons out painting their own houses, because it's cheaper than hiring it done. A real accomplishment). We ought to be scared stiff.

Now maybe, just maybe my colleague Harry Stine is right; that without any government investments the capital for space development will be forthcoming from the private sector; the Third Industrial Revolution will proceed apace, without stimulation from Washington. Maybe. I hope so. But I don't see many signs of it. I don't have a lot of faith in corporate management.

Here is a question for the Ph.D. Qualifying Examinations in Management Science:

The aliens have landed, and they are every bit as powerful as we imagined. The guards we place around them are merely to keep them from being annoyed. They spend a few weeks studying us; then their leader makes an offer.

"We will make you wealthy," it says. "Wealth beyond the dreams of avarice, sufficient wealth that every child, woman, and man on Earth will have the equivalent of a million dollars. Each of you will have perfect health for five hundred years, after which you will have a quick and painless death. No senility and no lingering illnesses."

They mean it, too. Assume further that we have ways to verify this, perhaps by direct communication with the Galactic Federation. They can give us wealth, health, and longevity. They will also be able to exact the price, and we won't be able to fudge on it. They always do what they say.

"Knowledge, too," they offer. "We will tell you everything you want to know about the Cosmos. How stars work, and where the solar neutrinos have gone, and if the universe is open or closed, and how many elementary particles there are (you'll be surprised at the answer . . .)"

"What's the price?" we ask.

"We want your solar system. But we're in no hurry at all to collect it. All this we do for you; but after 1000 years exactly every human will be born sterile."

QUESTION: Should we accept or reject that offer? Use cost/benefit ratio theory to justify your answer.

The interesting part is not that everyone I know believes we ought to reject the offer, but that current management theory provides no reason why we should—at least I've seen none.

Current management theory doesn't give any good reasons for investing in space. Investments that don't mature for twenty years simply don't figure in Return on Investment (ROI) and Position in the Industry (PII) charts; while ten year maturity investments are hedged about with all sorts of caveats.

Looking out for the long term good ("To promote the general welfare, and insure the blessings of liberty to ourselves and our posterity") must be the province of government, because no manager who does that will long keep his job in industry. Managers are trained to look at, not just the bottom line on the annual report, but on *quarterly* earnings. The modern corporate notion of long-range planning is to look ahead two years.

But then politicians who look a generation ahead aren't likely to be rewarded either. Our political system gives jobs for life to judges and low to medium level bureaucrats, but never to political leaders or high-level decision makers; nor indeed do we have much of a mechanism for making long-term plans and carrying them out.

So while I'd like to believe Harry Stine is right, and that the space moguls will come up with the cash, I'm also a bit worried because I don't see many on the horizon.

Which brings me back to the central point: we, the readers of this book, are more important than perhaps we think. True, not all of us look ahead to the future: but most of us do, *and we may be most of the people doing that.*

Scary, isn't it?

So what can we do?

Alas, nothing I haven't said before; nothing spectacular like marching on Washington. But we do have to organize. (My favorite organization, not surprisingly, is the L-5 Society, 1060 E. Elm, Tucson AZ 85619, $30/year.)

We must, somehow, convince Washington that the future has a real constituency; that we're not just a bunch of mild-mannered nuts out here, but people who are determined; that we can get together and change the results of elections; that space and high technology and investment in the future are issues that really do count, and politicians too blind to see that can be punished.

And, slowly, we are doing that. Not as quickly, not as dramatically as we'd like; but we're getting a hearing.

Our immediate goal is to get into the next State of the Union message. The long-term goal is to get official Washington to understand that when you're on a binge you can't get out of, and facing bankruptcy anyway, flinging a few percent into high-flying investments may be the only way out. It's not that far-out an idea. Anyone can understand it. Except maybe an economist.

Part Two: The Voodoo Sciences

"I wouldn't know anything about politics," my friend said the other day. "I'm only an engineer."

He happens to be a very good engineer, but he named his profession as if ashamed of it. I see this a lot. The social scientists are automatically assumed to know more about society and politics than the hard scientists—even when the subject matter is something like nuclear power.

I wouldn't be so sure.

I hear a lot recently about "voodoo economics." The term is most often employed by Democrats in reference to President Reagan's economic policies; but I've also heard professional economists use the term "voodoo economics" in a way that implies there is a real science of economics in contrast to "Reaganomics."

Certainly the official policy is that economics is a science. We have by law a Council of Economic Advisors to report to the President, while the Congress has Alice Rivkin and her staff of economists to tell them what they should do.

From all the evidence I've seen, we'd do as well to give the President a Council of Voodoo Practitioners, and let the Congress consult its Chief Astrologer. In fact, I suspect that a chief *hungan* and *mamba* would do less harm than our present economists: we'd be less likely to take them seriously. However much our Chief Voodoo Advisor protested that his work was scientific, we'd demand some kind of track record, some evidence that his predictions might once in a while come true; while we impose no such burdens on economists, which is just as well for them, since their track record is one of universally dismal failure.

One of the first things they teach stock brokers is to stay out of the stock market. Brokers make their pile from selling advice, and from commissions on stock transactions. They can't predict the market, and few risk their own money. They, at least, only affect their clients' fortunes. Economists, though, can ruin the lot of us with their advice—yet if no science can predict a relatively closed system like the stock market, how the devil are you going to "fine tune" something as large as the American economy? I'd think it arrogant to try; as arrogant as the man with three illiterate drug-addicted spoiled brats writing a book on parenting.

But there's worse to come: to the extent that there is a "science of economics", its practitioners must behave in ways that other professions would brand unethical. Example: the Corporate Economist of a large aircraft company is going to give a speech. He has made his analysis (cast lots? examined tea leaves?) and he forsees nothing but bad news. We're in a "downside cycle" and there ain't much to be done about it. So he goes to a meeting of, say, the Airline Owners, and of course when asked for his predictions he gives his honest professional opinion—

In a pig's eye, he does. If he told what he thinks is the truth, he'd be fired. Worse, the Securities Exchange Commission would look at all his financial records and probably charge him with manipulating the value of his company's stock. It would be sure to fall; and if he'd prudently sold any shares recently he would likely go to jail.

No: his speech is predictable. He'll give some nodding acknowledgement to current hard times, predict an upswing, and tell his audience they better be prepared to buy a lot of airplanes.

Dr. Milton Friedman has a Nobel Prize in economics; one assumes he must know something about the subject. He once said, "Every economist knows that minimum wages cause unemployment. That's not a principle, it's a definition." The logic seems clear enough, at least when applied to home economics: if I can get the yard cut for a couple of bucks, I'll pay it; raise the minimum wage to $17.50 an hour, and I'll cut it myself, or let it grow. Whomever I'd have hired will go jobless.

Of course not all economists agree with that. After all, it's not only possible, but *likely* that the Nobel Prize in economics will go in alternate years to people who disagree on nearly every fundamental. I have a textbook on macroeconomics, and every chapter essentially cancels out the last, as each "school" presents its theories—and proves the others wrong.

In point of fact, the economists don't have the foggiest notion of what's wrong with our economy or what to do about it; and the very best economics textbook have almost nothing to say about science, engineering, research, development, and technology.

Arthur Schlesinger Jr. recently said, "The collapse of economic analysis is demonstrated by the hopeless cacophony of economic forecasting, where experts generally disagree with each other and nearly all turn out wrong—a circumstance that, alas, discourages neither economists from making forecasts nor the rest of us from believing them."

So: will someone tell me what, other than one's political preferences, is the difference between "professional" and "voodoo" economics? And why we pay a Council of Economic Advisors while neglecting to have a Chief Astrologer?

Go to any U.S. university. You will hear lamentation and wailing and gnashing of teeth. Washington has become unfeeling and stupidly refuses to support higher education: don't those idiots on the Potomac know that education is investment in the future? Don't they know that human resources are our most valuable resources, that public higher education is necessary preparation for a democratic future? That we must invest in the future?

But now wander about the campus, and look at how our typical university allocates that all-important investment dollar. You will find that the "social science" departments are far larger than the "hard sciences," and indeed have more students than are enrolled in liberal arts. You will find that even in states with tens of thousands of unemployed teachers, the Department of Education is among the very largest departments on campus.

The social sciences will be large and important departments, with many members of faculty and much classroom space. One wonders what it is that graduates in the social sciences are prepared to do. It must be an important skill; we are spending a large part of our scarce but all-important investment funds to acquire it. Oddly enough, though, we're not training so many engineers and scientists, physicists and mathematicians. Why?

But of course the answer is well known. In most universities, our education investment funds are allocated by entering freshmen. They go to a kind of oriental bazaar, where they are seduced into choosing a major; the number of majors then determines the department's share of the university's budget funds. It does seem an odd way to allocate an important resource.

One might suppose a better way: that the legislature, or other public authority, determine the number of engineers, biologists, physicists, medicos, sociologists, etc., that might reasonably be required in future, and allocate public funds among the departments accordingly. Students wishing to declare various majors could so do; but when the number that the taxpayers will support is exceeded, the next student to enroll in that major gets to pay tuition accordingly. If tax supported higher education is an investment—and what other theory justifies sending the tax collector, policeman, and ultimately the public hangman to extort funds from the taxpayers?—then might we have some care in the way that investment is allocated? The present scheme looks like a bad parody invented by an inept science fiction writer. Who'd believe it if it weren't happening?

At least, though, the present scheme should give us plenty of social scientists, as well as lots of professional teachers. With all those behavioral scientists we shouldn't have any problems teaching the young to read and write: even if the teachers have problems, the sociologists and psychologists can devise a scientific education program.

Only they don't. They don't even try. And when someone does succeed, as for example Marva Collins of Chicago who built quality private schools in what she called "the allegedly fetid ghetto", the "professional educators" put out reams of material calling her a "hoax" who was "carefully constructed as a media event." It really infuriates the educational professionals to find someone able to do the job they claim they can do.

Mrs. Roberta Pournelle teaches in a juvenile detention facility. Her students are teenage illiterates. Most of them come with five pounds of paperwork that definitely *proves* that this kid cannot possibly learn to read. The schools, the psychologists, the educators haven't failed; there's something wrong with the kid. Roberta throws the paperwork away and teaches the kid to read. She hasn't failed yet.

Then there's the court system. In the history of trials, there must be about three cases in which the prosecution's psychiatrist said an accused pleading not guilty by reason of insanity was nuts, and none at all in which the defense's psychiatrist said he wasn't. Yet the taxpayers continue to pay for this all too predictable "scientific" expert testimony.

This is professionalism?

And yet: we not only excuse gross incompetence among social scientists, we let them give real scientists and engineers an inferiority complex. Somehow we've swallowed whole the myth that you can be well-rounded, an educated person, although knowing no science and mathematics whatever; but engineering and science majors are automatically uncultured boors, hardly fit for polite society.

We have a Council of Economic Advisors, and we debate economic policy, and everyone listens as these soothsayers pontificate about monetary policy; and meanwhile, the President's Science Advisor is a low ranking White House official, there is no Engineering Advisory Council, and there is no cabinet level post held by an engineer. More than a majority of seats in every major legislature in the land is held by lawyers (and we wonder why the law is so complex?); but there are about two engineers in Congress, and no cabinet-level post is held by an engineer or scientist.

Now go again to your typical university. Find an

engineering student and a social science student. I'll bet you anything you like that the engineer will have read about as much history and literature and genuine liberal arts as the social scientist; while the social scientist will know nothing of engineering and physics, little of biology, and no mathematics. He may protest that he "took stat"; which will mean that he knows how to do cookbook calculations to produce the mean, median, and mode of a bunch of numbers. Given a little help he may also be able to compute the standard deviation; and with a textbook and a bit of luck he might even be able to do a "T" test, although odds are that he won't have the foggiest notion of what the T test assumes.

Go now to a rally protesting a nuclear power plant. There'll be a lot of students there. How many will be engineers? And how many social scientists? Of the social scientists, how many will understand *anything* of nuclear physics? How many will know the difference between ionizing and non-ionizing radiation?

Engineering students may apologize for deficiencies in "culture." Social activists glory in their ignorance of science. The man who started the People's Lobby, the first of California's mass anti-nuclear groups, used to say proudly, "The only physics I ever took was Ex-Lax."

The fact is that engineers and scientists will have studied far more of the liberal arts than social scientists will have studied of physics or engineering. (And alas, neither will know any history.)

Isn't it about time we ended this farce? Granted, the social sciences have a tough subject matter; but it isn't made easier by involving us all in a conspiracy to act as if they'd skills they just haven't got. It would be a lot easier to respect them if they made their students take hard courses: calculus through differential equations, *real* probability and statistics, operations research, basic computer science. Of course if their students mastered those subjects, they'd probably get out of "social science" and into something useful. Meantime, though, they can stop trying to get the rest of us to act as if they know something we don't.

EDITOR'S INTRODUCTION TO:

PAX GALACTICA
Ralph Williams

I read this story not long after I returned from the Korean War; it takes place during that unhappy era, and makes use of characters and incidents of that war, and must therefore be considered an "alternate universe."

It could as easily be rewritten to take place tomorrow morning, or in the next century.

PAX GALACTICA
Ralph Williams

In North America, it was a bright, cool April night when Galactic Security, after several years of careful observation, decided the Solar Phoenix was a little too hot for Terrestrials to play with.

Early Warning, as was its function, made first contact as the ships flashed up over the northwestern horizon. The first report was disbelieved, it was off the grid and too high and too fast—but it was followed almost instantly by contact from three other sites. The controller made a rough mental plot from those first few tracks and did not like it at all. He gnawed his thumbnail for about thirty seconds, and by that time the tracks were going up in plot. The sight decided him. There was no time to be wrong about this, the strangers were closing too fast, better to take a chance on looking silly than to be caught short.

He scrambled everything he had and transmitted a full alert—

On the control deck of the lead ship of the second element, the captain and the task commander of the GS patrol stood watching Earth roll by them fifty miles below.

"We're being tracked," the watch officer said. He did not speak in English, of course, nor in any Earthly tongue. As a matter of fact, he did not speak at all, as we use the term.

The task commander nodded. "Let 'em track. This is task, not reconnaissance. They'll have plenty of reason to know we're here in a few minutes, anyway."

Below, off the starboard bow, a smudge of light marking an airfield suddenly winked out. "Rather effective security they have, at that," he added drudgingly, "considering their technical limitations."

"Coming on first target," the watch officer said.

The task commander glanced at the position plot and stepped over to his station. "Polka Dot Leader, Task Leader," he said, "coming on your target. Advise an execution."

"Polka Dot Leader, Roger," the speaker said, "coming on target." Thirty miles ahead, the first gleaming shape showed gaping holes along its belly as its bays slid open.

"On target," the speaker said.

An orderly array of stubby-winged projectiles drifted leisurely out of her belly.

"All clear, 1319 and a quarter," the speaker said.

"Roger," the task commander said. "Rendezvous." The empty bays of the big silver ship blinked shut and she stuck her nose up and began to climb. Below her, her progeny dipped and swung faster and faster toward Earth, while the remainder of the formation swept past above.

The task commander studied the position plot again. "Polka Dot Two," he said, "coming on your target."

The radar did not at first catch the drop, but when the lead ship left formation and began to climb, the controller smelled death on its way. Without thinking twice, he ordered Bomb Warning A. He had no way of knowing what was coming, but those ships up there were certainly nuclear powered, no chemical engine could drive that high and fast, and whatever they laid would be potent. For himself, and the personnel of plot, there was nothing he could do. They had to stay and keep trying. He did not, he thought somewhat gloomily, even have time to worry about it; at that moment the first tracks on the projectiles began to come through, as they separated from the formation, and he began to be very busy.

There was no use trying for the ships themselves, they went over at five times his interceptors' ceiling and six times their speed, he vectored everything he had in on the extrapolated drop course. Even this was useless, he soon found. As they closed with his fighters, the projectiles suddenly put on power and took evasive action. He had guessed they would, a free drop would hardly be made from that altitude and distance, but confirmation did not make him happy. The first projectile sizzled past the fighters at fifteen hundred miles an hour and streaked for the base—

Strategic Air Command alerted on the first flash, and by the time the GS patrol had made its second drop the heavies were rumbling-out onto the runways. They were armed and their eggs snuggled lethally in their bellies, but their pilots did not yet know their targets. Their mission was retaliatory, to get air-borne before the first strike hit them, and to see there were no bases for the enemy to return to. They would get their targets when the enemy was identified.

They never did get them. The first bomber was fifty miles out climbing on course when they got the bad news from their controller. A moment later their own radar picked up the bandit, closing fast from above. The turrets began to swivel, but they were not fast enough, they could not even track the enemy; as he flashed by at two thousand yards something flickered out to touch the big bomber, and it crumpled in on itself and lost speed and began to fall through the night just beginning to be touched by dawn.

The commanding general of SAC himself had observed the action by radar.

"Those weren't bomb-drops," he said. "They were fighter-drops. Fighter-bombers, probably. They'll be here next."

His words were prophetic. They were—

The GS patrol had flown into day, through it, and back into night again, on a course that roughly quartered the globe, by the time the last drop was made. Task Leader and Red Stripe Three pulled up to orbital altitude together and cut power. Polka Dot Leader had already made her pickup and the others were dropping down to do the same, but it would be some time before Red Stripe's parasites completed their missions.

Reports were coming in regularly, it was already obvious that the strike would be completely successful, and the task commander was in a jovial mood. There were losses, of course, even with a ten-to-one superiority in speed and an astronomical edge in armament a planet-wide action against an alert and savagely resistant foe cannot be fought without losses, but they were well within the calculated margin the commander had sent back to base in his preliminary estimate. He had done a good, workmanlike job, and he knew it. Adequate recognition would come at base, but in the meantime he wanted to explain just how good a job it was, and he could not very well do this to military personnel; they were all below him in rank so he sought out the civilian observer from the Department of Minorities and Backward Peoples.

"How do you like it?" he asked. "Good, fast, clean job, don't you think? All we have to do now is pick up our chicks, seed the inhibitor, and get out."

The Department man was somewhat dazed, he had never seen anything quite like this before. "Well, yes, I suppose so," he said. "How many casualties do you think there will be?"

The task commander pulled at his lip, mentally extrapolating the reported losses. "Not more than twenty," he said, confidently, "just over one per cent. Very cheap, really, for a planetary action of this scope."

"No, no," the Department man said impatiently. "I know our own losses are light. The others, I mean, the Terrestrials, how many of those do you think we're killing?"

"Well, I hadn't really tried to guess," the task commander said uneasily. He had not thought of the natives before as people, he was familiar with them, of course, from the years of observation and his briefing; but he had been thinking only in terms of installations to be destroyed.

"I suppose they'll run rather high," he said. "We've tried to avoid nonstrategic targets, but you can't rip the heart out of a heavily militarized planet without killing people. Yes, I suppose their casualties *will* be heavy."

He scratched thoughtfully at his nose. "Um-m-m . . . military crews . . . civilian personnel . . . we're pinpointing our strikes, you understand, but population is so *dense* in some areas, we can't confine fission products, vapors, dusts, and I don't suppose they are at all well protected . . . let's say three or four million, in all."

The Department man stared at him. "Three or four million? Do you suppose the Council knew that when they authorized this raid?"

"Of course they did," the task commander said impatiently. "You have to remember this planet is already heavily overpopulated, well over two billion, it's really bursting at the seams, these people breed like flies. Actually, four million is only two tenths of a per cent, or less, of the total population. A minor famine or epidemic could take that many, the next atomic war could have taken ten or twenty percent, if we hadn't pulled their teeth.

"It's bad, I'll grant you that," he added hastily, seeing the look on the Department man's face. "Even tragic. But you have to look at things like this rationally, from the long view. These people have to be controlled for their own good, we can't let them just run loose to slaughter each other and perhaps even destroy the planet.

"With the advanced weapons they had, they were like idiot children playing with machine guns."

The Pentagon was not, in the raiders' operations, a military target. In the midst of disaster and confusion, Intelligence and Communications still functioned, if not smoothly, at least adequately. The basic picture of the raid and its effect began to shape up almost before the last raider had slid up through the atmosphere to join the formation orbiting effortlessly above.

First, there was no longer in any part of the world, so far as careful reconnaissance could determine, any store of fissionable material nor any plant for processing such material. Where these had been were now boiling pits of liquid magma, with the air above and about lethally charged with radioactive debris. Either the raiders had perfect intelligence, or they had instruments able to sniff out the stuff with uncanny precision, in either event they had got them all.

Second, most of the nuclear technicians—and this included the best technical and scientific brains in the world—had gone with their works.

Third, the raiders were extraterrestrial. They had not spared any major nation, and they were too well-armed and well-organized, they did not fit in any Earthly technology.

Whence they had come, and whither gone, no one could say with assurance, but their purpose was clear—to see that men did not again use nuclear energy for either war or peace.

Forty-eight hours later, as the inhibitor settled down from the stratosphere, a secondary interdict became manifest. Men would also no longer use chemical explosives. Above a pressure of two hundred psi, chemical reactions were self-damping. Hydroelectric and steam plants functioned normally, low-compression engines and jets idled without power; but guns fizzled damply and high-compression engines stalled. A ceiling had been put on the compact power available to man.

Attempts were made at censorship, the enormity of the raid's implications were so obvious that the most stringent measures were indicated. Presses and editions were impounded, reporters locked up and even shot, a straight embargo on all nonmilitary long-distance communications was clamped down, security officers sprouted new ulcers and went sleepless. But it was too big, too sudden and unexpected, too spectacular. Even after years of indoctrination and screening and stringent regulation, there were too many poor security risks in the services, too many leaks, too many people who simply refused to understand the necessity for keeping their mouths and minds and eyes and ears closed in matters of military significance. And in every community there were the loud-mouths and wise-acres who could draw and spread conclusions from the fact that Oak Ridge and Brookhaven and Hanford and Los Alamos were hit, that their automobiles no longer ran, that guns would not shoot.

The news got out.

Men of good will had been talking disarmament for years. Now they had it, a free gift from heaven, somewhat roughly delivered but none the less effective.

After the first shock, thoughtful men everywhere began to consider what it might mean—

"It means," Paul Bonner said, "rescue at the eleventh hour, the Marines have landed, the courier has ridden up with the reprieve." He sipped appreciatively at his second preprandial martini. "These are very good, dear."

His wife, curled at his feet before the fireplace, nodded complacently.

"It means," he continued, "men can relax and live again. Here we were, sitting on a powder magazine, the few sane ones among us at the mercy of the brainless yuts giving each other hotfeet, and now suddenly some watchful intelligence, like a careful parent, has snatched the matches away."

"I'm going to miss our car," his wife sighed.

"I shan't," Bonner said positively. "There were too many cars, too many airplanes, too much speed. Man's machines evolved faster than he. We weren't built to cover miles in split minutes. Now we can slow down and catch up, consolidate our gains, live at a more natural pace, take time to think and really live. I say, it's a cheap price to pay."

And:

"The fact of disarmament itself," Professor Salton

wrote in his diary, "is of secondary significance, and must have been adjudged so by the raiders themselves. Had they been chiefly intent on demilitarizing the planet, they would not logically have confined themselves to the targets they chose. The logic of complete demilitarization would have included the dispersal of armies in the field and the destruction of all heavy industry which might contribute to the manufacture of munitions other than chemical and nuclear explosives. It is significant that stores of poison gas and biological warfare centers were not attacked.

"The inference can therefore be drawn that the raiders were socially sophisticated enough, and sufficiently well informed, to recognize the deep imbalance in our culture betwen the physical and social sciences.

"Their primary concern was to right this imbalance."

The professor turned a page and sat for a moment with poised pen, seeing not the blank sheet before him, but the panorama of western history, developing in tracings of ever more complex scope from the first few crabbed scribblings of the Sumerians.

"The focus of the main stream of human thought and inquiry," he wrote, "proceeds across the broad canvas of the plenum not in a steady progression, but in complicated pendulumlike sweeps from extreme to extreme—Hegelian thesis and antithesis, except that the final result is never a simple balancing, the synthesis results rather from the shading in of all areas between the opposite poles of thought until the distinction is lost and it all becomes one. This pendulum has multidimensional articulation, so that the trace is never a simple linear function, it never covers exactly the same area twice. Its movement is a complex function of all the things men have known or thought about since the beginning of time.

"The European Renaissance came as a reaction to the sterile perfectionism of Augustinian idealism. Because its impetus derived from an extreme of preoccupation with human behavior and morals, it not only swung wildly to the opposite extreme of rigidly objective experimentalism, but it spent its major force in the field of physical science. This was no accident, it was an inevitable outgrowth of the spirit of the times and the antecedents of our culture.

"We have now worked around the periphery of physical knowledge till we have again reached the pole of intuitive rationalism, where the universe melts into a confusing amorphism only scholars can feel at home in. Men of inquiring and independent minds must inevitably recoil into a simpler atmosphere where sight and touch again have meaning.

"The next swing should have directed us back to a concern with human motivation and activity.

"There were several indications that this trend was indeed developing.

"Men were wondering seriously why they thought like men, in a world engineered for the comfort of their animal bodies; as five hundred years earlier they had wondered why men had bodies, if only the soul were important. The development of the physical sciences had subtly loosened the hold of superstition on the minds of men, so that if they were unwilling to follow, they at least tolerated, students who classified the cherished opinions of themselves and others as phenomena in the physical universe, and called all the physical universe a valid field for objective inquiry. Scattered engineers and clinicians here and there were beginning to establish functional relations between pride and pay scales, human fellowship and production records, social status and sexual mores. The alchemistic mind-doctors were seeking the philosopher's stone which would transmute the dross of our individual foibles into shining gold—but stumbling here and there on factual discoveries scientists might later turn to good account. Perhaps Korzybski had written the 'Novum Organum' of a new Renaissance. And the germs of new mathematics that could handle the manifold variables were sprouting. The time was ready for a Newton.

"But it came too late. It needed fifty or a hundred years to get its growth, and with the helium bomb the world no longer had that time left.

"So the Raiders came. In effect, they moved the

clock of our conquest of the physical world back a hundred years. Before they came, we had passed the peak of the gasoline age and were moving into the atomic age. When they left, we were back in the age of steam.

"Undoubtedly, in the years to come, men will again discover energy sources as powerful as those they lost, but it will take time, perhaps not as long as the original hundred years, but still a breathing spell. And in that time the science of human behavior will have its chance. By the time we are ready to fly to the stars again, or have the power to blast whole armies out of existence, we will have means of controlling ourselves so that this power is used with cunning foresight for the good of man, rather than suicidally, like an idiot child playing with a machine gun.

"This is the best thing that could have happened to men."

And:

A writer who had dedicated the best years of his life to a crusade against the pointless stupidities and petty unthinking cruelties of his fellowmen, at two bits a word, was putting the finishing touches on a rush article.

"Pride," he wrote, "goeth before a fall—and men who thought they had tamed all nature, and were looking for new worlds to loot in the stars, have suddenly learned they have a master. The simple-minded barbarians who strutted valorously with the power of thousands of horses at their command have seen their most prized works crumble like sand castles before the tide.

"It was a lesson men sorely needed, the simple lesson of humility.

"In my own mind, for the first time since Hiroshima, is peace and good will and comfortable assurance that me and mine will live out our normal span in a world of men chastened and rendered less cocksure by this experience.

"I say, God bless the raiders—"

There were, of course, some who were not quite so sure—

*   *   *

On a hillside in Asia some two months after the raiders had come, Sergeant Albert Baker sat in the bright summer sun watching through glasses the mouth of a low pass. A cloud of dust rose there which came quickly down into the valley. Sparkles of light from burnished lance-tips flashed from the cloud. A Mongol swordsman with horsetails tied to his cap cantered out ahead and reined up to look around.

Baker's lips drew back in a snarl. This was the enemy. To them, the inhibitor had meant nothing. They threw their guns away, sharpened their lances, and whooped down upon the gun crews, tankers, and machine-gunners who clubbed useless carbines and threw rocks. The first few weeks had been massacre. After that the Americans recovered somewhat from their shock, began to reorganize and pick up edged weapons, to fight their way back to the sea. They were outnumbered and outmaneuvered, they could not in a few days learn a type of warfare devoid of firepower and mechanized supply, and the retreat was mostly a rout.

During that time, only men who moved fast and learned quickly survived. Baker was only nineteen, but he had come all the way, in this fighting he was an old hand, a veteran who knew all the tricks. He could hardly remember what it felt like to ride in a truck, sleep on a full belly, or command weapons that killed in great bursts of flame or sleets of lead. The tools he knew were knife and spear, arbalest and sword. His enemy was not a plane or a tank, it was the flat-faced horseman with sword or lance.

The Americans now stood with their backs to the sea, waiting for evacuation complicated by lack of Diesel- or gasoline-powered landing craft. Their situation was not bad, really, there were not very many of them left to evacuate, most were dead in the hills and plains of the interior; and to some extent supply had caught up with them here, they ate more often and they had a weapon to at least harass the horsemen.

The leading squadrons were well into the valley now, the point abreast of Baker. He moved his magneto box around between his knees and squatted over it, his glasses on the man standing on a spiny ridge at the lower end of the valley. Presently the man signaled, and Baker pressed the plunger. In the valley below, a thin vapor began to creep out from all sides toward the horsemen in the center. Baker carefully checked his sector with his glasses. All cylinders had fired—they almost had to, poison gas was cheap in the United States but dear here where the cylinders were brought up on men's backs, and they had been spread thin.

"All right," he said finally, "let's get out of here before those gooks spot us."

His men needed no urging, they had been uncomfortably aware of their exposed position for some time. They picked up their weapons and moved off at a swift walk along the hillside. There was a small gully they must cross, and here they donned masks before they scrambled down. The bank on the other side was steep, they needed to boost each other up to make it, and they were not all up when half a troop of the enemy, red-eyed and wheezing, came stampeding up out of the valley at them.

Baker saw them coming only a few hundred yards away, with his little force split, half on the bank and half below. He dropped his arbalest to cock it and shouted a warning.

There were three pikes in the party, twelve-foot shafts with heavy, wicked points of razor-ground steel armor scrap. The men had been using these to climb the bank, they snatched them away now and swung out to set them with drilled precision. The other men in the gully had captured swords and bayoneted M-1's, except for Baker and one other with arbalests of jeep springleaves and the airplane cable mounted on M-1 stocks. One man, a swordsman, was hanging on the edge of the bank by his elbows, on the verge of hoisting himself over, he twisted his head to look over his shoulder, hesitated a moment, and then slid back down to join them. Baker was glad to see him come, there was another arbalest on the bank, that was a good place for him, but the swordsmen and spearmen up there were useless. Still he could not order them back down, this looked like a death trap. Their left flank anchored on the bank, but their right hung in the air, he grabbed two spearmen and swung them around to give some protection, but there were just not enough of them to cover it adequately. He and the other arbalestier stepped in behind the pikemen and spearmen, who had dropped to their knees, and Baker slipped in a quarrel.

The enemy point swerved in at them, settling his lance, and at five yards Baker shot the horse in the throat. The other arbalestier took the second. A swordsman flashed by on the right and swung viciously at Baker, who parried with the stock of his weapon. At the same moment, from the corner of his eye he saw a horse caught on two of the pikes and one of his spearmen leaping out, yelling, over the pikemen and struggling horses to bayonet its rider. After that there was only dust and confusion and flashing steel and yelling men, and then sudden quiet. It took some minutes for Baker to realize the clash was over and he still alive—actually the enemy had not been anxious to press their charge home or turn his flank, they had only been trying to get out of the valley as quickly as possible and the platoon had been in the way.

Still, it had not been fun, the brief flurry had cost them men. Baker cursed the enemy and the raiders, both, thinking how much difference even one stinking Browning would have made—

After twenty years, the inhibitor against high-pressure chemical reaction lost its effectiveness and needed to be re-seeded. It was a routine task for one cruiser, there was no real reason for the former task commander, now deputy fleet admiral, to go along. At the moment, however, things were quiet and Galactic Security labored under an economy budget. The admiral needed the flight-time, and besides he was curious. He held a peculiar affection for Earth, the action of twenty years before had been his first independent task command, and still stood in his mind as a perfectly planned and executed job.

The civilian observer from the Department of Minorities and Backward Peoples went along because the Department wanted a check and he had asked for the assignment. He, too, was curious, this had been an unorthodox and controversial experiment from the start, and he was still unconvinced of its overall desirability.

They came in over the pole on almost the same course they had flown twenty years before, and the admiral was first to notice the change.

"No radar," he said, watching the instruments.

Where before a whole continent had quivered and reacted with alert savagery to their appearance, they now coasted alone through the bright sky, apparently unheeded and unknown to men. It made the admiral vaguely uneasy.

The seeding was to be done at two hundred thousand, in a crisscross pattern which would take several hours, and the Department observer wanted to go down in the tender and make some checks at a lower altitude. The admiral decided to go with him.

They glided down to five thousand feet before applying power, careless of who might see the disk-shaped flier drifting overhead; there was no particular reason to avoid observation now, this planet had already known them.

Over the northern United States, there was superficially little change, the admiral had little difficulty in orienting himself by the photo-charts made more than twenty years before, railroads and highways still cut in straight lines across the plains checker-boarded by wheatfields. Not till they came over the lakes region did they begin to notice significant differences. Here, small villages spotted crossroads where they had not appeared on the old charts, and cities had shrunk and drawn in upon themselves. Once again, the United States was a predominantly rural nation.

In the days immediately after the raid, there had been little change in those cities not directly affected. There were deaths from radiation sickness and poisoning as the debris of the raid sifted through the atmosphere, and film badges and gas masks became a part of the everyday costume of those who could afford them;

automobiles rusted where they stood and there were minor inconveniences; but the streetcars still ran, electric signs flashed, and the plumbing worked. In those first days, aside from the blasted areas, the farms and suburbs were hardest hit. Life there had tied itself tightly to the internal-combustion engine, to tractors and trucks and aircraft and Diesel engines.

There were not very many crops planted or harvested in North America that year.

As summer wore on, the cities also began to feel the pinch. Distribution was difficult without trucks, highlands and reservoirs needed helicopters and power boats for maintenance. Prices rose and inconveniences multiplied.

By fall, in the poorer sections, people were starving.

By the next spring, the population of the United States was less than sixty million and the machinery of civilization rusted unattended while people scrabbled for food. The bones of Paul Bonner and his pretty wife lay in a roadside ditch, with spring rains melting the ice and flesh from them.

That summer was bad, too, but the seeds of resurgence were sprouting. The federal gold hoard came out of its vaults to buy food men would not sell for paper, and when the hard yellow coin began to circulate people forgot their despair and their wits sharpened and they looked about for opportunity. Old stern-wheelers slid off the banks and creaked out of sloughs to push tons of Argentine beef and horses and grain up the inland waters from New Orleans. Independent train crews hauled loads for speculators out from St. Louis and Cincinnati and Kansas City. People drifted back to the cities to build steam tractors.

In another year the trains were running on schedules of a sort and a few turbine-powered automobiles and trucks were on the highways.

Five years after the raid, the country was back on its feet, but it was not the same country. Cultures, like individuals, discard patterns of behavior associated with defeat and cherish jealously those associated with gratification. The trauma of sudden almost mortal disaster is apt to intensify these reactions to the point of mania.

From five thousand feet, the country now looked green and prosperous, even the scars of Brookhaven were growing over. The admiral studied the peacefully pastoral scene, the bustling but not overcrowded cities, with approval.

From five thousand feet, he could not see the scavenger-gnawed skeletons still tangled in obscure briar-patches, nor the scars and bitterness and hatred still tangled in people's hearts. If he saw, he did not particularly note the little groups of hard-faced observers here and there who studied his craft through binoculars and carefully filmed its every move.

The Department observer could not see them either, but he was better versed in social phenomena than the military man, and he was not so sure.

"Let's see what Europe looks like," he said.

In Asia, after the debacle, the Americans evacuated about twelve thousand troops to Japan. Most of these, being veteran and reliable, were brought back to restore order when the domestic military establishment fell apart. Now again there were detachments in the Philippines and the Pacific Islands, and in Malaya to protect the growing rubber demand, but the mainland of Asia was left to the warlords and khans.

In Europe, defeat had not been so disastrous. The enemy there were almost as heavily mechanized as the NATO nations, and as discomfitted to find themselves suddenly disarmed. Also, they experienced internal troubles from those of their own peoples who had never taken kindly to statism. These troubles were compounded by the fact that the dissident elements were mainly just those who clung to and were most adept with yataghan and knife, bow and lance, horse and camel; many a Muscovite commissar fumbled uselessly with his pistol while Finnish knife or Montenegrin dagger or Ukrainian scythe bit into him.

Still, the enemy had numbers, and under the urge of famine he swept across Europe, looting and burning and killing to the Rhine, sending isolated raiding parties as far as the Pyrenees, then decomposed from internal stresses. His troops frittered away and disappeared, but Europe lacked the energy to recover. When the first great wave of horsemen from the steppes came, the only organized opposition they met was from the scattered American garrisons along the Rhine, and they foraged to the channel, so that in middle Europe hardly stone stood on stone and one might go for miles without seeing a living man.

Here, the admiral could see the skulls even from the air. In Potsdamer-Platz, they were piled in the neat Asiatic habit into a pyramid over fifty feet high.

They swung back across Bavaria then, and along the Rhine, staring wordlessly at the desolation below, livened only by the occasional disorderly gaggle of squat dark riders with their trains of loot. The admiral tugged uneasily at his collar and glanced sidelong at the civilian, but the latter said nothing, and then the admiral suddenly brightened. Away across the Rhine his trained eye had caught a hint of order, a flash of steel. He tapped the pilot's arm and pointed, and they swung down over a marching column of men, coming with burnished arms and steady step and even formation along a highway to cut behind a swarm of the savages.

Colonel Albert Baker pulled his horse off to the side and reined around to watch his regiment come up into the battle-line. They were rugged and tough, veterans with a sprinkling of husky recruits from midwestern prairies and Norman farms and Scotch hills, the fastest marching infantry since Grant's, and, with allowances for fire-power, perhaps the deadliest. Still, this was the time they were vulnerable, the next few minutes while they maneuvered directly from the column of march into the line. The colonel did not like it, but he was working on Evaluation's clockwork schedule, and there was nothing much he could do about it. The forward elements of his flanking archers began to drift out onto the plain, and he debated whether to throw them forward as a screen, slowing down his disposition but making a tactically sounder maneuver. Just then a squadron of dragoons jingled past at a trot, and he breathed easier. Corps had promised the cavalry screen, but he distrusted cavalry, they were always skittering off somewhere else when you needed them most, and he had not really believed they would show up.

The 103rd was next in the line, his right flank would rest on them, and he watched now as they moved into position smartly. When they were clear the colonel raised his hand, bugles screamed, and with drums beating to set the step his regiment swung out onto the plain and up into line. Standard-bearers ran forward and dressed and set guidons, squads and companies wheeled and marked time and countermarched, dust rose and swirled in choking clouds, lieutenants and sergeants back-pedaled anxiously and shouted hoarse commands and blew on whistles. The pattern began to fill in. Lines grew out of seeming chaos and weaved back and forth, dressing, and then the regiment was blocked solidly in its place, left flank on the river and right on the 103rd. The colonel eased himself in his saddle and lit a cigar, turning to survey the field as a whole.

For the first time since he had got his orders, he began to see how the battle would shape up. They had cut the hordes off from their train, he saw, far down the valley in his rear women and children, cook fires and wagons and pack animals tangled in a frightened mess. The enemy were strung up the valley, sucked up there probably by skirmishing cavalry, but pausing now to look back at the infantry who had come in behind them. It had been a tricky maneuver, but it had worked, and the enemy now must either fight or run. They would fight, the colonel knew, the horsemen would never leave their women and loot without a battle. He waited with cold confidence, knowing the light cavalry did not exist that could break a division of drilled heavy infantry solidly anchored with protected flanks.

He eased his right leg and studied his own men again. They were at ease now, their places marked by their weapons, some sitting, smoking or chewing field rations, breathing easy and in good shape. To their rear there was a sudden clatter as the batteries of steam centrifugals and mortars galloped up. Must be about time for things to start, the colonel thought sourly, it would be a miracle if artillery was actually spaded in and fired up by the time action joined. He trotted slowly back to his command post and joined his staff.

The horde made up its mind, bunched and began to drift back down the valley. Half a dozen blimps came up over the hills to the right and scattered napalm and spreading blobs of gas on the enemy, and suddenly they picked up speed and started coming like an avalanche, spread out over a half mile front, a wall of dust two hundred feet high surging along with them. The infantry were on their feet now, nervously stamping out butts, opening lanes for the dragoons to stream back through. Behind, there was a whine as the turbine-driven centrifugals came up to speed.

Baker spoke to his bugler. The bugle sang and the lines stiffened and solidified. Company officers ran back and forth dressing the front, and then suddenly the pikemen dropped and set their pikes and raised their shields. What had been an orderly array of men in infantry blue battle dress was now a solid line of glittering steel, reaching from river to cliffs on the far side, backed solidly by the lines of archers and swordsmen, file closers and mobile reserve, a heavy infantry division in line of battle. It made a grim, imposing sight. In the unnoticed flier overhead, the admiral almost fell out of his seat in his excitement, the fighting he knew was nothing like this, but he liked it.

The colonel was alert but unimpressed, he had seen it many times before, and he knew the rest would not be so pretty. He gauged the distance to the enemy, and spoke to his bugler again. The archers stepped out between the pikes and took their stand, leisurely setting their arrows in the ground in preparation for rapid fire. They were the elite, a pikeman or arbalestier could be trained in a few months but an archer needed to grow up with a longbow in his hands to use it effectively, and the colonel guarded them jealously, not because he loved them but because he couldn't get along without them. He wondered now, as he had often before, if the arbalest would ever be technically improved to the point of being a completely satisfactory missile weapon for light infantry.

The first ranks of oncoming horsemen were five hundred yards out now, and the mortars popped for the first time and sent a flood of lazy bombs arching overhead to burst and spread blazing napalm. The shouts of officers calling the range came dimly above the general racket, and then the first volley from the archers rose and fell in a cloud and slugs from the centrifugals began to whistle overhead, playing like hydraulic blasts on the onrushing enemy, eroding them away in patches and swathes. The archers were firing at will now, the air was solid with their shafts, it seemed impossible that horse or man could come through that hail and the sickening *plop* of the firebombs. Still they came, and there rose an answering swarm of arrows from their short stiff bows to rattle on the infantry's upraised shields. The archers skipped nimbly back into their ranks, and from between the now unobscured pikes the flame-throwers spat clouds and flame.

On Baker's front, the enemy broke, they dashed up against the pikes and recoiled, unable to force the flaming wall with its sharp steel core. Neither could they turn and face the gas cloud rolling threateningly in their rear, they raced in tangled streams back and forth parallel to the front, seeking a weak spot, while arbalestiers and centrifugals and flame-throwers poured fire relentlessly into them.

The 103rd was not having such good luck. Their front was broken in two places, and one serious melee developed into a momentary break-through. Baker alerted part of his reserve to help if necessary, but they closed up without aid and the cavalry in the rear finished off the few enemy who did come through.

The battle was over now, the rest slaughter. Baker turned his attention again to his own front, watching with cold appreciation the death his regiment was dealing.

The enemy was seeking only escape. Some tried to swim the river, where Baker's archers picked them off at leisure. Some scrambled up the cliffs on the other side, where they made equally good targets, and some drove recklessly back into the gas cloud to strangle. Very few got away. The mass thinned, and then there were only isolated riders racing madly past, and then nothing but a slowly settling cloud of dust, with an occasional limping figure drawing a flurry of fire, riderless horses stampeding aimlessly.

Baker looked at his watch. It was somewhat under two hours since he had ordered his men into action; less than two hours to annihilate a dozen hordes that had harried whole provinces for years—a good day's work.

The admiral settled back into his seat and drew a deep breath.

"Well," he said somewhat inadequately, "I'm afraid we didn't do such a good job of stopping war on *this* planet."

"We certainly lowered the population level that was worrying you Malthusians, though," the observer said. "That little tiff down there," he waved his hand, "must have helped by five or six thousand."

He rubbed wearily at his face. "No, it's no good," he said heavily. "We never should have permitted this experiment. You shoot-em-up boys are always too anxious to civilize people by gunfire. I am going to recommend that the Department question Security's stand in this matter at the next Council meeting, and urge we review the whole history of our contact with these people. It may not be too late to do something constructive yet."

"Now wait a minute," the admiral said stubbornly. "This may not have gone just according to plan, but it wasn't our plan, you long-hairs were the people who developed this theory that if we could block off the natives' physical expansion they'd be forced to develop a peaceful civilization, all Security did was to implement that plan. And there is *some* improvement. They may still be killing each other, but at least they aren't using mass weapons any more, it's man to man, between warriors. They aren't blowing up whole cities, women and children, the sick and peaceful along with the belligerent—"

The stretcher-bearers were working through the ranks now, picking up the dead and wounded, but they did not bother with the enemy. The dragoons were taking care of them. They were out front again, picking their way gingerly between the burning areas where the bombs had dropped, thrusting and hacking here and there as they found wounded, catching horses, dismounting to pick up an especially interesting bit of loot.

Let them have it, the colonel thought, what he wanted was the wagon train in the rear. There would be the real loot, women and stores and gold and all the stripped wealth of this land fine-combed again and again by the raiders. The colonel fought for his rank and his retirement and vaguer, higher, imponderables he felt but could not have put a name too, but his men fought for loot. There was no rotation in this army, only death or crippling wounds, retirement perhaps for a few who were lucky, at the end of a hard life of constant battle. They needed the occasional fierce satisfactions of stolen women, looted gold and wine, unopposed slaughter and destruction, to balance the hard discipline of their daily life. The colonel knew this, he did not begrudge them their fun, although for disciplinary reasons he liked to take his in quieter form. So now he sat, forgetting the battle already, estimating his chances, plotting cunningly how his regiment should be first to fall upon the camp.

He suddenly noticed some of the men looking up, and pointing, and he, too, looked up and for the first time saw the Galactic observation flier, hanging motionless over the battlefield. His mind went back twenty years, to the gully in Korea, to the hundred thousand men who had left their bones to whiten in that retreat, to his mother and father and brothers and sisters, who had lived near Oak Ridge before the raiders came, in an area still posted as radioactive.

He studied the flier carefully.

"You, too, boy," he thought. "Just wait a while, we'll get to you yet, we haven't forgotten—"

Professor Salton was writing in his diary—

"In retrospect," he wrote, "it is obvious that the effect of the raiders upon Terrestrial development was much more complex than at first appeared. They halted the explosive burgeoning of physical power available to man, and forced him to direct his energies in other directions. They gave man time and impetus to develop the social sciences he had forgotten in the sudden unfolding of physical power. But they altered his basic orientation.

"Before the raid, men lived in a world in which they were supreme, and had only each other to fear. The abrupt brutality of the raid, emphasized by its aftermath of famine and disruption, sharply reminded them that they were small fry in a shark-swarming, hostile universe, apt at any moment to be gulped up.

"Five hundred years earlier, they might have withdrawn into a shell of protective humility and prayer. A hundred years later, they might have understood the workings of their own mind well enough to preserve a balance. As it was, they reached instinctively, but in the pattern of an aggressive culture, aggressively.

"Since physical science had failed them, they cast it aside and snatched up the newer, subtler tools of thought and life. The new learning that might have taught men to live with each other was ground and sharpened for hostile uses.

"The millennium of peace, which seemed so close, has again been postponed—"

And:

"Colonel Baker," the general said, "I'd like you to meet Major Pellati. He's the man who set up your targets for you this afternoon, the chief of our corps evaluation staff."

"Well, you did a good job on that, major," the colonel said. "Everything folded together like a peddler's pack. I don't think a hundred of those devils got away."

"We didn't intend for very many to get away." The major looked around distastefully. "You like this racket?" he asked abruptly.

It *was* somewhat noisy. Division headquarters had been set up in an old building, a monolithic concrete relic of the atomic age, as indestructible without explosives as a mountain, and the junior officers had promptly organized a party. They had liberated a varied assortment of women and alcoholic beverages from the enemy camp and rounded up parts of three regimental bands, and the party was going strong.

At one end of the plank bar twenty company officers were harmonizing "Dinah," at the other end a small party of their seniors were rounding up candidates, amid shrieks of girlish laughter, to decorate with lipsticked kisses the shining bald head of the 103rd's colonel—who had gone to sleep, as was his habit, after the fifth drink. Half the band were following Baker's band leader in the "Tennessee Waltz" while the other half played something unidentifiable but certainly not the "Tennessee Waltz." As a finishing touch, three Marine observers within armlength of Baker and Pellati were defiantly bellowing "Zamboanga." It was quite a party.

"Why, yes," Baker said, "it is a little noisy."

With common consent, they picked up a bottle of Calvados from the bar and sought quieter surroundings. "Oops," Pellati said at the first door they tried and backed hurriedly out. "Occupied," he said briefly. They wandered down a long hall and found an alcove housing an ex-window, now ventilated agreeably by the fresh evening air. They sat down on the window ledge with the bottle between them.

"Yes, sir, that was a nice action," Baker said. Something that had been lurking in the back of his mind all day came to the fore. "Were you in Korea?" he asked.

"I was at Inchon. That's where we first used von

Neumann's mathematics to evaluate a large-scale operation. Worked pretty good."

"That was before my time. I got there just in time to be right in the middle when the raid hit and the gooks climbed all over us. That's what I was thinking about; this afternoon, I was thinking, 'Boy, I'll bet this learns you buggers a good lesson, I've been saving this twenty years for you.'"

He sucked gently at the bottle. "Did you say you were in Evaluation at Inchon?" he asked suddenly. "Didn't know they had anything like that then."

"Well, it was pretty crude stuff," the major said. "Experimental. Half mathematics and half good guessing."

"It still looks like magic to me."

"It isn't. Tactics isn't an art any more, or even science. It's just engineering. If your intelligence is good, and you know what you've got to work with, all you have to do is work up the equations. With those savages we were fighting today, you don't even have to make allowances for independent thought, they don't think, just react like machines. Once you know the basic pattern of that reaction, you can just about predict every move they'll make for the next six months. Then it's just a question of being in the right place at the right time."

"Did you see that raider flier this afternoon?" he asked abruptly.

Baker nodded.

"Those are the ones we'll have to sweat for," the major said.

"Well," Baker said piously, "I hope to live to see the day, but I don't know; they've got a pretty big edge on us in weapons—"

"Weapons don't mean a thing, colonel. Disparity in armament is simply one of the factors to which we assign weights in the tactical and strategic equations." He took a cigar from his pocket and lit it carefully, staring cross-eyed down his long nose.

"Twenty years ago, we put *our* faith in gadgets—radar and guns and engines and nuclear explosives—and you remember what happened. We learned our lessons. There's always somebody with bigger and better stuff. So now we learn to use what we do have with maximum effect, and stick to simple weapons we know won't fail us. Our hole card is the infantryman walking on his own two legs with good solid steel in his hands.

"We can't lose, because we don't depend on tools, we depend on knowing what *people* are going to do with tools, and adapt our own action to the circumstances. With the Latin-Americans we used a combination of force and economic and moral action. With the British, we used economic and political means. With these gooks, we use force at the moment, it's cheaper to kill them than to educate them. I don't know just what we'll use with the Raiders, but we'll take them, don't ever doubt that, all in good time, after we've cleaned our own house and have this planet organized.

"I worked on the initial evaluation, right after the raid, we had plenty of material to work up, and we learned enough even then to show they had weaknesses. Our biggest unit is still working on it, every time somebody comes up with a new refinement they work it down a little finer, every time we get new data it goes into the mill. The pictures we got of that fellow this afternoon are on the way back already. That's what we want now, little things, which side the pilot sits on, what part of the battle interested them, anything to fill in the picture.

"Some day, they'll land, get close enough for us to get our hands on them, and we'll be ready for them."

The major took the cigar out of his mouth and spat.

The watch chief socio-technician was monitoring reports by radio-fax, television, and voice; and keeping up a running fire of commentary for the evaluators and calculators who were screening the material and feeding it into the machines.

"Raider landing as predicted," he said, "near major urban center— Chicago. Bless *Bess*, what a ship, big as the *Queen Mary*—"

Machines clicked and chattered and hummed smoothly.

"Plan Sugar-fourteen, modification three on basis current information, just initiated."

"Somebody's dragging their feet," one of the calculators said. "I just cranked out modification five, and mod-4 was acknowledged by Field control at 2113."

"Log it," the watch chief advised. "They'll try to bounce it on us, they're always wrong but they keep hoping."

"Mod-4 coming up," he added. "Only three and a half minutes late, they're outdoing themselves today. That's old Fatso running to the ship instead of walking— Which stupid knothead took my coffee cup?"

On a balcony overlooking the control center, the commanding officer was explaining the operation to some high brass.

"Well, I can see you have a nice operation here," a general said. "Very smooth. But what I don't understand is how you Evaluation people are so sure the Raiders don't have something equivalent to our own Strategic and Tactical Evaluation. If they do, what are we going to do then?"

"They can't have," the CO said positively. "Remember, we've been evaluating these people for fifty years.

"In order to have STE, you have to have a basic science of human motivation. And they don't have it. The Raid itself is our basic evidence for that. There's no indication that they had anything whatever to gain from the raid, they did it to save us from self-destruction.

"A race that can destroy half a planet's population, forcibly impose its will on an alien race, not for the legitimate aim of self-preservation but because it wants to play God, can't possibly understand even the first rudiments of social control. That type of thinking is authoritarian, symptomatic of egotistic atomism.

"No, we'll take them all right. We have to. The universe isn't safe with people like that running loose, living in an insane world of subjective surrealism, but acting on men who live and die in the real world of objective events.

"They're like idiot children playing with a machine gun."

EDITOR'S INTRODUCTION TO:

THE PROPER STUDY OF MANKIND
J. E. Pournelle, Ph.D.

For a brief time there flourished *Destinies*, a series of books that were very like magazines; and they were wonderful. Edited by Jim Baen, with myself as science editor and columnist, *Destinies* was just that: an inquiry into possible destinies of the human race.

Indeed, the magazine could fairly have been called the official journal of the Advanced Planning Department of Humanity: not so much that it was so excellent as to earn that title, as that it had it by default. No one was interested in competing.

My part in *Destinies* was a series of columns called "New Beginnings." One of those was half tirade on the social sciences, and half suggestion as to what a social science might be.

Since I wrote that I've heard a lot about the "new" psychology, and "cognitive science." Its practitioners have high hopes; and since hope springs eternal, so do I. Alas, at the moment it's all hope; I've read a number of books and journals on the new sciences of the mind, and all I've seen so far is approach. There has been some healthy clearing of the sterile deadwood of behaviorism, but site clearing is not building. We can continue to hope.

Meanwhile, I see no need to revise this.

THE PROPER STUDY OF MANKIND
J. E. Pournelle, Ph.D.

"Know then thyself, presume not gods to scan. The proper study of mankind is man."

—Alexander Pope

We science fiction people often preen ourselves over SF's successful predictions. The famous visit by the FBI to John Campbell's office during World War II; rockets and space travel; TV; etc. And in fact we haven't done too badly in the technological forecasting business; no worse than anyone else, anyway.

But we don't often mention our "predictions" in the social sciences.

Remember the Golden Age of science fiction? Those were the days when "psycho-history" was an exact science using real math; computers manipulated the calculus of values, and matrix algebra, and all that good stuff. Psychiatrists "cured" criminals; judges were physicians, not lawyers. The social ills of the nation, the world, aye, the universe were plugged into computers (big, massive ones, not the dinky little things IBM and DEC make nowadays) and lo! the answers came forth.

Those stories had their effect, at least on me: I decided I was going to be the Hari Seldon of the XXth Century. I wanted to use the very best tools available, so I studied math and physics and hard sciences, then formal logic and Boole's Laws of Thought, and Carnap's sentential calculus, and once I was tooled up came a perfect orgy of psychology and sociology and anthropology that ended with what used to be called a "terminal degree" (meaning that thought ceases with the Ph.D.?).

I studied psychology at the University of Iowa, where they had not one but two schools of psychology, Hull's pseudo-mathematical "learning theory," and Kurt Lewin's "vector psychology." I kept wondering when they were going to *use* mathematics. Surely, thought I, there would come a time when they would give rigorous definitions; but no, what happened was that they took mathematical symbols and let them stand for some perfectly good English words—but without improving the precision of their definitions one whit. And even when they played math games with the resulting symbols (none of which could *really* be quantified), the most complicated function I ever saw was a simple algebraic equation.

But then there was statistics. That, we were told, is a tough subject. Well, given that it was taught daily at 0700 by a professor of education, it *seemed* tough; but in fact all that was taught was cookbook stat, how to compute mean, median, mode, standard deviation, and the like; and how to do cookbook tests using Student's "T-test," and a peek at the Chi-square—not at the Chi-square *distribution*, of course. Heaven forbid that psychology students learn real mathematics; so actual calculations of probability not covered in the cookbook were beyond my classmates, and I suspect that if you ask the average Ph.D. in psych or sosh or anthro or ed what a probability density is, you'll either get a blank stare or hear something mumbled about specific gravities.

In due time I wandered to the University of Washington. (Accident certainly plays a large part in one's life: I was in school on the Korean-type GI Bill, which paid a fixed sum per month; I hadn't lived with my parents since a year before I graduated from high school, but to save money I had to go to a state university as a resident; my parents had gravitated to Alaska, but the state of Washington had generously declared residents of Alaska to be Washingtonians; and therefore . . .)

The psychology department at the University of Washington had its schools, too: one was headed by a maniac who'd spent twenty years in the attic studying conditioned reflexes in chickens. The best-known man at Washington was Edwin Ray Guthrie, one of the "big three" in learning theory; at Iowa they'd taught us he was not merely wrong, but stupid. (My own opinion is that he was the only practical psychologist in the theory business; his theory can be stated in two sentences, and his practical deductions from the theory are almost absurdly simple; but they can be applied—and they work. That's another story for another time.) And finally there were a couple of professors who actually understood something of mathematics, and who seemed determined to apply real scientific method to the study of man.

One was Paul Horst, who had a contract from the US Navy; he was trying to predict the four-year grade point average of entering freshmen. Lest Proxmire read this and retroactively award Dr. Horst a Golden Fleece, let me point out that the Navy had—and has—a damned legitimate interest in predicting academic success. It costs a lot of money to send a recruit through specialized training such as electronics school; if you can choose from among the boots those likely to do well in the school, you'll save the cost of Dr. Horst's grant in no time.

Those were heady days. Horst's approach to the problem was to get every possible measure on every entering freshman, wait until they graduated, then flog hell out of the data. The goal was to find a series of weights to apply to each predictor such that when you did all the addition and multiplication you had an adequate prediction; and to do that for each of thirty possible majors! Here finally was a legitimate use for matrix algebra, which Horst required all of his students to take.

We also went to computer school, because inverting a 60 x 60 matrix is hairy. Of course the best computers in the world weren't very good; IBM thoughtfully gave the school a 650, but there weren't any programs to do what we wanted, and we grad students had to learn programming: not in easy languages like Basic or Fortran, which didn't exist; not even in modern assembly language; no, we had to do it in machine language.

Eventually it was done. (My part, as I recall, was a program that would invert triangular matrices; it took a whole summer to develop it, too.) Came the day when the great grade prediction program was to be run. Since the 650 had rather limited memory (on a drum at that) the programs made it punch intermediate answers on cards, which were then carried from the punch to the reader to be fed in again; we were up all night getting just part of the answer. But at last we had the equations: take an incoming freshman, subject same to a battery of tests, plug in high school grades and class standing, plug in a correction for the particular high school (and save the data, because that correction factor needed more cases from each school to give it more accuracy); put that into the computer; and out came a prediction of the grade that student would get after four years in each of about 30 major subjects.

Only predictions, of course; now there was nothing for it but to wait four years and let those students graduate. Obviously each case would count only toward the predictions made for the major actually chosen; but enough of those would validate the predictors. Eventually there'd be enough data to validate the method used.

I'd left before the first students graduated, but I'm told it looked very good indeed; good enough that the University decided to give incoming students their predictions to help them choose majors.

And it hit the fan.

I don't know the current status of the grade prediction program at the UW now; I gather it's moribund. It seems the predictions were racist. They were detrimental to some of the high schools (remember that correction factor?). They were also detrimental to certain departments, because they showed that students almost certain to flunk out in one of the difficult majors would do well in many of the soft sciences . . . (In certain majors there was not one single predicted flunk.)

So what's the point of all this?

Two points: one, it may just be possible to do really useful stuff in the social sciences; and two, it takes a lot of time, and it takes a lot of money; and if time and money shortages don't discourage that sort of thing, the next factor is almost certain to: it's *hard work*. It takes real knowledge of real hard stuff; much harder than sophomore stat and freshman calculus.

And do they require that sort of thing in social science departments? They do not. What they do require for a Ph.D. in psych is "History of Psychology"—a course in which you're required to learn, in great detail (the textbook was written by a man named Boring; portent enough, but the reality was worse), what all the "great thinkers" of the field believed. At the end of each section you find out why they were all wrong. It's as if to get a degree in chemistry you had to spend months learning about the phlogiston theory; as if physics required a three-week course in Democritus' beliefs about atomic structure. In other words, this required course is a confession: the discipline has so little content that they've invented this artificially difficult barrier so the doctorate won't be so easy to get.

Nor is that all: you can spend an entire quarter debating the difference between a "hypothetical construct" and an "intervening variable," a subject worth perhaps five minutes; you can learn a jargon designed to make your conversation incomprehensible, and which serves no purpose other than to see that someone from another discipline will be discouraged from trying his hand; and when it's all finished you are qualified to do what?

What indeed? What is a person with an undergraduate degree in psychology capable of doing? And psych is the tough one; if a B.S. in psychology is aptly named, what are we to make of sociology?

* * *

But maybe it's all just as well. Do you really *want* social science? Let me illustrate.

Probably the most controversial subject in the field involves IQ tests. What, if anything, do they mean? And since most IQ tests show a statistical difference between the races, shouldn't their use be forbidden? (Some courts have forbidden their use in university entry decisions for precisely that reason.)

And my Lord, the arguments that can develop! Nature versus nurture. Heredity versus environment. I listened to a paper on the subject presented by a Harvard professor at an AAAS meeting a couple of years ago, and by Roscoe the debate hasn't moved an inch since my undergraduate days.

Yet it wouldn't be hard to settle, would it? Not if the answer really were wanted.

When I took social sciences seriously, one experiment reported in the Tests and Measurement courses seemed really elegant: the twin studies. It's a simple experimental design. First locate a number of pairs of twins. What you want is identical twins reared together; identical twins reared apart; fraternal twins reared together; and fraternal twins reared apart. Those reared together shared roughly the same environment; while identical twins have identical heredity, unlike fraternal twins who are no more closely related than any other siblings. Go find a number in each category; not easy, but not so very difficult in this era of forms and dossiers.

Give them a number of tests. Ideally test everyone in their class at school, or job category at work, so that your subjects don't know they've been singled out. Then compare the results. What you're looking for is not absolute IQ, whatever that means, but point spread between pairs.

My Differential Psychology text reported such an experiment, and lo! the results were unambiguous. The least difference between pairs was identical reared together, as you'd expect; but then came identical reared apart, not fraternal together—suggesting strongly that heredity was more important than environment in determining what was being measured by the IQ tests.

I'm told that the classic experiment reported in my book was in error; that some of the data may have been fudged. Okay. That's possible. But instead of long debates with anecdotes, and speculations on whether those data were fudged, why not go do it again?

While we're at it, why not develop a really good grade prediction program? The computers exist. Lord knows there's enough money spent on tests. And there must be IQ data on millions of graduates of tax-supported institutions; that can be followed up to see if all that testing is worth anything. If it is, fine, use it to save time and effort and money; if not, fine again, abolish the silly tests; but what we actually do is ridiculous.

Maybe we don't want successful prediction? Might good predictions of academic success have a baleful effect on the republic?

Aha. We're now in the realm of political "science", which once a long time ago meant the study of political philosophy and involved a great deal of history; nowadays the rage is "behavior", meaning that what was faddish in psychology twenty years ago has now caught on in poly sci; with about the same utility. Not that all political science courses are a waste of time; there's considerable value in discovering that most of the ideas and movements and problems we think are unique to our age have cropped up again and again in other times and places. One can also learn something about statesmanship and diplomacy, and even a bit about how to win an election. But there's damned little science in it.

There's sometimes not even common sense. Take the business about a political "left" and "right". It's easy to prove it's nonsense. There's absolutely no variable underlying that "spectrum"; indeed, I pretty well proved in my dissertation that it takes at least two variables at right angles to each other to map even the broadest political groupings each to a unique point. The whole idea of a "left" and "right" is nonsense—but it's still with us, and it has important consequences in the very real world. What in the world do British labor unions have in common with Soviet communism other than the vague feeling that both are "the left"? Are the Czechs better off under Soviet occupation than they were under the Nazis? Of all the stupid notions in academia, the "left-right" model of politics is demonstrably among the silliest; to flog an already-used example, it's as if the chemistry department allowed the rest of the faculty to act as if they believed in phlogiston. If political science can't manage even to stamp out that nonsensical notion, what can it do?

And that at last brings me to the point of this polemic.

There isn't any "social science." None. There are no experts, not in the same sense in which one can be an expert in physics, or chemistry. To the extent that science fiction has encouraged the notion that a science of human behavior exists, we have harmed the world.

We can survive the sociologists. We may even be able to survive the psychologists. The political scientists are a bit more dangerous, but they don't have all that much power: mostly I think of good they could do (like using freshman poly sci to dispel some of the nearly-universal nonsense) and sigh over the waste.

Economists are another matter.

"It ain't what we don't know that hurts us, it's what we know for certain that ain't so."

The economists think they know. And between them and the lawyers, they run the country.

Hope springs eternal. Even after discovering that the useful content of academic psychology can be learned in under a year, and that political science, while enlightening and valuable for intellectual stimulation, was less scientific than psychology, I still yearned for Hari Seldon's laws. Perhaps economics? Economists at least say they're scientific. Grad students in economics talk about input-output models, aggregate economic analyses, "fine tuning" the economy; even in my day, they had complex equations systems which, once they had computers, they could solve . . .

Alas, it's worse there than elsewhere. Look at some of those splendid computer models—and look at the results. They don't predict a damned thing. Hell's bells, as I write this they're wondering whether we're in a recession or not! Now sure, economists can *explain* everything after it's happened—but so can any of the social sciences. And the trouble with acting as if economists have some special knowledge is that they get in the way of common sense.

Look: it doesn't take much genius to see that minimum wages cause unemployment of the unskilled. You wouldn't hire at three dollars an hour someone capable of doing only two dollars' worth of work; why think anyone else will? Now sure, politicians might act cynically: raise the minimum wage, and count on inflation to negate the effect; but that's not science.

It's not a lot harder to see that high taxes encourage people to spend rather than save; if you want to curb inflation, reduce the tax rate.

They give Nobel Prizes in economics. The award is political, of course; people with diametrically opposite views have won it. If one's right, the other must be wrong. Or they both are.

The theory of state-supported education is that it's an investment in the future. The future citizens should have intelligent opinions and useful skills.

Some think this is the most important investment we can make.

So who allocates this most important investment? Why, the people objectively least qualified to do so, of course: incoming freshmen. Department budgets are closely correlated with number of majors. Thus we have a kind of oriental bazaar, with each department trying to woo as many of the frosh as possible. Each also wants to have one or more courses required for graduation; that too boosts enrollment and thus budget.

There's another way.

Wouldn't it make more sense to subsidize departments in proportion to the republic's need for their graduates? And while we're at it, to use our new powerful computers to generate really good predictions of success in the field? Now true, that would mean some students wouldn't get into the department of their first choice; at least not at public expense. But is that any worse than the present situation, which looks like a bad parody of manpower allocation?

Over five years ago I was asked to testify to a legislative committee investigating diminishing resources; at the time I said the most critical diminishing resource was trained talent. I've had no reason to change my opinion.

In the 50's we thought it shameful that almost 20% of our population was in some degree illiterate. We debated what to do about it. The social scientists promised that all it would take was some Federal Aid to Education; a couple of billion dollars would solve the problem nicely.

Three years ago we lamented our 30% functional illiteracy. Now we have a Department of Education. When do we reach 50%? Anyone want to bet we won't?

Mrs. Pournelle is a reading specialist; her students are illiterate teen-agers, many of whom have thick files proving "scientifically" that they can't possibly learn to read. They've "got dyslexia" (which translates to "reading difficulties;" reminds me of my friend who was much relieved when the physician told him his lower backache was lumbago). She tips the files into the waste can and teaches the kids to read. She is also required by law to take various university classes on how to do her job; thus I'm exposed to the journals and textbooks, and they are simply unbelievable. What passes for research would be laughable if it didn't cost so much—and so thoroughly affect people's lives.

So what's to be done about it? I don't know. My agreement with Baen entitles me to an occasional tirade, and this has been it. Years ago E. C. Banfield said, "The existence of a body of nonsense which is treated as if it were a grand principle ought not to be regarded by reasonable critics as equivalent to a grand principle," and I'd like to think I could persuade some of the more honest academicians to take that seriously.

Because it is serious.

We have big computers now. We have analytical tools which might, just might, allow some real science in the social sciences. Hari Seldon's psycho-history probably isn't possible; but something short of it may yet be developed by people trained in scientific method and equipped with modern tools; who know something of computer science and the capabilities of both large and small machines, and also know enough mathematics to have something to program.

But that won't happen if we continue to insist that students learn the nonsense that fills today's social science texts. If they spend their time on nonsense they won't have time to learn anything else.

ALL ENDS OF THE SPECTRUM
An Appendix

One reason Jim Baen keeps me around is that he likes to talk. We have endless telephone discussions of column topics, and they tend to spill over to anything else going on. In the course of one conversation we got to the subject of the Ayatollah Kockamamie, and Jim said something about "all ends of the political spectrum . . . er, points."

"Curious you should put it that way," I replied. "I wrote my dissertation in political science on a proof that the political spectrum has more than one dimension; that the old left-right category doesn't really work."

"Now there's a column," Jim said. And on reflection I agree. At least it makes a good appendix to my tirade on what's wrong with the social sciences.

The notion of a "left" and a "right" has been with us a long time. It originated in the seating arrangement of the French National Assembly during their revolution. The delegates marched into the Hall of Machines by traditional precedence, with the aristocrats and clergy entering first, then the wealthier bourgeois, and so on, with the aristocracy seated on the Speaker's right. Since the desire for radical change was pretty well inversely proportionate to wealth, there really was, for a short time, a legitimate political spectrum running from right to left, and the concept of left and right made sense.

Within a year it was invalidated by events. New alliances were formed. Those who wanted no revolutionary changes at all were expelled (or executed). There came a new alignment called "The Mountain" (from their habit of sitting together in the higher tiers of seats). Even for 18th Century France the "left-right" model ceased to have any theoretical validity.

Yet it is with us yet; and it produces political absurdities. No one can possibly define what variable underlies the "left-right" continuum today. Is it "satisfaction with existing affairs?" Then why are reactionaries, who most definitely want fundamental changes in the system, called "right wing"? Worse, the left-right model puts Fascism and Communism at opposite ends— yet those two have many similarities. Both reject personal freedom. Some would say they are more similar than different.

What are we to make of Objectivists and the radical libertarians? They've been called "right wing anarchists," which is plain silly, a total contradiction in terms.

Nor is this all academic trivia. "There is no enemy to the Left" is a slogan taken very seriously by many intellectuals. "Popular Front" movements uniting "the Left" (generally socialists and communists) have changed the destinies of nations. Conservatives swallow hard and treat kindly other members of "the Right" even when the others seem despicable by Conservative standards. The left-right model, although nonsensical by any theoretical analysis, has had very real political consequences.

Some years ago I set out to replace the old model with one that made more sense. I studied a number of political philosophies and tried to see what underlying concepts separated them from their political enemies. Eventually I came up with two variables. I didn't then and don't now suggest these two are all there is to political theory. I'm certain there are other important ones. But my two have this property: they map every major political philosophy and movement onto one unique place.

The two I chose are "Attitude toward the State," and "Attitude toward planned social progress."

The first is easy to understand: what think you of government? Is it an object of idolatry, a positive good, necessary evil, or unmitigated evil? Obivously that forms a spectrum, with various anarchists at the left end and reactionary monarchists at the right. The American political parties tend to fall toward the middle.

Note also that both Communists and Fascists are out at the right-hand end of the line; while American Conservatism and US Welfare Liberalism are in about the same place, somewhere to the right of center, definitely "statists." (One should not let modern anti-bureaucratic rhetoric fool you into thinking the US Conservative has really become anti-statist; he may want to dismantle a good part of the Department of Health, Education, and Welfare, but he would strengthen the police and army.) The ideological libertarian is of course left of center, some all the way over to the left with the anarchists.

That variable works; but it doesn't pull all the political theories each into a unique place. They overlap. Which means we need another variable.

"Attitude toward planned social progress" can be translated "rationalism"; it is the belief that society has "problems," and these can be "solved"; we can take arms against a sea of troubles.

Once again we can order the major political philosophies. Fascism is irrationalist; it says so in its theoretical treatises. It appeals to "the greatness of the nation" or to the volk, and also to the fuhrer-prinzip, i.e., hero-worship. Call that end (irrationalism) the "bottom" of the spectrum and place the continuum at right angles to the previous "statism" variable.

Call the "top" the attitude that all social problems have findable solutions. Obviously Communism belongs there. Not far below it you find a number of American Welfare Liberals: the sort of people who say that crime is caused by poverty, and thus when we end poverty we'll end crime. Now note that the top end of the scale, extreme rationalism, may not mark a very rational position: "knowing" that all human problems can be "solved" by rational actions is an act of faith akin to the anarchist's belief that if we can just chop away the government, man truly free will no longer *have* problems. Obviously I think both top and bottom positions are whacky; but then one mark of Conservatism has always been distrust of highly rationalist schemes. Burke advocated that we draw "from the general bank of the ages," because he suspected that any particular person or generation has a rather small stock of reason; thus where the radical argues "we don't understand the purpose of this social custom; let's dismantle it," the conservative says "since we don't understand it, we'd better leave it alone."

Anyway, those are my two axes; and using them does tend to explain some political anomalies. For example: why are there two kinds of "liberal" who hate each other? But the answer is simple enough. Both are pretty thorough-going rationalists, but whereas the XIXth Century Liberal had a profound distrust of the State, the modern variety wants to use the State to Do Good for all mankind. Carry both rationalism and statism out a bit further (go northeast on our diagram) and you get to socialism, which, carried to its extreme, becomes communism. Similarly, the Conservative position leads through various shades of reaction to irrational statism, i.e., one of the varieties of fascism.

On the anti-statist end of the scale we can see the same tendency: extreme anti-rationalism ends with the Bakunin type of anarchist, who blows things up and destroys for the sake of destruction; the utterly rationalist anti-statist, on the other hand, persuades himself that somehow there are natural rights which everyone ought to recognize, and if only the state would get out of the way we'd all live in harmony; the sort of person who thinks the police no better than a band of brigands, but doesn't think that in the absence of the police, brigands would be smart enough to band together.

The whole thing looks like Figure One. (Page 370)
Now I do not claim this is *the* model of modern

politics; I do claim that it is a far better model than the one we're using, and in fact I go farther and claim that the "left-right" model so ubiquitous amongst us is harmful. And while I understand that some ideologues find the "left-right" model useful to their cause, and thus have a powerful incentive to gloss over its failures, what puzzles me is why so-called objective political "scientists" don't try to abolish it, at least in freshman political science classes.

But then I've already admitted I don't understand the "social sciences" to begin with, and I needn't say all that again.

EDITOR'S NOTE:

Never before have I felt called upon to add to one of the redoubtable Dr. Pournelle's columns, but Jerry has been guilty of that most heinous of auctorial sins: modesty.

Seriously, Jerry seems to have come up with a useful, predictive, *scientific* measuring device for the social so-called sciences, and passed it off as an "Appendix," forsooth! In politics alone the results of the widespread use of the Pournelle Axes would be revolutionary: pols would be required not only to declare themselves but to reveal precisely and literally their political position—and live with it. For example Teddy Kennedy from his own pronouncements cannot be less than a 4.5/4.5'—how many people in this country would vote for a 4.5/4.5' once it was revealed for what it was? Give me a 2/4' any day! (That's what *I* am; once you have analyzed your own position, you may find your own political choices becoming remarkably simplified. Reagan and Crane, both at 4/2', make me a little nervous. Bush, at 3/3', looks pretty good.)

Note also the odd sympathy and support between the diagonally facing quadrants, as opposed to the antipathy between contiguous ones—at first blush diagonals would seem to make natural enemies, yet artists, intuitive by definition and anti-statist almost by definition, yearn for a world where true art is replaced by Socialist Realism—

while *libertarians* provide the theoretical groundwork for right-wing dictatorships! Odd, very odd.

Note also how one can define "reasonable" as any position no farther from 3/3' than one's own: those farther out in one's own quadrant are pleasantly dotty; those farther out in another, unpleasantly so . . .

But it's not my aim to analyze the Pournelle Axes in depth; any such attempt by me would be necessarily superficial. One of these days I'll get another column from him on this subject. My point is that for *this* column Jerry Pournelle is guilty. Guilty as sin. Of modesty.

—Baen

THE POURNELLE AXES

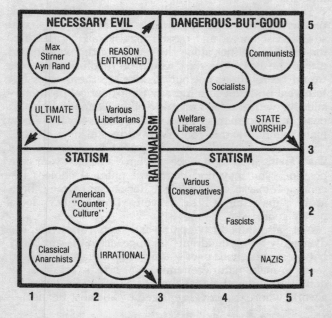

NECESSARY EVIL	DANGEROUS-BUT-GOOD	5
Max Stirner Ayn Rand / REASON ENTHRONED	Communists	
	Socialists	4
ULTIMATE EVIL / Various Libertarians	Welfare Liberals / STATE WORSHIP	3
STATISM	STATISM	
	Various Conservatives	
American "Counter Culture"		2
	Fascists	
Classical Anarchists / IRRATIONAL	NAZIS	1
1 2 3	4 5	

RATIONALISM

AN AFTERWORD ON THE FUTURE

Destinies isn't the only work James Patrick Baen and I have created in collaboration. When he was over at another publishing house we together generated a series of anthologies which I wanted to call *Future Men of War*; but which Jim insisted on calling *There Will Be War* despite vigorous arguments that the title would kill all its sales.

He must have done something right: the series is in six volumes with a million copies in print; and we are at work on volumes seven and eight.

That, of course, is the genesis of *Imperial Stars*: a series that might be called *There Will Be Government*. Of course that doesn't sound so exciting. Or does it? Empires rise and fall; republics come and go; we seek perfection, and we may or may not find it; but the manner of our seeking is terribly important.

The next volume of this series will be called *Republic and Empire*; and will contain stories and essays on the strengths and weaknesses of those forms of government, and of the conflicts and wars between them. We will look at the matter of conscription, and what obligations (if any) a free citizen owes to government. We will continue my speculations about all ends of the political spectrum, and our search for a real science of politics.

We'll do all this our way, which is with good stories that entertain as well as instruct.

EDITOR'S INTRODUCTION TO:

FINGER TROUBLE
Edward P. Hughes

Everyone knows how we came to be. There was a primordial Big Bang that created the Universe from nothing. This made a lot of hydrogen and helium, which sort of clumped into stars, which cooked new higher elements and eventually exploded. New stars formed, and planets; and on some of those planets there was a kind of organic soup, and—

There was a cartoon once. Three white-coated scientists looked at a blackboard covered with equations. Step by step the equations proceeded, until, in about the middle, were written the words: "And then a miracle occurs." The equations continued. The caption was, "Now, Dr. Hanscomb, about that eighteenth step . . ."

After life swam out of the organic soup we had Darwinian evolution. Everyone knows what that is. And of course it must be correct; after all, our schools are now required to teach it.

Sir Fred Hoyle, who knows a little about the origins of the universe, has some harsh words for all this. For example:

". . . nothing remains except a tactic that ill befits a

grand master but which was widely used by staunch club players, namely to blow thick black pipe tobacco smoke in our faces. The tactic is to argue that although the chance of arriving at the biochemical system of life as we know it [through random action] is utterly minuscule, there is in Nature such an enormous number of other chemical systems which could also support life that any old planet like Earth would inevitably arrive sooner or later at one or another of them.

"This argument is the veriest nonsense."

In their work *Evolution From Space* Sir Fred Hoyle and Chandra Wickramasinghe argue that life throughout the universe has arisen by *design*. They don't deny that most life on Earth, including human beings, evolved from simple forms that first appeared on the planet some millions of years ago; but they claim that the evolution was *directed*. Darwin was simply wrong.

This isn't as new an hypothesis as you might think. After all, most of us were taught in high school biology the cellular theory: "Omnia cellula e cellula," said Schleiden and Schwann. All cells come from other cells. There is no spontaneous generation of life. This was accepted well into this century. Arrhenius, Nobel Prize winner for chemistry in 1903, argued that life pervades the universe, and is carried across it in spore form. Life was no more spontaneously generated in Earth's primordial organic soup than is the serpent of Egypt born in the mud "by the action of the Sun." Thus believed Pasteur; thus believed everyone. Except they didn't.

Hoyle and Wickramasinghe: "Yet by a remarkable piece of mental gymnastics biologists were still happy to believe that life started on Earth through spontaneous processes. Each generation was considered to be preceded by a previous generation, but only so far back in time. Somewhere along the chain was a beginning, and the beginning was a spontaneous process.

"Most but not all. Even in the nineteenth century there were a few scientists who felt the situation to be contradictory. If spontaneous generation could not happen, as Louis Pasteur had claimed to the French Academy, then it could not happen. Every generation of every living creature had to be derived from a previous generation, going backward in time to a stage before the Earth itself existed. Hence it followed that life must have come to the Earth from outside."

And indeed, according to Hoyle and Wickramasinghe, that is exactly what happened. Not only that: although there is a chance element in evolution, we continue to receive new genetic material from space to this very day. There is Evolution From Space, and it is not yet completed.

Their conclusion is remarkable: there is only one chance in ten to the fortieth—ten followed by forty zeroes—that life arose spontaneously by chance.

After all: if you put all the parts of a watch into a barrel, you can shake the barrel until doomsday and the parts will not fall together into a watch. If you find a watch in the woods, does that not imply a watchmaker? And if you find a watchmaker?

It simply isn't true that if forty million monkeys sat at typewriters they would eventually produce all the works in the British Museum. If every molecule in the universe were a monkey complete with typewriter; if those monkeys had all begun typing at the moment of the Big Bang, and each monkey had produced one English character each second—the chances are no more than one in ten to the twentieth that among them they would have produced one of Shakespeare's plays.

But of course. Shakespeare produced Shakespeare's plays.

Precisely. And how probable was Shakespeare?

We need not settle this here, which is as well, because we're not going to. My point is that evolution *could* proceed from design. Of course we already know that: we're already doing gene splicing and other experiments with DNA. Add to that some of the discoveries we've made about electric eels and think how we might improve upon them; stir together into a mixture containing old and new civilizations; recall that many people know little about their own history; and you have the ingredients for a whacking good story. Edward Hughes has done just that.

FINGER TROUBLE
Edward P. Hughes

Make Ready Jones was lying low with the dogniks
aboard a sunken houseboat in Kelmet Old Dock when
his finger first began to ache.

He showed it to his dognik friend, Fide O'Reilly. The
tip of his index digit had swollen. The skin was black,
shiny, and angry-looking.

Fide sniffed the offending object. Dogniks were normally short on hygiene, but Fide knew about the sep-
tic. He cocked his head on one side, whining. "Did you
prick it on anything dirty?"

Make Ready screwed up his face, trying to recall past
events. One day ran unrecognizably into another. He
scowled his frustration. "Can't remember." He glared
at the offending digit. "It scares me, Fide."

Fide laid back his ears. The dognik was fond of this
hairless whelp who had taken shelter with the pack. He
growled deep in his throat. "You ought to let the medsin
see it. It could be the gangreeny.'

Make Ready held the finger to his nose. "It don't
smell bad."

Fide showed his canines. "I wouldn't risk it, M'kreddy.

If that black skin spreads, your finger's a goner . . . maybe your whole hand . . . your arm." Fide rolled his eyes. "Even . . . you!"

Make Ready surveyed the houseboat's canting desk, the rotting bulwarks, the black Kelmet river scummed with effluent from the chemplant upstream . . . and sighed. Life was too pleasant to hazard recklessly. He said, "If I go to the medsin . . . who pays?"

Fide O'Reilly scratched a flank with blunted talons. "Healer Grumm don't charge much if you're short of frons. And he comes this way, regular."

Make Ready had seen Healer Grumm . . . a near-standard man, sharp of tongue, but tolerant with orphan dogniks. Perhaps the man could be wheedled into a finger inspection in exchange for a few errands?

The click of rowlocks and the splashing of an oar floated over the water. They leaped together for dry land.

Fide yelped. "It's Healer Grumm. He's sculling in." The dognik waved his arms. "Chuck us a line, Messer Grumm!"

Make Ready caught the healer's rope. Together they took the strain, holding the boat against the current, then hauling it towards the pilings. When Grumm's craft bobbed below them, Fide threw a hitch around a bollard and made fast.

Healer Grumm tossed up a bag of clinking instruments, then climbed the rusting ladder to the dockside, the scabbard of his short sword clinking against the stonework. He grunted, "Thanks, lads. I ran out of mazoo halfway over the river. Would've had to walk back from Garbage if the current had got me."

They clucked in sympathy. The sea-dump where Kelmet's rubbish went was a three hour walk downstream.

Make Ready grabbed the medsin's bag. "Carry your tools, Messer?"

Grumm took the bag from him. "I can manage it, lad." His eyes narrowed. "What you done to your finger?"

Make Ready put the hand behind his back. The healer's interest embarrassed him. "Tain't nothing, Messer Grumm."

The healer extracted a shiny dixer from his pocket. He spun it in the sunlight. "I suppose you want a tip for pulling me in?"

Make Ready stuck out a ready palm.

"T'other one!" Grumm commanded. "Or the dixer goes back in my pocket."

Make Ready's left hand crept from concealment. Grumm inspected the swollen digit. "How long it's been like this?"

"Three—four days."

"Can you move it? Bend it?"

Make Ready tried to curve his finger. "Only at the bottom knuckle."

Grumm gripped his wrist. He took the swollen digit between thumb and forefinger, and squeezed gently. "Does that hurt?"

Make Ready winced. "I can stand it."

"You got any other symptoms?"

Make Ready looked blank.

Grumm gave him back his hand—with the dixer. "Better come up to my dispensary. I'll take a proper look at it."

Startled, Make Ready glanced at Fide. Going with Grumm meant abandoning the pack. Would they let him back afterwards?

Fide wagged his tail. "Go with the healer, M'kreddy. He'll fix that finger."

Make Ready tarried. "Can I come back, after?"

Fide O'Reilly whined. "I'll speak for the others. It'll be okay."

Make Ready sighed. He flicked the dixer to Fide, then turned and followed the medsin.

At Haut Chateau on the Mont des Chênes above Kelmet, court officials packed a labour room to witness the birth of Dame Dimsina Persay's second son. Present by ducal edict, were the court's annalist, lyricist, geneticist, priest, police chief, tutor, strangler, a wet nurse, and the midwife.

Of Dame Dimsina's husband, Duke Corwen Persay, Grand Maitre de Marécage, Maréchal de Haut Barbarie, there was no sign. Rumor had it that his lordship was out shooting corbies in the chateau woods.

Clem Gamble, obstetrician, elevated a syringe to squeeze out a drop of fluid, murmuring to the midwife, "Pray for a paragon, Martha. If his little lordship's anything less than perfect, the duke will have us flayed."

Bregonif, court tutor, undersized and wizened, scuttled back and forth behind a forest of legs, trying to catch a glimpse of the event. Only that very morning, the duke had promised, "If the boy satisfies Greville, you can have another fifteen years." Bregonif badly wanted those fifteen years.

Larry Greville, genetist, and a man who required no admonition from his master, stood before the witnesses, and watched the child slide into the world. Without emotion, he noted one head, two arms, two legs and a penis—all in their proper places. His back straightened. In appearance, the child was a true paragon. There remained the tests. Greville snipped a microscopic sample from the squawling infant's left heel, and hurried to his laboratory.

Annalist Clippy Cummins noted the time of birth, the sex, color of eyes, number and disposition of limbs, and waited for the midwife to announce the weight.

Genevieve Demain, lyricist, and Hector Garman, chef de police, were silent, absorbed in their own thoughts. Genevieve with rhymes for a sonnet to the new heir, Garman with plans for the heir's security.

On the bed, Dame Dimsina gave drowsy thanks to the Double Helix for a safe delivery. Having now doubly secured the succession, the duke might permit her a daughter. There was little fun in dressing boy babies.

The Duchess of Mary Cage went to sleep sucking her thumb.

James Laporte, strangler, folded his arms and waited. The geneticist's approval was required before he could leave the chamber.

But Larry Greville returned to the delivery room shaking his head. He made a sign to Laporte, then left. Gently, Laporte removed the child from the wet nurse's arms . . .

And Formal Crowfoot, the duke's confessor, knelt to mutter a prayer, tears running down his cheeks. The Double Helix gave, but High Barbary took away.

Hector Garman, who combined a spy's role with that of chief of police, began composing a message for transmission to his other master on a distant world: a message reporting that the latest heir to the Duchy of Marécage was inadequate and . . . unsatisfactory.

Healer Grumm's dispensary occupied one room of his home in the upper branch of a live timber shopping mall in downtown Kelmet. The dispensary overlooked a short order caff run by ophids. Grumm's shingle vied with a luminous sign advertising the caff.

Make Ready followed Grumm inside to discover a nest of carpetted and furnished rooms. Since Make Ready's more recent pieds-a-terre had included a disused pig-stye, a rubbish-choked cellar, a dockside packing case and an empty tomb in St. Diennay's churchyard, Grumm's home seemed palatial. He tried to conceal his feeling of awe.

Grumm said, "You don't have to tip-toe about, lad. The tree won't collapse if you breathe." Grumm shed his jacket, revealing a pair of muscular arms, and a down-covered chest. He hung his sword-belt and weapon on the back of the door, grinning. "Must get meself plucked, soon. Plumes ain't good for business. Folk like to believe their medsin's a near-paragon. Them vermy fugers in partic wouldn't let me near 'em if they knew I grew feathers."

Make Ready's eyes grew saucer-shaped. A feathered healer was a long way from standard. He said, "If you let them grow—could you fly?" Fide O'Reilly, with a yard of canine DNA in his genes couldn't urinate on demand.

Grumm flapped his elbows. "Guess I'm more of an osprich or an emug. Too much ballast for flight." He studied the silent youngster. "Not funny? Never mind. Don't suppose you'd say no to a spot of dinner before I check that finger?"

Make Ready shook his head. No adult had addressed

him so civilly for years. And no dognik ever refused food.

Over bacon and eggs, Grumm continued. "And what's a lad like you doing with those dogniks? You in trouble with the flix?"

Make Ready wagged his head again, mouth full of delicious food.

Grumm raised his eyebrows. "Not the recruiters, is it? You ain't old enough to be took for the militia."

Make Ready lowered his eyes. He had fled the tomb in St. Diennay's churchyard when his smouldering fire attracted the attention of Duke Corwen's impress sergeant.

"I'm near seventeen," he muttered.

"But you don't fancy carrying a pike against the chelonians, eh?" Grumm's voice was jovial. "Not that I blame you, lad. They say as how Colly Caswell's turtles cut themselves a slice of Mary Cage last month, up Whernmoor way."

Make Ready cleared his mouth of food. He set his jaw. "Why should I fight for the duke? He ain't never fought for me."

Healer Grumm brandished a fork approvingly. "True, lad. I don't suppose our duke even knows you exist." He cocked his head. "Though perhaps Messer Garman's men might be happy to make your acquaintance?"

Make Ready shrugged. "They'll be lucky to catch me."

"So?" The healer smiled. "How do you dodge them?"

Make Ready grinned in reminiscence. "Over the side of the houseboat—with breathing straws."

Grumm mopped his plate with a wedge of bread, unimpressed. "In that scum?"

Make Ready filled his mouth again. He recalled Rexy Donovan emerging from a skulking session foamy as a toothpaste ad. Make Ready sniffed. "It ain't always scummy. Weekends, it's clean."

They finished eating, and Grumm took him into the dispensary. The healer boiled a panful of water over a gas jet, and put in some instruments to sterilize. He dabbed stinging antiseptic on Make Ready's blackened finger.

Make Ready bit his lip, and made no sound.

Grumm took up his forceps, gripped a fragment of epidermis, and tugged.

Make Ready screamed.

Unperturbed, Grumm put down the forceps. "Tain't ready yet, lad. You'll have to come back tomorrow."

Make Ready nursed the tender digit. "You ain't going to chop it off, then?"

The healer packed away his instruments. He whistled a little tune. "What's your dad's name, lad?"

Make Ready stared hard at his finger. What had his father's identity to do with a possibly gangreeny finger? He said, "My mère told me he was called Messer Jones."

Grumm nodded, as though comprehending more than he had been told. "And your mère? What's she called?"

"I don't remember much about her. She was a Lonten Franchy called Semmy Laduce. They let her out of prison to come here."

Grumm latched his bag, and stowed it under the table. Lontaine France still used Omkrit III as a combined rubbish dump and penal planet. He decided not to ask what crime Make Ready's mother had committed. He said, "Did your mère work as a chamber maid at the Castle on Rue des Percées?"

Make Ready's mouth hardened. The healer was getting far too warm. He mumbled, "Don't remember no Castle."

In Make Ready's memory, the Castle Hotel's domestic quarters had been a warm nest. He had lived there with his mother until old enough to be wished onto a band of roving chip smugglers.

"Well, where did you live?"

After the Castle, where? The smugglers had been like gypsies, wandering the realms of Arcadia, from Mary Cage to Montynose, to Entendy, to Varek, to the Far Nighlands and then round them all again. He had stayed with them, absorbing the illicit mysteries of electronics, until, weary of the surreptitious life, he had run off with a gang of street thieves in Kelmet, his home town.

He muttered, "We shifted around a lot."

Grumm stared at him, eyes calculating. "Do you know that your father might—just might—have been a paragon!"

Make Ready ignored the bait. The mère had always insisted that his DNA was out of the top drawer . . . as if it mattered. Personally, he didn't care if his genes came off a second-hand stall. The dogniks hadn't queried his ancestry.

Grumm persisted. "But don't let that bother you, lad. There's a deal more unrecombined DNA about on Omkrit III than folk credit." He paused. "You don't know where your mère is?"

Make Ready fidgetted with his sore finger. What had all this to do with whether Grumm chopped it off or not? He said, "I haven't seen her for years."

Grumm's expression softened. "We'll manage without her. If your father was who I suspect, you could be an aristo." The healer scratched his head. "Maybe you'd better stay the night here. We can try that finger again tomorrow."

Make Ready's suspicions grew into convictions. Grumm was too interested in parents. A real dognik growl rumbled in his throat. "What do you know about my father? Do you know who he was?"

Grumm ignored the warning signals. "I might, lad. I'm just not sure enough to call 'em facts. You kip on the sofa tonight. We'll talk some more in the morning."

Duke Corwen Persay was told the news of his child's inadequacies when he returned from shooting. He stared, haggard, at the geneticist. "Is it me?"

Greville faced him, eyes expressionless. "No, sire. The infant's DNA was defective. The finger code was impaired."

"Well, if the fault's not mine—whose is it?"

Greville's face was impassive. "I have long had doubts, sire. I feel we were fortunate with Lord Mardy's conception. Perhaps Dame Dimsina should not be permitted to breed again."

The duke was silent for a moment. "Very well. And the child?"

"I gave it to Laporte, sire."

The duke heaved a convulsive sigh. He pulled off his gloves and shooting jacket. The fingerstall on his right hand had come loose. He retied the knot. "Please tell Lord Mardy I would like a word with him."

On Whernmoor, five hundred kilometres to the north, where Duke Corwen's levees strove to stem the chelonian tide, General Lord Cledger Persay had begun to suspect he was in difficulties. The pocket brigade despatched by the duke to halt the turtlebacks was irritatingly outnumbered. And, from an aerial inspection, Lord Cledger had just learned, was also being outmaneuvered.

In the grounds of Dormenville's only school, where the general had set up headquarters, soldiers of headquarters troop winched his captive balloon to earth.

"Steady with that basket!" roared a sashed and epauletted lieutenant to the crew of four-arms on the guide ropes. "Mind you don't shake his lordship!"

The bullet-proof basket came within reach of extended hands, and was eased to safety.

General Lord Cledger Persay cocked a leg over the side, and vaulted to the ground. Young Lord Cledger was proud of his fitness, his command, and his uncle Corwen's trust. He stabbed a leather-stalled finger at the troop-lined ridge above the township, addressing his equerry. "The bastards are as thick as bilberries on the far side of that hill!"

A cannon in the battery which had dug into the football field roared as he spoke, lobbing one of his lordship's explosive novelties over the ridge. His lordship gave the equerry's ears time to stop ringing, then swung up his arm to point east. "The bastards have also infiltrated along our left flank!"

While the lieutenant stood, stricken by the revelation, Lord Cledger brought his arm round in a half circle. "And on our right flank, too!"

He frowned. "Tell the major we are evacuating immediately. Lord Markey's bombardiers will provide covering fire to troops withdrawing from the ridge. Send a message with my instructions. We can't hold this position another hour!"

The equerry jerked like a marionette. "At once, milord. Er—where are we evacuating to?"

Lord Cledger dragged a map from his belt case. A nearby corporal bent to give him a back. The general spread his map on the corporal, searching it diligently. He stabbed the chart. "Here! We'll stand on the Lemon river, by the bridge." He stared about him. "Where's that captain of sappers? I want that bridge mined."

General Lord Cledger Persay's headquarters troop moved out of Dormenville within twenty minutes, followed by a hurriedly unemplaced field gun battery. Lord Cledger rode at their head on his all white gremgaur, blue and silver banner flying. Captain Fogelman's unit of mounted skirmishers, fuming smokepots hanging from their stirrups, waited behind to escort the retreating infantry as they fell back from the ridge. Dormenville was left to be sacked by the turtlebacks.

At the Lemon river bridge, Lord Cledger had his balloon put up again in an attempt to see over the billowing smoke which refused to blow away when it was no longer needed. As the dun-colored bubble rose above the dark billows, an enterprising chelonian sharpshooter in the branches of a tree which poked shrapnel-torn foliage through the smoke chanced a long shot, and brought the Lord Cledger down with a bullet through the head . . .

Word of the Persay babe's death—but not that of Lord Cledger at Whernmoor—was being shouted in the street when Make Ready awoke the following morning. Grumm sent him out to buy a paper. Make Ready returned, head in the pages.

"Dame Dimsina's child died soon after birth," he

reported. "It lived long enough to be helixed by the duke's pastor. Funeral's tomorrow."

Grumm snatched the paper. "I'll do my own reading, if you don't mind!" The medsin studied the printed columns. Nowhere was it reported that the duke's annalist, lyricist, obstetrician, tutor, priest and midwife were now confined to the Chateau at his lordship's pleasure. Nor was there mention of a wet nurse, too anxious to return to her own child, who now bobbed silently down to Garbage. Persay secrets were dangerous possessions. But Grumm had his suspicions. Infant deaths were abnormal on Omkrit III. But the Persays could get their DNA cocked up as easy as anyone else.

The medsin threw down the paper. "Here, lad—let's have another squint at that finger."

Make Ready held out his hand. He was no longer fooled. Grumm knew the cause of the blackened tip.

The healer peered at the finger, making no attempt to detach any dead skin. "Hmm! Still not ready, lad. Reckon you'd better hang on here a while."

Make Ready studied his digit. Not ready for what? Grumm had used the expression twice. Why was his finger so important to the healer? Why was he anxious to let a scruffy dognik stay in his house? And would he let the dognik go, if he didn't want to stay?

Make Ready said, "Am I a prisoner, Messer Grumm?"

The healer raised his eyebrows. Make Ready felt like a germ under a microscope. Grumm frowned. "Where'd you get that idea, lad?"

Make Ready scowled back. "Am I, sir?"

Grumm's face grew gloomy. "You can buzz off any time you like. But you'll be sorry if you do."

Make Ready's eyes became accusing slits. "You knew my finger wouldn't be ready this morning!"

Grumm avoided his gaze. "Suppose I did?"

Make Ready's voice was triumphant. "Ready for what? You tell me!"

Grumm squirmed on his seat. "I suppose you'll have to be told, sooner or later. If my guess is right, your sire's name wasn't Jones—it was Persay, the Grand

Maitre himself. And that what's bugging you is the Persay doigt!"

Make Ready caught his breath. His finger the Persay doigt?

For generations Persay digiteurs had defended Mary Cage against invaders from Entendy, Varek, and Montynose. He glanced anxiously at the blackened digit. "But that would make me . . ."

Grumm grinned. "Precisely, my little lord. A pettiduc, in the argot. More precisely, a precious little bastard. But we need expert opinion. I'll admit it crossed my mind to make a dublin or two out of your affliction, but this morning's news alters matters. If the duke's lost his new heir, he might look favorably on a byblow what already has the Persay doigt. What do you say? Would you like to be the duke's son? I've a contact at the Chateau that could pronounce for sure on your finger."

His tongue wouldn't move. Grumm was mad. *Him*—a duke?

Grumm let the boy stew. If Mary Cage didn't get another digiteur—and Healer Grumm peripheral benefits—out of this gambit, Healer Grumm would stand to be kicked!

Lord Mardy Persay knocked at the door of his father's study. From the haggard air, the duke had spent the night brooding. He motioned his son to a chair. "You heard the bad news?"

"About the child?"

The duke snarled. "No, you fool. About young Cledger getting himself killed at Whernmoor."

Lord Mardy nodded. "Bregonif told me. I suppose you want me to go out there, and pull the chestnuts out of the fire for you?"

Duke Corwen scowled. "Someone has to take his place. We can't let Colly Caswell's turtlebacks walk all over us. And you're the only digiteur I have to spare. But, before you take off—I want advice from you. We still require a backup heir for the duchy. I haven't the heart to try for another natural son. In any case, where would I go? Greville rules out your mère."

Lord Mardy examined his shiny toecaps. "Back to the cell banks, I imagine. Where else?"

The duke thumped his desk. "You haven't absorbed much in twenty years, Mardy. We don't let clones inherit." Lord Corwen sighed. "Though rules are made to be broken. Whom do you suggest?"

His son shrugged. "Whoever you like, sir."

The duke's lips compressed. "It ain't who I like! You're supposed to take an interest. Great Helix—it'll be your duchy when they put me in a bottle. Consider who's eligible. Your great grandpère? He's entitled to another term after fifty years in the bank. But he was a flop as Grand Maitre. His only sensible act was siring my father. We can't let him at the controls again."

Lord Mardy tried to show interest. "Further back, then?"

The duke frowned. "That's Bregonif's period. And he's been twice round already—although only me and Greville know it. Brecon IV was a pain in the derrière when he was boss. Greville chipped the doigt sequence out of his DNA before we cloned him the second time. His time's nearly up, anyway. I've already warned him."

"I mean back before Brecon IV, sir."

The duke gaped in alarm. "You wouldn't clone those murderous madmen! Lontaine France was still dumping its illicit experiments here in those days. Your grandpère six times removed had a wolf's head, and ate children. Greville needed three generations to excise that lupus sequence from the family's genes."

Lord Mardy's eyebrows lifted. "Greville? In those days?"

The duke waved away the query. "Larry Greville has his own way of surviving. As long as he takes care of the Persays, I don't ask no questions. He's got us as near standard as anyone would wish to be."

Lord Mardy became engrossed in his fingertips. "Are you sure you really want my advice, sir?"

The duke blew a gust of breath. "Dammit, Mardy—you're right. It's my job, and I'm shirking it. I just wish Dimsina's child had matched up to our requirements. I don't fancy a clone succeeding me. I want my own progeny in the driving seat."

Lord Mardy found a smile. "You still have me, father."

His parent cackled. "By the Helix, son—so I do, so I do. Don't I tend to overlook the obvious?" He paused. "Now, don't go acting reckless up at Whernmoor. Use your pikemen. They're steady. And the shellbacks don't like cold steel. Give them a bloody nose, and come home safe. Colly Caswell should know better than to try to invade me!"

Lord Mardy rose. "I'll take good care, father."

His father rose. "I'll talk to Larry Greville, then."

The duke stumped off to the laboratory. Greville would advise him on whom to reincorporate. The Persay's welfare was the man's prime concern. He could rely on Larry Greville.

Make Ready didn't doubt the healer's ability to achieve such a bizarre objective. As a child, Make Ready had ignored his mère's fantasies of a paragon lineage. Was he truly a Persay bastard? Or was it just a genetic accident which had produced a facsimile Persay doigt? What matter, if the results were identical?

He said, "Would I have to stay at the Chateau?" It would be a blow to leave the dogniks and the houseboat.

"You'd be better away from that scummy sewer." Grumm's expression was virtuous, as though Make Ready's welfare were his only concern.

Make Ready sulked. "It ain't all scummy. There's a channel over by the far bank where we swim."

Grumm shuddered. "Don't say I didn't warn you. Dogniks is different to us near-standards. Their bodies can cope with disease. I'm a medsin—I know."

Make Ready let it pass. His dognik friends were cleaner than most of Kelmet's citizens. He said, "Who do we contact at the Chateau?"

Grumm's face went blank. "My business, lad. You tell me if you want me to get him here to see that doigt of yours."

Oh, what the Helix! He could slide out if things got

too hot. It might be a lark to confront the Grand Maitre with a bastard he had forgotten!

Make Ready met the healer's gaze with innocent eyes. "Okay, Messer Grumm. I'll give it a go."

Lord Mardy Persay was in no hurry to dash off to Whernmoor. Cledger's second in command had reported that the Persay force was holding on the Lemon river, with the bridge still unblown. Dalliance at Haut Chateau was a deal more attractive than campaigning in the northern boondocks with an army of sweaty four-arms. And there were other ways of killing cats . . .

Lord Mardy headed for the Chateau's telecommunications centre. He found the duty corporal at his desk outside the aviary. The man saluted with an upper arm, while unsuccessfully attempting to conceal a comic book behind his back with the lower ones.

"At ease, corporal," Mardy ordered, smiling. "This visit ain't official until I put on my cap."

The corporal stared, noting that Lord Mardy carried no cap. He relaxed. "Can I help you, sir."

Mardy pointed his stalled index finger at the aviary door. "Can you get a message into Entendu for me?"

The corporal straightened. "That's easy, sir. I have a couple of Entendy birds in there. Would you want to get in touch with the earl himself? The birds are from his stable."

Mardy nibbled at a thumb nail. "Would the earl know who sent the message?"

"Only if you tell him, sir. The birds was took from a catman courier who was trying to smuggle them into Varrick through Mary Cage territory."

"So, if I were to send a message by one of your birds, Earl Elder would believe it came from his own agent in Varek?"

"If you didn't tell him different, sir."

Lord Mardy rubbed his hands together. "Excellent, corporal. How do I send a message?"

The corporal opened the lid of his desk, and got out a sheaf of flimsies. "If you'll write it out on this special paper, sir. I'll do the rest."

Mardy weighed the flimsies in his hand. "Won't the type of paper give us away?"

The corporal grinned. "We captured those flimsies with the birds, sir. We made copies before we replaced them—with our own birds . . . and our own agent!"

Lord Mardy whistled his admiration of the devious strategy. "So Earl Elder's messages from Varek will come to us?"

The corporal shrugged modestly. "Shouldn't be surprised, sir."

Lord Mardy bent over the soldier's desk. On the top flimsy he wrote: "An army of 3,000 shellbacks, with artillery and cavalry have invaded Marécage. Suggest prime opportunity for strike on Varek. Area around Mossum completely undefended."

He left the message unsigned. Folding the flimsy, he found the corporal offering him a minute container.

"Pop it in there, sir. I'll fix it to the bird straight-away, and send it off."

Lord Mardy screwed up the flimsy beneath the one he had used, and casually scribbled over the next lower sheet with the blunt end of his pen. "I'd like to see it go, corporal, if I may."

The corporal unlocked the aviary door. "We've no secrets from you, milord. You hold the message tube while I get the bird."

"That will do nicely, corporal," Lord Mardy agreed.

He went back to his own quarters in the Chateau humming happily. The message should be enough to spur Jark Elder into a raid on Caswell's territory, thereby creating a demand for the immediate recall of the turtlebacks from Whernmoor. And Lord Mardy Persay could stay snug at Haut Chateau, keeping an eye on the machinations of one Larry Greville. When it came to deciding on fresh additions to the Persay line, the heir apparent ought not to be left out in the cold.

Almost a week passed before Grumm was able to speak to his contact at the Chateau. Make Ready filled the time by helping around the dispensary, learning to compound traditional antibiotics, salves, and unguents.

On the eve of Haut Chateau's weekly market, Grumm showed Make Ready a note. He read, "Will visit you tomorrow."

He gave the it back to Grumm. "Your contact?"

Grumm nodded.

Make Ready fumbled under his jerkin. "You'd better have this back, then."

He handed Grumm a scalpel.

The medsin stared. "Where'd you get that?"

Make Ready shrugged elaborately. "I was going to get Fide O'Reilly to chop my finger off if your contact wouldn't play."

Face pale with anger, the healer placed the knife in a rack. "Why didn't you slip it back without telling me—like when you nicked it?"

Make Ready said nothing. He knew the healer knew why. Nobody pulled Make Ready Jones' strings. Dogniks—even honorary dogniks—get by on their own efforts. And now the healer knew it.

The contact was elderly and shrivelled. He paraded a cock's comb headpiece, webs between his fingers, and feathers dangled from beneath his cape. Make Ready was not deceived. When the man had unbuttoned his cloak, Make Ready had observed a dagger sheath jewelled and crested. The man was no cockalorum.

Healer and stranger shook hands High Barbary fashion, palms not quite touching. The stranger's pupils flicked from side to side, like a wary animal. He pulled off his finger webs. "One is forced into deceit, Grumm. Bit of a putsch on up the hill since the death of Dimsina's infant. I'm not supposed to be out without one of Garman's lackeys. Where's your candidate?"

Grumm signalled Make Ready from the dispensary. "Show the gentlesir your finger, boy."

Make Ready extended the blackened digit. The stranger inspected it closely, sniffing it, turning it over. He squeezed the crazed skin. Make Ready bit his lip. The stranger cocked an eye at the medsin. "This doigt has a long way to go."

Grumm gestured apologetically. "I guessed that. But

it gives us time to think, don't it? Would Grand Maitre be interested?"

The stranger studied Make Ready. Clad in a pair of Grumm's cut-down britches and a clean shirt, Make Ready felt he was making quite an impression.

The stranger wrinkled his nose. "How old are you, lad?"

Make Ready chose civility. "I'm not sure, sir. Sixteen or seventeen, I think."

The stranger turned to Grumm. "He'd have to be cleaned up before I could take him near the duke."

Grumm said, poker-faced, "I'll dress him like a lord if you'll fix him up with an audience."

The stranger sat down, and removed his headpiece. "What's the story? I can give you ten minutes."

Grumm related what he knew of Make Ready's antecedents, and his suspicions of what might have occurred between Make Ready's mother and a younger Duke Corwen Persay.

The stranger made noises like a trapped fly. "Daren't make too much of that. Grand Maitre is sensitive about his youthful peccadilloes. But he's anxious to secure another heir, having lost the child. I, also, must declare an interest. I was due for the cell banks this year, but the duke has given me a respite until he decides what to do about a backup heir. So I'm all for the lad being accepted. A new pettiduc at court could guarantee me another five years as his tutor."

"You'll push for him, then?"

The stranger pulled on his finger webs. "Leave it with me, Grumm. Old Breg can still pull a string or two. . ." The stranger paused.

Grumm frowned. "What's up?"

The stranger pointed a shaking finger, web dangling. "It's the wrong blessed doigt!"

Grumm bridled. "What d'you mean? It's his forefinger, ain't it?"

"But it's on the wrong hand! It's on his *left* hand!"

Grumm caught Make Ready's startled expression, then turned back to the stranger. "So what? He's a bastard— bar sinister, and all that—ain't he?"

The stranger hopped up and down with irritation, his tail feathers bobbing. "Don't quote bleedin' heraldry at me, Grumm! This might alter the whole picture. There's never been a left-handed digiteur."

"There's got to be a first time for everything."

"Don't *argue* with me, either! I'll have to make that point with the duke and that bloody Greville."

Grumm relaxed in his chair. "So you'll still try for him?"

The stranger dabbed a balding scalp. "Helix! Of course I will. How else do I stay out of the cell banks? But it isn't going to be easy!"

Make Ready and Grumm watched the stranger strut down the street. Neither of them paid much attention to the cloaked figure which drifted after him.

Make Ready said, "Who's Greville?"

Grumm told him what was known and rumored about the duke's geneticist.

"So Greville is really the boss?"

"No. The duke is the boss. But when Greville pronounces on anything to do with genetics, he can generally make it stick."

"Could he rule me out because it's my left finger?"

"He could rule you out because you fart too loud, son. He might bar you because your mère was a quadroon."

"Does the color show?"

"No way, lad. But Greville can tell you things about yourself what you never suspected."

Make Ready pondered briefly. "Then it would be best to keep out of Messer Greville's way?"

Grumm sniffed. "You couldn't have put it clearer, lad."

Below Dormenville in Whernmoor, at the bridge over the Lemon river, where the Persay forces were dug-in, shielded lanterns had been lit against the night. A face-blackened soldier presented himself to the guard at the headquarters tent, and requested admittance.

Colonel Kelp, temporary custodian of Lord Cledger's command, called, "Bring him in!"

Within the tent, the soldier grounded his ironwood musket, and saluted with the regulation arm. "Beg to report, colonel sir—the turtlebacks are pulling out."

Colonel Kelp frowned. He was daily expecting the arrival of a Persay replacement to relieve him of this hot potato of a command, and he wasn't keen on doing much more than sit on his butt and hold that Helix-damned bridge.

"You sure of that, soldier?" he demanded, hardly able to believe his ears.

"Their guns started moving out when the light went, sir. There can't be anything but their cavalry rearguard left over there by now."

Colonel Kelp knew he should take action. In his mind, he could hear a Persay voice snarling, "And what did you do about it, man?"

He turned to his aide-de-camp. "Ask Major Mottel to step across."

Major Mottel presented himself with the remains of supper clinging to his moustache.

Kelp addressed the soldier. "Tell the major what you've told me."

The soldier repeated his report.

"Now, Charles," said the colonel. "What are we to do?"

The major tugged his moustache while he thought. Charles Mottel had few inhibitions about taking action in any situation whatever. Unfortunately, he had little experience of handling brigade-sized forces.

He said, "We could put a strong patrol over the bridge to test their reaction. Might even bag a few of their cavalry before they all escape."

The colonel's face cleared. "Capital, Charles. Please arrange it, immediately." If the scout's report was accurate, he might even get the credit for routing the shellbacks, as well as capturing a few prisoners.

Half an hour later, a line of Persay infantrymen, armed and accounted, crept silently over the bridge, ears alert for the tramp of hooves or the clink of metal.

On the far side of the bridge, a turtleback sapper, his carapace liberally mud-smeared, lay prone, the silhouettes of the Persay infantry on the bridge just visible to him against the darkened sky. Every now and again, he tugged a cord which caused a cluster of gremgaur shoes hanging from a distant tree to jingle faintly.

When the sapper observed that the bridge was full from end to end with creeping Persay soldiers, he pressed a wire to the terminal of a wet cell on the ground beside him.

The Lemon river bridge blew skyward in a flash of light which displayed flying timbers, flailing arms, legs, bodies, heads, helmets, muskets and other impedimenta. The chelonian sapper picked up his battery, mounted a tethered and muffled gremgaur in the peculiar chelonian fashion, and speeded after his unit.

On the other side of the Lemon river, Colonel Kelp heard the explosion, and trembled . . .

The Grand Maitre sent for Bregonif.

"Well?" he challenged. "You blew it, didn't you?"

Bregonif feigned incomprehension. "Blew what, sire?"

The duke scowled. "Don't play the fool with me, Breg! I can't stand a rogue acting the innocent. And I hate cross-breeders. Something odd about a fellow who's not content with his own kind."

"I—I don't follow you, sire."

The duke thumped the desk top. "By the Helix, no! But someone followed you! Sneaking off to Kelmet tarted up as a mock cockalorum! Were you looking for another queer to ruffle your feathers?"

Bregonif drew himself unimpressively erect. "Nothing of the kind, sire. I wore cockalorum disguise to help me to follow a lead which might be of benefit to you."

The duke sighed. He hadn't been listening. "Might as well tell you. I've decided on a clone, instead of a natural son. This sex business is too chancy. It'll be Derzey, the youngest son of great uncle Armaduc. The lad got himself perforated by a Grogue raiding party before he was twenty, so he didn't have much fun. We reckon he deserves another go-round. Greville is picking a clone-mère for him. I had intended you to stay on as tutor, but if you've turned into a blasted queer . . ."

Bregonif trembled with rage. Not too difficult to guess who had been spying on him. He gabbled protests. "Sire—it was essential that I went disguised to Kelmet. Garman's men would have insisted in accompanying me in my own persona. I chose to dress as a cockalorum because they are easily imitated. A false comb, finger webs—"

The duke raised a hand. "Point taken. You've been disobedient, not queer. I forgive you, so don't harp on about it. Why go to Kelmet?"

Bregonif glanced around the room, looking for cover. Within the next minute, an old Persay retainer who must have lost his marbles might lose the rest of his assets. He said, "I went to meet your bastard son, sire." Then Bregonif closed his eyes, and waited for the lightning to strike.

He heard the duke's laugh. "Is my reputation so dire, Breg?"

Bregonif opened his eyes, relief showing. "I'm afraid so, sire."

"Tell me about this bastard."

Bregonif told his lord about Make Ready. He added quickly, "The youth might fail on one count—the doigt is on his left hand."

The duke was inattentive. He murmured, "She never told me." He chewed a lip in thought. "Is the lad presentable? Does he have manners? Any learning?"

Bregonif affected disinterest. "M'kreddy is an orphan who has run wild for years, sire. He has a native cunning which might indicate intelligence. He could be made presentable. He had manners enough to hold his tongue while I spoke to his sponsor."

"Who is his sponsor?"

"A Kelmet medsin I have known for years."

The duke grew pensive. "The lad could save us a deal of time." He glanced furtively at Bregonif. "If he has the doigt, we daren't ignore it. He must be either acknowledged or eliminated."

Bregonif should not have cared what happened to the duke's bastard. With a cloned heir already selected, he was sure of a tutor's job. But nine months was a long time. Fortunes could vanish and alliances burgeon while Greville brought his clone to birth. An heir in the hand was worth ten clones in the future. Bregonif said, "I think you should acknowledge your son, sire."

The duke knuckled his forehead. "I can't acknowledge him until I've had a good look at him."

"Agreed, sire. And one doesn't socialize with street arabs."

"Precisely. So what do we do?"

Bregonif appeared to cogitate, although his plan had been cooking for days. "Sire, I can arrange for the boy to be brought to the Chateau next market day. Perhaps you might find yourself on the Mendicants steps about noon? I could ensure that the lad passed close enough for you to scrutinize him without your purpose being apparent."

Duke Corwen Persay grunted his satisfaction. "That's quite neat, Breg. We'll do it that way."

Bregonif felt the sweat trickling down his nape. "Thank you, sire. Will that be all?"

The duke's eyes became gimlets. "Unless you have further shocks for me?"

"No, sire. No more shocks." Bregonif backed out of his lord's presence, knees decidedly shaky. It had gone smoother than he had anticipated. There was no point in pushing his luck.

When Duke Corwen received the report from Whernmoor, he went in search of his son.

Lord Mardy was trouncing Mim Bonner, his aide, at tennis when the duke arrived on court. One glance at the duke's purple face prompted Bonner to abandon the match, and the court.

The duke waved the message flimsy at his son. "Dammit, Mardy—you promised me you'd go to Whernmoor!"

Lord Mardy wiped his palms on a towel. "I promised to pull your chestnuts out of the fire, sir—which I did."

The duke fumed. "By the Holy Helix—don't bandy words with me!"

Lord Mardy stood his ground. When Duke Corwen was in a temper, it was either stand or grovel. Mardy said patiently, "I got the turtlebacks out of Mary Cage, sir. What more did you require?"

The duke flourished the avigram. "That fool Kelp allowed them to escape. *And* let them blow the bridge while a troop of musketeers were crossing—*with him and the brigade on the wrong side of the river!*"

Lord Mardy swung his racquet like a flail. "Kelp always was a fool, sir. He'd never have made second-in-command but for Cledger wanting him."

The duke rumbled like a distant thunderstorm. "Well, what are you going to do about it? Do I have to clean up the mess myself?"

Lord Mardy sighed. "You'll have to lend me the floater, sir. It's the only way to get to Whernmoor fast enough."

Duke Corwen blinked furiously at his son. The duke's floater, unlike most modern gimmicks in Mary Cage—such as electric batteries, hard metal muskets, and the like—was home-grown; not smuggled or imported from the mystery makers in the south. Part animal, part tree, the floater had been nurtured in Greville's own laboratory. Three younger planimals were maturing in the rose garden, but they wouldn't be ready for some years.

"Dammit, Mardy, the creature's just getting to know me!"

"It'll take three days to reach Whernmoor by gremgaur, sir. Helix knows what stupidities Kelp could commit in that time. The floater is three times as fast as any of our sixlegs."

The duke dug his toes into gravel. "You'd better take good care of that beastie, son!"

Lord Mardy spun his racquet. "I will, sir. And the run will do it good. It doesn't get enough exercise from you."

"*I'll* decide that," grunted the duke. "And, before you go—some news for you."

Lord Mardy's racquet ceased revolving. "Sir?"

"Bregonif's found a Persay byblow what has the doigt!"

Lord Mardy raised his eyebrows, and waited.

The duke looked vaguely uncomfortable. "A young

chap from Kelmet. Bit of a rough diamond, according to Breg."

Lord Mardy hid his amusement. "One of your indiscretions, sir?"

The duke harrumphed. "That's something we needn't go into."

Mardy stared thoughtfully at the sky. "I've often fancied a kid brother. Could be fun. I'm sorry I didn't see the babe before it died."

The duke's expression was unreadable. "Can't have a grown man watch his mère in parturition."

And just as well, he thought. The fewer complications, the better. Of those witnessing the birth, only an unnamed midwife had been unwilling to recall the child dying in Formal Crowfoot's arms. That one had followed the wetnurse on a one way trip to Garbage. And Hector Garman's men had proved their loyalty by diligently failing to discover who had disposed of the woman.

Duke Corwen was well served. He said, "The byblow appears for inspection next Saturday noon before the Mendicant Steps. If he's atall presentable, I'm prepared to accept him. But Greville's attitude may be different—he's keen on a clone of Derzey Persay."

. . . who was an idiot, Lord Mardy added to himself. Perhaps it would be wise to speed up to Whernmoor, deal with Colonel Kelp, and get back as quickly as possible. Saturday noon, at the Mendicant Steps might be the place to be, if you were sold on securing a stepbrother for yourself.

Bregonif said, "Does the boy know the duke?"

Grumm laughed. "Little Bastard ain't been out of the stews of Kelmet."

Bregonif turned towards Make Ready. "The duke will be on the steps before the Mendicant Door. He will wear a lime green, high necked, gold belted tunic. You may miss the stall on his finger, since he will have long, lace cuffs. He may wear a flat cap. His breeks will be red, buckled below the knee. There will be at least two Chateau guards with him. Approach no closer than six feet. Do not look at him. Do not address him. Walk the length of the alley between the market stalls and the Chateau, pass the steps slowly, then get the hell out of sight. And for Helix's sake, wipe that silly grin off your face!"

Make Ready's visage froze. "Yes, sir." He hesitated. "Sir— have you told the duke that my doigt ain't mature yet?"

Bregonif eyed the healer and the youth for a moment. Then he said, "You had both better understand what kind of fire you are playing with. I happen to know that Greville wants a Persay clone which he has already chosen. So M'kreddy's appearance on the scene could upset his plans. If he were to learn that the doigt wasn't ripe, he might take steps to eliminate you both. So, unless the Grand Maitre accepts M'kreddy, I can't answer for your safety."

Grumm tried to smile. "We never thought it'd be a cakewalk."

Bregonif toyed with the wattles depending from his cock's comb. "What did you expect to get out of the scheme, anyway?"

Grumm shrugged. "Supplier of herbs and medicals to the Chateau? Perhaps healer to the domestics?"

"And if the lad doesn't satisfy?"

Grumm's face grew gloomy.

Bregonif continued remorselessly. "You must appreciate the alternative. The duke can't ignore a contender with the doigt. He either accepts or rejects him. If *he* opts for rejection—he'll have to reject the sponsor, too!"

Grumm shot a furtive glance at Make Ready. "I—I have friends in Varrick."

Bregonif shook his head in doubt. "You'd have to be quick."

"The duke won't blight no one in public."

Bregonif fiddled with the catch on his cloak. "Don't be too sure. He has a quick temper. I'll have three gremgaurs tethered at the foot of the Demidrop Stairs, waiting for you. We might all need to be quick."

Grumm swallowed hard. He nodded in silent assent.

"So—turn the lad out smart, and hope for the best."

Make Ready kept quiet. What if you had no friends handy in Varrick? What if, anyway, you'd done enough running in your short life? What if you fancied letting the great Duke Corwen Persay see what you thought of absentee fathers? It would take more than a fast gremgaur to get you clear of the commotion that indiscretion would cause!

Lord Mardy Persay relaxed his pressure on the goad, allowing the floater to slow. Ahead, at the foot of the hill, lay the Lemon river. On the nearer bank, rows of tents advertised the presence of Lord Cledger's brigade.

Feeling the tiller pull against his palm, Mardy let the planimal drift unguided towards a nearby copse, where it nuzzled a tree, and settled.

No Persay patrol appeared to challenge their arrival.

"This'll do," Mardy told his escort. "That's Kelp's camp below."

He jumped from the driving seat, motioning his men out with him. "Watch our beastie, corporal," he ordered. "This won't take long."

The corporal nodded. "Aye, sir." He tucked his imported metal musket under one arm, and vanished among the trees. Lord Mardy set off downhill with the other two guardsmen.

Duke Corwen had given no precise instructions about the fate of Colonel Kelp. Lord Mardy had little doubt about what would happen to the colonel in his father's hands.

Followed by his guards, he paced along the line of tents towards the marquee flying the Persay banner. Beside them, the river bank swarmed with coveralled sappers. The skeleton of a two-lane bridge already stretched towards the farther bank. On the farther bank, refugees from the stricken township of Dormenville huddled, many in bloody bandages.

"Holy Helix!" Mardy's men being his personal bodyguard, were permitted a looseness of discipline he considered justified by their absolute loyalty to him. "Why don't the colonel do something for them poor bastards?"

The other guardsman grimaced. "Reckon them sappers will be digging a grave or two before we go back to Kelmet."

His companion nodded agreement. He raised his voice, "Permission to fix bayonets, sir?"

Mardy shook his head. His men were doubtless ready to fight the whole brigade, should it venture to disagree with any of his judgments. Mardy grinned. "We don't want to frighten them too much." Like all Persay nobles, Lord Mardy went unarmed, except for an ornamental dagger. The Persay doigt was all that was required to instill fear into his enemies.

The guard on the marquee threw up his musket, then, recognizing Lord Mardy, lowered it, and stood back.

Mardy thrust aside the flap, and entered the tent.

A coterie of officers sat around a campaign table, glasses before them. In Duke Corwen's army, a colonel wore two silver stars below a coronet on his shoulders. The officer carrying this weight of metal paused in the act of tipping a bottle over a glass, and turned.

"Dammit, soldier, I said we were not to be bothered—!"

"Except by me, colonel," Mardy interrupted. "I've come to collect the account of your stewardship."

Color drained from Kelp's face. He lowered the bottle to the table. The officers behind him got hurriedly to their feet, buttoning tunics.

"Are we celebrating a victory?" Mardy asked, face innocent.

"Er—no, sir," gasped the colonel.

"Then why are we not outside, getting on with the war? Why were there no patrols to challenge me when I arrived? Why are there wounded and homeless, unhoused and untreated, on the far bank of the Lemon?" Mardy paused for breath. "Why are you still in command, Colonel Kelp?"

The colonel gaped, wordless, eyes on Lord Mardy's stalled digit.

Mardy raised his index finger, pointing. "Can you

give me one good reason why you should continue to command Lord Cledger's brigade?"

"Sire—!" protested a moustached major behind Kelp.

The menacing digit moved from the colonel to the major. "Were you invited to speak, sir?"

The major shook his head, suddenly mute.

Mardy's eyes were bright. This sorry crew, who had permitted poor, idiotic Cledger to expose himself to enemy fire, deserved all that was coming to them. "Don't despair, major," he advised. "Your turn will come."

He turned back to Kelp. "Step forward, colonel, so that I may touch you."

Like a puppet jerked by strings, the colonel approached Lord Mardy.

"Close enough, colonel." Mardy reached out, hooked his finger under Kelp's epaulette, and ripped it loose from its button. Then he grabbed the dangling cloth, and tore it from the colonel's shoulder.

"Remain still, colonel," he ordered, "so that I may reach your other shoulder."

Tucking both epaulettes into his pocket, Mardy said, "Messer Kelp, you are now a civilian, and have no more power over this brigade. In my father's name, I now banish you under pain of death from the Duch of Mary Cage. When I am done here, you will be boated over the river, and left to your own devices. For your sake, I hope they serve you better than you served Milord Cledger!"

Kelp closed his eyes. "Sire, I have a wife and children—!"

Mardy's face was merciless. "So had Milord Cledger—and probably those troopers who were killed on the bridge."

Kelp opened his blazing eyes. His hand went to the hilt of his hanger.

Mardy heard the click of a musket trigger behind him.

He put out a restraining palm. "Messer Kelp, I would not take your sword from you, since a sword is every citizen's right. But, if you put your hand on it again in my presence, you will not live to draw it."

An hour later, the men of Lord Cledger's brigade watched six disgraced ex-officers ferried across the river. A young captain of musketeers, dazzled by the prospect of swapping a star for a coronet, had promised Lord Mardy to get the bridge finished, the refugees succoured, and the brigade home in good order.

Feeling sick, because he had come within an ace of blighting Kelp, Lord Mardy motioned to his bodyguard. "That's it, lads. Let's go home."

On Boulevard Trounoir, the healer paused before the window of a Gentlesires Outfitters. "Do as they tell you in there," he warned. "The fellow owes me a favour, but it won't stop him charging me a packet. So don't give him any excuse for jacking up his prices any higher than they already are."

The man who came to greet them wore two arms and two well-camouflaged stumps. Why a hero should choose amputation to emulate the paragon shape was beyond Make Ready. He had often envied the extra pair of arms the hexos owned.

Grumm and tailor flourished palms. Grumm muttered, "Good of you, Maddy. This is M'kreddy. M'kreddy, Maddy Dearboy is going to dress you for the pageant. Behave yourself, and do what he tells you."

The tailor gripped Make Ready's sleeve, holding him fast. He faced Grumm. "Float for a couple of hours. We don't like an audience."

He led Make Ready into a room where many hexos worked tailoring machines.

"You're getting priority, lad," he said. "Helix knows why. So busy we are. I must be going soft in the head." He pushed Make Ready onto a turntable, and produced a tape measure. "Get those rags off," he ordered.

Make Ready stripped off Grumms jacket and shirt.

Maddy Dearboy's hands fluttered. "Everything, laddie. I wouldn't put muttoncloth over that rag of a shirt."

Flushing, Make Ready removed Grumms britches and his own skimpy underwear.

The tailor eyed the fingerstall Grumm had supplied. "You can't want your glove fitted over that?"

Make Ready put his hand behind his back. To remove the stall would betray his blackened finger. If a Kelmet medsin could divine the significance of the digit, why not a Kelmet tailor. He said, "Over the stall, messer."

The tailor shrugged his indifference. "Messer Grumm didn't say, laddie—do you want polypop fibre or cultstuff? Cultured fabric is guaranteed not to crease or wear out during its life, but on humid days it tends to grow faster than the programmed shrinkage, and you get a baggy fit."

Make Ready observed Dearboy's unconcerned pose. Sackcloth or hessian would have held equal interest for the tailor. Make Ready set his jaw. Grumm looked for a profit from their venture. Why endanger it by skimping!

Make Ready said, "Haven't you got nothing better?"

Dearboy inflated his chest. "Laddie, we have a trad cotton velvet ideally suited for your rigout. It's guaranteed both to crease and wear out—eventually. But, until it does, it will disguise you as a gentlesir. It is, unfortunately, more expensive that the materials I suggested. Messer Grumm would no doubt regard it as too expensive for a single wearing."

Make Ready hesitated. Dress him like a lord, Grumm had promised Bregonif. Well, why not? Make Ready put a match to his boats. "I may have to make more than one appearance. Do me in velvet."

Dearboy vibrated like a butterfly. "You sure Messer Grumm won't mind, dear lad?"

Make Ready smothered his misgivings. "Messer Grumm wants the best. He gave me carte blanche."

Dearboy beamed. "Very well, sir. Now—about the trimmings . . ."

Sunlight bounced off market stall roofs on the Guards Parade at Haut Chateau. Make Ready, swathed in drapes raped from Grumm's dispensary, sweated beside a simmering medsin. The avenue before them, which separated the market from the chateau, was known as the

Alée des Dames, and was, by tradition, reserved for the ladies of the court.

A door opened along the allée. Four figures emerged into the sunlight, to stand idly on the steps before the door, as though lingering to watch the busy market. Two of the figures wore Chateau Guard stripes, one a soiled smock, and the fourth a lime green jacket and plum red breeches.

Grumm glanced at his watch, then gave Make Ready a push. "There he is. Get going! And walk proper. Don't rush."

Make Ready stumbled forward, feeling the drapes pulled from his shoulders. The healer may have disapproved of his madness at the tailors, but Grumm wasn't going to waste its fruit.

Make Ready surveyed the group on the steps. His spirits sank. What could they care about a presumptious bastard from Kelmet's slums? Too late, now, to back out. He squared his shoulders. Placing one foot neatly before the other, the way he had practised, Make Ready walked decorously towards the Mendicant Steps, where waited Duke Corwen Persay, Grand Maitre de Marécage, his guards, and . . . who?

The man in the soiled smock stretched his arms, and yawned. Who would dare to act so casually, dress so slovenly, in the duke's presence? Make Ready's heart leaped in a convulsion which set him trembling. Wearing that laboratory smock . . . it had to be Greville, the duke's geneticist!

Make Ready became aware of silence in the Market alleyways. Shoppers were staring at the youth who presumed to promenade the exclusive allée. The duke had turned to watch him. And Greville? Why was he with the duke? What were those gestures his hands were making? Make Ready's memory flew back to days with the street thieves, recalling a fagin directing minions to a gull. *Greville was signalling in finger code!*

Make Ready's pace faltered. Who did Greville signal to? And why? There were rumours aplenty of the geneticist's ruthlessness. Had he decided to get rid of a rival doigt in full view of the duke? Make Ready's back felt bare, exposed. A ball from a concealed musket could snuff him out, and no blame attach to the geneticist.

Make Ready halted before the steps. Raising his left hand, he pointed a stalled digit at the geneticist.

"Messer Greville!" His voice was shrill. "Stop what you are doing—or I'll make an end of you now!"

The man in the smock grew pale.

Behind him, the Mendicant Door opened. Lord Mardy Persay, in white court dress, appeared, buttoning his jacket. Voice light, amused, he asked, "Am I late for the party?"

Duke Corwen ignored his son's arrival. He said, "Get behind me, Greville."

Eyes on Make Ready, the duke brought up his right hand.

Lord Mardy thrust past the guard, reaching out a hand. "Not yet, sire. Ask the youth why."

Make Ready swallowed. Despite the menacing doigt, this was no ogre to fear. This was his father. His nervousness passed. He said, "Sire, your gene-man signals to someone. I fear he wishes me ill."

The duke frowned. "Why should Messer Greville wish you ill, boy?"

Make Ready responded in his mère's old penal patois. "*Sieur, sh'm'appelle*—I am called Mercredi, son of Semée La Douce, who was a transportee from Pont des Larmes in Lontaine France. My mère loved an *inconnu* who abandoned her with an unborn child."

The duke raised his eyebrows. "That is not an unusual story, lad. Why choose to tell me?"

Make Ready hoped he had the right answer. "Because, sire, the child inherited a finger which right now is scaring your scruffy vassal silly."

Lord Mardy, still gripping the duke's arm, whispered, "Sir—he's claiming to have the doigt!"

"Helix!" the duke snapped. "I know that. What do I do about him? I don't want to lose Greville. This wild youth wants to blight him."

Lord Mardy's eyes gleamed with wariness. "If he can do that, we don't want to lose him either." He raised his voice. "Lad! Put down your doigt! I guarantee your life."

Make Ready felt perspiration on his forehead. Greville was eyeing him with open malevolence. The duke still dithered over his execution. Lord Mardy's eyes pleaded. Make Ready slowly lowered his threatening finger.

Larry Greville's glance flicked along the allée. His fingers moved swiftly. Faster still, Lord Mardy's hand came up Lightning hissed from the tip of his doigt, stabbing at a figure which had appeared in the allée. The figure dropped a musket, and crumpled, cloak smoking.

"Greville!" snarled the duke. "That's enough. Send your men away. Then leave us."

They watched the geneticist go. Lord Mardy examined a hole in his fingerstall. He grinned at Make Ready. "That's a new doigt-clout you owe me, brother."

The duke surveyed Make Ready grimly. "My son seems to have made up his mind somewhat prematurely. Did you intend to blight my gene man?"

Make Ready's mind raced. How should a street arab respond to a noble parent of brief acquaintance, who was surely bound to discover that he had been hoodwinked about a crucial part of that urchin's anatomy?

Only the truth would do. Make Ready went down on one knee. "Sire," he confessed. "I couldn't do no harm to Messer Greville. My doigt hasn't yet come on song. But Messer Greville didn't know that."

Duke Corwen Persay shook his head in reproof. "A risky trick, boy. But for Lord Mardy, you'd be carrion now."

Out of the corner of his eye, Make Ready saw them carrying the smoking corpse from the allée. He inched his gaze upwards from the duke's shoes. "I was hoping you'd see fair play, sir."

The duke's eyebrows climbed towards his flat cap. "Oh—an arbiter, am I? Between my loyal retainers and any young hoodlum who chooses to threaten them?"

Make Ready lowered his eyes again. "No, sir. But I thought you wouldn't see one of your subjects killed without reason."

The duke grunted. "Boy, I've killed dozens of my subjects, myself, without a shred of reason. If you had so much as pointed that dummy doigt in my direction my guards would have cut you down without any objection from me."

Make Ready kept his head down. "You are the duke, sir, and you can get away with it. Messer Greville don't have your authority."

The duke glanced at Lord Mardy. "By Helix—a pocket diplomat, too!" His voice grew harsh. "Boy, how did you come by a copy of my costume?"

Make Ready kept a quaver out of his voice. "Sir, I was told how you would be dressed. I thought I couldn't have a better model."

"*And* a courtier!" The duke scowled. "You must have allies in the Chateau. Who is your accomplice?"

Make Ready thought of Bregonif, waiting anxiously with the gremgaurs. The man would be in trouble enough, without help from him. He stammered, "I—I'd rather not say, sir."

"And loyal, to boot!" The duke sighed. "I have efficient torturers, boy. Would you face them?"

Make Ready began to tremble. Too late now, to cut and run. What price his smartalick ideas of embarrassing the Grand Maitre! He said, "I'm not keen, sir."

He heard the duke's laugh. Felt himself pulled to his feet. The duke spoke in the old penal tongue. "*Leve-toi, garçon!* Get up, boy. Where did you learn the langue? I haven't used it for years."

Make Ready responded in the same patois. "Sir, it was my mère's tongue when she first came to High Barbary."

The duke's face saddened. "That's true. I recall teaching her how to pronounce some fairly useless phrases in our modern argot. Where is she now?"

Make Ready shrugged. "Sir, I haven't seen, nor heard, from her since I was seven years old."

"And you are now?"

"Seventeen—I think, sir."

"Show me your doigt!"

Make Ready pulled off the fingerstall. The duke took

the blackened digit gently in his hand. He turned to his elder son. "This has a few years to go, Mardy. Yet the lad scared the mighty Greville with it!"

Lord Mardy was grinning. "A genuine chip off the Persay block, sir. No one else would dare that kind of trick."

The duke extended his arms to Make Ready. "Come, son, we have tormented you enough. It's time you took your rightful place in the world."

Make Ready went with him, reckless of the consequences.

And the watcher at the end of the allée turned away. Skirting the market stalls, he made circuitously for the sunken garden below the Chateau. Pausing by a marble ballustrade, he waved to the cloaked man who waited at the foot of the steps with three gremgaurs. Bregonif would be pleased to know that the sixlegs wouldn't be required. That his extra five years were a certainty.

The healer smiled. There might be benefits for others who had helped, too.

Hector Garman, when he heard the news, hurried home to report to his secret masters that a new doigt had been found to replace Lord Cledger's.

And, as daylight faded, Make Ready stepped out into the Chateau gardens. Omkrit II, the evening star, gleamed above the treetops.

Make Ready shook his fist at it. What was fantasy for a Kelmet street arab might be possible for a noble of Mary Cage. One day, he would discover who lived up there in Lontaine France—and why they had sent his mère to exile in High Barbary.

EDITOR'S INTRODUCTION TO:

YELLOW RAIN AND SPACE WARS
Adrian Berry

Science may save us; it also has its dangers.

I first met Adrian Berry at one of the scientific cocktail parties Larry Niven and I give at the annual meetings of the American Association for the Advancement of Science. Adrian is the Science Correspondent for the London *Daily Telegraph* and a Fellow of the Royal Astronomical Society. His book *The Iron Sun* is magnificent, as is the older *The Next Ten Thousand Years*. If you haven't discovered Adrian Berry, go out and do so immediately. You'll do yourself quite a favor.

Adrian Berry writes of real futures: of real star wars; and it is no accident that these two essays are presented together.

YELLOW RAIN
Adrian Berry

He will practise against thee by poison.

"As You Like It"

For centuries, communities from Europe to Asia died in agony in huge numbers when their bread became polluted by virulent fungus poisons. Soviet scientists isolated these poisons in the 1930s, and have since been mass-producing them as a means of mass murder.

Most of the advanced nations, it is true, either manufacture or carry out research into chemical weaponry. But the Soviet Union and its allies have outstripped all others in the intensity of their devotion to the development and use of poison.

What are these substances? The most lethal toxins used in modern warfare are still the hideous natural poisons that one associates with the Dark Ages, rather than any synthetic material created in the laboratory.

Democratic countries have been pitifully slow to recognize and counteract the advances which Eastern dictatorships have made in this field. It comes as a dark surprise to today's Western mind that the technological societies of the Communist bloc are but a veneer on a base of mediaeval barbarism, in which poisons extracted from herbs, fungi, snakes, amphibians, and fishes are often the most favored way of getting rid of an enemy.

It was in this tradition that the Soviet Union began its 1980 invasion of Afghanistan with the most terrible arsenal of offensive chemical weapons used by any army in history. Countless Moslem rebels died in convulsions from attacks by clouds of "yellow rain".

Nor should there be too much surprise at the manner of their death. To quote from an excellent book on chemical warfare, "the Red Army demonstrates a military psychology that makes it possible to use war poisons without hesitation, as simply another weapon."*

Let us look at the history of one such poison: ergot, a fungus toxin which has been known for nearly 3,000 years. An Assyrian tablet of 600 BC first mentions it as a noxious pustule found on ears of grain. It probably caused the plague which nearly destroyed Athens during the Peloponnesian Wars, when starving people were forced to eat bad bread. It caused mayhem in Duisberg, Germany, in 857 AD, and in wide areas of France in 943.

A French chronicler of that year speaks of people "shrieking and writhing, rolling like wheels, foaming in epileptic convulsions, their limbs turning black and bursting open." Then he explains: "The bread of the people of Limoges became transformed upon their tables. When it was cut it proved to be wet, and the inside poured out as a black, sticky substance."

The cause of these horrors which became endemic among the ignorant peasantry was bad harvesting and grain storage, that permitted fungal growths on bread. Ergot, and similar fungal poisons, specially treated in Soviet laboratories, are nowadays used against rebel villages in Laos and Afghanistan, as Mr. Seagrave's book reveals in detail.

*Yellow Rain: A Journey through the terror of Chemical Warfare, Sterling Seagrave (M. Evans and Co., New York).

For mass killings or for individual murder, the ancient poisons are proving most efficacious. The Bulgarian exile Georgi Markov, hated in Sofia for his BBC broadcasts, was murdered in London in 1978 by an agent using an umbrella tipped with ricin, from the castor bean, which the murderer had boasted in a telephone threat to Markov "is a poison the West cannot detect or treat."

The greatest danger of all is that some group of ill-intentioned people might seek to combine the ancient poisons with the techniques of modern science to create a new weapon of unprecedented frightfulness.

It could happen like this. Genetic engineering, the laboratory manufacture of microbes through the alteration of genes, promises much for better medicines. But this hopeful new technology could be perverted to make a "monster microbe" that would colonize the human intestine with "pili," or tentacles, with which to adhere to its walls. For such a poison, there might be neither treatment nor antidote, and anti-bodies would accept it as being normal. A vial of it dropped in the water supply of a few major cities could, within days, produce a catastrophe to rival the Black Death.

One scientist who has warned of just such a danger is Professor Donald B. Louria, of the New Jersey Medical School. Explaining his worst fears, Professor Louria has said: "One microbiologist with whom I discussed this scenario said it could not happen because the experimenters themselves could not avoid becoming victims. 'But this is nonsense. They could immunize themselves against pili before the toxins were added, so that the bacteria could not take hold in their intestinal tracts. I believe there are those among us on this planet so venal, so committed to achieving power, or simply so mentally warped, that they would do exactly as I have outlined."

One doesn't have to be a geographical genius to predict just who these people might be. That is, if they thought they could get away with it.

* * *

SPACE WARS

This decade is likely to present greater dangers to mankind than any since the end of World War II. If the Soviet Union succeeds in placing an operational laser battle station in orbit while the Americans fail to do the same, the free world will be at the mercy of its enemies, most of its strategic weapons rendered useless.

The reason is simple. A laser beam fired in the vacuum of space can, or will soon be able to, punch fist-sized holes in metal objects at a range of hundreds of miles. This means that American intercontinental ballistic missiles, which make some of their journey through space, could all be destroyed before they reach their targets.

Nor will Western missiles that travel to their targets without leaving the Earth's atmosphere, like the Cruise and the Lance, be necessarily safe from enemy battle stations in orbit. While the energy of laser beams can dissipate in air, especially on cloudy days, this is not true of weapons which shoot beams of charged particles.

Polaris submarines will soon be at risk from spy satellites. For many years they have been safe in the secret depths of the oceans, able to inflict more damage on the Soviet Union in the space of four minutes than Hitler did in four years. But this is unlikely to be true for much longer. The Russians have a large and growing fleet of space-borne anti-submarine satellites, with a developing ability to detect the infra-red "scar" which a submarine leaves on the surface, enabling them to track its movements.

In short, with space warfare, strategic weapons are entering a new realm of technology. Thanks to four inactive years during the Carter Administration, the Russians have gained a substantial advantage in their efforts to acquire the ability to destroy Western strategic forces totally and without warning. Unless America acts with determination, we may be faced in this decade with the choice between surrender or destruction.

Not being privy to the councils of the Pentagon, we cannot be sure whether the Americans are reacting to this crisis with sufficient speed and vigour. It is only possible to be certain of one thing: that the space shuttle, a quarter of whose flights will be military in purpose, will add enormously to America's ability to place weapons in orbit. And weapons there are needed above all else.

Only if the new Soviet threat is successfully countered can there be hope for continuing the mutual balance of terror, which has prevented war between the superpowers for more than 30 years, and which now is trembling so dangerously.

The old balance, consisting of thousands of missiles in their silos, will give way to dependence on electromagnetic weapons which move their targets, not at a cumbrous 17,000 mph, but at the speed of light, 670 million mph. This, like previous great advances in military technology, is likely to lead in turn to new social developments. Let us try to predict what they will be.

The first consideration is that the existence of opposing laser battle stations in orbit, each holding the strategic forces of their client state in pawn, will not be the end of the cold war in space. Battle stations can themselves be attacked, and those weapons which threaten them will in turn be vulnerable to assault. The race will be on to construct the "ultimate" space weapon, a battle station so powerful and with such impregnable defences that all objects in low Earth orbit will be at its mercy.

One of the two safe places to install such a weapon will be beneath the surface of the moon. On the moon? At first sight, the idea must seem crazy, but it is being seriously considered as a long-term contingency plan by specialist groups at the Redstone Arsenal in Huntsville, Alabama, and at Strategic Air Command in Omaha, Nebraska.

Consider the advantages of a manned lunar laser battle station. The only remaining technical obstacle is the creation of a laser with sufficient power and narrowness of beam to destroy space vehicles at a range of 238,000 miles. But once installed it would be almost

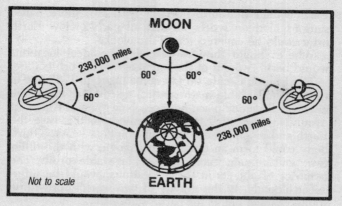

Laser guns on the moon and in Lagrangian orbits.

impossible to find, since it could be hidden anywhere among the moon's craters and canyons. It could not be destroyed by an opposing laser, since the enemy would not know where to fire. Nor could it be immobilized by a nuclear missile, since the approaching warhead would itself be vulnerable to the laser.

Building the station will, of course, require considerable preparations which can be observed by telescope. Would this reveal its intended location? Perhaps not. We speak now of a period 20 to 50 years hence, when civilian activity is likely to be taking place on the moon on a large scale. In this situation, military construction can be concealed. Peaceful technology is likely to follow the military lead into space, as it has in so many fields. As in the empires of old, the merchant will walk in the tracks of the army.

But the lunar battle station will have one disadvantage. It will only be effective in deterring aggression for about half the day. Anyone can verify, by playing with a small globe, that there are several missile flight-paths between Russia and key Western targets which, for some parts of the day, will not be in line of sight of the moon.

A Superpower desiring absolute command over the

Earth would therefore need at least two more battle stations in deep space, so that all parts of low Earth orbit could be covered round the clock.

Where should they be placed? The ideal locations would be in two out of the four Lagrangian orbits.

The French Comte de Lagrange made in 1788 one of the few remarkable mathematical discoveries about the universe that took place between Newton and Einstein. Around two orbiting celestial bodies—in this case the Earth and moon—there are four points at which a third body could form an equilateral triangle with the other two, and remain there forever in stable orbit. The behavior of objects in these locations, would be influenced equally by the gravity of two worlds, providing stable vantage points for battle stations.

The pattern of war, and of preparations for war, may be extended ever more deeply into space in the distant future—with all man's activities—until the Earth itself ceases to be the target and the prize.

But whether we can survive to inhabit that distant future depends on decisions being made now; on recognizing that Earth-bound weapons will soon no longer deter aggression, and on deciding swiftly what to do about this fact.

EDITOR'S INTRODUCTION TO:

THAT SHARE OF GLORY
C. M. Kornbluth

Machiavelli has been accused on the one hand of killing political philosophy, and on the other of inventing the first science of politics. Here is James Burnham:

"Machiavelli's name does not rank in the noble company of scientists. In the common opinion of men, his name itself has become a term of reproach and dishonor . . .

"Why should this be? If our reference is to the views that Machiavelli in fact held, that he stated plainly, openly, and clearly in his writings, there is in the common opinion no truth at all. . . . It is true that he has taught tyrants, from almost his own days—Thomas Cromwell, for example, the lowborn Chancellor whom Henry VIII brought in to replace Thomas More when More refused to make his conscience a tool of his master's interests, was said to have a copy of Machiavelli always in his pocket; and in our time Mussolini wrote a college thesis on Machiavelli. But knowledge has a disturbing neutrality in this respect. We do not blame the research analyst who has solved the chemical mysteries of a poison because a murderer made use of his treatise . . .

"We are, I think, and not only from the fate of Machiavelli's reputation, forced to conclude that men do not really want to know about themselves . . . Perhaps the full disclosure of what we really are and how we act is too violent a medicine.

"In any case, whatever may be the desires of most men, it is most certainly against the interests of the powerful that the truth should be known about political behavior. If the political truths stated by Machiavelli were widely known, the success of tyranny would become much less likely. If men understood as much of the mechanism of rule and privilege as Machiavelli understood, they would no longer be deceived into accepting that rule and privilege, and they would know what steps to take to overcome them.

"Therefore the powerful and their spokesmen—all the 'official' thinkers, the lawyers and philosophers and preachers and demagogues—must defame Machiavelli. Machiavelli says that rulers lie and break faith: this proves, they say, that he libels human nature. Machiavelli says that ambitious men struggle for power: he is apologizing for the opposition, the enemy, and trying to confuse you about us, who wish to lead you for your own good and welfare. Machiavelli says that you must keep strict watch over officials and subordinate them to the law: he is encouraging subversion and the loss of national unity. Machiavelli says that no man with power is to be trusted: you see that his aim is to smash all your faith and ideals.

"Small wonder that the powerful—in public—denounce Machiavelli. The powerful have long practice and much skill in sizing up their opposition. They can recognize an enemy who will never compromise, even when that enemy is so abstract as a body of ideas."

—*The Machiavellians*

No one has ever built a social order on that kind of political science. No one in the real world. Here Cyril Kornbluth turns Machiavelli loose on the stars.

THAT SHARE OF GLORY
C. M. Kornbluth

Young Alen, one of a thousand in the huge refectory, ate absent-mindedly as the reader droned into the perfect silence of the hall. Today's lesson happened to be a word list of the Thetis VIII planet's sea-going folk.

"*Tlon*—a ship," droned the reader.

"*Rtlo*—some ships, number unknown.

"*Long*—some ships, number known, always modified by cardinal.

"*Ongr*—a ship in a collection of ships, always modified by ordinal.

"*Ngrt*—the first ship in a collection of ships; an exception to *ongr*."

A lay brother tiptoed to Alen's side. "The Rector summons you," he whispered.

Alen had no time for panic, though that was the usual reaction to a summons from the Rector to a novice. He slipped from the refectory, stepped onto the north-bound corridor, and stepped off at his cell, a minute later and a quarter mile farther on. Hastily, but meticulously, he changed from his drab habit to the heraldic robes in the cubicle with its simple stool, washstand, desk, and paperweight or two. Alen, a level-headed young fellow, was not aware that he had broken any section of the Order's complicated Rule, but he was aware that he could have done so without knowing it. It might, he thought, be the last time he would see the cell.

He cast a glance which he hoped would not be the final one over it; a glance which lingered a little fondly on the reel rack where were stowed: "Nicholson on Martian Verbs," "The New Oxford Venusian Dictionary," the ponderous six-reeler "Deutche-Ganymediche Konversasionslexikon" published long ago and far away in Leipzig. The later works were there, too: "The Tongues of the Galaxy—an Essay in Classification," "A Concise Grammar of Cephean," "The Self-Pronouncing Vegan II Dictionary"— scores of them, and, of course, the worn reel of old Machiavelli's "The Prince."

Enough of that! Alen combed out his small, neat beard and stepped onto the southbound corridor. He transferred to an eastbound at the next intersection and minutes later was before the Rector's lay secretary.

"You'd better review your Lyran irregulars," said the secretary disrespectfully. "There's a trader in there who's looking for a cheap herald on a swindling trip to Lyra VI." Thus unceremoniously did Alen learn that he was not to be ejected from the Order but that he was to be elevated to Journeyman. But as a Herald should, he betrayed no sign of his immense relief. He did, however, take the secretary's advice and sensibly reviewed his Lyran.

While he was in the midst of a declension which applied only to inanimate objects, the voice of the Rector—and what a mellow voice it was!—floated through the secretary's intercom.

"Admit the novice, Alen," said the Master Herald.

A final settling of his robes and the youth walked into the Rector's huge office, with the seal of the Order blazing in diamonds above his desk. There was a stranger present; presumably the trader—a black-bearded fellow whose rugged frame didn't carry his Vegan cloak with ease.

Said the Rector: "Novice, this is to be the crown of your toil if you are acceptable to—?" He courteously turned to the trader, who shrugged irritably.

"It's all one to me," growled the blackbeard. "Somebody cheap, somebody who knows the cant of the thievish Lyran gem peddlers, above all, somebody *at once.* Overhead is devouring my flesh day by day as the ship waits at the field. And when we are spaceborne, my imbecile crew will doubtless waste liter after priceless liter of my fuel. And when we land the swindling Lyrans will without doubt make my ruin complete by tricking me even out of the minute profit I hope to realize. Good Master Herald, let me have the infant cheap and I'll bid you good day."

The Rector's shaggy eyebrows drew down in a frown. "Trader," he said sonorously, "our mission of galactic utilitarian culture is not concerned with your margin of profit. I ask you to test this youth and, if you find him able, to take him as your Herald on your voyage. He will serve you well, for he has been taught that commerce and words, its medium, are the unifying bonds which will one day unite the cosmos into a single humankind. Do not conceive that the College and Order of Heralds is a mere aid to you in your commercial adventure."

"Very well," growled the trader. He addressed Alen in broken Lyran: "Boy, how you make up Vegan stones of three fires so Lyran women like, come buy, buy again?"

Alen smoothly replied; "The Vegan triple-fire gem finds most favor on Lyra, and especially among its women when set in a wide glass anklet if large, and when arranged in the Lyran 'lucky five' pattern in a glass thumb-ring if small." He was glad, very glad, he had come across—and as a matter of course memorized, in the relentless fashion of the Order—a novel which touched briefly on the Lyran jewel trade.

The trader glowered and switched to Cephean—apparently his native tongue. "That was well-enough said, Herald. Now tell me whether you've got guts to man a squirt in case we're intercepted by the thieving so-called Customs collectors of Eyolf's Realm between here and Lyra?"

Alen knew the Rector's eyes were on him. "The noble mission of our Order," he said, "forbids me to use any weapon but the truth in furthering cosmic utilitarian civilization. No, master trader, I shall not man one of your weapons."

The trader shrugged. "So I must take what I get. Good Master Herald, make me a price."

The Rector said casually: "I regard this chiefly as a training mission for our novice; the fee will be nominal. Let us say twenty-five percent of your net as of blastoff from Lyra, to be audited by Journeyman-Herald Alen."

The trader's howl of rage echoed in the dome of the huge room. "It's not fair!" he roared. "Who but you thievish villains with your Order and your catch-'em-young and your years of training can learn the tongues of the galaxy? What chance has a decent merchant busy with profit and loss got to learn the cant of every race between Sirius and the Coalsack? It's not fair! It's not fair and I'll say so until my dying breath!"

"Die outside if you find our terms unacceptable," said the Rector. "The Order does not haggle."

"Well I know it," sighed the trader brokenly. "I should have stuck to my own system and my good father's pump-flange factory. But no! I had to pick up a bargain in gems on Vega! Enough of this—bring me your contract and I'll sign it."

The Rector's shaggy eyebrows went up. "There is no contract," he said. "A mutual trust between Herald and trader is the cornerstone upon which cosmoswide amity and understanding will be built."

"At twenty-five percent for an unlicked pup," muttered blackbeard to himself in Cephean.

None of his instructors had played Polonius as Alen, with the seal of the Journeyman-Herald on his brow, packed for blastoff and vacated his cell. He supposed they knew that twenty years of training either had done their work or had not.

The trader taking Alen to the field where his ship waited was less wise. "The secret of successful negotiation," he weightily told his Herald, "is to yield willingly. This may strike you as a paradox, but it is the veritable key to my success in maintaining the profits of my good father's pump-flange trade. The secret is to yield with rueful admiration of your opponent—but *only in unimportant details*. Put up a little battle about delivery date or about terms of credit and then let him have his way. But you never give way a hair's breadth on your asking price unless—"

Alen let him drivel on as they drove through the outer works of the College. He was glad the car was open. For the first time he was being accorded the doffed hat that is the due of Heralds from their inferiors in the Order, and the grave nod of salutation from equals. Five-year-old postulants seeing his brow-seal tugged off their headgear with comical celerity; fellow novices, equals a few hours before, uncovered as though he were the Rector himself.

The ceremonial began to reach the trader. When, with a final salutation, a lay warder let them through the great gate of the curtain wall, he said with some irritation: "They appear to hold you in high regard, boy."

"I am better addressed as 'Herald,' " said Alen composedly.

"A plague descend on the College and Order! Do you think I don't know my manners? Of course, I call a Herald 'Herald,' but we're going to be cooped up together and you'll be working for me. What'll happen to ship's discipline if I have to kowtow to you?"

"There will be no problem," said Alen.

Blackbeard grunted and trod fiercely on the accelerator.

"That's my ship," he said at length. "*Starsong*. Vegan registry—it may help passing through Eyolf's Realm, though it cost me overmuch in bribes. A crew of eight, lazy, good-for-nothing wastrels—agh! Can I believe my eyes?" The car jammed to a halt before the looming ship and blackbeard was up the ladder and through the port in a second. Settling his robes, Alen followed.

He found the trader fiercely denouncing his chief engineer for using space drive to heat the ship; he had seen the faint haze of a minimum exhaust from the stern tubes.

"For that, dolt," screamed blackbeard, "we have a thing known as electricity. Have you by chance ever heard of it? Are you aware that a chief engineer's responsibility is the efficient and *economical* operation of his ship's drive mechanism?"

The chief, a cowed-looking Cephean, saw Alen with relief and swept off his battered cap. The Herald nodded gravely and the trader broke off in irritation. "We need none of that bowing and scraping for the rest of the voyage," he declared.

"Of course not, sir," said the chief. "O'course not. I was just welcoming the Herald aboard. Welcome aboard, Herald. I'm Chief Elwon, Herald. And I'm glad to have a Herald with us." A covert glance at the trader. "*I've* voyaged with Heralds and without, and I don't mind saying I feel safer indeed with you aboard."

"May I be taken to my quarters?" asked Alen.

"Your—?" began the trader, stupefied.

The chief broke in: "I'll fix you a cabin, Herald. We've got some bulkheads I can rig aft for a snug little space, not roomy, but the best a little ship like this can afford."

The trader collapsed into a bucket seat as the chief bustled aft and Alen followed.

"Herald," the chief said with some embarrassment after he had collared two crewmen and set them to work, "you'll have to excuse our good master trader. He's new to the interstar lanes and he doesn't exactly know the jets yet. Between us we'll get him squared away."

Alen inspected the cubicle run up for him—a satisfactory enclosure affording him the decent privacy he rated. He dismissed the chief and the crewmen with a nod and settled himself on the cot.

Beneath the iron composure in which he had been trained, he felt scared and alone. Not even old Machiavelli seemed to offer comfort or counsel: "There is nothing more difficult to take in hand, more perilous to conduct, or more uncertain in its success, than to take the lead in the introduction of a new order of things," said Chapter Six.

But what said Chapter Twenty-Six? "Where the willingness is great, the difficulties cannot be great."

Starsong was not a happy ship. Blackbeard's nagging stinginess hung over the crew like a thundercloud, but Alen professed not to notice. He walked regularly fore and aft for two hours a day greeting the crew members in their various native tongues and then wrapping himself in the reserve the Order demanded—though he longed to salute them man-to-man, eat with them, gossip about their native planets, the past misdeeds that had brought them to their berths aboard the miserly *Starsong*, their hopes for the future. The Rule of the College and Order of Heralds decreed otherwise. He accepted the uncoverings of the crew with a nod and tried to be pleased because they stood in growing awe of him that ranged from Chief Elwon's lively appreciation of a Herald's skill to Wiper Jukkl's superstitious reverence. Jukkl was a low-browed specimen from a planet of the decadent Sirius system. He outdid the normal slovenliness of an all-male crew on a freighter—a slovenliness in which Alen could not share. Many of his waking hours were spent in his locked cubicle burnishing his metal and cleaning and pressing his robes. A Herald was never supposed to suggest by his appearance that he shared moral frailties.

Blackbeard himself yielded a little, to the point of touching his cap sullenly. This probably was not so much awe at Alen's studied manner as respect for the incisive, lightning-fast job of auditing the Herald did on the books of the trading venture—absurdly complicated books with scores of accounts to record a simple matter of buying gems cheap on Vega and chartering a ship in the hope of selling them dearly on Lyra. The complicated books and overlapping accounts did tell the story, but they made it very easy for an auditor to erroneously read a number of costs as far higher than they actually were. Alen did not fall into the trap.

On the fifth day after blastoff, Chief Elwon rapped, respectfully but urgently, on the door of Alen's cubicle.

"If you please, Herald," he urged, "could you come to the bridge?"

Alen's heart bounded in his chest, but he gravely said: "My meditation must not be interrupted. I shall join you on the bridge in ten minutes." And for ten minutes he methodically polished a murky link in the massive gold chain that fastened his boat-cloak—the "meditation." He donned the cloak before stepping out; the summons sounded like a full-dress affair in the offing.

The trader was stamping and fuming. Chief Elwon was riffling through his spec book unhappily. Astrogator Hufner was at the plot computer running up trajectories and knocking them down again. A quick glance showed Alen that they were all high-speed trajectories in the "evasive action" class.

"Herald," said the trader grimly, "we have broken somebody's detector bubble." He jerked his thumb at a red-lit signal. "I expect we'll be overhauled shortly. Are you ready to earn your twenty-five percent of the net?"

Alen overlooked the crudity. "Are you rigged for color video, merchant?" he asked.

"We are."

"Then I am ready to do what I can for my client."

He took the communicator's seat, stealing a glance in the still-blank screen. The reflection of his face was reassuring, though he wished he had thought to comb his small beard.

Another light flashed on, and Hufner quit the operator to study the detector board. "Big, powerful, and getting closer," he said tersely. "Scanning for us with directionals now. Putting out plenty of energy—"

The loudspeaker of the ship-to-ship audio came to life.

"What ship are you?" it demanded in Vegan. "We

are a customs cruiser of the Realm of Eyolf. What ship are you?"

"Have the crew man the squirts," said the trader softly to the chief.

Elwon looked at Alen, who shook his head. "Sorry, sir," said the engineer apologetically. "The Herald—"

"We are the freighter *Starsong*, Vegan registry," said Alen into the audio mike as the trader choked. "We are carrying Vegan gems to Lyra."

"They're on us," said the astrogator despairingly, reading his instruments. The ship-to-ship video flashed on, showing an arrogant, square-jawed face topped by a battered naval cap.

"Lyra indeed! We have plans of our own for Lyra. You will heave to—" began the officer in the screen, before he noted Alen. "My pardon, Herald," he said sardonically. "Herald, will you please request the ship's master to heave to for boarding and search? We wish to assess and collect Customs duties. You are aware, of course, that your vessel is passing through the Realm."

The man's accented Vegan reeked of Algol IV. Alen switched to that obscure language to say: "We were not aware of that. Are you aware that there is a reciprocal trade treaty in effect between the Vegan system and the Realm which specifies that freight in Vegan bottoms is dutiable only when consigned to ports in the Realm?"

"You speak Algolian, do you? You Heralds have not been underrated, but don't plan to lie your way out of this. Yes, I am aware of some such agreement as you mentioned. We shall board you, as I said, and assess and collect duty in kind. If, regrettably, there has been any mistake you are, of course, free to apply to the Realm for reimbursement. Now, heave to!"

"I have no intentions of lying. I speak the solemn truth when I say that we shall fight to the last man any attempt of yours to board and loot us."

Alen's mind was racing furiously through the catalog of planetary folkways the Rule had decreed that he master. Algol IV—some ancestor worship; veneration of mother; hand-to-hand combat with knives; complimentary greeting, "May you never strike down a weaker foe"; folk-hero Gaarek unjustly accused of slaying a cripple and exiled but it was an enemy's plot—

A disconcerted shadow was crossing the face of the officer as Alen improvised: "You will, of course, kill us all. But before this happens I shall have messaged back to the College and Order of Heralds the facts in the case, with a particular request that your family be informed. Your name, I think, will be remembered as long as Gaarek's—though not in the same way, of course; the Algolian whose hundred-man battle cruiser wiped out a virtually unarmed freighter with a crew of eight."

The officer's face was dark with rage. "You devil!" he snarled. "Leave my family out of this! I'll come aboard and fight you man-to-man if you have the stomach for it!"

Alen shook his head regretfully. "The Rule of my Order forbids recourse to violence," he said. "Our only permissible weapon is the truth."

"We're coming aboard," said the officer grimly. "I'll order my men not to harm your people. We'll just be collecting customs. If your people shoot first, my men will be under orders to do nothing more than disable them."

Alen smiled and uttered a sentence or two in Algolian.

The officer's jaw dropped and he croaked, after a pause: "I'll cut you to ribbons. You can't say that about my mother, you—" and he spewed back some of the words Alen had spoken.

"Calm yourself," said the Herald gravely. "I apologize for my disgusting and unheraldic remarks. But I wished to prove a point. You would have killed me if you could; I touched off a reaction which had been planted in you by your culture. I will be able to do the same with the men of yours who come aboard. For every race of man there is the intolerable insult that must be avenged in blood.

"Send your men aboard under orders not to kill if you wish; I shall goad them into a killing rage. We shall be massacred, yours will be the blame, and you will be disgraced and disowned by your entire planet." Alen

hoped desperately that the naval crews of the Realm
were, as reputed, a barbarous and undisciplined lot—

Evidently they were, and the proud Algolian dared
not risk it. In his native language he spat again: "You
devil!" and switched back into Vegan. "Freighter
Starsong," he said bleakly, "I find that my space fix was
in error and that you are not in Realm territory. You
may proceed."

The astrogator said from the detector board, incredu-
lously: "He's disengaging. He's off us. He's accelerating, Herald, *what* did you say to him?"

But the reaction from blackbeard was more gratify-
ing. Speechless, the trader took off his cap. Alen acknowledged the salute with a grave nod before he started
back to his cubicle. It was just as well, he reflected,
that the trader didn't know his life and his ship had
been unconditionally pledged in a finish fight against a
hundred-man battle cruiser.

Lyra's principal spaceport was pocked and broken,
but they made a fair-enough landing. Alen, in full heraldic robes, descended from *Starsong* to greet a handful of port officials.

"Any metals aboard?" demanded one of them.

"None for sale," said the Herald.

"We have Vegan gems, chiefly triple-fire." He knew
that the dull little planet was short of metals and,
having made a virtue of necessity, was somehow preju-
diced against their import.

"Have your crew transfer the cargo to the Customs
shed," said the port official studying *Starsong*'s papers.
"And all of you wait there."

All of them—except Alen—lugged numbered sacks
and boxes of gems to the low brick building designated.
The trader was allowed to pocket a handful for samples
before the shed was sealed—a complicated business. A
brick was mortared over the simple ironwood latch that
closed the ironwood door, a pat of clay was slapped
over the brick and the port seal stamped in it. A me-
chanic with what looked like a pottery blowtorch fed by

powdered coal played a flame on the clay seal until it glowed orange-red and that was that.

"Herald," said the port official, "tell the merchant to sign here and make his fingerprints."

Alen studied the document; it was a simple identification form. Blackbeard signed with the reed pen provided and fingerprinted the document. After two weeks in space he scarcely needed to ink his fingers first.

"Now tell him that we'll release the gems on his written fingerprinted order to whatever Lyran citizens he sells to. And explain that this roundabout system is necessary to avoid metal smuggling. Please remove *all* metal from your clothes and stow it on your ship. Then we will seal that, too, and put it under guard until you are ready to take off. We regret that we will have to search you before we turn you loose, but we can't afford to have our economy disrupted by irresponsible introduction of metals." Alen had not realized it was that bad.

After the thorough search that extended to the confiscation of forgotten watches and pins, the port officials changed a sheaf of the trader's uranium-backed Vegan currency into Lyran legal tender based on man-hours. Blackbeard made a partial payment to the crew, told them to have a good liberty and check in at the port at sunset tomorrow for probable take-off.

Alen and the trader were driven to town in an unlikely vehicle whose power plant was a pottery turbine. The driver, when they were safely out on the open road, furtively asked whether they had any metal they wanted to discard.

The trader asked sharply in his broken Lyran: "What you do you get metal? Where sell, how use?"

The driver, following a universal tendency, raised his voice and lapsed into broken Lyran himself to tell the strangers: "Black market science men pay much, much for little bit metal. Study, use, build. Politicians make law no metal, what I care politicians? But you no tell, gentlemen?"

"We won't tell," said Alen. "But we have no metal for you."

The driver shrugged.

"Herald," said the trader, "what do you make of it?"

"I didn't know it was a political issue. We concern ourselves with the basic patterns of a people's behavior, not the day-to-day expressions of the patterns. The planet's got no heavy metals, which means there were no metals available to the primitive Lyrans. The lighter metals don't occur in native form or in easily split compounds. They proceeded along the ceramic line instead of the metallic line and appear to have done quite well for themselves up to a point. No electricity, of course, no aviation, and no space flight."

"And," said the trader, "naturally the people who make these buggies and that blowtorch we saw are scared witless that metals will be imported and put them out of business. So naturally they have laws passed prohibiting it."

"Naturally," said the Herald, looking sharply at the trader. But blackbeard was back in character a moment later. "An outrage," he growled. "Trying to tell a man what he can and can't import when he sees a decent chance to make a bit of profit."

The driver dropped them at a boardinghouse. It was half-timbered construction, which appeared to be swankier than the more common brick. The floors were plate glass, roughened for traction. Alen got them a double room with a view.

"What's that thing?" demanded the trader, inspecting the view.

The thing was a structure looming above the slate and tile roofs of the town—a round brick tower for its first twenty-five meters and then wood for another fifteen. As they studied it, it pricked up a pair of ears at the top and began to flop them wildly.

"Semaphore," said Alen.

A minute later blackbeard piteously demanded from the bathroom: "*How* do you make water come out of the tap? I touched it all over but nothing happened."

"You have to turn it," said Alen, demonstrating. "And

that thing—you pull it sharply down, hold it, and then release."

"Barbarous," muttered the trader. "Barbarous."

An elderly maid came in to show them how to string their hammocks and ask if they happened to have a bit of metal to give her for a souvenir. They sent her away and, rather than face the public dining room, made a meal from their own stores and turned in for the night.

It's going well, thought Alen drowsily: going very well indeed.

He awoke abruptly, but made no move. It was dark in the double room, and there were stealthy, furtive little noises nearby. A hundred thoughts flashed through his head of Lyran treachery and double-dealing. He lifted his eyelids a trifle and saw a figure silhouetted against the faint light of the big window. If a burglar, he was a clumsy one.

There was a stirring from the other hammock, the trader's. With a subdued roar that sounded like "Thieving villains!" blackbeard launched himself from the hammock at the intruder. But his feet tangled in the hammock cords and he belly-flopped on the floor.

The burglar, if it was one, didn't dash smoothly and efficiently for the door. He straightened himself against the window and said resignedly: "You need not fear. I will make no resistance."

Alen rolled from the hammock and helped the trader to his feet. "He said he doesn't want to fight," he told the trader.

Blackbeard seized the intruder and shook him like a rat. "So the rogue is a coward too!" he boomed. "Give us a light, Herald."

Alen uncovered the slow-match, blew it to a flame, squeakily pumped up a pressure torch until a jet of pulverized coal sprayed from its nozzle, and ignited it. A dozen strokes more and there was enough heat feeding back from the jet to maintain the pressure cycle.

Through all of this the trader was demanding in his broken Lyran: "What make here, thief? What reason thief us room?"

The Herald brought the hissing pressure lamp to the window. The intruder's face was not the unhealthy, neurotic face of a criminal. Its thin lines told of discipline and thought.

"What did you want here?" asked Alen.

"Metal," said the intruder simply. "I thought you might have a bit of iron."

It was the first time a specific metal had been named by any Lyran. He used, of course, the Vegan word for iron.

"You are particular," remarked the Herald. "Why iron?"

"I have heard that it possesses certain properties—perhaps you can tell me before you turn me over to the police. Is it true, as we hear, that a mass of iron whose crystals have been aligned by a sharp blow will strongly attract another piece of iron with a force related to the distance between them?"

"It is true," said the Herald, studying the man's face. It was lit with excitement. Deliberately Alen added: "This alignment is more easily and uniformly effected by placing the mass of iron in an electric field—that is, a space surrounding the passage of an electron stream through a conductor." Many of the words he used had to be Vegan; there were no Lyran words for "electric," "electron," or "conductor."

The intruder's face fell. "I have tried to master the concept you refer to," he admitted. "But it is beyond me. I have questioned other interstar voyagers and they have touched on it, but I cannot grasp it— But thank you, sir; you have been very courteous. I will trouble you no further while you summon the watch."

"You give up too easily," said Alen. "For a scientist, much too easily. If we turn you over to the watch, there will be hearings and testimony and whatnot. Our time is limited here on your planet; I doubt that we can spare any for your legal processes."

The trader let go of the intruder's shoulder and grumbled: "Why you no ask we have iron, I tell you no. Search, search, take all metal away. We no police you. I sorry hurted you arms. Here for you." Blackbeard brought out a palmful of his sample gems and picked out a large triple-fire stone. "You not be angry me," he said, putting it in the Lyran's hand.

"I can't—" said the scientist.

Blackbeard closed his fingers over the stone and growled; "I give, you take. Maybe buy iron with, eh?"

"That's so," said the Lyran. "Thank you both, gentlemen. Thank you—"

"You go," said the trader. "You go, we sleep again."

The scientist bowed with dignity and left their room.

"Gods of space," swore the trader. "To think that Jukkl, the *Starsong*'s wiper, knows more about electricity and magnetism than a brainy fellow like that."

"And they are the key to physics," mused Alen. "A scientist here is dead-ended forever, because their materials are all insulators! Glass, clay, glaze, wood."

"Funny, all right," yawned blackbeard. "Did you see me collar him once I got on my feet? Sharp, eh? Good night, Herald." He gruntingly hauled himself into the hammock again, leaving Alen to turn off the hissing light and cover the slow-match with its perforated lid.

They had roast fowl of some sort or other for breakfast in the public dining room. Alen was required by his Rule to refuse the red wine that went with it. The trader gulped it approvingly. "A sensible, though backward people," he said. "And now if you'll inquire of the management where the thievish jewel-buyers congregate, we can get on with our business and perhaps be off by dawn tomorrow."

"So quickly?" asked Alen, almost forgetting himself enough to show surprise.

"My charter on *Starsong*, good Herald—thirty days to go, but what might not go wrong in space? And then there would be penalties to mulct me of whatever minute profit I may realize."

Alen learned that Gromeg's Tavern was the gem mart and they took another of the turbine-engined cabs through the brick-paved streets.

Gromeg's was a dismal, small-windowed brick barn with heavy-set men lounging about, an open kitchen at one end and tables at the other. A score of smaller, sharp-faced men were at the tables sipping wine and chatting.

"I am Journeyman-Herald Alen," announced Alen clearly, "with Vegan gems to dispose of."

There was a silence of elaborate unconcern, and then one of the dealers spat and grunted: "Vegan gems. A drug on the market. Take them away, Herald."

"Come, master trader," said Alen in the Lyran tongue. "The gem dealers of Lyra do not want your wares." He started for the door.

One of the dealers called languidly: "Well, wait a moment. I have nothing better to do; since you've come all this way I'll have a look at your stuff."

"You honor us," said Alen. He and blackbeard sat at the man's table. The trader took out a palmful of samples, counted them meaningfully, and laid them on the boards.

"Well," said the gem dealer, "I don't know whether to be amused or insulted. I am Garthkint, the gem dealer—not a retailer of *beads*. However, I have no hard feelings. A drink for your frowning friend, Herald? I know you gentry don't indulge." The drink was already on the table, brought by one of the hulking guards.

Alen passed Garthkint's own mug of wine to the trader, explaining politely: "In my master trader's native Cepheus it is considered honorable for the guest to sip the drink his host laid down and none other. A charming custom, is it not?"

"Charming, though unsanitary," muttered the gem dealer—and he did not touch the drink he had ordered for blackbeard.

"I can't understand a word either of you is saying—too flowery. Was this little rat trying to drug me?" demanded the trader in Cephean.

"No," said Alen. "Just trying to get you drunk." To Garthkint in Lyran, he explained, "The good trader was saying that he wishes to leave at once. I was agreeing with him."

"Well," said Garthkint, "perhaps I can take a couple

of your gauds. For some youngster who wishes a cheap ring."

"He's getting to it," Alen told the trader.

"High time," grunted blackbeard.

"The trader asks me to inform you," said Alen, switching back to Lyran, "that he is unable to sell in lots smaller than five hundred gems."

"A compact language, Cephean," said Garthkint, narrowing his eyes.

"Is it not?" Alen blandly agreed.

The gem dealer's forefinger rolled an especially fine three-fire stone from the little pool of gems on the table. "I suppose," he said grudgingly, "that this is what I must call the best of the lot. What, I am curious to know, is the price you would set for five hundred equal in quality and size to this poor thing?"

"This," said Alen, "is the good trader's first venture to your delightful planet. He wishes to be remembered and welcomed all of the many times he anticipates returning. Because of this he has set an absurdly low price, counting good will as more important than a prosperous voyage. Two thousand Lyran credits."

"Absurd," snorted Garthkint. "I cannot do business with you. Either you are insanely rapacious or you have been pitifully misguided as to the value of your wares. I am well-known for my charity; I will assume that the latter is the case. I trust you will not be too downcast when I tell you that five hundred of those muddy, undersized, out-of-round objects are worth no more than two hundred credits."

"If you are serious," said Alen with marked amazement, "we would not dream of imposing on you. At the figure you mention, we might as well not sell at all but return with our wares to Cepheus and give these gems to children in the streets for marbles. Good gem trader, excuse us for taking up so much of your time and many thanks for your warm hospitality in the matter of the wine." He switched to Cephean and said: "We're dickering now. Two thousand and two hundred. Get up; we're going to start to walk out."

"What if he lets us go?" grumbled blackbeard, but he

did heave himself to his feet and turn to the door as Alen rose.

"My trader echoes my regrets," the Herald said in Lyran. "Farewell."

"Well, stay a moment," said Garthkint. "I am well-known for my soft heart toward strangers. A charitable man might go as high as five hundred and absorb the inevitable loss. If you should return some day with a passable lot of *real* gems, it would be worth my while for you to remember who treated you with such benevolence and give me fair choice."

"Noble Lyran," said Alen, apparently almost overcome. "I shall not easily forget your combination of acumen and charity. It is a lesson to traders. It is a lesson to me. I shall *not* insist on two thousand. I shall cut the throat of my trader's venture by reducing his price to eighteen hundred credits, though I wonder how I shall dare tell him of it."

"What's going on now?" demanded blackbeard.

"Five hundred and eighteen hundred," said Alen. "We can sit down again."

"Up, down—up, down," muttered the trader.

They sat, and Alen said in Lyran: "My trader unexpectedly endorses the reduction. He says, 'Better to lose some than all'—an old proverb in the Cephean tongue. And he forbids any further reduction."

"Come, now," wheedled the gem dealer. "Let us be men of the world about this. One must give a little and take a little. Everybody knows he can't have his own way forever. I shall offer a good, round eight hundred credits and we'll close on it, eh? Pilquis, fetch us a pen and ink!" One of the burly guards was right there with an inkpot and a reed pen. Garthkint had a Customs form out of his tunic and was busily filling it in to specify the size, number and fire of gems to be released to him.

"What's it now?" asked blackbeard.

"Eight hundred."

"Take it!"

"Garthkint," said Alen regretfully, "you heard the firmness and decision in my trader's voice? What can I do? I am only speaking for him. He is a hard man but perhaps I can talk him around later. I offer you the gems at a ruinous fifteen hundred credits."

"Split the difference," said Garthkint resignedly.

"Done at eleven-fifty," said Alen.

That blackbeard understood. "Well done!" he boomed at Alen and took a swig at Garthkint's winecup. "Have him fill in 'Sack eighteen' on his paper. It's five hundred of that grade."

The gem dealer counted out twenty-three fifty-credit notes and blackbeard signed and fingerprinted the release.

"Now," said Garthkint, "you will please remain here while I take a trip to the spaceport for my property." Three or four of the guards were suddenly quite close.

"You will find," said Alen dryly, "that our standard of commercial morality is no lower than yours."

The dealer smiled politely and left.

"Who will be the next?" asked Alen of the room at large.

"I'll look at your gems,'" said another dealer, sitting at the table.

With the ice-breaking done, the transactions went quicker. Alen had disposed of a dozen lots by the time their first buyer returned.

"It's all right," he said. "We've been tricked before, but your gems are as represented. I congratulate you, Herald, on driving a hard, fair bargain."

"That means," said Alen regretfully, "that I should have asked for more." The guards were once more lounging in corners and no longer seemed so menacing.

They had a midday meal and continued to dispose of their wares. At sunset Alen held a final auction to clean up the odd lots that remained over and was urged to stay to dinner.

The trader, counting a huge wad of the Lyran manpower-based notes, shook his head. "We should be off before dawn, Herald," he told Alen. "Time is money, time is money."

"They are very insistent."

"And I am very stubborn. Thank them and let us be on our way before anything else is done to increase my overhead."

Something did turn up—a city watchman with a bloody nose and split lip.

He demanded of the Herald: "Are you responsible for the Cephean maniac known as Elwon?"

Garthkint glided up to mutter in Alen's ear: "Beware how you answer!"

Alen needed no warning. His grounding included Lyran legal concepts—and on the backward little planet touched with many relics of feudalism "responsible" covered much territory.

"What has Chief Elwon done?" he parried.

"As you see," the watchman glumly replied, pointing to his wounds. "And the same to three others before we got him out of the wrecked wineshop and into the castle. Are you responsible for him?"

"Let me speak with my trader for a moment. Will you have some wine meantime?" He signaled and one of the guards brought a mug.

"Don't mind if I do. I can use it," sighed the watchman.

"We are in trouble," said Alen to blackbeard. "Chief Elwon is in the 'castle'—prison—for drunk and disorderly conduct. You as his master are considered responsible for his conduct under Lyran law. You must pay his fines or serve his penalties. Or you can 'disown' him, which is considered dishonorable but sometimes necessary. For paying his fine or serving his time you have a prior lien on his services, without pay—but of course that's unenforceable off Lyra."

Blackbeard was sweating a little. "Find out from the policeman how long all this is likely to take. I don't want to leave Elwon here and I do want us to get off as soon as possible. Keep him occupied, now, while I go about some business."

The trader retreated to a corner of the darkening barnlike tavern, beckoning Garthkint and a guard with him as Alen returned to the watchman.

"Good keeper of the peace," he said, "will you have another?"

He would.

"My trader wishes to know what penalties are likely to be levied against the unfortunate Chief Elwon."

"Going to leave him in the lurch, eh?" asked the watchman a little belligerently. "A fine master you have!"

One of the dealers at the table indignantly corroborated him. "If you foreigners aren't prepared to live up to your obligations, why did you come here in the first place? What happens to business if a master can send his man to steal and cheat and then say: ' 'Don't blame *me*—it was *his* doing!' "

Alen patiently explained: "On other planets, good Lyrans, the tie of master and man is not so strong that a man would obey if he were ordered to go and steal or cheat."

They shook their heads and muttered. It was unheard-of.

"Good watchman," pressed the Herald, "my trader does not *want* to disown Chief Elwon. Can you tell me what recompense would be necessary—and how long it would take to manage the business?"

The watchman started on a third cup which Alen unostentatiously signaled for. "It's hard to say," he told the Herald weightily. "For my damages, I would demand a hundred credits at least. The three other members of the watch battered by your lunatic could ask no less. The wineship suffered easily five hundred credits' damage. The owner of it was beaten, but that doesn't matter, of course."

"No imprisonment?"

"Oh, a flogging, of course"—Alen started before he recalled that the "flogging" was a few half-hearted symbolic strokes on the covered shoulders with a light cane—"but no imprisonment. His Honor, Judge Krarl, does not sit on the night bench. Judge Krarl is a new-fangled reformer, stranger. He professes to believe that mulcting is unjust—that it makes it easy for the rich to commit crime and go scot-free."

"But doesn't it?" asked Alen, drawn off-course in

spite of himself. There was pitying laughter around him.

"Look you," a dealer explained kindly. "The good watchman suffers battery, the mad Cephean or his master is mulcted for damages, the watchman is repaid for his injuries. What kind of justice is it to the watchman if the mad Cephean is locked away in a cell unfined?"

The watchman nodded approvingly. "Well-said," he told the dealer. "Luckily we have on the night bench a justice of the old school, His Honor, Judge Treel. Stern, but fair. You should hear him! 'Fifty credits! A hundred credits and the lash! Robbed a ship, eh? Two thousand credits!' " He returned to his own voice and said with awe: "For a murder, he never assesses less than *ten thousand credits!*"

And if the murderer couldn't pay, Alen knew, he became a "public charge," "responsible to the state" —that is, a slave. If he could pay, of course, he was turned loose.

"And His Honor, Judge Treel," he pressed, "is sitting tonight? Can we possibly appear before him, pay the fines, and be off?"

"To be sure, stranger. I'd be a fool if I waited until morning, wouldn't I?" The wine had loosened his tongue a little too far and he evidently realized it. "Enough of this," he said. "Does your master honorably accept responsibility for the Cephean? If so, come along with me, the two of you, and we'll get this over with."

"Thanks, good watchman. We are coming."

He went to blackbeard, now alone in his corner, and said: "It's all right. We can pay off—about a thousand credits—and be on our way."

The trader muttered darkly: "Lyran jurisdiction or not, it's coming out of Elwon's pay. The bloody fool!"

They rattled through the darkening streets of the town in one of the turbine-powered wagons, the watchman sitting up front with the driver and the trader and the Herald behind.

"Something's burning," said Alen to the trader, sniffing the air.

"This stinking buggy—" began blackbeard. "Oops," he said, interrupting himself and slapping at his cloak.

"Let me, trader," said Alen. He turned back the cloak, licked his thumb, and rubbed out a crawling ring of sparks spreading across a few centimeters of the cloak's silk lining. And he looked fixedly at what had started the little fire. It was an improperly covered slow-match protruding from a holstered device that was unquestionably a hand weapon.

"I bought it from one of their guards while you were parleying with the policeman," explained blackbeard embarrassedly. "I had a time making him understand. That Garthkint fellow helped." He fiddled with the perforated cover of the slow-match, screwing it on more firmly.

"A pitiful excuse for a weapon," he went on, carefully arranging his cloak over it. "The trigger isn't a trigger and the thumb-safety isn't a safety. You pump the trigger a few times to build up pressure, and a little air squirts out to blow the match to life. Then you uncover the match and pull back the cocking-piece. This levers a dart into the barrel. *Then* you push the thumb-safety which puffs coaldust into the firing chamber and also swivels down the slow-match onto a touchhole. *Poof*, and away goes the dart if you didn't forget any of the steps or do them in the wrong order. Luckily, I also got a knife."

He patted the nape of his neck and said, "That's where they carry 'em here. A little sheath between the shoulder blades—wonderful for a fast draw-and-throw, though it exposes you a little more than I like when you reach. The knife's black glass. Splendid edge and good balance.

"And the thieving Lyrans knew they had me where it hurt. Seven thousand, five hundred credits for the knife and gun—if you can call it that—and the holsters. By rights I should dock Elwon for them, the bloody fool. Still, it's better to buy his way out and leave no hard feelings behind us, eh, Herald?"

"Incomparably better," said Alen. "And I am amazed that you even entertained the idea of an armed jail delivery. What if Chief Elwon had to serve a few days in a prison? Would that be worse than forever barring yourself from the planet and blackening the names of all traders with Lyra? Trader, do not hope to put down the credits that your weapons cost you as a legitimate expense of the voyage. I will not allow it when I audit your books. It was a piece of folly on which you spent personal funds, as far as the College and Order of Heralds is concerned."

"Look here," protested blackbeard. "You're supposed to be spreading utilitarian civilization, aren't you. What's utilitarian about leaving one of my crewmen here?"

Alen ignored the childish argument and wrapped himself in angry silence. As to civilization, he wondered darkly whether such a trading voyage and his part in it was relevent at all. Were the slanders true? Was the College and Order simply a collection of dupes headed by cynical oldsters greedy for luxury and power?

Such thoughts hadn't crossed his mind in a long time. He'd been too busy to entertain them, cramming his head with languages, folkways, mores, customs, underlying patterns of culture, of hundreds of galactic peoples—and for what? So that this fellow could make a profit and the College and Order take a quarter of that profit. If civilization was to come to Lyra, it would have to come in the form of metal. If the Lyrans didn't want metal, *make* them take it.

What did Machiavelli say? "The chief foundations of all states are good laws and good arms; and as there cannot be good laws where the state is not well-armed, it follows that where they are well-armed, they have good laws." It was odd that the teachers had slurred over such a seminal idea, emphasizing instead the spiritual integrity of the weaponless College and Order—or was it?

The disenchantment he felt creeping over him was terrifying.

"The castle," said the watchman over his shoulder, and their wagon stopped with a rattle before a large but unimpressive brick structure of five stories.

"You wait," the trader told the driver after they got

out. He handed him two of his fifty-credit bills. "You
wait, you get many, many more money. You understand, wait?"

"I wait plenty much," shouted the driver delightedly.
"I wait all night, all day. You wonderful master. You
great, great master, I wait—"

"All right," growled the trader, shutting him off.
"You wait."

The watchman took them through an entrance hall lit
by hissing pressure lamps and casually guarded by a
few liveried men with truncheons. He threw open the
door of a medium-sized, well-lit room with a score of
people in it, looked in, and uttered a despairing groan.

A personage on a chair that looked like a throne said
sharply, "Are those the star-travelers? Well, don't just
stand there. Bring them in!"

"Yes, your honor, Judge Krarl," said the watchman
unhappily.

"*It's the wrong judge!*" Alen hissed at the trader.
"This one gives out jail sentences!"

"Do what you can," said blackbeard grimly.

The watchman guided them to the personage in the
chair and indicated a couple of low stools, bowed to the
chair, and retired to stand at the back of the room.

"Your honor," said Alen, "I am Journeyman-Herald
Alen, Herald for the trading voyage—"

"Speak when you're spoken to," said the judge sharply.
"Sir, with the usual insolence of wealth you have chosen
to keep us waiting. I do not take this personally; it
might have happened to Judge Treel, who—to your
evident dismay—I am replacing because of a sudden
illness, or to any other member of the bench. But as an
insult to our justice, we cannot overlook it. Sir, consider your reprimanded. Take your seats. Watchman,
bring in the Cephean."

"Sit down," Alen murmured to the trader. "This is
going to be bad."

A watchman brought in Chief Elwon, bleary-eyed,
tousled, and sporting a few bruises. He gave Alen and
the trader a shamefaced grin as his guard sat him on a
stool beside them. The trader glared back.

Judge Krarl mumbled perfunctorily: "Letbattlebe joinedamongtheseveralpartiesinthisdisputeletnoman quesstionourimpartialawardingofthevictoryspeaknowif youyieldinsteadtoourjudgment. *Well?* Speak up, you watchmen!"

The watchman who had brought the Herald and the trader started and said from the back of the room: "I yieldinsteadtoyourhonorsjudgment."

Three other watchmen and a battered citizen, the wineshop keeper, mumbled in turn; "Iyieldinsteadtoyour honorsjudgment."

"Herald, speak for the accused," snapped the judge.

Well, thought Alen, I can try. "Your honor," he said, "Chief Elwon's master does not yield to your honor's judgment. He is ready to battle the other parties in the dispute or their masters."

"What insolence is this?" screamed the judge, leaping from his throne. "The barbarous customs of other worlds do not prevail in this court! Who spoke of battle—?" He shut his mouth with a snap, evidently abruptly realizing that *he* had spoken of battle in an archaic phrase that harked back to the origins of justice on the planet. The judge sat down again and told Alen, more calmly: "You have mistaken a mere formality. The offer was not made in earnest." Obviously, he didn't like the sound of that himself, but he proceeded, "Now say 'I yieldinsteadtoyourhonorsjudgment,' and we can get on with it. For your information, trial by combat has not been practiced for many generations on our enlightened planet."

Alen said politely: "Your honor, I am a stranger to many of the ways of Lyra, but our excellent College and Order of Heralds instructed me well in the underlying principles of your law. I recall that one of your most revered legal maxims declares: 'The highest crime against man is murder; the highest crime against man's society is breach of promise.' "

Purpling, the judge snarled: "Are you presuming to bandy law with me, you slippery-tongued foreigner? Are you presuming to accuse me of the high crime of breaking my promise? For your information, a promise consists of an offer to do, or refrain from doing, a thing in return for a consideration. There must be the five elements of promiser, promisee, offer, substance, and consideration."

"If you will forgive a foreigner," said Alen, suddenly feeling the ground again under his feet, "I maintain that you offered the parties in the dispute your services in awarding the victory."

"An empty argument," snorted the judge. "Just as an offer with substance from somebody to nobody for a consideration is no promise, or an offer without substance from somebody to somebody for a consideration is no promise, so my offer was no promise, for there was no consideration involved."

"Your honor, must the consideration be from the promisee to the promiser?"

"Of course not. A third party may provide the consideration."

"Then I respectfully maintain that your offer was a promise, since a third party, the government, provided you with the considerations of salary and position in return for you offering your services to the disputants."

"Watchmen, clear the room of disinterested persons," said the judge hoarsely. While it was being done, Alen swiftly filled in the trader and Chief Elwon. Blackbeard grinned at the mention of a five-against-one battle royal, and the engineer looked alarmed.

When the doors closed leaving the nine of them in privacy, the judge said bitterly: "Herald, where did you learn such devilish tricks?"

Alen told him: "My College and Order instructed me well. A similar situation existed on a planet called England during an age known as the Victorious. Trial by combat had long been obsolete, there as here, but had never been declared so—there as here. A litigant won a hopeless lawsuit by publishing a challenge to his opponent and appearing at the appointed place in full armor. His opponent ignored the challenge and so lost the suit by default. The English dictator, one Disraeli, hastily summoned his parliament to abolish trial by combat."

"And so," mused the judge, "I find myself accused in

my own chamber of high crime if I do not permit you five to slash away at each other and decide who won."

The wineshop keeper began to blubber that he was a peaceable man and didn't intend to be carved up by that blackbearded, bloodthirsty star-traveler. All he wanted was his money.

"Silence!" snapped the judge. "Of course there will be no combat. Will you, shopkeeper, and you, watchmen, withdraw if you receive satisfactory financial settlements?"

They would.

"Herald, you may dicker with them."

The four watchmen stood fast by their demand for a hundred credits apiece, and got it. The terrified shopkeeper regained his balance and demanded a thousand. Alen explained that his blackbearded master from a rude and impetuous world might be unable to restrain his rage when he, Alen, interpreted the demand and, ignoring the consequences, might beat him, the shopkeeper, to a pulp. The asking price plunged to a reasonable five hundred, which was paid over. The shopkeeper got the judge's permission to leave and backed out, bowing.

"You see, trader," Alen told blackbeard, "that it was needless to buy weapons when the spoken word—"

"And now," said the judge with a sneer, "we are easily out of *that* dilemma. Watchmen, arrest the three star-travelers and take them to the cages."

"Your honor!" cried Alen, outraged.

"Money won't get you out of *this* one. I charge you with treason."

"The charge is obsolete—" began the Herald hotly, but he broke off as he realized the vindictive strategy.

"Yes, it is. And one of its obsolete provisions is that treason charges must be tried by the parliament at a regular session, which isn't due for two hundred days. You'll be freed and I may be reprimanded, but by my head, for two hundred days you'll regret that you made a fool of *me*. Take them away."

"A trumped-up charge against us. Prison for two

hundred days," said Alen swiftly to the trader as the watchmen closed in.

"Why buy weapons?" mocked the blackbeard, showing his teeth. His left arm whipped up and down, there was a black streak through the air—and the judge was pinned to his throne with a black glass knife through his throat and the sneer of triumph still on his lips.

The trader, before the knife struck, had the clumsy pistol out, with the cover off the glowing match and the cocking piece back. He must have pumped and cocked it under his cloak, thought Alen numbly as he told the watchmen, without prompting: "Get back against the wall and turn around." They did. They wanted to live, and the grinning blackbeard who had made meat of the judge with a flick of the arm was a terrifying figure.

"Well done, Alen," said the trader. "Take their clubs, Elwon. Two for you, two for the Herald. Alen, don't argue! I had to kill the judge before he raised an alarm—nothing but death will silence his breed. You may have to kill too before we're out of this. Take the clubs." He passed the clumsy pistol to Chief Elwon and said: "Keep it on their backs. The thing that looks like a thumb-safety is a trigger. Put a dart through the first one who tries to make a break. Alen, tell the fellow on the end to turn around and come to me slowly."

Alen did. Blackbeard swiftly stripped him, tore and knotted his clothes into ropes, and bound and gagged him. The others got the same treatment in less than ten minutes.

The trader holstered the gun and rolled the watchmen out of the line of sight from the door of the chamber. He recovered his knife and wiped it on the judge's shirt. Alen had to help him prop the body behind the throne's high back.

"Hide those clubs," blackbeard said. "Straight faces. Here we go."

They went out, single file, opening the door only enough to pass. Alen, last in line, told one of the liveried guards nearby: "His honor, Judge Krarl, does not wish to be disturbed."

"That's news?" asked the tipstaff sardonically. He put

his hand on the Herald's arm. "Only yesterday he gimme a blast when I brought him a mug of water he asked me for himself. An outrageous interruption, he called me, and he asked for the water himself. What do you think of that?"

"Terrible," said Alen hastily. He broke away and caught up with the trader and the engineer at the entrance hall. Idlers and loungers were staring at them as they headed for the waiting room.

"I wait!" the driver told them loudly. "I wait long, much. You pay more, more?"

"We pay more," said the trader. "You start."

The driver brought out a smoldering piece of punk, lit a pressure torch, lifted the barn-door section of the wagon's floor to expose the pottery turbine, and preheated it with the torch. He pumped squeakily for minutes, spinning a flywheel with his other hand, before the rotor began to turn on its own. Down went the hatch, up onto the seats went the passengers.

"The spaceport," said Alen. With a slate-pencil screech the driver engaged his planetary gear and they were off.

Through it all, blackbeard had ignored frantic muttered questions from Chief Elwon, who had wanted nothing to do with murder, especially of a judge. "You sit up there," growled the trader, "and every so often you look around and see if we're being followed. Don't alarm the driver. And if we get to the spaceport and blast off without any trouble, keep your story to yourself." He settled down in the back seat with Alen and maintained a gloomy silence. The young Herald was too much in awe of this stranger, so suddenly competent in assorted forms of violence, to question him.

They did get to the spaceport without trouble, and found the crew in the Customs shed, emptied of the gems by dealers with releases. They had built a fire for warmth.

"We wish to leave immediately," said the trader to the port officer. "Can you change my Lyran currency?"

The officers began to sputter apologetically that it was late and the vault was sealed for the night—

"That's all right. We'll change it on Vega. It'll get back to you. Call off your guards and unseal our ship."

They followed the port officer to *Starsong's* dim bulk out on the field. The officer cracked the seal on her with his club in the light of a flaring pressure lamp held by one of the guards.

Alen was sweating hard through it all. As they started across the field he had seen what looked like two closely spaced green stars low on the horizon toward town suddenly each jerk up and toward each other in minute arcs. The semaphore!

The signal officer in the port administration building would be watching too—but nobody on the field, preoccupied with the routine of departure, seemed to have noticed.

The lights flipped this way and that. Alen didn't know the code and bitterly regretted the lack. After some twenty signals the lights flipped to the "rest" position again as the port officer was droning out a set of take-off regulations: bearing, height above settled areas, permissible atomic fuels while in atmosphere—Alen saw somebody start across the field toward them from the administration building. The guards were leaning on their long, competent-looking weapons.

Alen inconspicuously detached himself from the group around *Starsong* and headed across the dark field to meet the approaching figure. Nearing it, he called out a low greeting in Lyran, using the noncom-to-officer military form.

"Sergeant," said the signal officer quietly, "go and draw off the men a few meters from the star-travelers. Tell them the ship mustn't leave, that they're to cover the foreigners and shoot if—"

Alen stood dazedly over the limp body of the signal officer. And then he quickly hid the bludgeon again and strolled back to the ship, wondering whether he'd cracked the Lyran's skull.

The port was open by then and the crew filing in. He was last. "Close it fast," he told the trader. "I had to—"

"I saw you," grunted blackbeard. "A semaphore message?" He was working as he spoke, and the metal port closed.

"Astrogator and engineer, take over," he told them.

"All hands to their bunks," ordered Astrogator Hufner. "Blast-off immediate."

Alen took to his cubicle and strapped himself in. Blast-off deafened him, rattled his bones, and made him thoroughly sick as usual. After what seemed like several wretched hours, they were definitely space-borne under smooth acceleration, and his nausea subsided.

Blackbeard knocked, came in, and unbuckled him.

"Ready to audit the books of the voyage?" asked the trader.

"No," said Alen feebly.

"It can wait," said the trader. "The books are the least important part, anyway. We have headed off a frightful war."

"War? We have?"

"War between Eyolf's Realm and Vega. It is the common gossip of chancelleries and trade missions that both governments have cast longing eyes on Lyra, that they have plans to penetrate its economy by supplying metals to the planet without metals—by force, if need be. Alen, we have removed the pretext by which Eyolf's Realm and Vega would have attempted to snap up Lyra and inevitably have come into conflict. Lyra is getting its metal now, and without imperialist entanglements."

"I saw none," the Herald said blankly.

"You wondered why I was in such haste to get off Lyra, and why I wouldn't leave Elwon here. It is because our Vegan gems were most unusual gems. I am not a technical man, but I understand they are actual gems which were treated to produce a certain effect at just about this time."

Blackbeard glanced at his wrist chronometer and said dreamily: "Lyra is getting metal. Wherever there is one of our gems, pottery is decomposing into its constituent aluminum, silicon, and oxygen. Fluxes and glazes are decomposing into calcium, zinc, barium, potassium, chromium, *and iron*. Buildings are crumbling, pants are dropping as ceramic beltbuckles disintegrate—"

"It means chaos!" protested Alen.

"It means civilization and peace. An ugly clash was in the making." Blackbeard paused and added deliberately: "Where neither their property nor their honor is touched, most men live content."

"*The Prince*, Chapter 19. You are—"

"There was another important purpose to the voyage," said the trader, grinning. "You will be interested in this." He handed Alen a document which, unfolded, had the seal of the College and Order at its head.

Alen read in a daze: "Examiner 19 to the Rector— final clearance of Novice—"

He lingered pridefully over the paragraph that described how he had "with coolness and great resource" foxed the battle cruiser of the Realm, "adapting himself readily in a delicate situation requiring not only physical courage but swift recall, evaluation, and application of a minor planetary culture."

Not so pridefully he read: "—inclined toward pomposity of manner somewhat ludicrous in one of his years, though not unsuccessful in dominating the crew by his bearing—"

And: "—highly profitable disposal of our gems; a feat of no mean importance since the College and Order must, after all, maintain itself."

And: "—cleared the final and crucial hurdle with some mental turmoil if I am any judge, but did clear it. After some twenty years of indoctrination in unrealistic nonviolence, the youth was confronted with a situation where nothing but violence would serve, correctly evaluated this, and applied violence in the form of a truncheon to the head of a Lyran signal officer, thereby demonstrating an ability to learn and common sense as precious as it is rare."

And, finally, simply: "Recommended for training."

"Training?" gasped Alen. "You mean there's more?"

"Not for most, boy. Not for most. The bulk of us are what we seem to be: oily, gun-shy, indispensable adjuncts to trade who feather our nest with percentages. We need those percentages and we need gun-shy Heralds."

Alen recited slowly: "Among other evils which being unarmed brings you, it causes you to be despised."

"Chapter 14," said blackbeard mechanically. "We leave such clues lying by their bedsides for twenty years, and they never notice them. For the few of us who do—more training."

"Will I learn to throw a knife like you?" asked Alen, repelled and fascinated at once by the idea.

"On your own time, if you wish. Mostly it's ethics and morals so you'll be able to weigh the values of such things as knife-throwing."

"Ethics! Morals!"

"We started as missionaries, you know."

"Everybody knows that. But the Great Utilitarian Reform—"

"Some of us," said blackbeard dryly, "think it was neither great, nor utilitarian, nor a reform."

It was a staggering idea. "But we're spreading utilitarian civilization!" protested Alen. "Or if we're not, what's the sense of it all?"

Blackbeard told him: "We have our different motives. One is a sincere utilitarian; another is a gambler—happy when he's in danger and his pulses are pounding. Another is proud and likes to trick people. More than a few conceive themselves as servants of mankind. I'll let you rest for a bit now." He rose.

"But you?" asked Alen hesitantly.

"Me? You will find me in Chapter Twenty-Six," grinned blackbeard. "And perhaps you'll find someone else." He closed the door behind him.

Alen ran through the chapter in his mind, puzzled, until—that was it.

It had a strange and inevitable familiarity to it as if he had always known that he would be saying it aloud, welcomingly, in this cramped cubicle aboard a battered starship:

"God is not willing to do everything, and thus take away our free will and that share of glory which belongs to us."

THE STARS AT WAR
Jerry Pournelle

The Soviet Army has no recruiting posters. It doesn't need them. Not only are there no volunteers in the ranks of the Soviet Army, there can't be. There's no provision for volunteering for the ranks.

There's no need for volunteers, because every male Soviet citizen is conscripted at age 18. Every six months, approximately one million young men enter the system. They stay in for two years of training, after which they remain in the reserve registers until they reach the age of 50. They can be called up at any time.

There are always nearly two million men in the Land Forces alone; within ten days, these could be expanded to some 21 million. The Land Forces contain 123 divisions and 47 independent regiments of motor-rifle divisions. Each division has 23 tank companies and 67 artillery batteries.

There are also 47 Tank divisions, plus independent regiments and battalions. All in all, the Tank Army forces have some 54,000 tanks.

The Soviet Strategic Rocket Forces muster some 325,000 troops. There are at least 1,400 land-based

ICBM rockets. Five hundred intermediate range missiles (IRBM) are deployed in the Western USSR; this includes 315 mobile SS-20's. The SS-20 can be reloaded, and many of the launchers already have at least one nuclear-tipped reload weapon.

In 1944, General Patton raced across France with his 3rd Army. The 16 divisions of First and Third Armies were supported by 5,600 trucks of the Red Ball Express. In 1975, the North Vietnamese Army moved south against Saigon. Its 20 divisions were supported by over 10,000 trucks and vehicles, nearly all of them sent into North Viet Nam from the Soviet Union. Those were the transport vehicles the Soviets could spare from their military establishment. The Red Army today has access to nearly half a million supply vehicles.

Germany entered World War II with 57 submarines. Britain had 58, Japan 56, and the United States 99. In 1941, the Soviet Union had 212 submarines in commission. They have about 275 submarines now, *in addition to* 83 Strategic Nuclear Forces nuclear subs. Of their 275 "regular navy" subs, at least 100 are nuclear powered.

We could continue, but surely the point is clear? The Soviet Union has built an enormous military machine, the largest peacetime military establishment in the history of mankind, and continues to maintain it. The expenses are great, but the Kremlin's control over the Soviet Empire is strong; apparently, the expense does not greatly concern the Politburo and its secret inner circle, the Defense Council.

We don't have to look into Soviet motives to conclude that the United States must respond to this enormous military buildup. The official policy of the Soviet Union is "world liberation." One may argue that they don't really mean it, and that their revolutionary ardor long ago expired, but world revolution remains their official aim. If it is immoral to tempt a poor man by making theft easy, it seems no less so to tempt the Soviets by making conquest cheap and bloodless.

In fact, it is pointless to debate the issue. No responsible President or Congress can or will advocate leaving the United States helpless in the face of the growing Soviet strategic threat. Unilateral disarmament may be a subject for debate within the population, but it has been overwhelmingly and repeatedly rejected by the American people, and our political leaders know this.

Granted that we must respond to the Soviet military threat, though there remains the problem of what the response should be. It is no good responding ineffectively.

We could, if we chose, attempt to match the Soviets in men, machines, and weapons. Their military machine costs much less than ours, of course. As an example, they pay their soldiers no more than $25 U.S. a month. Even so, the United States is far wealthier than the Soviet Union, and there is no question of our ability to *afford* a military establishment equal to or greater than theirs.

The costs would be high. Taxes would rise, and there would be real cuts in our standard of living; but we could do it. We could match the Soviets gun for gun, tank for tank, plane for plane, ship for ship.

We aren't likely to do that. Indeed, the events of the past two years demonstrate that the Congress isn't likely to do half that. Current administration efforts to bring the defense budget up to the proportions it held under John F. Kennedy have not been successful. Moreover, although the courts have held universal conscription to be constitutional, it certainly wouldn't be popular; and without universal conscription, we could never match the Soviets. We aren't *that* rich

This, too, is a pointless debate; in the absence of some clear and unambiguous provocation, such as a massive invasion of Western Europe, or direct attack on Israel, the American people are not prepared to make the necessary sacrifices. We won't give up consumer goods, cosmetics, and the myriad luxuries we enjoy, nor will we opt for universal conscription. There is just no way that we'll respond to the Soviets by building a peacetime military establishment similar to theirs.

Unfortunately, although we have rejected matching the Soviet military establishment, we have not seized upon any viable alternative. Instead, we putter about, building some of this and some of that, hoping that our technological superiority will somehow do the trick even though we have no clearcut strategy of technology.

This has not always brought about good results. As Congressman Newt Gingrich, among others, has repeatedly pointed out, simply throwing money at the Pentagon is wasteful. Given money but no marching orders, the Pentagon almost always buys more M-1 tanks for the Army, more carriers for the Navy, wings of F-16's for the Air Force. They buy "things people can ride on," as one analyst recently put it.

Left to its own direction, the military is very conservative. Military establishments tend to keep the old, while flirting with the new and glamorous; to buy one or two armored cars, but keep horses for the cavalry. To put catapults and seaplanes on battleships, but reject aircraft carriers as not needed.

The result is a lack of direction. As the *Wall Street Journal* put it in November 1982, "The Pentagon is an enormously inefficient nationalized industry. Its decisions are less the implementation of a coherent strategy than a matter of three services dividing a patronage pie. The most predictable result has been to deaden innovation."

The bold new systems are shunted aside; or, if the Pentagon is forced to deal with them, they are studied, tested, restudied, and retested. Then, suddenly, often as much a result of the geographical location of the factory that makes them as of strategic necessity, some of the most glamorous systems are procured.

We end up with weapons that no one is trained to use, aircraft with no spare parts and few trained pilots, communications systems that don't quite work, ships without trained sailors to man them, and missiles that work splendidly in test situations, but have profound problems on the battlefield.

I do not mean here to argue against high-technology weapons systems. One of the clearest lessons of the Viet Nam War was that high technology pays off. From "Blackbird" gunships to smart bombs and automatic mortars, high-technology weapons proved to have high effectiveness, and to be relatively cheap compared to the results they achieved.

The Falklands battles demonstrated the same point. High-technology weapons are essential for modern warfare. Moreover, the weapons must be in the hands of trained, able, and dedicated troops. It is not enough that we design and develop high technology weapons systems. We must build them, deploy them, bring them to operational effectiveness, and maintain them. Anything short of that invites disaster.

However, it is not enough merely to recognize that high technology is vital to our future. There must also be a strategic focus. As Stefan Possony and I have argued elsewhere, we must have strategic direction to our military research and development. We must have a strategy of technology.

That won't be developed overnight. Most analysts believe it will require a grueling and painful reorganization of the entire defense establishment. That will generate great opposition. There are too many vested interests for things to be otherwise.

It will also require time. We may not have that time. Military establishments, ours among them, have *always* been inefficient, and better organized for the last war than the next. If we wait for perfection, we may well wait forever.

Thus three facts stand out:

1. The Soviets have an enormous military establishment, and we are not going to match it tank for tank and gun for gun.

2. Our present course of buying some of this and some of that, more tanks here and more planes there, isn't an adequate, or indeed reasonable, response to the threat, and "reform of the Pentagon" and other efforts to "trim the fat and reduce waste" aren't likely to succeed very quickly, if at all.

3. We have to do *something* and soon.

* * *

This reasoning was the starting point for Lt. General Daniel O. Graham's strategic analysis. If what we're doing isn't going to work, and we have to do something, where can we go? Graham concluded that we needed a bold new approach, a strategic sidestep; that we had to stop competing with the Soviets in areas in which we can't win, and begin to compete where we have the advantage.

His analysis led him through high technology to space; to the High Frontier. As Dan Graham has repeatedly said, he didn't start with any prejudices toward space as a decisive frontier. All his training and experience pointed him elsewhere. It was the search for strategic initiatives which led him to his conclusions.

The above was written as the preface to General Daniel O. Graham's book *High Frontier*. That book presents, in detail, a bold new strategy for the defense of the United States and Western Civilization. The concepts of High Frontier are very new and different, but the plans suggested were realistic. Some of the nation's best engineers and development scientists have examined Project High Frontier. Many began their analysis convinced that High Frontier couldn't work, or would cost too much, or would take too long. As they became more involved, they changed their minds.

I know, because I was one of them. I am not any longer a professional scientist, but I stay in touch with the aerospace community. When I was first told of High Frontier, I searched among those I respected for engineers and scientists opposed to the plan, and introduced them to the team of equally respectable advisors assisting General Graham. In some cases I was privileged to sit in on the resulting debates.

Certain conclusions emerged. First, we do hold the advantages in space. Our technology is more advanced and more reliable, and the Soviet "brute force" approach to problems creates as many difficulties as it solves when applied to the space environment. We don't have everything our way in space, but we are clearly better off in a high technology competition than trying to match their conventional military establishment.

Secondly, High Frontier will work. There can be arguments over details, costs, and schedules. As with all strategic plans there will remain uncertainties: the first thing taught to career officers is the maxim "No battle plan ever survives contact with the enemy." But it will work, and those who all too predictably argue that High Frontier's supporters don't understand the laws of physics are cordially invited to present their case—not to Dan Graham, who *doesn't* understand the laws of physics, but to the prize-winning physicists aboard General Graham's team.

In *The Strategy of Technology*, Stefan Possony and I argued that the United States ought to abandon the doctrine of Mutual Assured Destruction, sometimes known as MAD, in favor of a strategic doctrine of "Assured Survival"; that as a Western nation adhering to the Judeo-Christian tradition, we should be more concerned with preserving our nation than with assuring another's destruction.

I concluded that: Project High Frontier presents a practical way to achieve that goal.

In fact, we builded better than we knew. Part of the High Frontier analysis was a presentation to President Ronald Reagan. It must have been convincing, because on March 23, 1983, the President made his famous "Star Wars" speech, in which he asked the scientists and technologists of the United States to end the terrible fears of our strategy of Mutual Assured Destruction, and adopt a new strategy of Assured Survival.

I've discussed that in some detail in *Mutual Assured Survival* by Jerry Pournelle and Dean Ing (Baen Books).

In 1970 Stefan Possony and I published *The Strategy of Technology*. The most important point made in that book was that technology can be directed by a strategist; that *technological breakthroughs* can be created on demand if sufficient technological resources are focussed in a rational way on strategic problems.

The "Star Wars" speech proved that we were more right than we'd known. Once the technological community became focussed on the problem of making the

ICBM "impotent and obsolete," it turned out to be rather easier than we'd thought. The Manhattan Project turned up three ways to make atomic weapons; all worked.

Strategic Defense Initiative research turned up five ways. General James Abrahamson, SDI Director, has confessed to an *embarrass d' richess*. He has to choose among strongly competing alternatives, all of which will work.

One of the most important discoveries was that ground-based lasers are not only feasible, but a likely way to defend a nation. We speak here of *enormous* lasers; lasers built near, say, Hoover Dam, and capable of turning the enormous output of that dam into laser energy. This is combined with new techniques that unfocus the laser beam at the ground, so that the atmospheric distortions *refocus the beam*. The result is that the laser beam is perfectly focussed when it gets above the atmosphere.

With lasers that large, and a mirror in orbit to redirect the energy, it's not necessary to "point and shoot"; you can *raster* the entire target area; sweep the beam in a deadly conical pattern to sterilize the whole ICBM corridor from the USSR to the U.S. For good measure these lasers can be used against submarine-launched missiles.

Finally, enormous lasers like these can launch ships from the ground. Arthur Kantrowitz invented that technique way back in the '60's; the ground-based laser provides the energy for a rapidly climbing rocket. It's almost as if the light beam pushes the ship to orbit. The result is that ships get to orbit for fuel costs alone.

There are other ways to destroy incoming ICBM's. As Professor Greg Benford said when I told him of some new breakthroughs: "Really, if you stop to think about it, if you can spend ten million bucks a shot, why is it surprising that you can shoot down a delicate little thing like an ICBM? Not much has to go wrong to keep the ICBM from working. . . ."

*　　　*　　　*

The technology is there. It isn't simple technology, and it isn't cheap; but it has already been demonstrated. We can build enormous lasers, on the ground or in space.

Note too that if we put them on the ground they can be extremely powerful; as I said above, you can put the laser next to a dam. The "planetary defenses" beloved of the old imperial-style science fiction have just become a reality. Planet-based laser beams can reach out as far as the moon to engage and destroy armored space ships.

The technology is there. It will be built. The only real question is, who will build it? If we delay long enough, there will be imperial stars all right: but they will be red stars.

ROBERT A. HEINLEIN

"Heinlein knows more about blending provocative scientific thinking with strong human stories than any dozen other contemporary science fiction writers."
—*Chicago Sun-Times*

"Robert A. Heinlein wears imagination as though it were his private suit of clothes. What makes his work so rich is that he combines his lively, creative sense with an approach that is at once literate, informed, and exciting."
—*New York Times*

Seven of Robert A. Heinlein's best-loved titles are now available in superbly packaged new Baen editions, with embossed series-look covers by artist John Melo. Collect them all by sending in the order form below:

REVOLT IN 2100, 65589-2, $3.50 □

METHUSELAH'S CHILDREN, 65597-3, $3.50 □

THE GREEN HILLS OF EARTH, 65608-2, $3.50 □

THE MAN WHO SOLD THE MOON, 65623-6, $3.50 □

THE MENACE FROM EARTH*, 65636-8, $3.50 □

ASSIGNMENT IN ETERNITY**, 65637-6, $3.50 □

SIXTH COLUMN***, 65638-4, $3.50 □

*To be published May 1987. **To be published July 1987. ***To be published October 1987. Any books ordered prior to publication date will be shipped at no extra charge as soon as they are available.

Please send me the books I have checked above. I enclose a check or money order for the combined cover price for the titles I have ordered, plus 75 cents for first-class postage and handling (for any number of titles) made out to Baen Books, Dept. B, 260 Fifth Avenue, New York, N.Y. 10001.

GORDON R. DICKSON

Winner of every award science fiction and fantasy to offer, Gordon Dickson is one of the major authors of this century. He creates heroes and enemies, not just characters in books; his stories celebrate bravery and virtue and the best in all of us. Collect some of the very best of Gordon Dickson's writing by ordering the books below.

FORWARD!, 55971-0, 256 pp., $2.95 ☐

HOUR OF THE HORDE, 55905-2, 256 pp., $2.95 ☐

INVADERS!, 55994-X, 256 pp., $2.95 ☐

THE LAST DREAM, 65559-0, 288 pp., $2.95 ☐

MINDSPAN, 65580-9, 288 pp., $2.95 ☐

SURVIVAL!, 55927-3, 288 pp., $2.75 ☐

WOLFLING, 55962-1, 256 pp., $2.95 ☐

LIFESHIP (with Harry Harrison), 55981-8, 256 pp., $2.95 ☐

WE'RE LOOKING FOR
TROUBLE

Well, feedback, anyway. Baen Books endeavors to publish only the best in science fiction and fantasy—but we need you to tell us whether we're doing it right. Why not let us know? We'll award a Baen Books gift certificate worth $100 (plus a copy of our catalog) to the reader who best tells us what he or she likes about Baen Books—and where we could do better. We reserve the right to quote any or all of you. Contest closes December 31, 1987. All letters should be addressed to Baen Books, 260 Fifth Avenue, New York, N.Y. 10001.